ISBN 978-0-483-62747-5
PIBN 10792674

FB &c Ltd, Dalton House, 60 Windsor Avenue, London, SW19 2RR.
Company number 08720141. Registered in England and Wales.

For support please visit www.forgottenbooks.com

Technical and Bibliographic Notes / Notes techniques e

The Institute has attempted to obtain the best original copy available for filming. Features of this copy which may be bibliographically unique, which may alter any of the images in the reproduction, or which may significantly change the usual method of filming, are checked below.

L'Institut a n lui a été poss exemplaire bibliograph reproduite, dans la mé ci-dessous.

- [x] Coloured covers/ Couverture de couleur
- [ ] Covers damaged/ Couverture endommagée
- [ ] Covers restored and/or laminated/ Couverture restaurée et/ou pelliculée
- [ ] Cover title missing/ Le titre de couverture manque
- [ ] Coloured maps/ Cartes géographiques en couleur
- [x] Coloured ink (i.e. other than blue or black)/ Encre de couleur (i.e. autre que bleue ou noire)
- [ ] Coloured plates and/or illustrations/ Planches et/ou illustrations en couleur
- [ ] Bound with other material/ Relié avec d'autres documents
- [ ] Tight binding may cause shadows or distortion along interior margin/ La reliure serrée peut causer de l'ombre ou de la distorsion le long de la marge intérieure
- [ ] Blank leaves added during restoration may appear within the text. Whenever possible, these have been omitted from filming/ Il se peut que certaines pages blanches ajoutées lors d'une restauration apparaissent dans le texte, mais, lorsque cela était possible, ces pages n'ont pas été filmées.

- [ ] Pages
- [ ] Pages Pages
- [ ] Pages Pages
- [x] Pages d Pages
- [ ] Pages Pages
- [x] Showth Transp
- [ ] Quality Qualité
- [ ] Contin
- [ ] Include

Title on Le titre

- [ ] Title pa Page de
- [ ] Caption Titre de
- [ ] Génériq

ks

L'exemplaire filmé fut reproduit grâce à la générosité de:

Bibliothèque nationale du Canada

Les images suivantes ont été reproduites avec le plus grand soin, compte tenu de la condition et de la netteté de l'exemplaire filmé, et en conformité avec les conditions du contrat de filmage.

Les exemplaires originaux dont la couverture en papier est imprimée sont filmés en commençant par le premier plat et en terminant soit par la dernière page qui comporte une empreinte d'impression ou d'illustration, soit par le second plat, selon le cas. Tous les autres exemplaires originaux sont filmés en commençant par la première page qui comporte une empreinte d'impression ou d'illustration et en terminant par la dernière page qui comporte une telle empreinte.

Un des symboles suivants apparaîtra sur la dernière image de chaque microfiche, selon le cas: le symbole → signifie "A SUIVRE", le symbole ▼ signifie "FIN".

Les cartes, planches, tableaux, etc., peuvent être filmés à des taux de réduction différents. Lorsque le document est trop grand pour être reproduit en un seul cliché, il est filmé à partir de l'angle supérieur gauche, de gauche à droite, et de haut en bas, en prenant le nombre d'images nécessaire. Les diagrammes suivants illustrent la méthode.

3

1

2

MICROCOPY RESOLUTION TEST CHART

(ANSI and ISO TEST CHART No. 2)

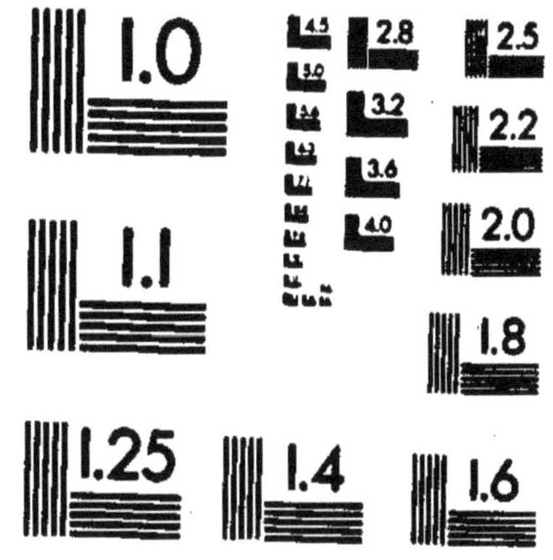

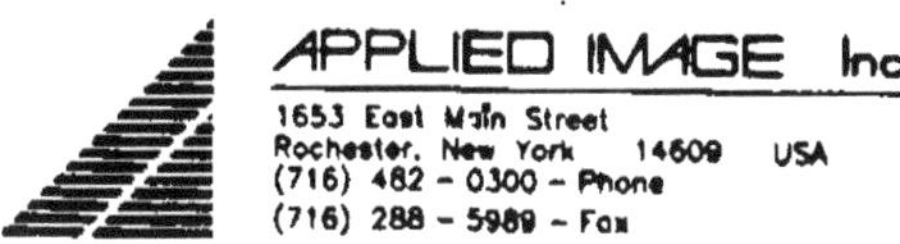

THE COIL OF CARNE

THE COIL OF CARNE

BY

JOHN OXENHAM

AUTHOR OF "THE LONG ROAD"

TORONTO
THE COPP, CLARK CO. LIMITED
1911

TO

RODERIC DUNKERLEY, B.A., B.D.

"And what are you eager for, Mr. Eager?"

"Men, women, and children—bodies and souls."

Intra, page 53.

"By God's help we will make men of them, the rest we must trust to Providence."

Intra, page 66.

"Catch them young!"

Intra, page 67.

"No man is past mending till he's dead, perhaps not then."

Intra, page 82.

CONTENTS

BOOK I

CHAPTER		PAGE
I.	THE HOUSE OF CARNE	1
II.	THE STAR IN THE DUST	9
III.	THE FIRST OF THE COIL	14
IV.	THE COIL COMPLETE	22
V.	IN THE COIL	29

BOOK II

VI.	FREEMEN OF THE FLATS	40
VII.	EAGER HEART	50
VIII.	SIR DENZIL'S VIEWS	57
IX.	MORE OF SIR DENZIL'S VIEWS	63
X.	GROWING FREEMEN	67
XI.	THE LITTLE LADY	76
XII.	MANY MEANS	83
XIII.	MOUNTING	94
XIV.	WIDENING WAYS	101
XV.	DIVERGING LINES	108

CHAPTER		PAGE
XVI.	A CUT AT THE COIL	110
XVII.	ALMOST SOLVED	118
XVIII.	ALMOST SOLVED AGAIN	120
XIX.	WHERE'S JIM?	124
XX.	A NARROW SQUEAK	131
XXI.	A WARM WELCOME	137
XXII.	WHERE'S JACK?	143

BOOK III

XXIII.	BREAKING IN	149
XXIV.	AN UNEXPECTED GUEST	155
XXV.	REVELATION AND SPECULATION	164
XXVI.	JIM'S TIGHT PLACE	166
XXVII.	TWO TO ONE	169
XXVIII.	THE LINE OF CLEAVAGE	180
XXIX.	GRACIE'S DILEMMA	185
XXX.	NEVER THE SAME AGAIN	190
XXXI.	DESERET	193
XXXII.	THE LADY WITH THE FAN	201
XXXIII.	A STIRRING OF MUD	207
XXXIV.	THE BOYS IN THE MUD	213
XXXV.	EXPLANATIONS	216
XXXVI.	JIM'S WAY	227
XXXVII.	A HOPELESS QUEST	230
XXXVIII.	LORD DESERET HELPS	234

CHAPTER		PAGE
XXXIX.	OLD SETH GOES HOME	240
XL.	OUT OF THE NIGHT	245
XLI.	HORSE AND FOOT	253
XLII.	DUE EAST	255
XLIII.	JIM TO THE FORE	262
XLIV.	JIM'S LUCK	266
XLV.	MORE REVELATIONS	271
XLVI.	THE BLACK LANDING	277
XLVII.	ALMA	284
XLVIII.	JIM'S RIDE	290
XLIX.	AMONG THE BULL-PUPS	294
L.	RED-TAPE	300
LI.	THE VALLEY OF DEATH	304
LII.	PATCHING UP	309
LIII.	THE FIGHT IN THE FOG	313
LIV.	AN ALLY OF PROVIDENCE	318
LV.	RETRIBUTION	321
LVI.	DULL DAYS	328
LVII.	HOT OVENS	331
LVIII.	CHILL NEWS	335
LIX.	TOUCH AND GO FOR THE COIL	338
LX.	INSIDE THE FIERY RING	346
LXI.	WEARY WAITING	352
LXII.	FROM ONE TO MANY	355
LXIII.	EAGER ON THE SCENT	361
LXIV.	THE LONG SLOW SIEGE	366

CHAPTER

LXV. THE CUTTING OF THE COIL . . .

LXVI. PURGATORY . . . .

LXVII. THE BEGINNING OF THE END . .

LXVIII. HOME AGAIN . . . . . .

LXIX. "THE RIGHT ONE" . . . .

LXX. ALL'S WELL . . . . . .

THE COIL OF CARNE

BOOK I

CHAPTER I

THE HOUSE OF CARNE

IF by any chance you should ever sail on a low ebb-tide along a certain western coast, you will, if you are of a receptive humour and new to the district, receive a somewhat startling impression of the dignity of the absolutely flat.

Your ideas of militant and resistant grandeur may have been associated hitherto with the iron frontlets and crashing thunders of Finisterre or Sark, of Cornwall or the Western Isle. Here you are faced with a repressive curbing of the waters, equal in every respect to theirs, but so quietly displayed as to be somewhat awesome, as mighty power in restraint must always be.

As far as eye can reach—sand, nothing but sand, illim'table, overpowering by reason of its immensity, a very hara of the coast. Mighty levels stretching landward and eaward—for you are only threading a capricious channel mong the banks which the equinoctials will twist at their leasure, and away to the west the great grim sea lies growling ı his sandy chains until his time comes. Then, indeed, he ill swell and boil and seethe in his channels till he is full eady, and come creeping silently over his barriers, and then—p and away over the flats with the speed of a racehorse, and death to the unwary. You may see the humping back of him among the outer banks if you climb a few feet up your mast. Then, if you turn towards the land, you will see, far away across the brown ribbed flats, a long rim of yellow sand backed by bewildering ranges of low white hummocks, and farther away still a filmy blue line of distant hills.

Here and there a fisherman's cottage accentuates the loneliness of it all. At one point, as the sun dips in the west, a blaze of light flashes out as though a hidden battery had suddenly unmasked itself; and if you ask your skipper what it is, he will tell you that is Carne. Then, if he is a wise man, he will upsail and away, to make Wytham or Wynsloe before it is dark, for the shifting banks off Carne are as hungry as Death, and as tricky as the devil.

For over three hundred years the grim gray house of Carne has stood there, and watched the surface of all things round about it change with the seasons and the years and yet remain in all essential things the same. When the wild equinoctials swept the flats till they hummed like a harp, the sand-hills stirred and changed their aspects as though the sleeping giants below turned uneasily in their beds. For, under the whip of the wind, grain by grain the sand-hills creep hither and thither and accommodate themselves to circumstances in strange and ghostly fashions. So that, after the fury of the night, the peace of the morning looked in vain for the landmarks of the previous day.

And the cold seabanks out beyond were twisted and tortured this way and that by the winds and waves, and within them lay many an honest seaman, and some maybe who might have found it difficult to prove their right to so honourable a title. But the banks were always there, silent and deadly even when they shimmered in the sunshine.

And generations of Carrons had held Carne, and had even occupied it at times, and had passed away and given place to others. But Carne was always there, grim and gray, and mostly silent.

The outward aspects of things might change, indeed, but at bottom they remained very much the same, and human nature changed as little as the rest, though its outward aspects varied with the times. What strange twist of brain or heart set its owner to the building of Carne has puzzled many a wayfarer coming upon it in its wide sandy solitudes for the first time. And the answer to that question answers several others, and accounts for much.

It was Denzil Carron who built the house in the year Queen Mary died. He was of the old faith, a Romanist of the Romanists, narrow in his creed, fanatical in his exercise of it, at once hot- and cold-blooded in pursuit of his aims. When Elizabeth came to the throne he looked to be done by as he had done, and had very reasonable doubts as to the quality of the mercy which might be strained towards him. So he quietly withdrew from London, sold his houses and lands in other counties, and sought out the remotest and quietest spot he could find in the most Romanist county in England. And there he built the great house of Carne, as a quiet harbourage for himself and such victims of the coming persecutions as might need his assistance.

But no retributive hand was stretched after him. He was Englishman first and Romanist afterwards. Calais, and the other national crumblings and disasters of Mary's short reign, had been bitter pills to him, and he hated a Spaniard like the devil. He saw a brighter outlook for his country, though possibly a darker one for his Church, in Elizabeth's firm grip than any her opponents could offer. So he shut his face stonily against the intriguers, who came from time to time and endeavoured to wile him into schemes for the subversion of the Crown and the advancement of the true Church, and would have none of them. And so he was left in peace and quietness by the powers that were, and found himself free o indulge to the full in those religious exercises on the trict observance of which his future state depended.

His wife died before the migration, leaving him one son,

Denzil, to bring up according to his own ideas. And a dismal time the lad had of it. Surrounded by black jowls and gloomy-faced priests, tied hand and foot by ordinances which his growing spirit loathed, all the brightness and joy of life crushed out by the weight of a religion which had neither time nor place for such things, he lived a narrow monastic life till his father died. Then, being of age, and able at last to speak for himself, he quietly informed his quondam governors that he had had enough of religion to satisfy all reasonable requirements of this life and the next, and that now he intended to enjoy himself. Carne he would maintain as his father had maintained it, for the benefit of those whom his father had loved, or at all events had materially cared for. And so, good-bye, Black-Jowls! and Ho for Life and the joy of it!

He went up to London, bought an estate in Kent, ruffled it with the best of them, married and had sons and daughters, kept his head out of all political nooses, fought the Spaniards under Admiral John Hawkins and Francis Drake, and died wholesomely in his bed in his house in Kent, a very different man from what Carne would have made him.

And that is how the grim gray house of Carne came to be planted in the wilderness.

Now and again, in the years that followed, the Carron of the day, if he fell on dolorous times through extravagance of living—as happened—or suffered sudden access of religious fervour—as also happened, though less frequently—would take himself to Carne and there mortify flesh and spirit till things, financial and spiritual, came round again, either for himself or the next on the rota. And so some kind of connection was always maintained between Carne and its owners, though years might pass without their coming face to face.

The Master of Carne in the year 1833 was that Denzil Carron who came to notoriety in more ways than one during the Regency. His father had been of the quieter strain, with a miserly twist in him which commended the wide, sweet solitude and simple, inexpensive life of Carne as exactly suited to his close humour. He could feel rich there on very little; and after the death of his wife, who brought him a very ample fortune, he devoted himself to the education of his boy and the enjoyment, by accumulation, of his wealth. But a short annual visit to London on business affairs afforded the boy a glimpse of what he was missing, and his father's body was not twelve hours underground before he had shaken off the sands of Carne and was posting to London in a yellow chariot with four horses and two very elevated post-boys, like a silly moth to its candle.

There, in due course, by processes of rapid assimilation and lavish dispersion, he climbed to high altitudes, and breathed the atmosphere of royal rascality refined by the gracious presence of George, Prince of Wales. For the replenishment of his depleted exchequer he married Miss Betty Carmichael, only daughter and sole heiress of the great Calcutta nabob. She died in child-birth, leaving him a boy whose education his own diversions left him little time or disposition to attend to. He won the esteem, such as it was, of the Prince Regent by running through the heart the Duke of Astrolabe, who had, in his cups, made certain remarks of a quite unnecessarily truthful character concerning Mrs. Fitzherbert, whom he persisted in calling Madame Belicis; and lost it for ever by the injudicious insertion of a slice of skinned orange inside the royal neck-cloth in a moment of undue elevation, producing thereby so great a shock to the royal system and dignity as to bring it within an ace of an apoplexy and the end of its great and glorious career.

Under the shadow of this exploit Carron found it judicious to retire for a time to the wilderness, and carried his boy with him. He had had a racketing time, and a period of rest and recuperation would be good both for himself and his fortunes.

He had hoped and believed that his trifling indiscretion

would in time be forgotten and forgiven by his royal comrade. But it never was. The royal cuticle crinkled at the very mention of the name of Carron, and Sir Denzil remained in retirement, embittered somewhat at the price he had had to pay for so trivial a jest, and solacing himself as best he could.

Once only he emerged, and then solely on business bent.

In the panic year, when thousands were rushing to ruin, he gathered together his accumulated savings, girded his loins, and stepped quietly and with wide-open eyes into the wild mêlée. He played a cautious, far-sighted game, and emerged triumphant over the dry-sucked bodies of the less wary, with overflowing coffers and many gray hairs. He was prepared to greet the royal back with showers of gold once more. But the royal neck, though it now wore the ermine in its own right, could not forget the clammy kiss of the orange, and Carron went sulkily back to Carne.

When the Sailor Prince stepped up from quarter-deck to throne, he returned to London and took his place in society once more. But ten years in the desert had placed him out of touch with things; and with reluctance he had to admit to himself that if the star of Carron was to blaze once more, it must be in the person of the next on the roll.

And so, characteristically enough, he set himself to the dispersal of the flimsy cloudlet of disgrace which attached to his name by seeking to win for his boy what the royal disfavour had denied to himself.

Now, indeed, that the royal sufferer was dead, the rising generation, when they recalled it, rather enjoyed the crinkling of the royal skin. They would even have welcomed the crinkler among them as a reminder of the hilarities of former days. But the fashion of things had changed. He did not feel at home with them as he had done with their fathers, and he who had shone as a star, though he had indeed disappeared like a rocket, had no mind to figure at their feasts as a lively old stick.

Young Denzil's education had been of the most haphazard

during the years his father was starring it in London. On the retirement to Carne, however, Sir Denzil took the boy in hand himself and inculcated in him philosophies and views of life, based upon his own experiences, which, while they might tend to the production of a gentleman, as then considered, left much to be desired from some other points of view.

He bought him a cornetcy in the Hussars, supplied him freely with money, and required only that his acquaintance should be confined to those circles of which he himself had once been so bright an ornament.

The young man was a success. He was well-built and well-featured, and his manners had been his father's care. He had all the family faults, and succeeded admirably in veiling such virtues as he possessed, with the exception of one or two which happened to be fashionable. He was hot-headed, free-handed, jovial, heedless of consequences in pursuit of his own satisfactions, incapable of petty meanness, but quite capable of those graver lapses which the fashion of the times condoned. With a different upbringing, and flung on his own resources, Denzil Carron might have gone far and on a very much higher plane than he chose.

As it was, his career also ended somewhat abruptly.

At eight-and-twenty he had his captaincy in the 8th Hussars, and was in the exuberant enjoyment of health, wealth, and everything that makes for happiness—except only those things through which alone happiness may ever hope to be attained. He had been in and out of love a score of times, with results depressing enough in several cases to the objects of his ardent but short-lived affections. It was the fashion of the times, and earned him no word of censure. He loved and hated, gambled and fought, danced and drank, with the rest, and was no whit better or worse than they.

At Shole House, down in Hampshire, he met Lady Susan Sandys, sister of the Earl of Quixande—fell in love with her through pity, maybe, at the forlornness of her state, which might indeed have moved the heart of a harder man. For Quizande was a warm man, even in a warm age, and Shole was ante-room to Hades. Carron pitied her, liked her—she was not lacking in good looks—persuaded himself, indeed, that he loved her. For her sake he summarily cut himself free from his other current feminine entanglements, carried her hot-foot to Gretna—a labour of love surely, but quite unnecessary, since her brother was delighted to be rid of her, and Sir Denzil had no fault to find either with the lady or her portion—and returned to London a married, but very doubtfully a wiser, man.

Lady Susan did her best, no doubt. She was full of gratitude and affection for the gallant warrior who had picked her out of the shades, and set her life in the sunshine. But Denzil was no Bayard, and it needed a stronger nature than Lady Susan's to lift him to the higher level.

For quite a month—for thirty whole days and nights, counting those spent on the road to and from Gretna—Lady Susan kept her hold on her husband. Then his regimental duties could no longer be neglected. They grew more and more exigent as time passed, and the young wife was left more and more to the society of her father-in-law. Sir Denzil accepted the position with the grace of an old courtier, and did his duty by her, palliated Captain Denzil's defections with cynical kindness, and softened her lot as best he might. And the gallant captain, exhausted somewhat with the strain of his thirty days' conservatism, resumed his liberal progression through the more exhilarating circles of fashionable folly, and went the pace the faster for his temporary withdrawal.

The end came abruptly, and eight months after that quite unnecessary ride to Gretna Lady Susan was again speeding up the North Road, but this time with her father-in-law, their destination Carne. Captain Denzil was hiding for his life, with a man's blood on his hands; and his father's hopes for the blazing star of Carron were in the dust.

CHAPTER II

THE STAR IN THE DUST

AND the cause of it all?—Madame Damaris, of Covent Garden Theatre, the most bewitching woman and the most exquisite dancer of her time. Perhaps Captain Denzil's handsome face and gallant bearing carried him farther into her good graces than the others. Perhaps their jealous tongues wagged more freely than circumstances actually justified. Anyway, the rumours which, as usual, came last of all to Lady Susan's ears caused her very great distress. She was in that state of health in which depression of spirits may have lasting and ulterior consequences. There were rumours too of a return of the cholera, and she was nervous about it; and Sir Denzil was already considering the advisability of a quiet journey to that quietest of retreats, the great house of Carne, when that happened which left him no time for consideration, but sent him speeding thither with the forlorn young wife as fast as horses could carry them.

There was in London at this time a certain Count d'Aumont attached to the French Embassy. He was a man of some note, and was understood to be related in some roundabout way to that branch of the Orleans family which force of circumstance had just succeeded in seating on the precarious throne of France. He cut a considerable figure in society, and had most remarkable luck at play. He possessed also a quick tongue and a flexibility of wrist which so far had served to guard his reputation from open assault.

He had known Madame Damaris prior to her triumphant descent on London, and was much piqued when he found himself ousted from her good graces by men whom he could have run through with his left hand, but who could squander on her caprices thousands to his hundreds. Head and front of the offenders, by reason of the lady's partiality, was Denzil Carron, and the two men hated one another like poison.

Denzil was playing at Black's one night, when a vacancy was occasioned in the party by the unexpected call to some official duty of one of the players. D'Aumont was standing by, and to Denzil's disgust was invited by one of the others to take the vacant chair.

He had watched the Frenchman's play more than once, and had found it extremely interesting. In fact, on one occasion he had been restrained with difficulty from creating a disturbance which must inevitably have led to an inquiry and endless unpleasantness. Then, too, but a short time before, hearing of some remarks D'Aumont had made concerning Madame Damaris and himself, Denzil, in his hot-headed way, had sworn that he would break the Frenchman's neck the very first time they met.

It is possible that these matters were within the recollection of Captain O'Halloran when he boisterously invited D'Aumont to his partnership at the whist-table that night. For O'Halloran delighted in rows, and was ready for a "jule," either as principal or second, at any hour of the day or night. He was also very friendly with D'Aumont, and it is possible that the latter desired a collision with Carron as a pretext for his summary dismissal at the point of the sword. However it came about, the meeting ended in disaster.

The play ran smoothly for a time, and the onlookers had begun to believe the sitting would end without any explosion, when Carron rose suddenly to his feet, saying:

"At your old tricks, M. le Comte. You cheated!"

"Liar!" said the Count.

Then Carron laid hold of the card-table, swung it up in his powerful arms, and brought it down with a crash on the Frenchman's head. The remnants of it were hanging round his neck like a new kind of clown's ruffle before the guineas had ceased spinning in the corners of the room.

"He knows where to find me," said Denzil, and marched

out and went thoughtfully home to his quarters to await the Frenchman's challenge, which for most men had proved equivalent to a death-warrant.

Instead, there came to him in the gray of the dawn one of his friends, in haste, and with a face like the morning's.

"Ha, Pole! I hardly expected you to carry for a damned Frenchman. Where do we meet, and when?" said Carron brusquely, for he had been waiting all night, and he hated waiting.

"God knows," said young Pole, with a grim humour which none would have looked to find in him. "He's gone to find out. He's dead!"

"Dead!—Of a crack on the head!"

"A splinter ran through his throat, and he bled out before they could stop it. You had better get away, Carron. There'll be a deuce of a row, because of his connections, you see."

"I'll stay and see it through. I'd no intent to kill the man—not that way, at any rate."

"You'll see it through from the outside a sight easier than from the inside," said young Pole. "You get away. We'll see to the rest. It's easier to keep out of the jug than to get out of it."

Carron pondered the question.

"I'll see my father," he said, with an accession of wisdom.

"That's right," said young Pole. "He'll know. Go at once. I'm off."

It was a week since Denzil had been to the house in Grosvenor Square, and when he got there he was surprised to find, early as it was, a travelling-chariot at the door, with trunks strapped on, all ready for the road.

He met his father's man coming down the stairs with an armful of shawls.

"Sir Denzil, Kennet. At once, please."

"Just in time, sir. Another ten minutes and we'd been gone. He's all dressed, Mr. Denzil. Will you come up, sir?"

"Ah, Denzil, you got my note," said Sir Denzil at sight of him. "We settled it somewhat hurriedly. But Lady Susan is nervous over this cholera business. What's wrong?" he asked quickly, as Kennet quitted the room.

Denzil quietly told him the whole matter, and his father took snuff very gravely. He saw all his hopes ruined at a blow; but he gave no sign, except the tightening of the bones under the clear white skin of his face, and a deepening of the furrows in his brow and at the sides of his mouth.

"The man's death is a misfortune—as was his birth, I believe," he said, as he snuffed gravely again. "Had you any quarrel with him previously?"

"I had threatened, in a general way, to break his head for wagging his tongue about me."

"They may twist that to your hurt," said his father, nodding gravely. "In any case it means much unpleasantness. I am inclined to think you would be better out of the way for a time."

"I will do as you think best, sir. I am quite ready to wait and see it through."

"You never can tell how things may go," said his father thoughtfully. "It all depends on the judge's humour at the time, and that is beyond any man's calculation. . . . Yes, you will be more comfortable away, and I will hasten back and see how things go here. . . . And if you are to go, the sooner the better. . . . You can start with us. We will drop you at St. Albans, and you will make your way across to Antwerp. You had better take Kennet," he continued, with the first visible twinge of regret, as his plans evolved bit by bit. "He is safe, and I don't trust that man of yours—he has a foxy face. If they follow us to Carne, you will be at Antwerp by that time. Send us your address, and I will send you funds there. Here is enough for the time being. Oblige me by ringing the bell. And, by the way, Denzil, say a kind word or two to Susan. You have been neglecting her somewhat of late, and she has felt it. . . . Kennet, tell Lady Susan

I am ready, and inform her ladyship that Mr. Denzil is here, and will accompany us."

And ten minutes later the travelling-chariot was bowling away along the Edgware Road; and the hope which had shone in Lady Susan's eyes at sight of her husband was dying out with every beat of the horses' hoofs and every word that passed between the two men. For the matter had to be told, and the time was short. Sir Denzil had intended to stop for a time at Carne. Now he must get back at the earliest possible momet. And, though they made light of the matter, and described Denzil's hurried journey as a simple measure of precaution, and a means of escaping unnecessary annoyance, Lady Susan's jangled nerves adopted gloomier views, and naturally went farther even than the truth.

Denzil did his best to follow his father's suggestion. His conscience smote him at sight of his wife's pinched face and the shadows under her eyes—shadows which told of days of sorrow and nights of lonely weeping, shadows for which he knew he was as responsible as if his fists had placed them there.

"I am sorry, dear, to bring this trouble on you," he said, pressing her hand.

"Let me go with you, Denzil," she cried, with a catch of hope in her voice. "Let me go with you, and the trouble will be as nothing."

How she would have welcomed any trouble that drove him to her arms again! But she knew, even as she said it, that it was not possible. That lay before her, looming large in the vagueness of its mystery, which sickened her, body and soul, with apprehension. But it was a path which she must travel alone, and already, almost before they were fairly started, she was longing for the end of the journey and for rest. The jolting of the carriage was dreadful to her. The trees and hedges tumbled over one another in a hazy rout which set her brain whirling and made her eyes close wearily. She longed for the end of the journey and for rest—peace and quiet and rest, and the end of the journey.

"We will hope the trouble will soon blow over," said Sir Denzii. "But we lose nothing by taking precautions. I shall return to town at once and keep an eye on matters, and as soon as things smooth down Denzil will join you at Carne." At which Denzil's jaw tightened lugubriously. He had his own reasons for not desiring to visit Carne.

"Old Mrs. Lee," continued Sir Denzil—for the sake of making talk, since it seemed to him that silence would surely lead to hysterics on the part of Lady Susan—"will make you very comfortable. She is a motherly old soul, though you may find her a trifle uncouth at first; and Carne is very restful at this time of year. That woman of yours always struck me as a fool, my dear. I think it is just as well she decided not to come, but she might have had the grace to give you a little longer warning. That class of person is compounded of selfishness and duplicity. They are worse, I think, than the men, and God knows the men are bad enough. Your man is another of the same pattern, Denzil. They ought to marry. The result might be interesting, but I should prefer not having any of it in my service."

At St. Albans they parted company. Denzil pressed his wife's hand for the last time in this world, hired a post-chaise, and started across country in company with the discomfited Kennet, who regarded the matter with extreme disfavour both on his own account and his master's, and Sir Denzil and Lady Susan went bumping along on the way to Carne.

CHAPTER III

THE FIRST OF THE COIL

A WOMAN trudged heavily along the firm damp sand just below the bristling tangle of high-water mark, in the direction of Carne. She wore a long cloak, and bent her head and humped her shoulders over a small bundle which she hugged tight to her breast.

She had hoped to reach the big house before it was dark. But a north-east gale was blowing, and it caught up the loose tops of the sand-hills and carried them in streaming clouds along the flats and made walking difficult. The drift rose no higher than her waist; but if she stood for a moment to rest, the flying particles immediately set to work to transform her into a pillar of sand. If she had stumbled and been unable to rise, the sweeping sand would have covered her out of sight in five minutes.

The flats stretched out before her like an empty desert that had no end. The black sky above seemed very close by reason of the wrack of clouds boiling down into the west. Where the sun had set there was still a wan gleam of yellow light. It seemed to the woman, when she glanced round now and again through her narrowed lids to make sure of her whereabouts, as if the sky was slowly closing down on her like the lid of a great black box. On her right hand the sand-hills loomed white and ghostly, and were filled with the whistle of the gale in the wire-grass and the hiss of the flying sand.

Far away on her left, the sea chafed and growled behind its banks.

Her progress was very slow, but she bent doggedly to the gale, stopped now and again and leaned bodily against it, then drew her feet out of the clogs the sand had piled round them and pushed slowly on again. At last she became aware, by instinct or by the instant's break in the roar of the wind on her right, that she had reached her journey's end. She turned up over the crackling tangle, crossed the ankle-deep dry sand of the upper beach, and stopped for breath under the lee of the great house of Carne.

It was all as dark as the grave, but she knew her way, and after a moment's rest she passed round the house to the back. Here in a room on the ground floor a light shone through a window. The window had neither curtain nor shutter, but was protected by stout iron bars. The sill was piled high with drifted sand.

The sight of the light dissipated a fear which had ber- in the woman's heart, but which she had crushed resolutely out of sight. At the same time it set her heart beating tumultuously, partly in the rebound from its fear and partly in anticipation of the ungracious welcome she looked for. She stood for a moment in the storm outside and looked at the tranquil gleam. Then she slipped under a stone porch, which opened towards the south-west, and knocked on the door. The door opened cautiously on the chain at last, six inches or so, and a section of an old woman's head appeared in the slit and asked gruffly:

"Who's it?"

"It's me, mother—Nance!"

The door slammed suddenly to, as though to deny her admittance. But she heard the trembling fingers inside fumbling with the chain. They got it unsnecked at last, and the door swung open again. The woman with the burden stepped inside and shut out the drifting sand.

The room was a stone-flagged kitchen; but the light of the candle, and the cheery glow of a coal fire, and the homeliness of the white-scrubbed table and dresser, and the great oak linen-press, mellowed its asperities. After the cold north-easter, and the sweeping sand and the darkness, it was like heaven to the traveller, and she sank down on a rush-bottomed chair with a sigh of relief.

"So tha's come whoam at last," was the welcome that greeted her, in a voice that was over-harsh lest it should tremble and break. The old woman's eyes shone like black beads under her white mutch. She sniffed angrily, and dashed her hand across her face as though to assist her sight. She spoke the patois of the district. Beyond the understanding of any but natives even now, it was still more difficult then. It would be a sorry task to attempt to reproduce it.

"Aye, I've come home."

"And brought thy shame with thee!"

"Shame?" said the other quickly. "What shame? He married me, and this is his boy." And as she straightened up, the cloak fell apart and disclosed the child. She spoke boldly, but her eyes and her face were not so brave as her speech.

"Married ye?" said the old woman, with a grim laugh that was half sob and half anger. "I know better. The likes o' him doesna marry the likes o' you."

Holding the sleeping child in her one arm, the girl fumbled in her bodice and plucked out a paper.

"There's my lines," she said angrily.

The old woman made no attempt to read it, but shook her head again, and said bitterly:

"The likes o' him doesna marry the likes o' you, my lass."

"He married me as soon as we got to London."

But the old woman only shook her head, and asked, in the tone of one using an irrefutable argument:

"Where is he?"

At that the girl shook her head also; but she was saved further reply by the baby yawning and stretching and opening his eyes, which fastened vacantly on the old woman's as she bent over to look at him in spite of herself.

"You might ha' killed him and yoreself coming on so soon," she said gruffly.

"I wanted to get here before he came," said the girl, with a choke, "but I couldna manage it. I were took at Runcorn, seven days ago."

"An' yo' walked from there! It's a wonner yo're alive. Well, well, it's a bad job, but I suppose we mun mak' best o' it. Yo're clemmed!"

"Ay, I am, and so is he. I've not had much to give him, and he makes a rare noise when he doesn't get what he wants."

The baby screwed up his face and proved his powers. His mother rocked him to and fro, and the old woman set herself to getting them food. She set on the fire a pannikin of goats' milk diluted with water to her own ideas, and placed bread and cheese and butter on the table. The girl reached for the food and began to eat ravenously. The old woman dipped her finger into the pannikin and put it into the child's mouth. It sucked vigorously and stopped crying. She drew it out of the girl's arms and began to feed it slowly with a spoon.

"If he married yo', why did he leave yo' like this?" she asked presently, as she dropped tiny drops of food into the baby's mouth and watched it swallow and strain up after the spoon for more.

"He was ordered away with his regiment. He left me money and said he'd send more. But he never did. I made it last as long's I could, but it runs away in London. I couldna bear the idea of—of it up there, an' I got wild at him not coming. I tried to find him, and then I set off to walk here. I got a lift on a wagon now and again. But when I got to Runcorn I could go no further. There was a woman there was good to me. Maybe I'd ha' died but for her. Maybe it'd ha' been best if I had. But"—she said doggedly—"he married me all the same."

The old woman shook her head hopelessly, but said nothing. The baby was falling asleep on her knee. Presently she carried him carefully into the next room and left him on the bed there.

"I nursed him on my knee," she said when she came back, "before you came. If I'd known he'd take you from me I'd ha' choked him where he lay."

The girl felt and looked the better for her meal. She nodded her head slowly, and said again, "All the same he married me." Her persistent harping on that one string—which to her mother was a broken string—angered the old woman.

"Tchah!" she said, like the snapping of a dog, and was about to say a great deal more when a peremptory knocking on the door choked the words in her throat. Her startled yes turned accusingly on the girl; what faint touch of colour er face had held fled from it, and her lips parted twice in uestioning which found no voice. Her whole attitude mplied the fear that there was something more behind the irl's story than had been told and that now it was upon them.

The knocking continued, louder and still more peremptory.

The girl strode to the door, loosed the chain and drew back he bolts, and flung it open. A tall man, muffled in a travelling-cloak, strode in with an imprecation, and dusted the sand ut of his eyes with a silk handkerchief.

"Nice doings when a man cannot get into his own house," e began. Then, as his blinking eyes fell on the girl's face, he topped short and said, "The deuce!" and pinched his chin etween his thumb and forefinger. He stood regarding her in nomentary perplexity, and then went on dusting himself, with is eyes still on her.

He was a man past middle age, but straight and vigorous till. His clean-shaven face, in spite of the stubble of three lays' rapid travel on it, and the deep lines of hard living, was ndeniably handsome—keen dark eyes, straight nose, level rows, firm hard mouth. An upright furrow in the forehead, nd a sloping groove at each corner of the mouth, gave a look f rigid intensity to the face and the impression that its owner as engaged in a business distasteful to him.

"Ah, Mrs. Lee," he said, as his eyes passed from the girl t last and rested on the old woman.

"Yes, Sir Denzil." And Mrs. Lee attempted a curtsey.

"A word in your ear, mistress." And he spoke rapidly to r in low tones, his eyes roving over to the girl now and ain, and the old woman's face stiffening as he spoke.

"And now bustle, both of you," he concluded. "Fires first, en something to eat, the other things afterwards. I will ing her ladyship in."

He went to the door, and the old woman turned to her ughter and said grimly:

"There's a lady with him. Yo' mun help wi' the fires."

She closed the door leading to the bedroom where the baby lay sleeping soundly, and then set doggedly about her duties. The two women had left the room carrying armfuls of firing when Sir Denzil came back leading Lady Susan by the hand, muffled like himself in a big travelling-cloak. He drew a chair to the fire, and she sank into it. He left her there and went out again, and as the door opened the rattle of harness on chilling horses came through.

Lady Susan bent shivering over the fire and spread her hands towards it, groping for its cheer like a blind woman. Her face was white and drawn. Her eyes were sunk in dark wells of hopelessness, her lips were pinched in tight repression. Any beauty that might have been hers had left her; only her misery and weariness remained. Her whole attitude expressed extremest suffering both of mind and body.

A piping cry came from the next room, and she straightened up suddenly and looked about her like a startled deer. Then she rose quickly and picked up the candle and answered the call.

The child had cried out in his sleep, and as she stood over him, with the candle uplifted, a strange softening came over her face. Her left hand stole up to her side and pressed it as though to still a pain. A spasmodic smile crumpled the little face as she watched. Then it smoothed out and the child settled to sleep again. Lady Susan went slowly back to her seat before the fire, and almost immediately Sir Denzil came in again, dusting himself from the sand more vigorously than ever.

"How do you feel now, my dear?" he asked.

"Sick to death," she said quietly.

"You will feel better after a night's rest. The journey has been a trying one. Old Mrs. Lee will make you comfortable here, and I will return the moment I am sure of Denzil's safety. You agree with the necessity for my going?"

"Quite."

"Every moment may be of importance. But the moment

he is safe I will hurry back to see to your welfare here. I shall lie at Warrington to-night, and I will tell the doctor at Wynsloe to come over first thing in the morning to see how you are going on. Ah, Mrs. Lee, you are ready for us?"

"Ay. The oak parlour is ready, sir. I'll get you what I con to eat, but you'll have to put up wi' short farin' to-night, sin' you didna let me know you were coming. To-morrow——"

"What you can to-night as quickly as possible. Lady Susan is tired out, and I return as soon as I have eaten. See that the post-boy gets something too."

"Yo're non stopping?" asked the old woman in surprise.

"No, no, I told you so," he said, with the irritation of a tired man. "Come, my dear!" and he offered his arm to Lady Susan, and led her slowly away down the stone passage to a small room in the west front, where the rush of the storm was barely heard.

An hour later Sir Denzil was whirling back before the gale on his way to London, as fast as two tired horses and a none too amiable post-boy could carry him. His usual serene self-complacency was disturbed by many anxieties, and he carried not a little bitterness, on his own account, at the untowardness of the circumstances which had dragged him from the ordered courses of his life and sent him posting down into the wilderness, without even the assistance of his man, upon whom he depended for the minutest details of his bodily comfort.

"A most damnable misfortune!" he allowed himself, now that he was alone, and he added some further unprofitable moments to an already tolerably heavy account in cursing every separate person connected with the matter, including a dead man and the man who killed him, and an unborn babe and the mother who lay shivering at thought of its coming.

CHAPTER IV

THE COIL COMPLETE

IN the great house of Carne there was a stillness in strange contrast with the roaring of the gale outside. But the stillness was big with life's vitalities—love and hate and fear; and, compared with them, the powers without were nothing more than whistling winds that played with shifting sands, and senseless waves that sported with men's lives.

It was not till the new-comer was lying in her warm bed in the room above the oak parlour, shivering spasmodically at times in spite of blankets and warming-pans and a roaring fire, that she spoke to the old woman who had assisted her in grim silence.

The silence and the grimness had not troubled her. They suited her state of mind and body better than speech would have done. Life had lost its savour for her. Of what might lie beyond she knew little and feared much at times, and at times cared naught, craving only rest from all the ills of life and the poignant pains that racked her.

It was only when Mrs. Lee had carefully straightened out her discarded robes, and looked round to see what else was to be done, and came to the bedside to ask tersely if there was anything more my lady wanted, that my lady spoke.

"You'll come back and sit with me?" she asked.

"Ay—I'll come."

"Whose baby is that downstairs?"

"It's my girl's," said the old woman, startled somewhat at my lady's knowledge.

"Did she live through it?"

"Ay, she lived." And there was that in her tone which implied that it might have been better if she had not. But my lady's perceptions were blunted by her own sufferings.

"Is she here?"

"Ay, she's here."

"Would she come to me too?"

But the old woman shook her head.

"She's not over strong yet," she said grimly. "I'll come back and sit wi' yo'."

"How old is it?"

"Seven days."

"Seven days! Seven days!" She was wondering vaguely where she would be in seven days.

"It looked very happy," she said presently. "Its father was surely a good man."

"They're none too many," said the old woman, as she turned to go. "I'll get my supper and come back t' yo'."

"Who is she?" asked her daughter, with the vehemence of an aching question, as she entered the kitchen.

Mrs. Lee closed the passage door and looked at her steadily and said, "She's Denzil Carron's wife." And the younger woman sprang to her feet with blazing face and the clatter of a falling chair.

"Denzil's wife! I am Denzil Carron's wife."

"So's she. And I reckon she's the one they'll call his wife," said her mother dourly.

"I'll go to her. I'll tell her——" And she sprang to the door.

"Nay, you wun't," said her mother, leaning back against it. "T' blame's not hers, an' hoo's low enough already."

"And where is he? Where is Denzil?"

"He's in trouble of some kind, but what it is I dunnot know. Sir Denzil's gone back to get him out of it, and he brought her here to be out of it too."

"And he'll come here?"

"Mebbe. Sir Denzil didna say. He said he'd hold me responsible for her. She's near her time, poor thing! An' I doubt if she comes through it."

"Near——!" And the girl blazed out again.

"Ay. I shouldna be surprised if it killed her. There's the look o' it in her face."

"Kill her? Why should it kill her? It didn't kill me," said the girl fiercely.

"Mebbe it would but for yon woman you told me of. Think of your own time, girl, and bate your anger. Fault's not hers if Denzil served you badly."

"He connot have two wives."

"Worse for him if he has. One's enough for most men. But—well-a-day, it's no good talking! I'll take a bite, and back to her. She begged me come. Yo' can sleep i' my bed. There's more milk on th' hob there if th' child's hungry." And carrying her bread-and-cheese she went off down the passage, and the young mother sat bending over the fire with her elbows on her knees.

She had no thought of sleep. Her limbs were still weary from her long tramp, but the food and rest had given her strength, and the coming of this other woman, who called herself Denzil Carron's wife, had fired her with a sense of revolt.

The blood was boiling through her veins at thought of it all—at thought of Denzil, at thought of the boy in the next room, and this other woman upstairs. Her heart felt like molten lead kicking in a cauldron.

She got up and began to pace the floor with the savage grace born of a life of unrestricted freedom. Once she stopped and flung up her hands as though demanding—what?—a blessing—a curse—the righting of a wrong? The quivering hands looked capable at the moment of righting their own wrongs, or of wreaking vengeance on the wrongdoer if they closed upon him.

Then, as the movement of her body quieted in some measure the turmoil of her brain, her pace grew slower, and she began to think connectedly. And at last she drooped into the chair again, leaned her elbows on her knees and sat gazing into the fire. When it burned low she piled on wood mechanically, and sat there thinking, thinking. Outside, the storm raged furiously, and the flying sand hit the window like hailstones. And inside, the woman sat gazing into the fire and thinking.

She sat long into the night, thinking, thinking—unconscious of the passage of time;—thinking, thinking. Twice her child woke crying to be fed, and each time she fed him from the pannikin as mechanically almost as she had fed the fire with wood. For her thoughts were strange long thoughts, and she could not see the end of them.

They were all sent flying by the sudden entrance of her mother in a state of extreme agitation, her face all crumpled, her hands shaking.

"She's took," she said, with a break in her voice. "Yo' mun go for th' doctor quick. I connot leave her. Nay!"—as the other sat bolt upright and stared back at her—"yo' *mun* go. We connot have her die on our hands. Think o' yore own time, lass, and go quick for sake o' Heaven."

"I'll go." And she snatched up her cloak. "See to the child." And she was out in the night, drifting before the gale like an autumn leaf.

The old woman went in to look at the child, filled the kettle and put it on the fire, and hurried back to the chamber of sorrows.

The gale broke at sunrise, and the flats lay shimmering like sheets of burnished gold, when Dr. Yool turned at last from the bedside and looked out of the window upon the freshness of the morning.

He was in a bitter humour. When Nance Lee thumped on his door at midnight he was engaged in the congenial occupation of mixing a final and unusually stiff glass of rum and water. It was in the nature of a soporific—a nightcap. It was to be the very last glass for that night, and he had compounded it with the tenderest care and the most business-like intention.

"If that won't give me a night's rest," he said to himself, "nothing will."

But there was no rest for him that night. He had been on the go since daybreak, and was fairly fagged out. He greeted Nance's imperative knock with bad language. But when he heard her errand he swallowed his nightcap without a wink, though it nearly made his hair curl, ran round with her to the stable, harnessed his second cob to the little black gig with the yellow wheels, threw Nance into it, and in less than five minutes was wrestling with the north-easter once more, and spitting out the sand as he had been doing off and on all day long.

"There's one advantage in being an old bachelor, Miss Nancy," he had growled, as he flung the harness on the disgusted little mare: "your worries are your own. Take my advice and never you get married——" And then he felt like biting his tongue off when he remembered the rumours he had heard concerning the girl. She was too busy with her own long thoughts to be troubled by his words, however, and once they were on the road speech was impossible by reason of the gale.

When they arrived at Carne she scrambled down and led the mare into the great empty coach-house, where the post-horses had previously found shelter that night. She flung the knee-rug over the shaking beast, still snorting with disgust and eyeing her askance as the cause of all the trouble. Then she followed the doctor into the house. He was already upstairs, however, and, after a look at her sleeping boy, she sat down in her chair before the fire again to await the event, and fell again to her long, long thoughts.

And once more her thoughts were sent flying by the entrance of her mother. She carried a tiny bundle carefully wrapped in flannel and a shawl, and on her sour old face there was an expression of relief and exultation—the exultation of one who has won in a close fight with death.

"He were but just in time," she said, as she sat down

efore the fire. "I'm all of a shake yet. But th' child's ife anyway." And she began to unfold the bundle tenderly. Git me t' basin and some warm water. Now, my mannie, e'll soon have you comfortable. . . . So . . . Poor little nap! . . . I doubt if she'll pull through. . . . T' doctor's ursing high and low below his breath at state she's in . . . avelling in that condition . . . 'nough to have killed a ronger one than ever she was. . . . I knew as soon as ivver set eyes on her . . . A fine little lad!"—as she turned the ew-comer carefully over on her knee—"and nothing a-want-g 's far as I can see, though he's come a month before he ould."

She rambled on in the rebound from her fears, but the rl uttered no word in reply. She stood watching abstractedly, id handing whatever the old woman called for. Her oughts were in that other room, where the grim fight was ill waging. Her heart was sick to know how it was going. Ier thoughts were very shadowy still, but the sight of the oy on the old woman's knee showed her her possible way, ke a signpost on a dark night. She would see things earer when she knew how things had gone upstairs.

She must know. She could not wait. She turned towards e passage.

"I will go and see," she said.

"Ay, go," said the old woman. "But go soft."

The doctor was sitting at the bedside. He raised his nd when she entered the room, but did not turn. She ood and watched, and suddenly all her weariness came on r and she felt like falling. She leaned against the wall d waited.

Once and again the doctor spoke to the woman on the l. But there was no answer. He sat with furrowed face tching her, and the girl leaned against the wall and watched m both.

And at last the one on the bed answered—not the doctor, a greater healer still. One long sigh, just as the sun began to touch the rippled flats with gold, and it was over. The stormy night was over and peace had come with the morning.

The doctor got up with something very like a scowl on his face and went to the window. Even in the Presence he had to close his mouth firmly lest the lava should break out.

He hated to be beaten in the fight—the endless fight to which his whole life was given, year in, year out. But this had been no fair fight. The battle was lost before he came on the field, and his resentment was hot against whoever was to blame.

He opened the casement and leaned out to cool his head. The sweet morning air was like a kiss. He drank in a big breath or two, and, after another pained look at the white face on the pillow, he turned and left the room. The girl had already gone, and as she went down the passage there was a gleam in her eyes.

Her mother saw it as soon as she entered the kitchen.

"Well?" asked the old woman.

"She's gone."

"And yo're glad of it. Shame on yo', girl! And yo' but just safe through it yoreself!"

The girl made no reply, and a moment later the doctor came in.

"Now, Mrs. Lee, explain things to me. Whose infernal folly brought that poor thing rattling over the country in that condition? And get me a cup of coffee, will you? Child all right?"

"He's all right, doctor. He's sleeping quiet there"—pointing to a heap of shawls on the hearth. "It were Sir Denzil himself brought her last night."

"And why didn't he stop to see the result of his damned stupidity? It's sheer murder, nothing less. Make it as strong as you can,"—referring to the coffee—"my head's buzzing. I haven't had a minute's rest for twenty-four hours. Where is Sir Denali? He left word at my house to come over here first thing this morning. I expected to find him here."

"He went back wi' the carriage that brought 'em. There's rouble afoot about Mr. Denzil as I understond. He said t were life and death, and he were off again inside an hour."

"Ah!" said the doctor, nodding his head knowingly. 'That's it, is it? And you don't know what the trouble was?"

"'Life and death,' he said. That's all I know."

"Well, if he bungles the other business as he has done his it'll not need much telling which it'll be." And he blew on his coffee to cool it.

"I must send him word at once," he said presently, "and I'll tell him what I think about it. I've got his town address. You can see to the child all right, I suppose? Another piece of that bread, if you please. Any more coffee there? This kind of thing makes me feel empty."

"I'll see to t' child aw reet."

"Send me word if you need me, not otherwise. There's yphus down Wyvveloe way, and I'm run off my legs. A log's life, dame—little thanks and less pay!" And he buttoned ip his coat fiercely and strode out to his gig. "I'll send 'ohn Braddle out," he called back over his shoulder. "But doubt if we can wait to hear from Sir Denzil. However——" And he drove away, through the slanting morning unshine.

The white sand-hills smiled happily, the wide flats blazed ke a rippled mirror, the sky was brightest blue, and very far way the sea slept quietly behind its banks of yellow sand.

CHAPTER V

IN THE COIL

THE days passed and brought no word from Sir Denzil in reply to Dr. Yool's post letter. And, having waited as ng as they could, they buried Lady Susan in the little green urchyard at Wyvveloe, where half a dozen Carrons, who happened to have died at Carne, already rested. Dr. Yool and Braddle had had to arrange everything between them, and, as might have been expected under the circumstances, the funeral was as simple as funeral well could be, and as regards attendance—well, the doctor was the only mourner, and he still boiled over when he thought of the useless way in which this poor life had been sacrificed.

Braddle was there with his men, of course, but the doctor only just managed it between two visits, and his manner showed that he grudged the time given to the dead which was all too short for the requirements of the living. Yet it went against the grain to think of that poor lady going to her last resting-place unattended, and he made a point of being there. But his gig stood waiting outside the churchyard gate, and he was whirling down the lane while the first spadefuls were drumming on the coffin.

He thought momentarily of the child as he drove along. But, since no call for his services had come from Mrs. Lee, he supposed it was going on all right, and he had enough sick people on his hands to leave him little time for any who could get along without him.

The days ran into weeks, and still no word from Sir Denzil. It looked as though the little stranger at Carne might remain a stranger for the rest of his days. And yet it was past thinking that those specially interested should make no inquiry concerning the welfare of so important a member of the family.

"Summat's happened," was old Mrs. Lee's terse summing-up, with a gloomy shake of the head whenever she and Nance discussed the matter, which was many times a day.

Other matters too they discussed, and to more purpose, since the forwarding of them was entirely in their own hands. And when they spoke of these other matters, sitting over the fire in the long evenings, each with a child on her knee, hushing it or feeding it, their talk was broken, interjectional even at times, and so low that the very walls could have made little of it.

It was fierce-eyed Nance who started that strain of talk, nd at first her mother received it open-mouthed. But by legrees, and as time played for them, she came round o it, and ended by being the more determined of the wo. So they were of one mind on the matter, and the natter was of moment, and all that happened afterwards grew ut of it.

Both the children throve exceedingly. No care was lacking hem, and no distinction was made between them. What one ad the other had, and Nance, with recovered strength, layed foster-mother to them both.

Just two months after Lady Susan's death the two women vere sitting talking over the fire one night, the children being sleep side by side in the cot in the adjacent bedroom, when he sound of hoofs and wheels outside brought them to their eet together.

"It's him," said Mrs. Lee; and they looked for a moment nto one another's faces as though each sought sign of flinching n the other. Then both their faces tightened, and they eemed to brace themselves for the event.

An impatient knock on the kitchen door, the old woman astened to answer it, and Sir Denzil limped in. He was hinner and whiter than the last time he came. He leaned eavily on a stick and looked frail and worn.

"Well, Mrs. Lee," he said, as he came over to the fire d bent over it and chafed his hands, "you'd given up l fears of ever seeing me again, I suppose?"

"Ay, a'most we had," said the old woman, as she lifted e kettle off the hob and set it in the blaze.

"Well, it wasn't far off it. I had a bad smash returning London that last time. That fool of a post-boy drove to a tree that had fallen across the road, and killed himself d did his best to kill me. Now light the biggest fire you n make in the oak room, and another in my bedroom, and t me something to eat. Kennet"—as his man came in agging a travelling-trunk—"get out a bottle of brandy, and, as soon as you've got the things in, brew me the stiffest glass of grog you ever made. My bones are frozen."

He dragged up a chair and sat down before the fire, thumping the coals with his stick to quicken the blaze. The rest sped to his bidding.

Kennet, when he had got in the trunks, brewed the grog in a big jug, with the air of one who knew what he was about.

"Shall I give the boy some, sir?" he asked, when Sir Denzil had swallowed a glass and was wiping his eyes from the effects of it.

"Yes, yes. Give him a glass, but tone it down, or he'll be breaking his neck like the last one."

So Kennet watered a glass to what he considered reasonable encouragement for a frozen post-boy, and presently the jingling of harness died away in the distance, and Kennet came in and fastened the door.

Sir Denzil had filled and emptied his glass twice more before Mrs. Lee came to tell him the room was ready. Then he went slowly off down the passage, steadying himself with his stick, for a superfluity of hot grog on an empty stomach on a cold night is not unapt to mount to the head of even a seasoned toper.

Kennet, when he came back to the room, after seeing his master comfortably installed before the fire, brewed a fresh supply of grog, placed on one side what he considered would satisfy his own requirements, and carried the rest to the oak room.

It was when the girl Nance carried in the hastily prepared meal that Sir Denzil, after peering heavily at her from under his bushy brows, asked suddenly, "And the child? It's alive?"

"Alive and well, sir."

"Bring it to me in the morning."

The girl looked at him once or twice as if she wanted to ask him a question.

He caught her at it, and asked abruptly, "What the devil are you staring at, and what the deuce keeps you hanging round here?" Upon which sh . quitted the room.

There was much talk, intense and murmurous, between the two women that night, when they had made up a bed for Kennet and induced him at last to go to it. From Kennet and the grog, after Sir Denzil had retired for the night, Nance learned all Kennet could tell her about Mr. Denzil.

According to that veracious historian it was only through Mr. Kennet's supreme discretion and steadfastness of purpose that the young man got safely across to Brussels, and, when he tired of Brussels, which he very soon did, to Paris.

"Ah!" said Mr. Kennet. "Now, that *is* a place. Gay?—I believe you! Lively?—I believe you! Heels in the air kind of place?—I believe you! And Mr. Denzil he took to it like a duck to the water. London ain't in it with Paris, I tell you." And so on and so on, until, through close attention to the grog, his words began to tumble over one another. Then he bade them good night, with solemn and insistent emphasis, as though it was doubtful if they would ever meet again, and cautiously followed Nance and his candle to his room.

The flats were gleaming like silver under a frosty sun next morning, and there was a crackling sharpness in the air, when Sir Denzil, having breakfasted, stood at the window of the oak room awaiting his grandson.

"Tell Mrs. Lee to bring in the child," he had said to Kennet, and now a tap on the door told him that the child was there.

"Come in," he said sharply, and turned and stood amazed at sight of the two women each with a child on her arm.

"The deuce!" he said, and fumbled for his snuff-box.

He found it at last, a very elegant little gold box, bearing a miniature set with diamonds—a present from his friend George, in the days before the slice of orange, and most probably never paid for. He slowly extracted a pinch without removing his eyes from the women and children. He snuffed, still staring at them, and then said quietly, "What the deuce is the meaning of this?"

"Yo' asked to see t' child, sir," said Mrs. Lee.

"Well?"

"Here 'tis, sir."

"Which?"

"Both!"

"Ah!"—with a pregnant nod. Then, with a wave of the hand. "Take them away." And the women withdrew.

Sir Denzil remained standing exactly as he was for many minutes. Then he began to pace the room slowly with his stick, to and fro, to and fro, with his eyes on the polished floor, and his thoughts hard at work.

He saw the game, and recognized at a glance that no cards had been dealt him. The two women held the whole pack, and he was out of it.

He thought keenly and savagely, but saw no way out. The more he thought, the tighter seemed the cleft of the stick in which the women held him.

The law? The law was powerless in the matter. Not all the law in the land could make a woman speak when all her interests bade her keep silence, any more than it could make her keep silence if she wanted to speak.

Besides, even if these women swore till they were blue in the face as to the identity of either child, he would never believe one word of their swearing. Their own interests would guide them, and no other earthly consideration.

He could turn them out. To what purpose? One of those two children was Denzil Carron of Carne. Which?

The other—ah yes! The other was equally of his blood. He did not doubt that for one moment. He had known of Denzil's entanglement with Nance Lee, and it had not troubled him for a moment. But who, in the name of Heaven, could have foreseen so perplexing a result?

When he glanced out of the window, the crystalline morning, the white sunshine, the clear blue sky, the hard yellow flats, the distant blue sea with its crisp white fringe, all seemed to mock him with the brightness of their beauty.

How to solve the puzzle? Already, in his own mind, he doubted if it ever would be solved. And he cursed the brightness of the morning, and the women—which was more to the point, but equally futile,—and Densil, and poor Lady Susan, who lay past curses in Wyvveloe churchyard. And his face, while that fit was on him, was not pleasant to look upon.

Presently, with a twitching of the corners of the mouth, like a dog about to bare his fangs, he rang the bell very gently, and Kennet came in.

"Kennet," he said, as quietly as if he were ordering his boots, "put on your hat and go for Dr. Yool. Bring him with you without fail. If he is out, go after him. If he says he'll see me further first, say I apologise, and I want him here at once. Tell him I've burst a blood-vessel."

He had had words with the doctor the night before. He had stopped his post-chaise at his house and gone in for a minute to explain his long absence, and the doctor, who feared no man, had rated him soundly for the thoughtlessness which had caused Lady Susan's death.

He did not for a moment believe that the doctor or any one else could help him in this blind alley. But discuss the matter with some one he must, or burst, and he did not care to discuss it with Kennet. Kennet knew very much better than to disagree with his master on any subject whatever, and discussion with him never advanced matters one iota. Discussion of the matter with Dr. Yool would probably have the same result, but it could do no harm, and it offered possibilities of a disputation for which he felt a distinct craving.

Whether doctors could reasonably be expected to identify infants at whose births they had officiated, after a lapse of two months, he did not know. But he was quite prepared to uphold that view of the case with all the venom that was in him, and he awaited the doctor's arrival with impatience.

Dr. Yool drove up at last with Kennet beside him, and presently stood in the room with Sir Denzil.

"Hello!" cried the doctor, with disappointment in his face. "Where's that blood-vessel?"

"Listen to me, Yool. You were present at the birth of Lady Susan's children——"

"Eh? What? Lady Susan's child? Yes!"

"Children!"

"What the deuce! Children? A boy, sir—one!"

"You'd know him again, I suppose?"

"Well, in a general kind of way possibly. What's amiss with him?"

"According to these women here, there are two of him now."

"Good Lord, Sir Denzil! What do you mean? Two? How can there be two?"

"Ah, now you have me. I thought that you, as a doctor—as the doctor, in fact—could probably explain the matter."

The doctor's red face reddened still more.

"Send for the women here—and the children," he said angrily.

Sir Denzil rang the bell, gave his instructions to the impassive Kennet, who had not yet fathomed the full intention of the matter, and in a few minutes Mrs. Lee and Nance, each with a child on her arm, stood before them.

"Now then, what's the meaning of all this?" asked Dr. Yool. "Which of these babies is Lady Susan's child?"

"We don't know, sir," said Mrs. Lee, with a curtsey.

"Don't know! Don't know! What the deuce do you mean by that, Mrs. Lee? Whose is the other child?"

"My daughter's, sir. It were born a day or two before the other, and we got 'em mixed and don't know which is which."

"Nonsense! Bring them both to me."

He flung down some cushions in front of the fire, rapidly undressed the children, and laid them wriggling and squirming in the blaze among their wraps. He bent and examined them with minutest care. He turned them over and over, noticed all their points with a keenly critical eye, but could make nothing of it. They were as like as two peas. Dark-haired, dark-eyed, plump, clear-skinned, healthy youngsters both. The seven days between them, which in the very beginning might have been apparent, was now, after the lapse of two months, absolutely undiscoverable.

Sir Denzil came across and looked down on the jerking little arms and legs and twisting faces, and snuffed again as though he thought they might be infectious. For all the expression that showed in his face, they might have been a litter of pups.

"Well, I am ——!" said Dr. Yool, at last, straightening up from the inspection with his hands on his hips. "Now"—fixing the two women with a blazing eye—"what's the meaning of it all? Who is the father of this other child?"

"Denzil Carron," said Nance boldly, speaking for the first time. "He married me before he married her, and here are my lines," and she plucked them out of her bosom.

Dr. Yool's eyebrows went up half an inch. Sir Denzil took snuff very deliberately.

The doctor held out his hand for the paper, and after a moment's hesitation Nance handed it to him.

He read it carefully, and his good-humoured mouth twisted doubtfully. The matter looked serious.

"Dress the children and take them away," he said at last. When they were dressed, however, Nance stood waiting for her lines.

Dr. Yooi understood. "I will be answerable for them," he said; and she turned and went.

"A troublesome business, Sir Denzil," he said, when they were alone. "A troublesome business, whichever way you look at it. This"—and he flicked Nance's cherished lines—"may, of course, be make-believe, though it looks genuine enough on the face of it. That must be carefully looked into.

But as to the children—you are in these women's hands absolutely and completely, and they know it."

"It looks deucedly like it."

"They know which is which well enough; but nothing on earth will make them speak—except their own interests, and that," he said thoughtfully, "won't be for another twenty years."

"It's too late to make away with them both, I suppose," said Sir Denzil cynically.

"Tchutt! It's bad enough as it is, but there's no noose in it at present. Besides, they are both undoubtedly your grandsons——"

"And which succeeds?" asked the baronet grimly.

"There's the rub. Deucedly awkward, if they both live—most deucedly awkward! There's always the chance, of course, that one may die."

"Not a chance," said Sir Denzil. "They'll both live to be a hundred. They can toss for the title when the time comes. I'd sooner trust a coin than those women's oaths."

The doctor nodded. He felt the same.

"What about this?" he asked, reading Nance's lines again. "Will you look into it?" He pulled out a pencil and noted places and dates in his pocket-book.

"What good? It alters nothing."

"As regards your son?"

Sir Denzil shrugged lightly.

"He has shown himself a fool, but he is hardly such a fool as that. If he comes to the title, and she claims on him, he must fight his own battle. As to the whelps——" Another shrug shelved them for future consideration.

Nevertheless, when Dr. Yooi had driven away in the gig with the yellow wheels, Sir Denzil paced his room by the hour in deep thought, and none of it pleasant, if his face was anything to go by.

He travelled along every possible avenue, and found each a blind alley.

He could send the girl about her business, and the old woman too. But to what purpose? If they took one of the children with them, which would it be? Most likely Lady Susan's. But he would never be certain of it. That would be so obviously the thing to do that they would probably do the opposite. If they left both children, he would have to get some one else to attend to them, and no one in the world had the interest in their welfare that these two had.

If both children died, then Denzil might marry again, and have an heir about whom there was no possible doubt. That is, if this other alleged marriage of his was, as he suspected, only a sham one. He would have to look into that matter, after all.

If, by any mischance, the marriage, however intended, proved legal, then that hope was barred, and it would be better to have the children, or at all events one of them, live. Otherwise the succession would vest in the Solway Carrons, whom he detested. Better even Nance Lee's boy than a Solway Carron.

The conclusion of the matter was, that he could not better matters at the moment by lifting a finger. Not lightly nor readily did he bring his mind to this. He spent bitter days and nights brooding over it all, and at the end he found himself where he was at the beginning. Time might possibly develop, in one or other of the boys, characteristics which might tell their own tale. But that chance, he recognised, was a small one. Both boys took after their father, and were as like Denzil, when he was a baby, as they possibly could be.

In the spring he would look into that marriage matter. Till then, things must go on as they were.

Not a word did he say to the women. Not the slightest interest did he show in the children. He rarely saw them, and then only by chance. And in the women's care the children throve and prospered, since it was entirely to their interest that they should do so.

BOOK II

CHAPTER VI

FREEMEN OF THE FLATS

NOW we take ten years at a leap.

So small a span of time has made no difference in the great house of Carne, or in its surroundings. Many times have the sand-hills sifted and shifted hither and thither. Many times have the great yellow banks out beyond lazily uncoiled themselves like shining serpents, and coiled themselves afresh into new entanglements for unwary mariners. In the narrow channels the bones of the unwary roll to and fro, and some have sunk down among the quicksands. Times without number have the mighty flats gleamed and gloomed. And the great house has watched it all stonily, and it all looks just the same.

But ten years work mighty changes in men and women, and still greater ones in small boys.

A tall straight-limbed young man strode swiftly among the sand-hummocks and came out on the flats, and stood gazing round him, with a great light in his eyes, and a towel round his neck.

He had a lean, clean-shaven face, to which the hair brushed back behind his ears lent a pleasant eagerness. But the face was leaner and whiter than it should have been, and the eyes seemed unnaturally deep in their hollows.

"Whew!" he whistled, as the wonder of the flats struck home. "A change, changes, and half a change, and no mistake! And all very much for the better—in most respects. The bishop said I'd find it rather different from Whitechapel, and he was right! Very much so! Dear old chap!"

It was ten o'clock of a sweet spring morning. The brown ribbed flats gleamed and sparkled and laughed back at the sun with a thousand rippling lips. The cloudless blue sky was ringing with the songs of many larks.

The young man stood with his braces slipped off his shoulders, and looked up at the larks. Then he characteristically flung up a hand towards them, and cried them a greeting in the famous words of that rising young poet, Mr. Robert Browning, "God's in His heaven! All's well with the world! —Well! Well! Ay—very, very well!" And then, with a higher flight, in the words of the old sweet singer which had formed part of the morning lesson—"Praise Him, all His host!" And then, as his eye caught the gleam of the distant water, he resumed his peeling in haste.

"Ten thousand souls—and bodies, which are very much worse—to the square mile there, and here it looks like ten thousand square miles to this single fortunate body. . . . That sea must be a good mile away. . . . The run alone will be worth coming for. . . ."

He had girt himself with a towel by this time, and fastened it with a scientific twist. . . . "Now for a dance on the Doctor's nose," and he sped off on the long stretch to the water.

The kiss of the salt air cleansed him of the travail of the slums as no inland bathing had ever done. The sun which shone down on him, and the myriad broken suns which flashed up at him from every furrow of the rippled sand, sent new life chasing through his veins. He shouted aloud in his gladness, and splashed the waters of the larger pools into rainbows, and was on and away before they reached the ground.

And so, to the sandy scum of the tide, and through it to deep water, and a manful breasting of the slow calm heave of the great sea; with restful pauses when he lay floating on his back gazing up into the infinite blue; and deep sighs of content for this mighty gift of the freedom of the shore and the waves. And a deeper sigh at thought of the weary toilers among whom he had lived so long, to whom such things were unknown, and must remain so.

But there!—he had done his duty among them to the point almost of final sacrifice. There was duty no less exigent here, though under more God-given conditions. So—one more ploughing through deep waters, arm over arm, side stroke with a great forward reach and answering lunge. Then up and away, all rosy-red and beaded with diamonds, to the clothing and duty of the work-a-day world.

"Grim old place," he chittered as he ran, and his eye fell on Carne for the first time. "Grand place to live . . . if she lived there too. . . . Great saving in towels that run home. . . . Now where the dickens . . . ?"

He looked about perplexedly, then began casting round, hither and thither, like a dog on a lost scent.

"Hang it! I'm sure this was the place. . . . I remember that sand-hill with its hair all a-bristle."

He poked and searched. He scraped up the sand with his hands in case they should have got buried, but not a rag of his clothes could he find.

Stay! Not a rag? What's that? Away down a gully between two hummocks, as if it had attempted escape on its own account—a blue sock which he recognised as his own.

He pounced on it with a whoop, dusted one foot free of the dry, soft sand, and put the sock on.

"It's a beginning," he said, quaintly enough, "but——!" But obviously more was necessary before he could return home. He searched carefully all round, but could not find another thread. He climbed the sliding side of the nearest sand-hill, and looked cautiously about him. But the whole place was a honeycomb of gullies, and the clothing of a thousand men might have hidden in them and never been seen again.

He sat down in the warm sand and cogitated. He looked at his single towel, and at the wire-grass bristling sparsely through the sand, and wondered if it might be possible to construct a primitive raiment out of such slight materials. But his deep-set eyes never ceased their vigilant outlook.

Something moved behind the rounded shoulder of a hill in front. It might be only the loping brown body of a rabbit, but he was after it like a shot.

When he topped the hill he saw a naked white foot slipping out of sight into a dark hole like a big burrow. He leaped down the hill, and stretched a groping arm into the hole. It lighted on squirming flesh. His hand gripped tightly that which it had caught, and a furious assault of blows, scratches, bites, and the frantic tearings of small fingers strove to loosen it. But he held tight, and inch by inch drew his prisoner out—a small boy with dark hair thick with sand, and dark eyes blazing furiously.

He was stark naked, and held in his hand a small weapon consisting of a round stone with a hole in the centre, into which a wooden handle had been thrust and bound with string. With this, as he lay on his back, now that he had space to use it, he proceeded to lash out vigorously at his captor, who still held on to his ankle in spite of the punishment his wrist and arm were receiving.

"Well, I'll be hanged!" said the young man in the towel, dodging the blows as well as he could. "What in Heaven's name are you? Ancient Briton? Bit of the Stone Age?"

"Le' me go or I'll kill you," howled the prisoner.

"No, don't! You're strong: be merciful. Hello!" as a fresh attack took him in the rear, and his bare back resounded to the blows of a weapon similar to the one that was pounding his arm. "You young savages! Two to one, and an unarmed man!"

He loosed the ankle and made a quick dive at the brown thrashing arm, and, having secured it, lifted the wriggling youngster and tucked him under his arm like a parcel. Then, in spite of the struggles of his prisoner, he turned on the new-comer and presently held him captive in similar fashion.

They bit and tore and wriggled like a pair of little tiger-cats, but the arms that held them were strong ones if the face above was thin and worn and gentle.

"Stop it!" He knocked their heads together, and squeezed the slippery little bodies under his arms till the breath was nearly out of them, and took advantage of the moment of gasping quiescence to ask, "Will you be quiet if I let you down?"

They intimated in jerks that they would be quiet.

"Drop those drumsticks, then."

First one, then the other weapon dropped into the sand. He put his foot on them and stood the boys on their feet.

"Drumsticks!" snorted one, his sandy little nose all a-quiver.

"Well, neither am I a drum," said their captor good-humouredly. "Now what's the meaning of all this? Who are you? Or what are you?"

They were fine sturdy little fellows, of ten or eleven, he judged, their skins tanned brown and coated with dry sand, quick dark eyes and dark flushed faces all aglow still with the light of battle. They stood panting before him, no whit abashed either by their defeat or their lack of clothing. He saw their eyes settle longingly on the clubs under his feet. He stooped and picked them up, and the dark eyes followed them anxiously.

"Promise not to use them on me and I'll give them back to you."

The brown hands reached out eagerly, and he handed the weapons over.

"Now sit down and tell me all about it." And he sat down himself in the sand.

He saw them glance towards the mouth of their retreat, and shook his head.

"You can't manage it. I'd have you out before you were half way in. You're prisoners of war on parole. Now then, who are you?"

"Carr'ns."

"Carr'ns, are you? Well, you look it, whatever it means. Do you live in that hole?"

"Sometimes."

"Never wear any clothes?"

"Sometimes."

"I see. Much jollier without, isn't it? But, you see, I can't go home like this. So perhaps you won't mind telling me why you stole my things and where they are?"

"Carr'ns don't steal," jerked one.

"Carr'ns only take things," jerked the other.

"I see. It's a fine point, but it comes to much the same thing unless you return what you take. So perhaps you'll be so good as to turn up my things. Where are they?"

One of the boys nodded towards the burrow.

"That's the stronghold, is it? Not much room to turn about in, I should say."

They declined to express an opinion.

"May I go in and have a look?"

But that was not in the terms of their parole, and they sprang instantly to the defence of their hold. The young man of the towel was beginning to wonder if another pitched battle would be necessary before he could recover his missing property, when a diversion was suddenly created by an innocent outsider.

A foolish young rabbit hopped over the shoulder of a neighbouring sand-hill to see what all the disturbance was about. In a moment the round stone clubs flew and the sense was out of him before he had time to twinkle an eye or form any opinion on the subject. With a whoop the boys sprang at him and resolved themselves instantly into a pyrotechnic whirl of arms and legs and red-hot faces and flying sand, as they fought for their prey.

"Little savages!" said the young man, and did his best to separate them.

But he might as well have attempted argument with a Catherine wheel in the full tide of its short life. And so he took to indiscriminate spanking wherever bare slabs of tumbling flesh gave him a chance, and presently, under the influence of his gentle suasion the combatants separated and stood panting and tingling. The *casus belli* had disappeared beneath the turmoil of the encounter, but suddenly it came to light again under the workings of twenty restless little toes. They both instantly dived for it, and the fight looked like beginning all over again, when the long white arm shot in and secured it and held it up above their reach.

"I say! Are you boys or tiger-cats?" he asked, as he examined them again curiously.

"Carr'ne," panted one, while both gazed at the rabbit like hounds at the kill.

"Yes, you said that before, but I'm none the wiser. Where do you live when you're clothed and in your right minds?—if you ever are," he added doubtfully.

One of them jerked his head sharply in the direction of the great gray house away along the shore.

"There?"

Another curt nod. He had rarely met such unnatural reserve, even in Whitechapel, where pointed questions from a stranger are received with a very natural suspicion. Here, as there, it only made him the more determined to get to the bottom of it. But Whitechapel had taught him, among other things, that round-about is sometimes the only way home.

"Why do you want to fight over a dead rabbit?"

"I killed it."

"Didn't. 'Twas me."

"Well now, if you ask me, I should say you both killed it. How did you become such capital shots?"

But to tell that would have needed much talk, so they only stared up at him. He saw he must go slowly.

"These are first-rate clubs. Did you make them?"

Nods from both.

"Do you know?"—he picked one up and examined it carefully—"these are exactly what the wild men used to make when they lived here a couple of thousand years ago and used to go about naked just as you do." They listened eagerly, with wide unwinking eyes, which asked for more. "They used to stain themselves all blue"—the idea so evidently commended itself to them that he hastened to add—"but you'd better not try that or you'll be killing yourselves. They used the juice of a plant which you can't get and it did them no harm. Can you swim?"

Both heads shook a reluctant negative.

"Can't? Oh, you ought to swim. You can fight, I know, and you are splendid shots—and good runners, I'll be bound. Why haven't you learnt to swim?"

"Won't let us."

"Who won't let you?"

"Him."

"Who's 'him'?"

"Sir Denzil."

"Is that your father?"

"Gran'ther!"

"I see. I wonder if he'd let me teach you. Every boy ought to learn to swim. You'd like to?"

The black heads left no possible doubt on that point.

"Well, I'll call on him and ask his permission. Now, what are your names?"

"Denzil Carr'n."

"And you?"

"Denzil Carr'n."

"But you can't both be Denzil Carr'n."

"I'm Jack."

"I'm Jim."

"And how am I to tell who from which? You're as like as two peas."

They looked at one another as if it had never struck them.

"Stand up and let me see who's the biggest. No"—with a shake of the head, as they stood side by side—"that doesn't help. You're both of a size. Now, let me see. Jack's got a big bump on the forehead,"—at which Jim grinned with reminiscent enjoyment. "That will identify him for a few days, anyhow, and by that time I shall have got to know you. Why hasn't your grandfather let you learn to swim?"

"Devil of a coast," said Jack, loosing his tongue at last.

"Damned quicksands," said Jim in emulation. "Suck and suck and never let go."

"We must be careful, then. You must tell me all about them. My name's Eager—Charles Eager. I've come to take Mr. Smythe's place at Wyvveloe. Do you two go to school?"

Emphatically No from both shaggy heads, and undisguised aversion to the very thought of such a thing.

"But you can't go on like this, you know. What will you do when you grow up?"

"Go fighting," said Jack of the bumped forehead.

"Quite so. But you don't want to go as privates, I suppose. And to be officers you must learn many things."

This was a new view of the matter. It seemed to make a somewhat unfavourable impression. It provided food for thought to Eager himself also, and he sat looking at them musingly with new and congenial vistas opening before him.

He had in him a great passion for humanity—for the uplifting and upbuilding of his fellows. Here apparently was virgin soil ready to his hand, and he wanted to set to work on it at once.

"You know how to read and write, I suppose?"

"We can read *Robinson Crusoe*—round the pictures."

"Of course. Good old Robinson Crusoe! He's taught many a boy to read."

"He's in there," said Jim, nodding vaguely in the direction of their burrow.

"That's a good idea. Let us have a look at him." And Jim started off to fetch Robinson out. "And you might bring my things out too, Jim. My back's getting raw with the sun."

Jim grinned and crept into the hole, and reappeared presently with an armful of clothing and a richly bound volume.

Eager put on his other sock and his shirt and trousers, and then sat down again and picked up the book. It was an unusually fine edition of the old story, with large coloured plates, and had not been improved by its sojourn in the sand.

"Does your grandfather know you have this out here?"

Most decidedly not.

"I should take it back if I were you, or keep it wrapped in paper. It's spoiling with the sand and damp. It always hurts me to see a good book spoiled. Are there many more like this at the house?"

"Heaps,"—which opened out further pleasant prospects if the mine proved workable.

"Have you gone right through it?"

"Only 'bout the pictures."

"Well, if you're here to-morrow I'll begin reading it to you from the beginning. There must be quite three-quarters of it that you know nothing about. And as soon as I can, I'll call on your grandfather and have a talk with him about the swimming and the rest. Can you write?"

"Not much," said Jack.

"Sums?"

Nothing of the kind and no slightest inclination that way.

"Now I must get back to my work," said Eager, as he finished dressing. "This is my first morning, and it's been holiday. I've been living for the last five years in the

East End of London, where the people are all crowded into dirty rooms in dirty streets, and I came to have a look at the sea and the sands. It's like a new life. Now, good-bye," and he shook hands politely with each in turn. "I shall be on the look-out for you to-morrow."

He strode away through the sand-hills towards Wyvveloe, and the boys stood watching till he disappeared.

"My rabbit!" cried Jim, as his eye lighted on the old gage of battle lying on the sand, and he dashed at it.

"Mine!" and in a moment they were at it hammer and tongs. And the Rev. Charles went on his way, not a little elated at thoughts of this new field that lay open before him.

CHAPTER VII

EAGER HEART

"MRS. Jex," said Eager, to the old woman in whose cottage he had taken his predecessor's rooms, "who lives in yon big house on the shore?"

Mrs. Jex straightened her big white cap nervously. She had hardly got used yet to this new "passon," who was so very different from the last, and who had already in half a day asked her more questions than the last one did in a year.

"Will it be Carne yo' mean, sir?"

"That's it,—Carne. Who lives there, and what kind of folks are they?"

"There's Sir Denzil an' there's Mr. Kennet——"

"Who's Mr. Kennet?"

"Sir Denzil's man, sir. An' there's the boys——"

"Ah, then, it's the boys I met on the shore, running wild and free, without a shirt between them."

"Like enough, sir. They do say 'at——"

"Yes?"—as she came to a sudden stop.

"'Tain't for the likes o' me, sir, to talk about my betters," said Mrs. Jex, with a doubtful shake of the head.

"Oh, the parson hears everything, you know, and he never repeats what he hears. What do they say about the boys? Are they twins? They're as like as can be, and just of an age, as far as I could see."

"Well, sir," said Mrs. Jex, with another shake, "there's more to that than I can say, an' I'm not that sure but what it's more'n anybody can say."

"Why, what do you mean? That sounds odd."

"Ay, 'tis odd. Carne's seen some queer things, and this is one of 'em, so they do say."

"I'd like to hear. I rather took to those boys. They seem to be growing up perfect little savages, learning nothing and——"

"Like enough, sir."

"And I thought of calling on their grandfather and seeing if he'd let me take them in hand."

"Yo'd have yore hands full, from all accounts."

"That's how I like them. They've been a bit overfull for a good many years, but this offers the prospect of a change anyway."

"Well, yo'd best see Dr. Yool. If yo' con get him talking he con tell yo' more'n onybody else. He were there when they were born—one of 'em onyway."

"Worse and worse! You're a most mysterious old lady. What's it all about?"

"Yo'd better ask t' doctor. He knows. I only knows what folks say, and that's mostly lies as often as not. Yore dinner's all ready. Yo' go and see t' doctor after supper and ax him all about it."

After dinner he took a ramble round his new parish. He had arrived a couple of days sooner than expected and the head shepherd was away from home, so he had had to find his way about alone and make the acquaintance of his sheep as best he could.

Mrs. Jex, who had also acted as landlady for the departed Smythe, had already thanked God for the change. For Smythe, a lank, boneless creature, who cloaked a woeful lack of zeal for humanity under cover of an unwrinkling robe of high observance, had found the atmosphere of Wyvveloe uncongenial. It lacked the feminine palliatives to which he had been accustomed. He had grown fretful and irritable—"a perfec' whimsy!" as Mrs. Jex put it. The sturdy fisher-farmer folk laughed him and his ways to scorn, and the whole parish was beginning to run to seed when, to the relief of all concerned, he succeeded in obtaining his transfer to a sphere better suited to his peculiar requirements.

Mrs. Jex had had experience of Mr. Eager for one night and half a day, and she already breathed peacefully, and had thanked God for the change. And it was the same in every cottage into which the Rev. Charles put his lean, smiling face that day.

Those simple folk, who looked death in the face as a necessary part of their daily life, knew a man when they saw one, and there was that in Charles Eager's face which would never be in Mr. Smythe's if he lived to be a hundred—that keen hunger for the hearts and souls and lives of men which makes one man a pastor, and the lack of which leaves another but a priest.

And if the cottagers instinctively recognised the difference, how much more that bluff guardian—beyond their inclinations at times—of their outer husks, Dr. Yool!

When Jane Tod, his housekeeper, ushered the stranger into his room Dr. Yool was mixing himself a stiff glass of grog and compounding new fulminations, objurgative and expletive, tending towards the cleansing of Wynsloe streets and backyards.

Miss Tod was a woman in ten thousand, and had been specially created for the post of housekeeper to Dr. Yool. She was blessed with an imperturbable placidity which the irascible doctor had striven in vain to ruffle for over twenty years. When he came in of a night, tired and hungry and bursting with anger at the bovine stupidity of his patients, she let him rave to his heart's relief without changing a hair, and set food and drink before him, and agreed with all he said, even when he grew personal, and she never talked back. When she showed in Mr. Eager she simply opened the sitting-room door, said "New passon," and closed it behind him.

"Will you let me introduce myself, Dr. Yool, seeing that the vicar is not here to do it? I am Charles Eager, vice Smythe, translated. You and I are partners, you see, so I thought the sooner we became acquainted the better."

"H'mph!" grunted Dr. Yool, eyeing his visitor keenly over the top of the glass as he sipped his red-hot grog.

"Charles Eager, eh? And what are you eager for, Mr. Eager?"

"Men, women, children—bodies and souls."

"You leave their bodies to me," growled Dr. Yool in his brusquest manner. "Their souls 'll be quite as much as you can tackle."

But Eager saw through his brusquerie. A very beautiful smile played over the keen, earnest face as he said:

"When you separate them it's too late for either of us to do them any good."

"Separate them! Takes me all my time to keep 'em together."

"Exactly! So we'll make better headway if we work together and overlap."

"Right! We'll work together, Mr. Eager." And the doctor's big brown hand met the other's in a friendly grip. "You've got more bone in you than the late invertebrate. He was a sickener. Hand like a fish. Have some grog?"

"I don't permit myself grog. It wouldn't do, you know. But I'll have a pipe. I see you don't object to smoke."

"Smoke and grog are the only things a man can look forward to with certainty after a stiff day's work. The sooner you can get your flock to cleanse out the sheepfolds the better, Mr. Shepherd. We had typhus here ten years ago, and it gave them such a scare that for one year the place was fairly sweet. Now it stinks as bad as ever, and I'll be hanged if I can stir them."

"I'll stir them, or I'll know the reason why!"

Dr. Yool studied the deep-set eyes and firm mouth before him for a good minute, and then said:

"Gad! I believe you will if any man can."

"Do you know East London?"

"Not intimately. I've seen enough of it to strengthen my preference for clean sand."

"This is heaven compared with it. I'm going to open these people's eyes to their advantages."

"You'll be a godsend if you can."

"I want you to tell me all you think fit about two naked boys I came across on the shore this morning. Carr'ns, they called themselves. Fine little lads, and next door to savages, as far as I could judge. I tried to pump Mrs. Jex, and she referred me to you."

Dr. Yool puffed contemplatively, and looked at him through the smoke.

"That's the problem of Carne," he said slowly at last—"the insoluble problem."

"What's the problem? And why insoluble?"

"One of them is heir to Carne; the other is baseborn. No man on earth knows which is which."

"Any woman?"

"Ah—there you have it! Can you make a woman speak against her will—and her interest?" he added, as a hopeful look shot through Eager's eyes.

"It's a strong combination against one. All the same, there is no reason why those boys should grow up naked of mind as well as of body. They are surely close in age? They're as like as two peas—splendid little savages, both."

"There may be a week between them, not more." He

puffed thoughtfully for several minutes again, and then said slowly: "If you can clothe them, body and mind, it will be a good work and a tough one. It's virgin soil and a big handful, and one of them's got a place in the world. I'll tell you the story for your guidance. I can trust it in your keeping. The old man would curse me, no doubt, but his time is past and the boys' is only coming. They are of more consequence."

And bit by bit he told him what he knew of the strange happenings which had led to the problem of Carne.

Eager followed him with keen interest.

"And was that first marriage genuine?" he asked.

"Very doubtful. I worried the old man till he went off to look into it, but when he came back he would say nothing. It makes no difference, however, for we don't know one boy from the other."

"And the mother—the one who lived?" asked Eager, following out his own line of thought.

"She stayed on at Carne with her mother for about a year. Then she disappeared, and, as far as I know, nothing has been heard of her since. She could solve the problem doubtless, but if she swore to it no one would believe her."

"She believed in her own marriage, of course?"

"Doubtless. And the time may come when she will put in her claim, if she is alive."

"That's what I was thinking. And the father of the boys?"

"The man he killed—unintentionally, no doubt, still after threats—had powerful friends. They would have exacted every penalty the law permitted. Denzil no doubt considered he could enjoy life better in other ways. If he is alive he is abroad. He has never shown face here since."

"A complicated matter," said Eager thoughtfully, "and likely to become more so. Where would the old man's death land things?"

"God knows. I've puzzled over it many a day and night."

"And meanwhile Sir Denzil allows the youngsters to run to seed?"

"Exactly. He takes absolutely no interest in them. If one of them died it would be all right for the other. He would be Carron of Carne in due course and no questions asked. But the complication of the two has made him look askance at both."

"And the old woman—Mrs. Lee?"

"She lives on at Carne, biding her time. I have no doubt she knows which is her grandson, but she won't speak till the time comes."

"And how does Sir Denzil treat her?"

"They say he has never spoken to her for the last ten years—never a word since that day she and her daughter brought the two children in to him and started the game. She tends the house and does the cooking, and so on. Sir Denzil lives in his own rooms, and man K looks after him. a very long time I saw We never got It's together. He his that poor ennet dragging her [illegible] he did, and I [illegible] so. An[illegible] chose to say that I ought to have been able to recognise t'other baby from which. Much he knows about it," snorted the doctor.

"And what does he do with himself? Is he a student?"

"Drinks, I imagine. I meet his man about now and again, and if it's like master like man there's not much doubt about it."

"Poor little fellows! I must get hold of them, doctor. I must have them. Now, how shall I set about it?"

"Better call on the old man and see what he says. His soul's in your charge, you know. I have my own opinion as to its probable ultimate destination, in spite of you. It'll be an experience, anyway."

"For me or for him?"

"Well, I was thinking of you at the moment."

"And not an over-pleasant one, you suggest?"

"Oh, he's a gentleman, is the old man, if he is an old heathen. Gad! I'd like to go along with you, only it would upset your apple-cart and set you in the ditch."

"I'll see him in the morning," said Eager.

CHAPTER VIII

SIR DENZIL'S VIEWS

THE struggle between the boys, which began before Mr. Eager was well out of sight, resulted in a bump on Jim's forehead similar to the one which already decorated Jack's, in a few additional scratches and bruises to both brown little bodies, and in Jim's temporary possession of the rabbit.

That point decided for the time being, they sat down in the hot sand to recover their wind, Jim holding his prey tightly by the ears on his off side, since a moment's lack of caution would result in its instant transfer to another owner.

"I'm going to learn to swim," said Jack.

"HE won't let us," said Jim.

Then, intent silence as a sand-piper came hopping along a ridge. It stopped at sight of them, and fixed them first with one inquiring eye and then with the other. Their hands felt for their little clubs. The sand-piper decided against them, and flew away with a cheep of derision.

Jim had dropped the rabbit for his club. Jack leaned over behind him and had it in a second. Jim hurled himself on him, and they were at it again hammer and tongs, and presently they were sitting panting again, and this time the rabbit was on Jack's off side, and, for additional security, wedged half under his sandy leg.

"We could tell him we'd asked HIM and HE said Yes," said Jim, resuming the conversation as if there had been no break.

"He'll go and ask HIM himself, and HE'LL say No," said

Jack, with perfect understanding, in spite of the mixture of third persons.

"H'mph!" grunted Jim sulkily. "Wish HE was dead."

"There'd be somebody else."

From which remark you may gather that, where abstruse thinking met with little encouragement, Master Jack was the more thoughtful of the two.

"We'll go in and watch him when he goes in to-morrow," suggested Jim presently.

"They'd see us."

"Drat 'em! Let 'em. Who cares?"

"Means lickings. . . . And that Kennet he lays on a sight harder than he used to."

"Ever since we caught him in the rat-trap. He remembers it whenever he's licking us. . . . Soon as I'm a man I'm going to kill Kennet. It's the very first thing I shall do."

"I don't know," said Jack doubtfully. "He only licks us when HE tells him to."

"I should think so," snorted Jim, with scorn at the idea of anything else.

"HE always looks at us as if we were toads. Why does he?"

"Damned if I know," said Jack quietly. It sounded odd from his childish lips, but it had absolutely no meaning for him. It was simply one of the accomplishments they had picked up from Mr. Kennet.

An upward glance at the sun at the same moment suddenly accentuated a growing want inside him. He sprang up with a whoop, swinging his rabbit by the ears, and made for the hole in the sand-hill. Jim followed close on his heels, and presently, clad only in short blue knee-breeches of homely cut, and blue sailor jerseys, they were trotting purposefully through the shallows towards Carne and dinner, chattering brokenly as they went.

A grim old man watched them from an upper window till they padded silently round the corner out of sight. They ran in through the back porch, and so into the comfortable kitchen with its red-tiled floor and shining pans, and dark wood linen-presses round the walls.

Old Mrs. Lee, grandmother to one of them, turned from the fire to greet them.

"Ready for yore dinner, lads? And which on yo' killed to-day?"—as she caught sight of the rabbit.

"I did," from Jack.

"No—me," from Jim.

"Well, both of us, then," said Jack.

"Clivver lads! Now fall to." And they needed no bidding to the food she set before them. They were always hungry, and never criticised her provisioning.

Ten years had made very little change in Mrs. Lee. Indeed, if there was any change at all it was for the better. For, whereas in the previous times she had had grievous troubles and anxieties, during these last ten years she had had an object in life, not to say two, and lively subjects both of them.

The grim old man upstairs would have viewed the death of either of the boys with more than equanimity. At the first sudden upspringing of the trouble he had, indeed, fervently wished both out of the way. But consideration of the subject and much snuff brought him to just that much better a frame of mind that he ended by desiring short shrift for only one of them, and which one he did not care a snap. Either would be preferable to a Solway Carren, but the two together produced a complication which time would only intensify, unless Death stepped in and cut the knot.

In the beginning he watched Nance's and Mrs. Lee's treatment of them as closely as he could, without betraying his keen interest in the matter. His man, Kennet, had instructions to surprise, entrap, or coerce the secret out of the women in any way he could devise.

But the women laughed to scorn their clumsy attempts at espionage, and meted out equal justice and mercy to both boys alike. Never by one single word or look of special favour bestowed on either did master or man come one step nearer to the knowledge they sought.

Mr. Kennet, indeed, undertook, for a consideration, to make Nance his lawful, wedded wife, with a view to getting at the truth. But when he deviously approached Nance herself he received so hot a repulse, which was not by any means confined to mere verbal broadsides, that he beat a hasty retreat, with marks of the encounter on his face which took longer to heal than did his ardour to cool.

She was a handsome, strapping girl, with a temper like hot lava, and she honestly believed herself Densil Carron's lawful wife, though her mother still cast doubts upon it.

"You!" Nance labelled Mr. Kennet after this episode, and concentrated in that single word all the scorn of her outraged feelings; and thereafter, till she took herself off to parts unknown, made Mr. Kennet's life a burden to him, yet caused him to thank his stars that the matter had gone no farther.

And the grim old man upstairs? From the women's treatment of the boys—and he spied upon them in ways, and at times, and by means, of which they had no slightest idea—he had learned nothing. And so he waited and waited, with infinite patience, and hoped that time might bring some solution of the problem, even though it came by the hand of Death. And then, as Death stood aloof, and the boys grew and waxed strong, and developed budding personalities, he watched them still more keenly, in the hope of finding in their dispositions and tempers some indications which might help him in his quest.

Plain living was the order of those days at Carne; and he who had hobnobbed with princes, and had been notorious for his prodigality in times when excess rioted through the land, lived now as simply as the simplest yeoman of the shire. And that not of necessity, for his income was large, and, since he spent nothing, the accumulations were rollicking up into high figures. The candle had simply burnt itself out. He had not a desire left in life, unless it was to get the better of these women who had dusted his latter days with ashes.

Of his son, the origin of this culminating and enduring trouble, he had heard nothing for many years. He did not even know whether he was alive or dead, and, save for the confusion which lack of definite knowledge on that head might cause in the table of descent, he did not much care.

He had looked to the gallant captain to raise the house of Carne to its old standing in the world—a poor enough ambition indeed, but still all that was left him. By his hot-headed folly Captain Denzil had struck himself out of the running, and by degrees, as this became more and more certain, his father's interest in life transferred itself from the impossible to the remotely possible, even though the possibility was all of a tangle.

For a time he supplied the prodigal freely with money, and the prodigal dispensed it in riotous living. The fact that by rights he ought to have been cooling his heels in prison gave a zest to his enjoyments, and he denied himself none.

His father buoyed his hopes, as long as hope was possible, on his son's return in course of time to his native land, and to those aristocratic circles of which he had previously been so bright an ornament. But time passed and brought no amelioration of his prospects. Louis Philippe still occupied the French throne. The death of d'Aumont was not forgotten. Sir Denzil's quiet soundings of the authorities were always met with the invariable, and perfectly obvious, reply, that Captain Carron was at liberty to return at any time—at his own risk; a reply which only strengthened Captain Carron's determination to remain strictly where he was.

He lived for a time, as Kennet told us, in Paris, under an assumed name of course, but under the very noses of the men whose implacable memories debarred him from returning home. It was added spice to his already highly spiced life. But high living demands high paying, and Captain Denzil's demands grew and grew till at last his father—who would have withheld nothing for a definite object, but saw no sense in aimless prodigality—flatly refused anything beyond a [illegible] allowance. From that time communications ceased, and whether and how his son lived Sir Denzil knew not, and, from all appearances, cared little. He had ceased to be a piece of value in the old man's game.

Pending direction, from above or below or from the inside, Sir Denzil left the boys to develop as they might. A magnanimous, even a reasonably balanced nature would have assumed the burden and done its best for both alike, and trusted to Time and Providence for a solution of the problem. But no one ever miscalled Sir Denzil Carron to the extent of imputing to him any faintest trace of magnanimity. Time he had some hopes of, Providence he had no belief in. He was simply the product of his age: an unmitigated old heathen, with but one aim in life—the resuscitation of the house of Carne, and to that end ready to sacrifice himself, or any other, body, soul, and spirit.

That both boys were of his blood he was satisfied, but the unsolvable doubt as to which was the rightful heir cancelled all his feelings for them and set them both outside the pale of his doubtful favours.

At times, in pursuance of his search for leading signs, he had sent for the boys, talked to them, tried to get below the surface. But in his presence they crept into their innermost shells and became dull and dumb, and impervious even to his biting sarcasms on their appearances, tastes, and habits.

They feared and hated the grim old tyrant, with his peaked white face and thin scornful lips and gold snuff-box. There was no kindliness for them in the keen dark eyes, and they felt it without understanding why. They would slink out of his presence like whipped puppies, but once out of it he would hear their natural spirits rising as they raced for the kitchen, and their merry shouts as they sped across the flats to their own devices.

When that was possible he watched them unawares, on the

look-out always for what he sought. But such chances were few, for natural instinct caused the boys to remove themselves as far away from him as possible, and the sand-hills offered an inviting field and unlimited scope for their abilities.

CHAPTER IX

MORE OF SIR DENZIL'S VIEWS

ALL the next morning the boys lay in the wire-grass on top of their special sand-hill, on the look-out for their new friend. But he did not come.

Instead, he walked over to Carne, and coming first on the back door, rapped on it, and was confronted by Mrs. Lee. It seemed to him that she eyed him with something more than native caution, and after what he had heard from Dr. Yool he was not surprised at it.

"Can I see Sir Denzil?" he asked cheerily. "I'm the new curate."

The old woman's mouth wrinkled in a dry smile, as though the thought of Sir Denzil and the curate compassed incongruity.

"Yo' can try," she said. "Knock on front door and maybe Kennet 'll hear yo'." And Eager went round to the front.

Continuous knocking at last produced some result. The great front door looked as if it had not been opened for years. It opened at last, however, and Mr. Kennet stood regarding him with disfavour and surprise and a touch of relief on his hairless red face. Carne had few callers, and Kennet's first idea, when summoned to that door, was that Captain Denzil had come home, a return which could hardly make for peace and happiness.

"Can I see Sir Denzil?" asked Eager once more. "Tell him, please, that Mr. Eager, the new curate, begs the favour of an interview with him."

Kennet looked doubtful, but finally, remembering that he was a gentleman's gentleman, asked him to step inside while he inquired if Sir Denzil could see him.

The hall was a large and desolate apartment, flagged with stone and destitute of decoration or clothing of any kind, and was evidently little used. There was a huge fireplace at one side, but the bare hearth gave a chill even to the summer day. A wide oak staircase led up to a gallery off which the upper rooms opened, and from which Sir Denzil at times in the winter quietly overlooked the boys at their play down below, and sought in them unconscious indications of character.

And presently, Kennet came silently down the staircase and intimated that the visitor was to follow him. He ushered him into a room looking out over the sea, and Sir Denzil turned from the window, snuff-box in hand, to meet him.

There was an intimation of surprised inquiry in the very way he held his snuff-box. He bowed politely, however, and his eyebrows emphasised his desire to learn the reasons for so unexpected a visit.

"I trust you will pardon my introducing myself, Sir Denzil," said Eager. "I am taking Mr. Smythe's place, and the vicar is away."

"Ah!" said Sir Denzil, taking a pinch very elegantly, "I had not the pleasure of Mr. Smythe's acquaintance,"—and his manner politely intimated that he equally had not sought that of Mr. Smythe's successor.

"I have come with a very definite object," said Eager, cheerfully oblivious to the old man's frostiness, and going straight to his mark, as was his way. "I want you to let me take those two boys in hand. I met them on the sands yesterday. In fact, they amused themselves by hiding my clothes while I was in bathing, and I looked like having to go home clad only in a towel." And he laughed again at the recollection.

"They shall be punished——"

"My dear sir! You don't suppose I came for any such purpose as that! It broke the ice between us. I got my things and made two friends. I want to improve the acquaintance—with your sanction."

"To what end?"

"To the end of making men of them, Sir Denzil. There are great possibilities there. You must not neglect them, or the responsibility will be yours."

"That, I presume, is my affair."

"No—excuse me! In the natural course of things those boys will be here when you and I are gone. As their feet are set now, so will they walk then. If you leave them untrained the responsibility for their deeds will be yours. It is no light matter."

Sir Denzil extracted a pinch very deliberately and closed the box with a tap on the First Gentleman's snub nose.

"And suppose I prefer to let them run wild for the present?"

"Then you are not doing your duty by them, and sooner or later it will recoil upon your own head—or house."

"Yes; but, as you say, I shall probably not be here, and so I shall not suffer."

"Your name—the name of your house will suffer——"

Sir Denzil shedded the prospect with a shrug.

"Who set you on this business, Mr. Eager?" he asked, with a touch of acidity.

"God."

"Ah!"—snuffing with extreme deliberation. "Now we approach debatable ground."

"No, sir. We stand on the only ground that offers sound footing."

"Well, well! I suppose some people still believe such things."

"Fortunately, yes. Now about the boys. May I take them in hand?"

Sir Denzil regarded him thoughtfully while he shook his snuff-box gently and prepared another pinch.

"On conditions, possibly yes," he said at last.

"And the conditions?"

"What have you heard about those boys, Mr. Eager?"

"I think I may say everything."

"Egad! Then you know more than I do. You have wasted no time. Who told you the story?"

"Perhaps you will not press that question, Sir Denzil. Having got interested in the boys I naturally desired to learn what I could about them. It was from no idle curiosity, I assure you."

"So you went to Dr. Yool, I suppose. I felt sure he would be at the root of the matter."

"I assure you he is not. The root of the matter is simply my desire for those boys. I would like to try my hand at making men of them."

"Very well. You shall try—on this condition. As you are aware, one of them comes of high stock on both sides, the other of low stock on one side. The signs may crop out, must crop out in time. You will have opportunities, such as I have not, of observing them. What I ask of you is to bring all your intelligence and acumen to bear on the solution of my problem—which is which?"

"I understand, and I will willingly do my best. But you must remember, Sir Denzil, that there is no infallibility in such indications. The crossing of blue blood with red sometimes produces a richer strain than the blending of two thin blues."

"That is so. Still I hope there may be indications we cannot mistake, and then I shall know what to do. It is, as you can understand, a matter that has caused me no little concern."

"Naturally. By God's help we will make men of both of them. The rest we must trust to Providence."

Sir Denzil's pinch of snuff cast libellous doubts on Providence.

"You design them for the army, I presume?" asked Eager.

"Unless one should show an inclination for the Church," said the old cynic suavely. "Which I should be inclined to look upon as a clear indication of his origin."

"I'm not so sure of that," said Eager, with a smile. "The Church has its heroes no less than the army."

"You will find them difficult to handle."

"We shall soon be good friends. I'm going to begin by teaching them to swim."

Sir Denzil looked at him thoughtfully and said:

"That might undoubtedly relieve the situation. It is a dangerous coast. If you could drown one of them for me——"

"I am going to make men of them. I can't make a man out of a drowned boy. I will take every care of them, and some time you will be proud of them."

"Of one of them possibly. The question is, which?"

CHAPTER X

GROWING FREEMEN

THE Rev. Charles was greatly uplifted as he tramped through the sand to keep his appointment with the boys. He had succeeded beyond his hopes, and a most congenial field of work and study lay open to his hand.

"Catch them young," had been hammered into his heart and brain by his five years' work in East London. With heart and brain he had fought against the stolid indifference and active evil-mindedness of the grown-ups, till heart and brain grew sick at times. His greatest hopes had settled on the children, and here were two, of a different caste indeed, but as ignorant of the essentials as any he had met with—and they were given into his hand for the moulding. By God's help he would make men of them, high-born or base-born. The side-issue was nothing to him, but it would add zest to the work.

When he got, as he believed, into the neighbourhood of his previous day's adventure, he examined the ridge of sand-hills with care. But they were all so much alike that he could not be sure. He had hoped to find the boys on the look-out for him, but he saw no signs of them.

He struggled up the yielding side of the nearest hill and looked round. If he could find their hole he would probably find them inside it or not far away.

It was close on mid-day, baking hot, and the sand-hills seemed as deserted as Sahara. The sea lay fast asleep behind its banks, which reached to the horizon. When he looked back across the flats to Carne, he rubbed his eyes at sight of its stout walls bending and bowing and jigging spasmodically in an uncouth dance. The very wire-grass drooped listlessly. The only sound was the cheerful creak of a cricket.

The width, length, and height of it, the gracious spaciousness of it all filled him with fresh delight. It was all so very different from the heart-crushing straitness of the slums and alleys in which his last years had been spent. He stood drinking it all in, and then, seeing no signs of the boys, he turned his back to the shore and strode inland.

But within a few steps he caught sight of recent traces of them in fresh-turned yellow sand which the sun had not had time to whiten. He whistled shrilly, if perchance the sound might penetrate to their hold.

And then, to his astonishment, the ground in front of him cracked and heaved, and first one and then another dark sanded head and laughing face came out, and the boys sprang up from the shallow holes in which they had buried themselves and stood before him.

"You young rabbits," he laughed. "I had just about given you up. Thought I wasn't coming, I suppose."

Decisive nods from both black heads.

"Well, we'll make a start on that. Remember that I never break a promise, and I want you to do the same. The boy who makes up his mind that he'll never break his word is half a brave man."

They stared up at him with wide eyes, and whether they understood it he did not know. But he knew better than to say more just then.

"Now—why——?" And he looked from one to the other and then began to laugh. "Which of you is Jack and which is Jim? I was to remember Jack by a bump on the forehead, and now you've both got bumps. Been fighting again?"

Gleaming nods from both boys.

"We must find you something better to do. I've been seeing your grandfather, and he says I may teach you to swim."

Squirms of anticipation in the active brown bodies, and glances past him at the distant sea.

"No, not to-day. It's too late now, but it was worth spending the morning on. We'll make a start to-morrow. Can you be here at eight o'clock?"

Their energetic heads intimated that they could be there very much before eight if desired.

"Right! I'll be here. In the meantime you can be practising a bit on dry land. Here's the stroke"—and he laid himself flat on a convenient hummock and kicked out energetically, while the black eyes watched intently.

"Now try it. You first, Jack. That's right. Keep your hands a bit more sloped, and your toes more down. Thrust back with the flat of your feet as though you were trying to kick some one. First rate! Now, Jim!" But Jim was already hard at work on his own account. "That's right. Hands sloped, toes down. Draw your knees well up under your body. You'll find it easier in the water. Oh, you'll do. You'll be swimmers in no time. That'll do for just now.

Now—Jack," he looked at them both, but his eyes finally settled on Jim—"if you'll fetch Robinson out we'll make a start on him."

Jim turned to dive down the hill-side, and was instantly tripped by Jack, who flung himself on top of him. They rolled down together, fighting like cats, amid a cloud of flying sand. Eager sprang after them, found it useless, as before, to attempt to separate them by any ordinary means, so spanked them indiscriminately till they fell apart and stood up panting. And the odd thing about it all was that no slightest ill-will seemed born of their strife. The moment it was over they were friends again.

"He told me," panted Jack in self-justification.

"He looked at me," panted Jim.

"My fault, boys. I must tie a string round one of your arms till I get to know you. Now trot along one of you—no, you"—grabbing one by the shoulder as both started off again. "We haven't much time to-day. If I'm not home by one Mrs. Jex will be eating all my dinner."

So they sat in the soft sand, and he read, and explained what he read, till Robinson Crusoe came alive and began to be as real to them as one of themselves, and they knew him as they had never known him before.

When Eager was dodging about his sheepfold that afternoon he came upon Dr. Yool in the yellow-wheeled gig.

"Well, I've got 'em," said the curate.

"Got what? Measles, jumps——?"

"Those boys. I bearded the old man in his den this morning, and he has given me a free hand with them."

"You'll do," said Dr. Yool. "They'll keep you busy. Don't forget I want your help with these stinks"—pointing with his whip to the heaps of refuse lying about.

"I'm tackling stinks now. Tiger-pups in the morning, stinks in the afternoon, Dr. Yool in the evening. That's the order of service at present." And they parted the better for the meeting.

Eager had a chat with some of the wise men of Wynsloe, and got points from them as to shifting sands, and the sucking sands, and the other dangers of that treacherous coast, and in return incidentally dropped into their minds some seeds of wisdom respecting stinks and their consequences.

Five minutes to eight next morning found him a-perch of the highest sand-hill in the neighbourhood, on the look-out for his pupils.

Five minutes past eight found him somewhat disappointed at their non-appearance. They had seemed eager enough too, the day before. Perhaps the old man had thought better of it. Then he remembered his cynical hope that the swimming might prove of service in the solution of his great problem. And then a couple of war-whoops at each of his ears jerked him off his perch with so sudden a leap that the whoopers squirmed in the sand with delight.

"Thought we weren't coming?" grinned Jack.

"Well, I began to fear you'd been stopped——"

"We promised," grinned Jim; and Eager rejoiced to think that that seed at all events had taken root.

In two minutes they were trotting across the flats, and presently they were in the tide-way, and the little savages were revelling in a fresh acquirement and a new sense of motion.

There was little teaching needed. Eager took them out, one after the other, neck-deep, and turned their faces to the shore, and they swam home like rats, and yelled hilariously from pure enjoyment as soon as they found their breath.

Then he carried them out of their depths, and loosed them, and they paddled away back without a sign of fear. Fear, in fact, seemed absolutely lacking in them. The only thing on earth of which they stood in any fear, as far as he could make out, was the grim old man in the upper room at Carne, and even in his case it seemed to be as much distrust and dislike as actual fear.

But even fearlessness has its dangers, and, mindful of

his trust, Eager exacted from each of them a solemn promise not to go into the sea except when he was with them, for he had no mind to solve the old man's riddle for him in the way he had so hopefully suggested.

Those mornings on the sands and in the water proved the foundation on which he slowly and surely built the boys' characters.

A very few days of so close an intimacy stamped their individualities on his mind. After the third day he never again mistook one for the other. Time and again they tried to mislead him, but he saw deeper than they knew and never failed to detect them.

They were, at this time, remarkably alike in every way, and though, later on, each developed marked characteristics of his own, there all along remained between them resemblance enough to put strangers to confusion, a matter in which they at all times found extreme enjoyment.

But even now, like as they were, in face and body and the wild naturalness of their primeval ways, their respective personalities began to disclose themselves, as Eager broke them, bit by bit, to the harness of civilisation. And if their harnessing was no easy matter, either for themselves or their teacher, they came to realise very quickly that, though it might mean less of freedom in some ways, it meant also an immensely wider reach and outlook. Whereas their life had hitherto revolved in narrow grooves—with which indeed no man had taken the trouble to meddle, now it ran in courses that were ordered, but which also were spacious and lofty and filled with novelty and enterprise.

And as their natural characteristics began to develop in these more reasonable ways, Eager watched and studied them with intensest interest.

But little savages they remained in certain respects for a considerable time, and it was only by slow degrees that he managed to lead them out of darkness into something approaching twilight.

Jim, for instance, had a rooted detestation of every living thing he came across on the shore, and promptly proceeded to squash it with his bare foot or to pound it into jelly with his prehistoric club. From tiny delicate crab to senseless jelly-fish or screaming gull, if Jim came across it it must die if he could manage it.

To counteract, if he might, this innate lust for slaughter Eager took to explaining to them some of the more simple wonders and beauties of seashore life. He brought down a small pocket microscope and showed them things they had never dreamed of.

This appealed to Jack immensely. He became a devoted slave of the wonderful glasses, and never tired of poring over and peering into things. Jim, however, drew a double satisfaction from them. He smashed things first and then delighted in the examination of the pieces, and many a pitched battle they fought over the destruction and defence of flotsam and jetsam which formerly they would both have destroyed with equal zest.

It was all education, however, and Eager rejoiced in them greatly. He found them, in varying degrees and with notable exceptions, fairly easy to lead, but almost impossible to drive. He led them step by step from darkness towards the light, and meanwhile studied them with as microscopic a care as that with which he endeavoured to get them to study the tiny things of the shore.

Their wild free life about the sand-hills had trained their powers of observation to an unusual degree. True, the observation had generally tended to destruction, but the faculty was good, and the end and aim of it was a matter to be slowly brought within control.

They could tell him many strange things about the manners and customs of rabbits, and gulls, and peewits, and sand-pipers, and bull-frogs, and tadpoles, and so on. They could forecast the weather from the look of the sky and the smell of the wind, with the accuracy of a barometer. They could run as fast and farther than he could, for they had been breathing God's sweetest air all their lives, while he had been travelling alley-ways, with tightened lips and compressed nostrils. And they could fling their little stone clubs with an aim that was deadly. Jim indeed vaunted himself on having once brought down a seagull on the wing, but the actual fact rested on his sole testimony and Jack cast doubts on it, and thereupon they fought each time it was mentioned, but proved nothing thereby.

Eager told them of the wonders of the black man's boomerang; and they laboured long and practised much, but could not compass it. It was their ideal weapon, a thing to dream of and strive after, but it always lay beyond them.

One day he brought home under his arm, from the shop in Wyvveloe, a small parcel which he took up into his own room. He borrowed Mrs. Jex's scissors, and spent a very much longer time planning and cutting than the result seemed to warrant. Then he got Mrs. Jex, who would have shaved her scanty locks to please him, to do some hemming and stitching and to sew on some bits of tape, and next day he astonished his little savages by attiring himself and them in bright-red loin-cloths, before they started for their mile sprint to the water.

The boys were inclined to resist this innovation as an unnecessary cramping of their freedom. Jim averred that he couldn't stretch his legs, and that his garment burnt him, though when it was on it looked no bigger than his hand. Jack demanded reasons, and was told to wait and he would see. However, the brilliancy of the little garments somewhat condoned their offence, and once in the water they were soon forgotten, and as they flashed back and forth across the sands the startling effects they produced in the sunny pools by degrees reconciled their wearers to their use.

About a week after this, the boys were sitting one morning in the hollow Mr. Eager used as a dressing-room, wondering why he was later than usual.

"Gone to see HIM, maybe, 'bout yon books we brought out," growled Jack gloomily.

"Hmph!" grunted Jim. "I don't care—'sides, he wouldn't."

And then Eager strode in with a brighter face even than usual.

"Afraid I wasn't coming, were you?" he laughed.

"Thought maybe you'd gone to see HIM again," said Jack.

"Your grandfather? No; I've been seeing some one very much nicer. Jim, did you say your verse this morning?"

This was a gigantic innovation, and still much of a mere ritual. But it was a beginning, and the rest would follow. It was the first upward step towards those higher things which Charles Eager kept ever steadily in view.

"Forgot," grunted Jim.

This again was mighty gain. A month ago—if such a contingency had been possible—he would never have owned up. To his grandfather it is doubtful if he would have owned up even now.

"Well, oblige me by going behind that sand-hill and saying it now, and think what you're saying as well as you can. And you, Jack?"

"Said um," said Jack dutifully.

"Never saw you," said Jim, on his knees. Whereupon Jack dashed at him and rolled him over prayer and all, and they had a regular former-state set-to.

The Rev. Charles, grave of face, but internally convulsed, got them seperated at last, and as soon as Jim had performed his devotions they turned their faces towards the sea. Before the two boys could start out, as they usually did, like bolts from a cross-bow, however, he laid a detaining hand on each brown shoulder, and to their surprise whistled shrilly across the hills. In reply, a tiny figure in brilliant scarlet sped out from an adjacent nook, and shot, with flowing hair, and little white feet going like drumsticks, across the flats towards the sea.

The boys caught their breath and gaped in amazement.

"What is it?" gasped Jim.

"Whew! Who?" from Jack.

"My little sister. She only arrived last night. Now, let's see if we can catch her! Off you go!" And they tore away across the long ribbed sands after the flying streak of scarlet in front.

They caught her long before she reached the tide-lip, and her eyes flashed merriment as they raced alongside.

She had rare beauty even as a child—and no beauty of after-life ever quite equals that of a lovely child—and the two boys had never in their lives seen anything like her. They stumbled alongside, careless of holes and lumps, with sidelong glances for nothing but that radiant vision—scarlet-wrapped, streaming nut-brown hair, dancing blue eyes, white skin flushed with the run like a hedge-rose, little teeth gleaming pearls between panting, laughing lips, a little rainbow of beauty.

"Well run, Gracie! Keep it up, old girl!" panted Eager, almost pumped himself. And then they were in the water.

Grace, it appeared, could not swim yet. The boys fell to at once and fought for the honour of helping her, though neither would have dared to touch her. She screamed at sight of their brown bodies thrashing to and fro in the foam, but was comforted at sight of her brother's laughing face.

"Come along, Gracie. Never mind the boys. They enjoy a fight more than anything. Now kick away, and strike out as I showed you how on the footstool. I'll hold your chin up. That's it! Bravo, little one! You'll be a swimmer in a week."

CHAPTER XI

THE LITTLE LADY

AND so another element entered into the tiger-cubs' education, and one that, for so small a creature, exercised a mighty influence on them, both then and thereafter.

She was the joy of Charles Eager's heart and the light of his eyes. Other sisters and brothers there had been, but all were gone save this little fairy, and they two were alone in the world. While he wrought in the dark corners of the great city he had boarded her with some maiden aunts in the suburbs, and the weekly sight of her, growing like a flower, had helped to keep his heart fresh and sweet. Not the least of the joys of his translation to this wide new sphere was the fact that he could have her always with him.

Mrs. Jex wept with joy at sight of her, vowed she was the very image of her own little Sally, who died when she was eight; and proceeded to squander on her the pent-up affections of thirty childless years.

And the Little Lady, as Mrs. Jex styled her, lorded it over them all, then and thereafter, and was a factor of no small consequence in all their lives.

Over the slowly regenerating tiger-cubs she exercised a peculiarly softening and elevating influence. It was exactly what they needed, and all unconsciously it wrought upon the simple savageries of their boy-natures as powerfully as did the Rev. Charles's more direct and strenuous endeavours.

Both boys, in moments of excitement, which were many in the course of each day, had a habit of expression, picked up from Sir Denzil and Mr. Kennet, which was not a little startling on their juvenile lips. Eager promptly suppressed these whenever they slipped out. He knew well enough that they conveyed no special meaning to the boys beyond an idea of extra forcefulness, but, besides being unseemly, they grated horribly on his sensitive ear.

As for the Little Lady, Master Jim Carron did not soon forget the effect produced on her by one of his unconscious expletives.

When Dan Fell of Wynsloe got to the end of his bottle of Hollands gin sooner than he expected one dark night at the fishing, and hurled it overboard with a curse, his only feeling was one of disgust at the shortcomings of a friend

MICROCOPY RESOLUTION TEST CHART

(ANSI and ISO TEST CHART No. 2)

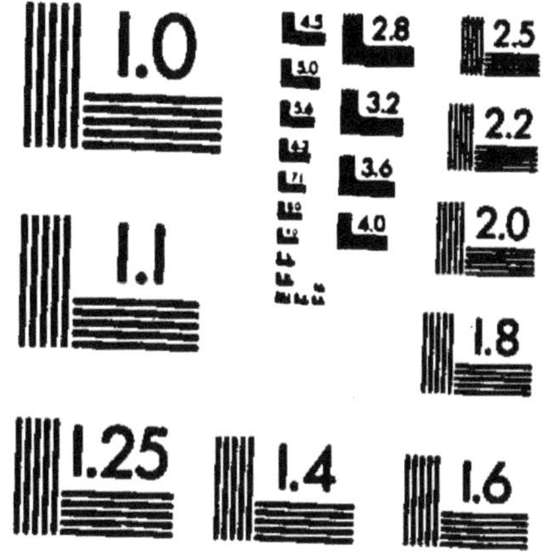

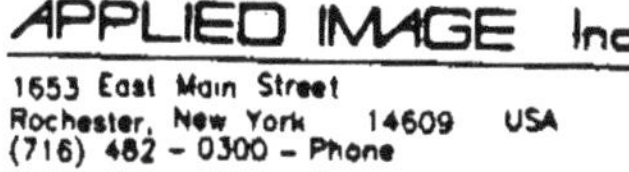

in time of need. If any one had told him that he was thereby assisting in the education of little Jim Carron of Carne he would have cursed more volubly still, under the impression that he was being made game of, which was a thing he could not stand. The bottle floated ashore, tried conclusions with a log of Norway pine thrown up hy the last equinoctials, distributed itself in razor-like spicules about the soft sand, and lay in wait for unwary feet.

Jim, racing home one day from the bathing alongside the Little Lady, and dazzled somewhat, perhaps, by the gleam of the little crimson robe and the damp little mane of flowing hair, set incautious foot on one of the razor spicules, jerked out an energetic and utterly unconscious "Damn!" and bit the sand.

The Little Lady heard the word, but missed the cause.

"Oh!" cried she, in a shocked voice, and sped away to her own apartment, and began to dress with trembling sodden pink fingers in extreme haste, as though clothing might possibly afford a certain amount of protection against the ill effects of flying curses.

By the time she had got on her tiny pink petticoat, a peep round the corner showed her her brother and Jack kneeling by the fallen utterer of oaths and curses, and she began to fear something had happened.

She had little doubt that punishment had promptly overtaken the sinner. But she liked the sinner in spite of his sin, and she stole back to see what was the matter. That it was something serious was evident by Charles's knitted brows as he bent over the foot which Jim held tightly between his hands. His lips were pinched very close, and his brown face was mottled with putty colour, and the sand below was red. The indurated little pad, hard as leather almost with much running on the sands—for the boys scoffed at shoes—was badly sliced and bleeding freely, but the worst of it was that the treacherous spicule had broken off short and stopped inside and they had no means of getting it out.

"Rags, Gracie," said Eager, at sight of the tearful face and clasped hands and pink petticoat, and she turned and sped, over sands that rocked like waves beneath her feet, to her dressing-room, and back with an armful of garments and a handkerchief the size of his hand.

He folded the handkerchief into a square pad, and ripped something white into strips and bound the foot tightly, issuing his orders as he did so.

"Jack, get into your things and run for Dr. Yool, and tell him to go to the house. Tell him there's glass inside that must come out. Gracie, put on your frock and sit here with Jim. I'll get some things on, and then I'll carry him home!"

And the Little Lady struggled mistily into her things behind Jim's back, and then sat down alongside him without speaking.

"Doesn't hurt a bit," said Jim, through clenched teeth and whitened lips.

The Little Lady sniffed and looked at the distant sea.

"Tell you it doesn't hurt," said Jim again.

The Little Lady made no response.

And presently—"Whew!" said Jim, with a frightful twist of the face, trying by instinct the other tack, "ah!—o-o-oh!" —but all to no purpose. The Little Lady's soft heart might be wrung, but at present she could not bring herself to speak to this dreadful sinner.

"Now," said Eager, running up. "Stand up, Jim. Put your arms round my neck. Now your feet up, so, and off we go. I must get old Bent to make sandals for you youngsters. We can't have this kind of thing, you know. It'll be ten days before you can use that foot, old man."

"Damn!"

"Jim!"

And the Little Lady fell solemnly into the rear.

She would not speak to him for two whole days, though she did not mind sitting within sight of him in the side of a sand-hill, and she silently allowed him to instruct her in the art of making sand waterfalls. But the current of her usual merry chatter was frozen at the fount, and the unconscious Jim could make nothing of it.

On the third day, tiring of an abstinence that was quite as irksome to herself as to her victim, she broke the ice by informing him of the painful fact that he was doomed to everlasting punishment. She put it very shortly and concisely.

"Jim," she said, "you'll go to hell."

"Um?" chirped Jim cheerfully, glad to hear her voice once more, even at such a price. "An' why?"

"'Cause you swear."

"Ho! Very well! So will HE"—the emphatic use of the third person singular in the boys' vernacular was always understood to stand for Sir Denzil Carron of Carne—"and so will Kennet, and so will Dr. Yool."

"I don't care about any of them," said Grace impartially, "unless, perhaps, Dr. Yool. I do rather like him. But it will be such a pity for you."

The prospect did not seem to trouble him greatly, perhaps because his views on the subject were not nearly so clearly defined as hers.

"Oh, well, I won't if you don't like," he answered cheerfully.

"Thank you," said the Little Lady; and from that time, simply to oblige her, and from no great fear of direr consequences, he really did seem to do his best to avoid the use of any words which might offend her. He even went so far as to assume an oversight of his brother's rhetorical flights, and many a pitched battle they had in consequence.

These encounters were so much a part of their nature that Eager found it impossible to stop them entirely. They had fought continually since ever they could crawl within arm's length of one another. Where other boys might have argued to ill-temper, these two simply closed without wasting a word, and having settled the momentary dispute, *vi et armis*, were as friendly as ever. They both possessed fiery tempers, and had never seen or dreamt of the necessity of controlling them. But on the other hand, they never bore malice, and the cause of dispute, and the blows that settled it, were forgotten the moment the god of battle had awarded the palm. They were very closely matched, and no great bodily harm came of it, though to the spectators it looked fearsome enough.

Bit by bit, utilising and turning to best account their natural powers and proclivities, Eager got hold of them, to the point at all events of inducing their feet into more reasonable upward paths. But as to coming one step nearer to the reading of Sir Denzil's puzzle, he had to acknowledge completest failure.

He studied the boys, from his own intense interest in them, as no other had ever had the opportunity of studying them. And he discussed his observation of them with Sir Denzil time and again. But, so far, there were no ultra indications of disposition in either of them so marked as to offer any reasonable basis for deduction.

For men without a single common view of life, he and Sir Denzil had become quite friendly. A verbal tussle with the old heathen, in which each spoke his mind without reserve, always braced him up, just as the boys' more primitive method of argument seemed to do them good.

The old gentleman always greeted him, over a pinch of snuff, with an expression of regret that he had not yet succeeded in settling the matter out of hand by drowning one of his pupils.

"Well, Mr. Eager," he would say, "no progress yet?"

"Oh, plenty. We're improving every day."

"H'mph! If you'd only drown one of them for me——"

"I've a better use for them than that."

"I doubt it. Ill stock on either side, though I say it."

"As the twig is bent——"

"Break one off and I'd thank you. Here is possibly a

further complication,"—tapping with his snuff-box a small news-sheet he had been reading when Eager came in.

"What is that, sir?"

"That fool Quixande has got into a mess in Paris—got a sword through his ribs."

"Quixande?" queried Eager, not perceiving the relevancy of the matter.

"He has no issue—none that can inherit, that is. One of those whelps is his only sister's son and so comes in for the title. Which?"

"H'm, yes. It's mighty awkward. I suppose you couldn't make one of them Earl of Quixande and the other Carron of Carne?"

"It would be a solution. But which? Which? Such matters are not settled by guesswork."

"We can only wait and see."

"If Quixande dies we cannot wait—the succession cannot."

"For his own sake we'll hope he'll pull through. He may repent of his sins."

"Quixande?"—with raised brows, and a shake of the head. "You don't know him."

"If I did, I'd try to bring him to his senses."

"Waste of time. With these cubs you may be able to do something, though I doubt it. Quixande's past mending."

"No man is past mending till he's dead. Perhaps not then——"

"Ah!"—with a pinch of snuff and a wave of the hand, "A hopeful creed, but with no more foundation than most others. It would, however, undoubtedly commend itself to Quixande on his death-bed."

"A hopeful creed is better than a hopeless one," said Eager, with emphasis.

"Undoubtedly, if you admit the necessity of such things."

"Thank God, I do."

"Well, well! However—what you are doing for those

boys should benefit one of them, though it's thrown away upon the other."

"And if you never solve the puzzle?"

"If one of them dies I accept the other in full. That's the solution."

There were times when all Eager's knocking on the great front door was productive of no result whatever. Then he would go round to the back and interview Mrs. Lee, but never with any satisfaction.

"Ay?" she would say to his statement, straightening up from her work, arms akimbo, and gazing steadily at him with her dark eyes. "Maybe they're out."

But he had never met Sir Denzil out, nor had any of the villagers ever encountered him, and Dr. Yool said brusquely that both the old gentleman and his gentleman were probably lying dead drunk in the upper rooms.

Eager never mentioned these abortive visits to Sir Denzil, and there was never anything in his appearance to justify Dr. Yool's assertions.

CHAPTER XII

MANY MEANS

EAGER spread his nets very wide for the capture for higher things of these two callow souls cast so carelessly into his hands. Carelessly, that is, on the part of Sir Denzil. For his own part he believed devoutly in the Higher Hand in the great game of life, and never for a moment doubted that here was a work specially designed for him by Providence.

He put his whole heart into the matter, as he did into all matters. He felt himself very much in the position of a missionary breaking up new ground, except, indeed, that here were no old beliefs to get rid of. It was absolutely virgin soil, and he felt and rejoiced in the responsibility.

Perfect little savages they were in many respects, and their training had to begin at the very beginning. Manners they lacked entirely, and their customs were simply such as they had evolved for themselves in their free-and-easy life on the flats. Their beliefs were summed up in a wholesome fear of Sir Denzil and his representative Mr. Kennet. These two were to them as the gods of the heathen: powers of evil, to be avoided if possible, and if not, then to be propitiated by the assumption of graces—such as unobtrusiveness, and if observed, then of meekness and conformability—which were no more than instantly assumed little masks concealing the true natures within, which true natures found their full vent and expression in the wilds of the sand-hills and the untrammelled freedom of the shore.

Old Mrs. Lee was a power of another kind, on the whole benevolent; provident, at all events, and not given to such incomprehensible outbreaks of anger and punishment as were the others at times.

They had known no coddling, had run wild with as little on as possible—and in their own haunts with nothing on at all—since the day they could crawl out of the courtyard down to the ribbed sand below. They were hard as nails, and feared nothing, except Sir Denzil and Mr. Kennet.

Eager's first and most difficult work was to break them off their evil habits—their natural lust for slaughter and destruction, the perpetual resort to fisticuffs for the settlement of the most trifling dispute, the use of language which conveyed no meaning beyond that of emphasis to their own minds, but which to other ears was terribly revolting.

Just as, if he had had a couple of wild colts to take to stable, he would have found it better to lead them than to drive, so he strove to win these two from the miry ways and pitfalls among which a shameful lack of oversight had left them to stray. He forced no bits into their mouths, laid no halters on their touchy heads. He just won their confidence and liking, till they looked up to him, trusted him, finally worshipped him, and followed, unquestioning, where he chose to lead them.

And—Providence or no Providence—they could not have fallen into better hands.

Charles Eager was one of the newer school, a muscular Christian if ever there was one, rejoicing greatly in his muscularity, and as wise as he was thorough in his Master's work. He had pulled stroke in his boat at Cambridge, and when he went there had looked forward to the sword as his oyster-opener. And so he had given much time to fitting himself adequately for an army career. He would have backed himself to ride, or box, or fence with any man of his time; and he had so unmistakable a bent for mechanics, and was so skilful a hand with lathe and tools, that there could not be a moment's doubt as to which branch nature designed him for.

And then, when he had perfected himself for the way he had chosen, a better way opened suddenly before him. Without a sign of the cost, he renounced all he had been looking forward to all his life, and dedicated himself whole-heartedly to the greater work.

All that he had acquired, however, with so different an end in view, remained with him, and helped to make him the man he was; and it was into such hands that, by the grace of God, these two wild Carron colts had fallen.

A missionary, when he sets out to turn his unruly flock from their old savageries, must, if he understands human nature and his work, provide other and less harmful outlets for the energies resulting from generations of tumult and slaughter. Eager taught his young savages boxing on the most scientific principles, and made the gloves himself. He taught them fencing with basket-hilted sticks, constructed under his own eyes by the old basket-weaver in the village. Prompt appeal to arms was still permitted in settlement of their endless disputes; but the business was regularised, and tended, all unconsciously on the part of the combatants, to education.

For their inexhaustible energies he found new and much-appreciated vent in games on the sands. And if these were crude enough performances, compared with their later developments familiar to ourselves, they still had in them those elements of saving grace which all such games teach in the playing—self-control, fair-play, honour And these be mighty things to learn.

In the summer they played cricket. The bat and ball Eager provided; the stumps he made himself.

He also instructed them in the mysteries of hare-and-hounds, which chimed mightily with their humour, especially when he supplemented it with a course of Fenimore Cooper. They became mighty hunters and notable trackers, their natural instincts and previous training standing them in excellent stead.

In the winter the flats rang to their shouts at football and hockey, crudely played, but mightily relished.

And always, in and alongside their play and in between, but so deftly administered that it seemed to them but a natural part of the whole, their education proceeded by leaps and bounds. They drank in knowledge unawares, and learned intuitively things that mere teaching is powerless to teach.

When he found them they were simply self-centred and selfish little savages—each for himself, and heedless of anything outside his own skin; and their manners and customs were such as naturally fitted their state.

As their minds opened to the larger things outside, and they began to be drawn away from themselves, their natural proclivities came into play. Like hardy wild-flowers, their rough outer sheaths began to open to the sun, revealing glimpses of the better things within.

And, all unconsciously to herself or to them, little Grace Eager was the sun to whom, in the beginning, their expansion was due.

Eager, watching them all with keenest interest, used to say to himself that she was doing as much for them as he, if not more.

She was so novel to them, so altogether sweet and charming. She supplied something that had hitherto been a-wanting in their lives, and of whose lack they had not even been aware, until she came into them, and made them conscious of the want by filling it.

Now and again at first, and presently almost as a matter of course, the tiger-cubs were invited up to Mrs. Jex's cottage for a homely meal, after some hotly contested game on the sands or some long chase after the tricky two legged hare or astute and elusive Redskin.

And, in the beginning, Indian brave who knew no fear, but knew almost everything else that was to be known in his own special line, and cunning hare and vociferous hound, and tireless champion of the bat and hockey-stick, and valiant fighters on all possible occasions, would sit mumchance and awkward, watching the Little Lady, with wide, observant eyes, as she dispensed her simple hospitalities with a grace and sweetness that set her above and apart from anything they had ever known.

And then she was so extraordinarily different indoors from what she was on the sands. There, at cricket or hockey, or football, she danced and shrieked with excitement, and was never still for a moment. Here, at the table, she suddenly became many years older, knew just what to do, and did it charmingly,—ordering even the Rev. Charles about, and beaming condescendingly on them all, from the lofty heights of her experience and knowledge of the world as learned from her aunts in London.

Painfully aware of deficiency, they began to strive to fit themselves for such occasions, repressed themselves into still greater awkwardness and silence, fought one another afterwards on account of too obvious lapses from what they considered proper behaviour and unkind brotherly comment thereupon, but all the time unconsciously absorbed the new atmosphere and by degrees became able to enjoy it without discomfort.

"Jim, my dear boy," she would say, on occasion, "are you comfortable on that chair?"

A quick nod from the conscious and obviously uncomfortable Jim.

"You shouldn't just nod your head, my dear. You should say, 'Yes, thank you,' or 'Not entirely,'—as the case may be. It's rude just to nod."

"Not entirely, then," blurted Jim, with a very red face, and many times less comfortable than before.

"I'm sorry, but they're all the same, and if you sit on the sofa you can't reach the table. And if you sit on the floor I can't see you."

"I can do, thank you."

"Who lives in that cottage we passed to-day, down along the shore by the Mere?" asked Eager, by way of diversion.

"Old Seth," from both boys at once, much relieved at being put into a position to answer a question that had nothing to do with themselves.

"Old Seth? I've not come across him yet. Old Seth what?"

"Old Seth Rimmer. He's a Methody," said Jack.

"It's a lonely place to live, away out there. Has he a wife,—any children?"

"Mrs. Rimmer's always in bed."

"An invalid. I must call and see her, Methody or no Methody."

"And there's young Seth and Kattie."

"I saw the girl peeping out after you'd passed. She's a nice-looking girl. I shall call and get to know her," said the Little Lady decisively.

"We'll go and make their acquaintance to-morrow," said her brother. "What does Mr. Rimmer do? Fishing?"

A nod from Jim. "Keeps his boat up in the river, two miles further on."

"And the Mere? Any fish there?"

"Ducks in winter. We got one once."

"Had to lie in the rushes all day," said Jack, with a reminiscent shiver.

"It was a good duck," said Jim.

And the next afternoon the Rev. Charles set out for the cottage, with Grace skipping about him in search of treasure-trove of beach and sand-hill.

It was a stoutly-built little wooden house, standing back in a hollow of the sand-hummocks, and its solitariness was enhanced by reason of the vast and lonely expanse of Wyn Mere, which lay just behind it. The shore of the Mere was thick with reeds and rushes. The long unbroken stretch of water silently mirroring the blue sky, with its margin of rustling reeds, possessed a beauty all its own, but something of loneliness and solemnity too.

Grace, standing on top of a sand-hill, with a high tide dancing merrily up the flats on the one side and the long silent Mere on the other, put it into words.

"How unhappy it looks, Charlie! I like the sea best. It laughs."

"It laughs just now, my dear, but sometimes it roars and thunders."

"All the same, I like it best. This other looks as if it drowned people."

"I don't suppose it ever drowned as many people as the sea, Gracie."

"Then it seems as if it thought more of those it has drowned. I wouldn't live here for anything. I'd cut a hole through the sand-hills and let the sea wash it all away."

"Better see what Mr. Rimmer thinks of it before you do that." And he laid a restraining hand on her arm as the door of the wooden house opened quietly, and a man came out backwards and stood for a moment with his head bent towards the door as if he were listening. His hair was long and of scanty grizzled gray. He wore a blue jersey and high sea-boots, and carried his sou'wester in his hand. Then he straightened up, clapped on his hat, and strode away round the house towards the Mere. Eager jumped down the sand-hill and ran after him, and caught him before he reached a flat-bottomed skiff drawn up on to the sedgy shore.

"Is this Mr. Rimmer?" he asked.

"Seth Rimmer, at yore service, sir." And there turned on them a fine old gray face, laced and seamed with weather-lines that told of bitter black nights on the sea, when the spume flew and the salt bit deep. The blue eyes, very deep under the bushy gray brows, were shrewd and kindly; the mouth, half hidden in gray moustache and beard, was set very firmly.

"He looked good but hard. But I liked him," was Gracie's comment afterwards.

"Yo' be the new curate," he said at once, taking in Eager in a large comprehensive gase.

"Charles Eager, the new curate, Mr. Rimmer. How is your wife to-day? I understand——"

"Ay, hoo's bed-rid. We're Wesleyans, but hoo'll be glad to see yo' and th' little lady." And he turned back to the house.

"An' what's yore name?"—to Gracie.

"Grace Eager."

"Yore sister?"

"All I have left. There have been many between, but we are the last, and so we're very good friends."

"An' so ye should. A fine name yon, Grace Eager. An' what are yore graces, an' what are yo' eager for, missie?"

"She's full of all graces and eager for all good, like her big brother. Isn't that it, Gracie?" laughed Charles, to cover her confusion at so pointed a questioning.

She nodded and squeezed his hand and skipped by his side, and so they came back to the house.

"Someun to see yo', Kattrin," he said, as he opened the door and ushered them in.

It was but a small room and the furnishings were of the simplest, but everything was spick-and-span in its ordered brightness. There was a small fire with a kettle on the hob, and in one corner was a bed with a sweet-faced woman in it, propped up with pillows so that she could look out of the window.

"Yo're welcome, whoever yo' are," she said.

"It's new curate, Mr. Eager, an' 's li'll sister."

"Ech, a'm glad to see yo', sir, though we don't trouble church much here. Nivver set eyes on last curate, nivver once."

"I apologise for him, Mrs. Rimmer; perhaps he found the long walk through the sand too much for him."

"Ay; he wasn't much of a man," said Rimmer quietly. "Yo're a different breed, I'm thinking. Yo're tackling them Carron lads, an' that's a good job. I seen yo' about the sands with 'em."

"Yes; they're worth tackling, aren't they?"

"Surely; and yo're the man for the job! Now I mun get along or I'll miss tide. Yo'll excuse me, an' if yo'll talk a while with the missus she'll be glad. She dunnot get too many visitors. Good-bye, wife!" And he went out quietly and tramped sturdily away to his work.

"He's a right good mon," said his wife fervently. "And he aye bids me good-bye in case he nivver comes back, and he aye says a prayer for me outside the door. It's a bad, bad coast this," she said, with a sigh. "It took his feyther, an' his grandfeyther, and it's aye on his mind that sometime it'll take him too. An' it may be onytime."

"He's in better hands than his own, Mrs. Rimmer," said Eager.

"Aye, I know, and so was they, an' it's no good thinking o' death and drownin's till you see 'em. But I seen so many it's not easy to get away from 'em, lying here all alone."

"Where's your little girl?" asked Gracie suddenly.

"Kattie? She should be in by this. She stops chattin' wi' th' neebors now an' then. It's lonesome here for childer, yo' see. I sometimes wish we was nearer folk, but we've lived here all our lives an' I wouldna like to move now."

"And who are your nearest neighbours, Mrs. Rimmer?" asked Eager.

"Oh, there's plenty across Mere—Bill o' Jack's, an' Tom o' Bob's o' Jim's, an'——" She stopped and lay listening. "That's her now." And presently a girl's voice lilting a song drew near from the direction of the Mere.

The door opened and she came in carrying a pail of milk.

"'Ello!" she jerked in her astonishment, and then lapsed into silence.

"Where's your manners, Kattie?" from her mother, as she stood staring at the strangers, especially at Gracie.

"How are you, Kattie?" said Eager. "I'm the new curate. This is my sister, Gracie. She saw you the other day and wanted to see you again."

Kattie put out the tip of a red tongue and smiled in rich confusion.

She was a remarkably pretty child, with large, dark-blue eyes, a mane of brown hair tumbling over her shoulders, and the healthy red-brown skin of the dwellers on the flats.

Like the boys of Carne, she obviously wore only what she had to wear of necessity. In her shy grace she was like a startled fawn, looking her first on man, and ready to bound away at smallest sign of advance.

"Where's yore manners, lass?" said her mother again; and Kattie drew in the tip of her tongue and twisted her little red mouth and stared at Gracie harder than ever.

"Suppose you two run away out and make one another's acquaintance," said Eager to Gracie, "and I'll have a chat with Mrs. Rimmer." And the girls slipped out contentedly.

"Ech, but you do wear a lot o' clothes!" jerked Kattie, the moment they got outside.

"It must be jolly to wear so few," said Gracie enviously. When I've lived here a bit perhaps I can too. You see I've always been used to wearing a lot.".

"They're gey pratty, but I'd liever not carry 'em."

"Is that your boat? Do you row it all by yourself?"

"O' course! I'll show you." And she sped down to the long-prowed shallop from which she had just landed, shoved it off, tumbled in, regardless of wet feet and display of bare leg, and sent the little craft bounding over the smooth dark mirror, her vivid little face sparkling with delight at this opportunity for the display of superior accomplishment.

Gracie meanwhile danced with desire on the sedgy shore.

"Me too, Kattie! Come back and take me too! What a love of a little boat! And you row like a man."

"I can scull too," cried Kattie vauntingly, and drew in one oar and slipped the other over the stern and came wobbling back with a manly swing that seemed to Gracie to court disaster.

"I like the rowing best," she gasped, as she crawled cautiously in over the projecting prow. "Let me try one."

And thereafter they were friends.

"I like Kattie," said Gracie exuberantly, as she danced along home holding Charlie's hand.

"She's a pretty little thing, but she seems very shy."

"She's not a bit shy when you know her. And she can row and swim, and once she shot a duck on the Mere. And she knows where they lay their eggs, and . . ."

And so, for better or worse, Kattie Rimmer came into the story.

CHAPTER XIII

MOUNTING

FOR the polishing of gems the dust of gems is necessary. And for the training of boys other boys are essential. Eager cast about for other boys against whom his colts might wear off some of their angles.

Some men have a wonderful power of attracting and drawing out all that is best in their fellows. Personal magnetism, we call it, and it is a mighty gift of the gods.

Charles Eager had that gift in a very remarkable degree, and with it many others that appealed to the most difficult of all sections of the community. Boys hate being made good. The man who can lift them to higher planes without any unpleasant consciousness thereof on their part is a genius, and more than a genius. We have, some of us, met such in our lives, and we think of them with most affectionate reverence and crown them with glory and honour, though, all too often, the world passes them by with but scant acknowledgment.

But diamond-dust alone will polish diamonds. Softer stuff is useless, and the supply of boy-diamond-dust in that neighbourhood was small. So he laid masterful hands on what there was.

Just outside Wyvveloe, between that and Wynsloe, lay Knoyle, the residence of Sir George Herapath, the great army contractor. He was a man of sixty-five, tall, gray-bearded, genial, enjoying a well-earned rest from a life of many activities. He had married late, and had one son, George, aged fifteen, and one daughter, Margaret, a year younger. His wife was dead.

The firm of Horspath & Handyside, and its trade-mark of interlocked H's, was as well known in army circles as the

War Department's own private mark. During the Napoleonic wars its business dealings were on a gigantic scale. It fed and clothed and sheltered armies in many lands, and carried out its every undertaking to the letter, cost what it might. The first consideration with the firm of H. and H. was perfect fulfilment of its obligations. None knew better how much depended on its exertions—how helpless the most skilful commander was unless he could count absolutely on his supplies. H. and H. never failed in their duty, and the firm reaped its reward, both in honours and in cash. But to both Herapath and his partner Handyside the honour they cherished most of all was the fact that their name and mark stood everywhere as a guarantee of reliability and fair dealing.

Handyside died five years after his partner's baronetcy, and left the bulk of his money to Herapath, having no near relatives of his own. And Sir George, desirous of rest before he grew past the enjoyment of it, took into partnership his right-hand man, Ralph Harben, who had grown up with the firm, strung another H on to the bar of the first big one, which represented himself—so that the mark of the firm came to look something like a badly made hurdle—and left the direction of affairs chiefly in his hands.

Eager, in the course of his duties, had called at Knoyle and had met with a congenial welcome. George and Margaret Herapath would be useful to his cubs now that they were licking into shape. His thoughts turned to them at once.

There had been another boy with them at church the previous Sunday, he noticed. The more the merrier. He would rope them all in, for games good enough with four are many times as good with eight or more.

"Yes, I heard you'd tackled the Carron colts," smiled Sir George. "Bit of a handful, I should say, from all accounts."

"I like bits of handfuls," said Eager. "I've got good material to work on. I shall make men of those two."

"You'll have done a good work. And how can Knoyle be of service to you, Mr. Eager?"

"In heaps of ways. I want your two in our games. Four are really not enough for proper work. Who's the new youngster I saw with you on Sunday?"

"That's young Harben, my partner's son. His father is in Spain just now, and his mother's dead, so I've taken him in for a time."

"The more the merrier! I wish you had another half-dozen."

"H'm! I don't. My two keep me quite lively enough."

"I want you to let me break my two in on some of your horses, too. You've got more than you can keep in proper condition, and the old curmudgeon at Carne flatly refuses to buy them ponies. I've done my best with him, and riding's about due with my two. They can fence and swim and box. They beat me at running. Boating's no good here, and wouldn't be much use to them later, anyway. They're for the army, of course. Your boy, too, I suppose?"

"Yes, George is for the army, and young Harben too, I judge, from his talk. Suppose you bring your two up, say, to-morrow, and they can have a fling at the ponies, and——"

"And you can form your own judgment of them," said Eager, with a quiet chuckle. "That's all right. They're presentable, or I should not have proposed it, and yours will help to polish them, and that's what I want."

"I see. To-morrow morning, then, and they can tumble off the ponies in the paddock to their hearts' content."

So—three very excited faces, and three pairs of very eager eyes, as they pressed up the avenue to Knoyle next morning, and keen little noses sniffing anxiously for ponies, for Gracie was not going to miss such a chance, and as for the boys, wild mustangs of the prairies would not have daunted them.

Life—what with swimming and fencing and boxing and cricket and hockey and football—had suddenly widened its bounds beyond belief almost, and now the crowning glory of horses loomed large in front.

Picture them in their scanty blue knee-breeches and blue

jerseys, no hats, but fine crops of black hair, their eager, handsome faces the colour of the sand, with the hot blood close under the tan, bare legs and homely leather sandals, black eyes with sparks in them; Gracie in a little blue jersey also and a short blue frock, bare-legged and in sandals too, for life on the sands had proved altogether too destructive of stockings; on her streaming hair, and generally hanging by its strings, a sunbonnet originally blue, but now washing out towards white.

"There they are!" gasped Gracie, dancing with excitement as usual. "In that field over there——"

"And here are Sir George and the others. Remember to salute him, boys; and look him straight in the eye when he speaks to you. He's a jolly old boy."

"And, for goodness' sake, don't fight if you can possibly help it!" said Gracie impressively.

"I congratulate you on your colts, Mr. Eager," said Sir George, as they followed the youngsters to the paddock. "They're miles ahead of what I expected. I had my misgivings, I confess, but now they are gone. You've done wonders with them already."

"Good material, Sir George. But there's plenty still to do. You can't cure the neglect of years in a few months."

"If any man could, you could. They're a well-set-up pair, and look as fit as fiddles."

"Their free life on the sands has done that for them at all events. If they've missed much, they have also gained much, and, by God's help, I'm going to supply the rest. There are the makings of two fine men there."

"You'll do it. Why! What are they up to now?"

"Only fighting," laughed Eager. "They rarely dispute in words, always *vi et armis*. Jack! Jim! Stop that! What's the matter now?" as the boys got up off the ground with flushed faces and dancing eyes. "A mighty good-looking pair!" thought Sir George to himself. "And which is which and which is t'other, I couldn't tell to save my life."

"I was going to help Gracie over, and he cut in," said Jack.

"I wanted to help her over too," grinned Jim.

"Sillies!" said Gracie. "I didn't need you. I got through. Oh, what beauties!" as a bay pony and a grey came trotting up to their master and mistress for customary gifts and caresses.

"This is mine," said Margaret, kissing the soft dark muzzle. "Dear old Graylock! Want a bit of sugar? There then, old wheedler!" And Graylock tossed his head and savoured his morsel appreciatively, with a mouth that watered visibly for more.

"Lend me a bit, Meg," begged her brother. "I forgot the greedy little beggars. You spoil 'em. Here you are, Whitefoot."

"Bridles only, at present, Bob," said Sir George, to a stable-boy who had come down laden with gear. "Let the youngsters begin at the beginning. Now you, Jack and Jim—I don't know which of you's which—have a go at them bare-backed, and let's see what you're made of." And the boys flung themselves over the ponies with such vehemence that Jim came down headlong on the other side while Graylock danced with dismay; and Jack hung over Whitefoot like a sack, but got his leg over at last, with such a yell of triumph that his startled steed shot from under him and left him in a heap on the grass.

But they were both up in a moment and at it again.

"Twist yer hand in his mane," instructed Bob, "an' hang on like the divvle. There y'are! Now clip him tight wi' yer knees an' shins. You're aw reet!" And Jim and Graylock went off down the paddock in a series of wild leaps and bounds, while Bob ran after them administering counsel.

"Loose yer reins a bit! Don't tickle him wi' yer toes!

. . . Stiddy then! Go easy, my lad! Don't fret 'im!"—as Jack and Whitefoot bore down upon him in like fashion.

"They'll ride aw reet," he said, as he came back crab-fashion to the lookers-on, with his eyes fixed on the riders. "Stick like cats, they do. And them ponies is enjoying theirselves."

"Promising, are they, Bob?" asked Sir George.

"They're aw reet. They'll ride," said Bob emphatically.

When the horsemen wore round towards the group they were in boastful humour.

"I was up first," from Jack.

"I was off first," from Jim.

"Ay—on ground!"

"Nay, on pony! You were sitting on grass."

"You fell over t'other side."

"I'll fight you!" And in a moment they were off their steeds and locked in fight, to the great scandal of Gracie.

"Oh you dreadful boys!" And she danced wildly about them. "Didn't I tell you——"

"Stop it, boys!" And Eager laughingly shook them apart.

"The old Adam will out," he said to Sir George, who was enjoying them mightily.

"They've no lack of pluck. Keep 'em on right lines, Mr. Eager, and you'll make men of them. Now then, who's for next mount? Rafe, my lad, what do you say to a bareback?"

"Sooner have a saddle, sir," said young Harben, and sat tight on the paling.

"You, missie?" as Gracie danced imploringly before him. "Saddle up, Bob. . . . Well, I'm——!" as the ponies went off down the field again with the boys struggling up into position. "Oh, they'll do all right. I like their spirit."

When the ponies were captured, Gracie had her ride under Margaret's care, and expressed herself very plainly on the subject of side-saddles and the advantages of being a boy.

And the boys took to saddle and stirrups as they had to the swimming.

"They'll ride," was Bob's final and emphatic verdict again.

Sir George insisted on their waiting for midday dinner, an experience which some of them enjoyed not at all and would gladly have escaped.

Gracie sat between Jack and Jim, and got very little dinner because of her maternal anxieties on their account. By incessant watchfulness on both sides at once she managed to keep them from any very dreadful exhibition of inexperience, but she got very red in the face over it, and rather short in the temper, which perhaps was not to be wondered at considering the state of her appetite and the many tempting dishes she had no time to do justice to.

The boys scuffled through somehow, with very wide eyes—to say nothing of mouths—for hitherto untasted delicacies. Mrs. Lee's commissariat tended to the solidly essential, and disdained luxuries for growing lads.

Master Harben made the Little Lady's ears tingle more than once with an appreciative guffaw at her protégés' solecisms, and if quick indignant glances could have pierced him he would have suffered sorely. As it was, Margaret frowned him back to decency, and George intimated in unmistakable gesture that punishment awaited him in the privacy of the immediate future.

But Jack and Jim, the prime causes of all this disturbance, ate on imperturbably, and followed the directions, conveyed by their monitress in brief fierce whispers and energetic side-kicks, to the best of their powers, so long as these imposed no undue restraint on the reduction of two healthy appetites.

And more than once Eager caught Sir George's eye resting thoughtfully on the pair, and knew what he was thinking.

"I suppose you know them apart?" he asked quietly, one time when Eager caught him watching them.

"Oh yes, I know them, but it took me a few days."

"A deuced troublesome business! No wonder the old man's gone sour over it. I don't see what he can do."

"He can do nothing but wait."

"And it's bitter waiting when the sands are running out."

On the way home the Little Lady blew away some of the froth of their exultation at their own prowess, by her biting comments on their shortcomings at table. But this new and grand addition to their lengthening list of acquirements overtopped everything else, and they exulted in spite of her.

"We stuck on barebacked, anyway," said Jim; "and what does it matter how you eat?"

"It matters a great deal if you want to be gentlemen," said Gracie vehemently.

"We're going to be soldiers," said Jack.

CHAPTER XIV

WIDENING WAYS

NEXT day, when the Rev. Charles was putting all his skill into underhand twisters for the overthrow of Jack, who, to Jim's great exasperation, had got the hang of them and was driving them all over the shore, and Gracie was dancing with wild exhortation to her brother to get him out, as it was her innings next—she stopped suddenly with a shout and started off towards the sand-hills. And the others, turning to see what had taken her, found the Knoyle party threading its way among the devious gullies, and presently they all came cantering through the loose sand to the flats.

"Morning, Mr. Eager; we've come for a game. Will you have us?" cried Sir George exuberantly.

"Rather! It's just what we wanted. You'll play, sir?"

"That's what I came for. Renew my youth, and all that kind of thing! See to the horses, Bob. Eh, what?"—at sight of the lad's eager face—"Like to take a hand too? Well, see if you can tether 'em—away from those bents. Bents won't do them any good. Now then, how shall we play?"

"Oh, Carne versus Knoyle," said Eager. "All to field, and Margaret goes in for both sides."

Knoyle beat Carne that time, thanks to George and Bob. Sir George "renewed his youth, and all that kind of thing." And young Ralph Harben entered vigorous protest every time he was put out, and argued the points till George punched his head for him.

After the game the boys were allowed to take the stiffness out of the ponies' legs. And altogether—as the first of many similar ones—that was a memorable day.

Eager rejoiced greatly in the success of his planning, for the close contact with these other bright and restless spirits had a wonderful effect on his boys. They toned down and they toned up, and it seemed to him that he could trace improvement in them each day.

He had his doubts now and again of the effects of young Harben on his own two. The lad was difficult and had evidently been much spoiled at home. Eager quietly did his best to remedy his more visible defects, and George Herapath seconded him with bodily chastisement whenever occasion offered.

Eager and Sir George were sitting resting in the side of a sand-hill one day, and watching the younger folk at a game in which Ralph was perpetually disputatious odd-man-out. It seemed impossible for him to get through any game without some wrangle.

Eager made some quiet comment on the matter and Sir George said:

"Yes, he's difficult. He's the only child, and his mother

spoiled him sadly. When she died his father sent him to a second-rate school, and this is the result. But I hope he'll pull round. We must do what we can for him. Harben is in treaty for the Scarsdale place just beyond Wynsloe, so you'll be able to keep an eye on the boy. Your two are marvels. I never see them squabbling."

"Oh, they never squabble. They just fight it out, and no temper in it. They're really capital boxers, and they're coming on in their fencing."

"You'll make men of those two yet."

"I'll do my best."

"And if the old man dies? What will happen then?"

"God knows. It's as hard a nut as I ever came across."

"That infernal old woman up at Carne could crack it if she would, I suppose?"

"I have no doubt; but she won't speak. And I'm afraid no one would believe her if she did."

"Deuced rough on the old man!" And Sir George lapsed into musing, and watched the riddles of Carne as they sped to and fro, as active as panthers and as careless as monkeys of the trouble they represented.

One day when they were all hard at it, Gracie suddenly sped from her post, as her manner was, heedless of the shouts of the rest, darted in among the hummocks, and came back dragging the not very reluctant Kattie Rimmer and insisted on her joining the game. And Kattie, nothing loth, succeeded in cloaking her lack of knowledge with such untiring energy that she proved a welcome recruit and was forthwith pressed into the company. For where numbers are few and more are needed, trifling distinctions of class lose their value. She was very quick and bright, too, and soon picked up the rules of the games; and when she was not flying after balls she was watching Margaret and Gracie with worshipful observant eyes, and assimilating from them a new code of manners for her own private use.

Gracie's usual behaviour in games, indeed, was that of

a pea on a hot shovel. But Margaret, no whit behind her in her zeal for the business on hand, bore herself with something more of the dignity and decorum of a young lady in her fifteenth year—except just on occasion, when, at a tight pinch, everything went overboard and she flung herself into things with the abandon of Gracie and Kattie combined.

Eager watched her with great appreciation. He could divine the coming woman in the occasional sweet seriousness of the charming face, and rejoiced in her as he did in all beautiful things.

And George Herapath, with much of his father in him, was always a tower of good-humoured common sense and abounding energy. He backed up Eager's efforts in every direction, licked Harben or the tiger-cubs conscientiously, as often as occasion arose, and brought to their play the experience and tone of the public schoolboy up to date. He was at Harrow, and his house was closed on account of an outbreak of scarlet fever, which all except the higher powers counted mighty luck and all to the good.

They soon dropped into the way of all bathing together of a morning, before starting their game—all except Sir George, whose sea-bathing days were over, and who preferred cantering over the sands with them, all racing alongside like a pack of many-coloured hounds, shouting aloud in the wild glee of the moment, splashing through the shimmering pools in rainbow showers, tumbling headlong into the tideway, and then in dogged silence breasting fearlessly out to sea, while Sir George rode his big bay into the water after them as far as his discretion would permit.

And at times they sped far afield over the countryside, when, if Jack and Jim were hares, they were never caught, and if they were hounds they picked up an almost invisible scent in a way that did credit to their powers and to Mr. Fenimore Cooper. They might be beaten at cricket or hockey, whose finer rules they were always transgressing, but in this wider play none could come near them.

It took the new-comers a very long time to distinguish between them; and even when they thought they had got them fixed at last, they were as often wrong as right, for the boys delighted to puzzle them, and even went the length of refusing to answer to their right names and assuming one another's with that sole end in view.

"They beat me," laughed Sir George, more than once. "I never know t'other from which, and when I'm quite sure of 'em I'm always wrong."

"They do it on purpose," said Gracie. "They're little rascals, but they're as different as different to me. I can't see any likeness in them, except that they're both rather bad at times—but nothing to what they used to be, I assure you, Sir George."

"Well, well! Perhaps I'll get to know them in time, my dear; and meanwhile you just wink at me when they're making game of the old man."

"I will," said Gracie solemnly. "But they don't really mean any harm, you know. It's just their fun."

From his upper windows in the house of Carne that other old man watched them also, with scowling face and twisted heart. The sands were running—running—running, and he was no nearer the solution of his life's puzzle than he had been ten years ago Farther away if anything, for babies die more easily than lusty, tight-knit, sun-tanned boys who never knew an ailment, and grew stronger every day.

But there were keener eyes still, sharpened by a vast craving love for the wakening souls committed to his care, watching them all the time, and eager for every sign of growth and development. Love blinds, they say, and so it may to that which it does not wish to see. But Love is a mighty revealer, too, and Doubt and Dislike attain no revelations but the shadows of themselves.

Charles Eager studied those boys with many times the eagerness and acumen that he had ever brought to his books. Here was a living enigma, and he found it fascinating. But the weeks grew into months, and he found himself not one step nearer its solution.

In all their moods and humours, in their outstanding virtues and their no less prominent defects, they were one. They had grown up in the equal practice of qualities drawn, on the one side at all events, from the same source.

Bodily fear seemed quite outside their ken. They lacked the imagination which pictures possible consequences behind the deed. If they wanted to do a thing, they did not stop to consider what might come of it, but just did it. The consequences when they came were accepted as matters of course.

They were generous to a fault. They would, indeed, fight between themselves for the most trifling possessions, but it was from sheer love of fighting. They never kept for the mere sake of having, and most of their belongings they held in common—jointly against the world as they had known it. And this feeling of being two against outsiders had undoubtedly fostered the communal feeling. As their circle widened and others were admitted into it, the feeling extended to them. They possessed little, but what they had all were welcome to.

And they were by nature eminently truthful. To their grandfather or Mr. Kennet they might on occasion assume masks which belied their feelings, but that was in the nature of a ruse to mislead an enemy who by gross injustice had forced them into unnatural ways. To them it was no more acting a lie than is the broken fluttering of a bird which thereby draws the trespasser from its nest. They were in a state of perpetual war with the higher powers, and to them all things were fair.

Their faults were the natural complements of these better things. They were headstrong, reckless, careless, hot-tempered—defects, after all, which as a rule entail more trouble on their owners than on others, and are therefore regarded by the world with a lenient eye.

For many months Eager found no shade of difference in their development. They had started level, and they progressed in equal degree, and progressed marvellously. The virgin soil brought forth an abundant harvest. But then, in spite of all, it was good soil, and ready for the seed.

The grim old man at Carne sent now and again for Eager, and received him always, snuff-box in hand, with a cynical, "Well, Mr. Eager, no progress?"

"Progress, Sir Denzil? Heaps! We are advancing by leaps and bounds. We are doing splendidly."

"You've still got the two of them, I see,"—as though they were puppies Eager was trying to dispose of.

"Still got the two, sir, and I couldn't tell you which is the better of them. There are the makings of fine men in both."

"Then you're just where you were as to which is which?"

"Just where you have been these ten years, sir."

"You have seen more of them in ten weeks than I've seen in ten years."

"They are developing every day, but so far they run neck to neck. But, candidly, Sir Denzil, I scarcely know what signs one could take as any decisive indication of their descent. Heredity is a ticklish thing to draw any certain inference from. It plays odd tricks, as you know."

"I had hoped somewhat from those swimming lessons——" and he snuffed regretfully.

Eager laughed joyously at his disappointment.

"Why, they swam like ducks the very first day. You really have no idea what fine lads they are, sir. They are lads to be proud of."

"Ay—if there was but one."

"It's a thousand pities we can't find the right way out of the muddle without thinking of such things."

"We cannot," said the old man grimly.

CHAPTER XV

DIVERGING LINES

AS time went on, however, Eager's careful oversight of the boys began to note slight points of divergence in the lines of their characteristics, which had so far run absolutely side by side.

Jack, for instance, began to develop a somewhat tentative kind of self-control. His brain seemed to become more active. At times he even attempted to subject Jim to discipline for lapses from his own view of the right way of things. And Jim took him on right joyously; and the pitched battles, which Eager had been striving to relegate to the background, were renewed with vehemence, within the strict limits of the new rules thereto ordained.

Gracie was distressed at this falling away. But Eager bade her be of good cheer, and watched developments with interest. Meanwhile, the boys' muscles and skill in self-defence grew mightily.

There was no doubt about it, Jack was harvesting his grain the quicker of the two—so far as could be seen, at all events. The difference between them when instruction was to the fore was somewhat marked. Jack gave his mind to it and took it in, evinced a desire to get to the bottom of things, even asked questions at times on points that were not clear to him. Jim, on the other hand, would sit gazing at the fount of wisdom with wide black eyes which presently wandered off after a seagull or a shadow, with a very visible inclination towards such things—or towards anything actively alive—rather than towards the passivity entailed by the pursuit of abstract knowledge.

Then again, Jack succeeded at times in forcing himself to

sit quite still for whole minutes on end, while Jim, after a certain limited number of seconds, was on the wriggle to be up and doing. And the moment he was loosed, the quiescence of seconds had to be atoned for by many minutes of joyous activity.

They were, in fact, beginning to take the lines of the good scholar and the bad. And yet Eager confessed to himself a very warm heart for careless, happy-go-lucky Jim.

"The other looks like making the deeper mark," he said to himself. "But I can't help loving old Jim. He's all one could wish except in the brain. Maybe it will come!"

As to any deductions to be based upon these growing differences between the boys, he could find no sound footing.

"Jack seems undoubtedly the more able," he would reason it out, "but what does that point to? Is it the high result of two blue-blooded strains, or the enriching of a blue blood with a dash of stronger red? Which would the stronger blend run to—activity of mind or activity of body?"

The latter, he was inclined to think, but found it impossible to pronounce upon with anything like certainty, and realised that every other indication would inevitably lead to the same result. The riddle of Carne would never be read thus. Time and Providence might cut the knot and give to Carne its rightful heir. Pure reason, or the questionable affirmation of interested parties, never would.

From that point of view he saw his commission from Sir Denzil doomed to failure. But that, after all, he said to himself, with a bracing shake, was, from his own point of view, of minor consequence. The great thing was to make men of his boys and fit them for the battle of life to the best of his powers and theirs.

CHAPTER XVI

A CUT AT THE COIL

TWICE, during the autumn, it seemed as though t riddle would be solved, or at all events the knot cut. George Herapath and young Harben had gone off to sch but the reduced company still took its fill of the freedom the sands. Sir George and Margaret rarely failed, and pla and work progressed apace.

Boating on that coast was all toil and little pleasure. With a tide that ran out a full mile, the care of a boat, unless for strictly business purposes, would have been a burden. Old Seth Rimmer and his fellows kept their craft in the estuaries up Wytham way and at Wynsloe, where, with knowledge of the ever-shifting banks and much labour, it was possible to get out to sea in most states of the tide.

But Eager, desirous of an all-round education for his cubs, managed to teach them rowing in Kattie Rimmer's shallop on the Mere, to Kattie's great delight, since there she shone at first alone.

And it was there they made the acquaintance of Kattie's brother, young Seth, a great loose-limbed giant of nineteen or so, who helped his father at the fishing at times, and at times went ventures of his own on less respectable lines. A good-humoured giant, however, who would lie asprawl on a sand-hummock by the Mere-side, and laugh loud and long at new-beginners' first clumsy attempts at rowing, and more than once waded waist-deep into the water to set right-side-up some unfortunate whose ill-applied vigour had capsized the crank little craft.

Some of young Seth's doings were a sore discomfort and mortification to the older folk in the little wooden house. But he took his own way outside with dogged nonchalance, bore himself well towards them except on these sore points of his own private concerns, and worshipped Kattie.

Old Seth, you see, had always ordered his little household on the strictest—not to say straitest—lines of right and wrong. Young Seth, when he grew too big for bodily coercion, kicked over the lines and took his own way, in spite of all his father and mother could do to prevent him. And his way led at times through strange waters and in strange company.

He was away sometimes for days on end, and then, whether the little house lay baaking in the sunshine or shaking in the gale, his mother would lie full of fears and prayers, and his father was quieter than ever in the boat, and Kattie, but half-comprehending the matter, would feel the gloom his absences cast and would question him volubly when he returned, but never got anything for her pains.

He would do anything for her or for any of them—except give up the ways he had chosen.

When the south-wester screamed over the flats for days at a time it set the ribbed sands humming with its steady persistence. Games were impossible then, and Eager's ready wit devised a means of turning the screamer to account.

He turned into Bob Ratchett's shed one day and said:

"Bob, I want some wheels—two big ones four feet across, and two about a foot smaller, and the tires of all must be a foot wide."

"My gosh, them's wheels! What'u yo' want 'em for?" grinned Bob admiringly.

"I'm going to make a boat——"

"Aw then, passon!—a boat now!"

"To run on the sands."

"Aw!" gasped Bob, and eyed "passon" doubtfully.

"You can make them?"

"Aw! I can mek 'em aw reet, but——"

"All right, Bob. You set to work, and I'll see to the rest."

"Passon's" boat became a great joke in the village. But bit by bit he worked it out, got his materials into shape, and with his own hands and the assistance, in their various degrees, of the boys and the excited oversight of Gracie, fitted it together into a somewhat nightmare resemblance to the skeleton of a boat.

Jack stuck pretty steadily to the novel work. Jim and Gracie fluttered about it, questioning, suggesting, doubting, went off for a game, came back, danced about, hindering more than helping, but always convinced in their own minds that but for them that boat would never have been built.

The two large wheels, rather wide apart, supported it abeam forward, and between them be stepped a stout little mast carrying jib and mainsail. The smaller wheels astern moved on a stout pin and acted as rudder, actuated by a long wooden tiller. A rough wooden frame abaft the mast offered precarious accommodation for passengers. And when at last, after many days, it was finished, the villagers crowded round it, and joked and laughed themselves purple in the face over the oddest and most unlikely craft that coast had ever seen.

Then willing hands took the ropes, and dragged it out of the village and through the gullies of the sand-hills with mighty labours, and so, at last, to the edge of the flats not far from Carne.

And there Eager climbed in by himself, with not a few fears that the doubts and laughter of the village might find their justification in him.

There was a strong wind blowing with a steady hum right on to the flats from the south-west. Eager hauled up his sails, lay down in the meagre cockpit, tiller in hand, and the scoffers started him off with a run.

They looked for him to come to a stop when they did; but instead, to their never-dying amazement, the wind gripped the sails, the clumsy-looking boat sped on, faster and faster, bumping over the hard-ribbed sands, rushing through the wind-rippled pools, and they stood gaping. In less than five minutes it was at the bend of the coast where it turns to the north-east, a good three miles away, and then, marvel of marvels for such a craft, just as they expected it to disappear round the corner, it ran up into the wind, came round on the other tack with a fine sweep and without a pause, and was rushing back towards them before their gaping mouths had closed. "Passon's" boat was a huge success, it raised him mightily in their opinions and inclined them to give ear even to his suggestions for the abolition of stinks, and to the boys and the rest it gave a new zest to life. Day after day, whenever the wind served, they were at it, and looked forward to the gray windy days as they had never done before.

Sir George had been away when the boat was launched, but he rode over the first morning after he got home, and after watching it for a time ventured on board himself, with Eager at the helm.

"Man!" he said, as he tumbled out after the run—blown and breathless and considerably shaken up—"that's wonderful! You ought to have been an engineer."

"So I am," laughed Eager, "and on a larger scale than most."

From the windows of Carne, Sir Denzil watched the novel craft careering wildly over the flats, and snuffed more hopefully.

"A sufficiently dangerous-looking toy, Kennet. It seems to me that it might quite well kill one or more of them if it upset at that speed. Let us hope for the best!" And he and Kennet watched the new goings-on with interest.

Incidentally, the sand-boat one day came very near to solving the riddle of Carne on the lines of Sir Denzil's highest hopes.

There was something in the wild headlong motion that appealed with irresistible power to Jim's half-tamed nature. The mad humping rush, with now one huge wheel barely skimming the ground, now the other; the hoarse dash through the pools, when, if the sun shone, you sat for a moment in a whirling rainbow of flying drops; the keen zest and delicious risks of the turn; the novel sense of power in the lordship of the helm; these things thrilled him through and through, and he could not get too much of them.

He made himself the devoted slave of the sand-boat—spent his spare time in anointing its axles with all the fat he could coax, or otherwise procure, from Mrs. Lee, till the great wheels almost ran of their own accord, scraped the long tiller till it was as smooth as a sceptre—handled the ropes till they were as flexible almost as silk.

It was he who insisted on naming the boat *Gracie*—"because it jumped about so," but in reality, of course, because the word *Gracie* represented to him the brightest and best that life had yet brought him.

They had all tried their hands at names. Sir George—*The Flying Dutchman*, because it certainly flew and was undoubtedly broad in the beam; Margaret—*The Sylph*, because it was so tubby; Gracie—*The Sand-fly*, because it flew over the sand; Jack, for abstruse reasons of his own—*Chingachgook*; Eager was quite content to leave it to them. But no matter what the others decided on, Jim always called it *Gracie*—to the real Gracie's immense satisfaction; and as he talked *Gracie* ten times as much as all the rest put together, *Gracie* it finally became.

When wind and weather put the *Gracie* out of action she lay under the walls of Carne, with folded wings and docked tail—for Jim always carried away the tiller into the house, for love of the very feel of it, and partly perhaps in token of proprietorship. It stood in a corner where he could always see it, and slept by his bedside.

No one, however, ever thought of meddling with the sand-boat. In the first place, she belonged to Mr. Eager, and they held "passon" in highest esteem. And, in the second place, Carne was a dangerous place to wander round at night. Mr. Kennet had a gun, with which he was no great shot, indeed, but even the wildest bullet may find unexpected billet in the dark.

It happened, one afternoon in the late autumn, that Eager was away on the confines of his wide sheepfold, about his Master's business. It had been wet and blusterous all day, and the boys were desultorily employed on their books in a corner of the kitchen; Jim with the *Gracie's* polished tiller twisting fondly in his hand, as a devoted lover toys with a ribbon from his mistress's dress; Jack somewhat absorbed in the doings of Themistocles and Xerxes at Salamis, in a great volume which he had abstracted from the library the day before.

The polished tiller wriggled more and more restlessly in Jim's hand, as though it longed to be up and doing.

He got up at last and strolled out just to have a look at the rest of the *Gracie*. Jack was too busy sinking Persian galleys in Salamis Bay to pay any heed to anything nearer home.

Jim found the wind blowing half a gale. It swept round the house with a scream, and seemed to meet again full on the *Gracie*, who quivered and throbbed as though longing to be off.

The jib had been wrapped round the forestay, and the wind, working at it as though of one mind with him, had loosened the clew, and it was thrashing to and fro in desperate excitement.

He climbed aboard, fitted the tiller, and sat in vast enjoyment. Why, it would only need a pull at a rope here and there, and he believed she would be off. The rain had hardened the soft sand, and there was a good slope down to the ribbed flats below. He had always longed for a run all by himself, and he knew the ropes and how to steer her as well as Mr. Eager did.

In sheer self-defence he captured the thrashing sheet and twisted it round a cleat. The jib untoggled itself from the stay, bellied out full, and the boat began to move slowly down the slope.

The joy of it sent the blood up into Jim's head and set it spinning. He would have a run—just a little run—all by himself, just to prove to himself that he could do it.

The boat went rocking down the slope. He hauled at the halyard in a frenzy, and the mainsail went jumping up. He made it fast, grabbed his beloved tiller, and the *Gracie*, with a roll and a shake, bounded away up the flats.

Faster and faster she went, the ribbed sands and the wind-whipped pools seemed to sweep along to meet her and fly beneath her all-devouring wheels, till Jim's head was spinning faster even than they. He yelled and waved his arms above his head, till the tiller banging him in the ribs nearly knocked him overboard and recalled him to his duties.

He was at the bend in the coast before he knew it. He threw his weight on to the tiller to bring her round on the curve which would allow her head to fall off on the other tack, but fooled it somehow, and instead she flew off at a tangent straight for the sea.

"Ecod!" said a watcher—for other purposes—in the sand-hills. "'Oo's gooin' reet to stick-sands!"—and started at a run after the *Gracie*.

Jim always stoutly maintained that if he had only had room enough he would have got her round all right. But space and time were wanting.

All in a moment the solid ground seemed to vanish from below the whirling wheels. One wheel sank down into comparative space, the other spun on horizontally; the *Gracie's* nose went down out of sight into a squirming mass of slimy sand, and Jim was flung head over heels into the midst of it.

He got his head up with his mouth full of watery sand which half choked him. Before he had coughed it out, fear and the clammy sand gripped him together. It clung to him like thick treacle. His feet and legs were bound and weighted—he could not move them. And when his arms got into it the deadly sand clasped them tightly. It was up to his chest, like cold dead giant arms folding him tighter and tighter in a last embrace, or the merciless coils of a boa-constrictor.

Presently it would have him by the throat, and the stuff would run into his mouth and choke him, and he would die and they would never find him.

He tried to shout, with little hope of any one hearing; but it was all he could do. The clammy death was at his throat, and the pressure on his chest was so great that his shout was of the feeblest.

Another minute and the riddle of Carne would have been solved. But feeble as was his shout, it was answered. The runner on the sands came panting up, and the sight of his anxious face was to Jim as the face of an angel out of heaven—and a great deal more, for Jim had never troubled much about angels.

"Help—Seth!"—he bubbled, through the sandy scum.

"Ay, ay, sir!" panted young Seth, and jumped on to the half-submerged *Gracie*, whipped out his knife from its sheath at his back, and sliced the stays of the mast and had it out in a twinkling.

"Lay holt!"—and he shoved it towards the disappearing Jim. "And hang on tight, if it teks yore skin off! That's it. Twist rope round yo'!" And he dug his heels deep into the firm sand beyond, and laid himself almost flat as he hauled at his end of the mast.

The sweat broke in beads on his forehead, and rolled down his red face like tears, before the sands would let go their prey. But, inch by inch, he gained on them, while Jim gave up his legs for lost, so tightly did the sands hold on to them.

Inch by inch he was drawn back to life, joints cracking, sinews straining. It seemed impossible to him that he should come out whole. But there—his neck was clear, his chest, his body, his knees, and then, with a "swook" from the "stick-sands" that sounded like a disappointed curse, the rest of him came out and he lay spent on the solid earth beyond.

He remembered no more of the matter, but learned afterwards how young Seth, after thriftily staking the mast in the sand and lashing the *Gracie* to it with a length of rope to prevent her sinking out of sight—had taken him over his shoulder, not quite sure whether he was dead or alive, but face downwards, so that if he were alive some of the sand and water might run out of him, and had set off with him so, for Carne.

CHAPTER XVII

ALMOST SOLVED

JACK, when presently he had seen the little affair at Salamis to a satisfactory conclusion, missed Jim and went out in search of him. He poked about the courtyard without finding him, and only when he got outside, and saw that the *Gracie* was gone, did it occur to him that Jim had gone with her. Then in the distance he saw young Seth Rimmer coming heavily over the sands with something over his shoulder, and he ran to meet him.

From his windows Sir Denzil had watched the sand-boat go racing wildly up the flats, and had wondered at its solitary occupant. He could see by the size of him that it was one of the boys, but could not tell which.

No matter which: if the thing would only come to grief and make an end of either of them, what an ending of trouble! What a mighty relief! Then his way would be clear.

And as he mused upon it, he saw the distant boat go over, and his bitter old heart quickened a beat or two with grim hope. Then he saw the runner on the sands, and knew that something serious was amiss, and his hopes grew. And when, after what seemed a long, long time, one came running heavily towards Carne, with a load upon his shoulder, he believed his wish was realised.

He went down the stairs and into the kitchen, and spoke to old Mrs. Lee for the first time in ten years.

"One of the boys is drowned. Young Rimmer is bringing home his body." And he eyed the old woman like a hawk, with an evil light of hope in his eye.

"Naay!" said she, not to be trapped.

"Old fool!" he said to himself, but kept an unmoved face and opened his snuff-box.

Young Seth came labouring into the courtyard, with Jim on his shoulder and Jack at his heels.

Sir Denzil never looked at them. He had eyes for nothing but old Mrs. Lee's face, which was hard-set and the colour of gray stone.

"What's happen't, Seth Rimmer?" she croaked as he came, peering through half-closed eyes at him and his burden.

"Sand-boat ran i' stick-sand. Nigh got 'im."

"Is hoo gone?"—as Seth laid the limp body on the table.

"Nay, I dunno' think hoo con be dead; but it wur sore wark gettin' 'im out—nigh pooed 'im i' two—an' hoo swallowed a lot o' stuff."

"Hoo'll do," she said, after a quick examination. "Yo' leave 'im to me." And she "shooed" them all out of the kitchen and proceeded to maltreat Jim tenderly back to life.

"H'm!" said Sir Denzil disappointedly, as he climbed the stairs again—"a good chance missed! D——d fools all! . . . I wonder if Lady Susan's mother would have kept as quiet a face! . . . Well . . . The deuce take one of them! . . . Which doesn't matter."

Young Seth waited till the tide washed up over the quicksand, and then with assistance from the village dragged the *Gracie* back to life and trundled her forlornly home. And Sir Denzil sent him out a guinea by Mr. Kennet—not for saving Jim's life, but for bringing back the means whereby one or other of his grandsons might still possibly come to a sudden end.

Jim, for the first time since he began to remember things, lay in bed for three whole days, but, thanks to Mrs. Lee's anointings and rubbings, suffered no further ill-effects from his adventure—except, indeed, many a horrible nightmare, in which he was perpetually sinking down into the clinging sands, with his hands and feet fast bound and the scum running into his mouth; from which he would awake with a howl which always woke Jack with a start, and the ensuing scrimmage had in it all the joy of new life.

Eager, when he hurried up to see Jim and hear all about it, exacted a promise from them both never to sail the *Gracie* single-handed again, and was satisfied the promise would be kept.

Sir Denzil, hearing he was there, sent for him, and received him as usual.

"Well, Mr. Eager, you came near to solving the puzzle for us."

"I can't tell you how sorry I am, sir——"

"Yes, 'twas a good chance missed. If that fool Rimmer had only let Providence work out its own ends——"

"Thank God, he was on the spot, or I'd never have forgiven myself. Providence will see to the matter in its own time and in its own way, Sir Denzil, and neither you nor I can help or thwart it."

"I'm not so sure of that. If I had my way now——"

"Providence always wins," said Eager, with a shake of the head and a cheerful smile. "If we blind bats had our own way, what a muddle we would make of things. You would surely regret it in the end, sir."

CHAPTER XVIII

ALMOST SOLVED AGAIN

DURING that winter two events happened, much alike in their general features, apparently quite disconnected, and yet not at all improbably resulting the one from the other. Either happening might well have solved the problem of Carne.

Jack, as we have seen, had developed a certain taste for information. He could lose himself completely in the doings of Hannibal or Alexander, and found the mighty realities of history—or what were accounted as such—more to his taste than the most thrilling imaginings of the story-tellers. Jim found them good also—as retailed to him by Jack—and would sit by the hour, with open mouth and eyes and ears, taking them all in at second-hand. But sit down to one of the big books, and worry them all out for himself, he would not.

And so it came that more than once when Jack was over head and ears in some delightfully bloody action of long ago, Jim would ramble off by himself in search of amusement more to his taste, until such time as the sponge, having filled itself full, should be ready to be squeezed.

That was how be came to be strolling along the beach one lowering windy afternoon, seeking desultorily in the lip of the tide for anything the waves might have thrown up.

It was always an interesting pursuit, for you never knew what you might light on. In former times Jack had been as keen a treasure-hunter as himself, but now he was digging it out elsewhere and otherwise.

They had never found anything of value, though many a thing of mighty interest was brought ashore by the waves. A girl's wooden doll, and a boy's wooden horse, for instance, had nothing very remarkable about them; but found within a dozen yards of each other on the beach after a storm, they set even boys not used to very deep thinking, thinking deeply. Coco-nuts and oranges, and a dead sheep, and an oar, and a ship's grating—that was about as much as they ever came across, except once, when it was the awful body of a dead black man, and then they ran home, with their heads twisting fearfully over their shoulders, as fast as their legs could carry them; and saw the hideous thick white lips of him for many a night afterwards.

But though you sought in vain for years, there was always the chance of coming upon a casket of jewels sooner or later; and if you never actually found it, the possibility of it was delightfully attractive.

Jim ambled on, kicking asunder lumps of seaweed which

might conceal treasure, stooping now and again to pick up and examine some find more closely, and so came to the bend in the coast out of sight of Carne.

And there he stopped suddenly, like a pointing dog.

Away along the shore, and as close in as the long shoal of the sands would permit, was a large fishing-smack. Between her and the beach a boat was plying, and when it grounded a string of men was rapidly passing its contents up into the sand-bills.

Jim guessed what that might mean. His ephemeral reading in books of adventure told him these must be smugglers, and he had unconsciously gathered from unknown sources the fact that out beyond there lay the Isle of Man, a place given up to freebooters and such-like gentry, though he had never happened to come across any so near home before. A matter therefore to be cautiously inquired into on the most approved Fenimore Cooper lines.

So he slipped in among the sand-hills and threaded a devious path parallel with the sea, now and again crawling like a snake up a hummock, and peering through the wire-grass to ascertain his position and make sure that the boat had not gone off. That was his only anxiety, that she would get away before he had the chance of a nearer view.

He was delighted with his adventure. Here was treasure-trove better than all the tantalising possibilities of the beach. Here was something real and new to set against Jack's musty, but still exciting, stories of old Greeks and Romans. He felt rich.

The short day was drawing in. The gray of the dusk was in his favour. He wriggled up a soft bank on his stomach, and found himself with a fair view of what was going on. He sank flat among the wire-grass and watched, and was Robinson Crusoe, and Deerslayer, and Chingachgook, and many others, all in one.

A growl of rough voices down below, the "slaithe" of spades in the soft sand, and he saw little barrels and neat little corded packages being rapidly buried, each in a little hole by itself, and evidently according to some recognised plan.

The boat had probably made another trip to the smack, for barrels and packages came pouring in and were deftly put out of sight. The light was so dim that he could not recognise any of the busy workers, and their occasional growls gave him no clue.

He was wondering vaguely who they might be, when a heavy hand descended on the back of his neck and lifted him up like a kicking rabbit.

"Dom yo'! What d' yo' want a-spyin' here for?"

His captor dragged him down into the centre of operations, and Jim found himself inside a wall of scowling, hairy faces.

"Now then, who are yo', and what'n yo' want here?"

The long rough fingers reached well round his throat, and he was almost black in the face, and sparks and things were beginning to dance before his eyes. He clutched at the big hand and tried to pull it away.

"I'm Jim Carron," he gasped.

"Yo' wunnot be Jim Carron long, then. Dig a hole there big enow to take him," he ordered—and Jim saw himself lying in it, alongside the little barrels and packages.

"I meant no harm. I only wanted to see," he urged sturdily.

"Yo' seen too much. I' th' sand yo'll see nowt an' yo'll talk none."

"I won't in any case. I promise you."

"We'se see to that, my lad. Yo'll be safest i' th' sand, and so 'ill we." And Jim, glancing scare-eyed up at the wall of rough faces, would have been mightily glad to be back in the warm kitchen at Carne with Jack and his old Greeks and Romans.

He looked very small and helpless among them. Some of them had little lads at home, no doubt; but there was much at stake, and it would never do to leave him free to talk. On the other hand, running goods free of duty was one thing, and killing a boy was another, and there arose a growling controversy among them as to what they should do with him.

It was ended suddenly by one wresting him masterfully from his original captor, and dragging him by the scruff of the neck towards the boat. It was emptied of its last load and ready to return for another. His new keeper tossed him in, tumbled in after him with three others, and pulled out to the smack.

CHAPTER XIX

WHERE'S JIM?

JACK, having lived through an unusually exciting time in the neighbourhood of Carthage, came back to himself in the kitchen at Carne and the first thought of Jim he had had for over an hour.

"Hello! Where's old Jim?" he asked.

"I d'n know. Yo'd better seek him or he'll be into some mischief. I nivver did see sich lads." And Jack strolled out to look for Jim.

He was in none of his usual places, and Jack stood gazing vaguely along the shore, wondering where he could have got to. He might have gone to Mr. Eager's. It was not usual with them of an afternoon, for then Mr. Eager was busy with his parish affairs. But Gracie was always an attraction—the warmest bit of colour in their lives—and she made them welcome no matter when they came.

As he turned to trot away inland, with a last look along the shore, a fishing-smack beat out from behind the distant bend and went thrashing out to sea with the waves flying white over her bows.

"Glad I'm not there, anyway," said Jack, and galloped away among the hummocks towards Wyvveloe.

"Oh, Jack, I *am* so glad to see you. I've got so tired of myself. Mrs. Jex has been showing me how to make crumpets, and you shall have one as soon as Charles comes in. If they're not very good you mustn't say so, because they're the first I've made, you see. What? Jim? No, he's not been here. What a troublesome boy he is!—always getting himself drowned or lost. Dear, dear, dear! What with you two, and Charles, and the vicar falling ill again—my hair will go quite white, I expect! And there's that Margaret never been near me all day, and if it hadn't been for Mrs. Jex and the crumpets I don't know what I would have done. . . . Thank you, Mrs. Jex, I'll come at once; but we must keep them hot for Charles, they do lie so heavy on your stomach when they're cold. He can't be long, Jack. You sit down there and look at that book." And the Little Lady went off to butter her crumpets, while Jack, at the end of his tether as regards Jim and his possible whereabouts, lay down contentedly on the hearthrug and lost himself in the book.

When Eager came in at last, tired with a long round among outlying parishioners, he was surprised to find the boy there and still more surprised to learn why he had come.

"Jim's a jimsa! He's always getting himself lost," was Gracie's contribution to the discussion, but it did not help much.

"Where can he have got to, Jack?" asked Eager, with a touch of anxiety. "When did you see him last?"

"I was reading in the kitchen, and when I looked up he'd gone. I looked in all the places I could think of, and then I came here." And that did not help much, either.

"Well, I must have a bite. I'm famished. And then we'll have another look. Maybe he's at home by this time. He wouldn't be likely to go to Knoyle, would he?"

Jack shook his head very decidedly.

"He wouldn't go alone."

"Seth Rimmer's?"

"I d'n know. He might."

"We'll call at Carne and then go along to Rimmer's. Oh-ho! hot buttered crumpets and coffee! And the crumpets made by a master-hand, unless I'm very much mistaken!" For Gracie had dumped them down before him herself with an air of triumphant achievement, and now stood waiting his first bite with visible anxiety.

"Excellent!" said the Rev. Charles, smacking his lips. "If there's one thing Mrs. Jex does better than another, where all is well done, it's hot buttered crumpets."

"They're not at all a bit heavy?"

"Heavy? Light as snowflakes—hot buttered snowflakes! That's what they are. How do you find them, Jack?"

"Fine!"

"I *am* glad. I was afraid they'd turn out a bit——"

"You don't mean to tell me you made them!"

"Yes, I did. All myself—with Mrs. Jex just looking on, you know!"

"Well! Two more, please, just like the last! Best crumpets I ever tasted in my life!"

And so they were—because Gracie made them; and the Rev. Charles would have pledged himself to that though they had choked him and given him indigestion for life. He had a pretty bad night of it—but that might have been the coffee,—but most likely it was Jim.

For presently they all set off in the riotous wind, Gracie skipping joyfully in the pride of accomplishment, and went first to Carne, hopeful of finding Jim there. But Mrs. Lee greeted their inquiry with a tart:

"'Oo's none here. Havena set eyes on him sin'—— Didn' yo' go out tegither?"—to Jack.

"No, I d'n know when he went."

"Where can th' lad ha' gotten to now? 'Oo's aye gett'n' i' mischief o' some kind."

'We'll go along to Seth Rimmer's, Mrs. Lee. He may have gone down there," said Eager.

"'C) mowt," she admitted unhopefully. And they set off in the windy darkness, with the roar of the sea and the long white gleam of the surf on one side. and on the other the fantastic hummocks of the sand-hills, which looked strangely desolate by night and capable of holding any mystery or worse.

Eager had wanted the children to wait at Carne till he returned, but they would not hear of it. Gracie was enjoying the spice of adventure. Jack wanted to find Jim. Eager himself was beginning to feel anxious, though he would not let the others see it.

"If he is not here—where?" he asked himself, as they ploughed through the sand and the crackling seaweed. And he had to confess that he did not know where to look next. The grim desolation of the sand-hills made him shiver to think of. Suppose the boy had damaged himself in some way and was lying there waiting for help. A thousand boys might lie there unfound till help was useless.

A glimmer in the distant darkness, and presently they were at Rimmer's cottage.

Kattie opened to them—both the door and her big blue eyes—and stood staring.

"Hello, Kattie! Is Jim here?" asked Eager cheerfully.

"Jim? No, Mr. Eager."

"Who's it, Kattie?" asked her mother anxiously, from her bed; for over the lonely cottage hung the perpetual fear of ill-tidings.

"It's only us, Mrs. Rimmer." And they stepped inside.

"Ech! Mr. Eager, and the little lady, and——"

"We're looking for Jim, and were hoping he might have come along here."

"Jim?" said Mrs. Rimmer, looking steadfastly at Jack. "I nivver con tell one from t'other; but none o' them's been here to-day."

"No? I wonder where the boy can have got to. Is Seth about? Maybe he could help us."

"Seth's away," said Mrs. Rimmer briefly; and Eager did not ask her where For "Seth's away" was an understood formula, and meant that young Seth was off on one of his expeditions, and the less said about it the better.

"I don't quite know where to look next," said Eager anxiously. "Can you suggest anything, Kattie?"

But Kattie shook her mane of hair and stared back at them nonplussed, and presently said:

"Jim knows his way; he couldn' get lost."

"I'm just afraid he may have got hurt somewhere—twisted his ankle, or something of that kind, and be lying out in the sand-hills; and it's as black as pitch outside, and going to be a bad night."

"Puir lad, I hopé not," said Mrs. Rimmer, with added concern in her face. "'T'will be a bad night for them that's on th' sea." Her face, in its setting of puckered white night-cap, looked very frail and anxious. "But they're aw in His hands, passon."

"And they couldn't be in better, Mrs. Rimmer," he said, more cheerfully than he felt.

"Ay, I know; but I wish my man were home. Whene'er th' wind howls like that, I aye think of them that's gone and them that has yet to go."

"Not one of them goes without His knowing. Your thoughts are prayers, and the prayers of a good woman avail much." And he pressed the thin white hand, and Gracie kissed her and Kattie, and they went out into the night.

The wind hummed across the flats till their heads hummed in unison. More than once the drive of it carried them off their course, and brought them up against the ghostly hummocks, where the long, thin wire-grass swirled and swished with the sound of scythes. The grim desolation beyond struck a chill to Eager's heart, as he imagined Jim lying out there, calling in vain for help against the strident howl of the gale.

There was just the possibility that he had got home during their absence, however; so, in anxious silence, they made for Carne.

"No, I hanna seen nowt of him," said Mrs. Lee, and stood glowering at them with set, pinched face.

"I had better see Sir Denali. Shall I go up? You wait here with Jack, Gracie." And he went off along the stone-flagged passage, and climbed the big staircase, and knocked on the door leading to Sir Denzil's rooms.

Mr. Kennet opened to him at last, with so much surprise that he was, for the moment, unable to recognise the unexpected visitor, and stood staring blankly at him.

"I want to see Sir Denzil, Kennet—Mr. Eager. One of the boys is missing——"

"Eh?—Ah!—Missing?—Tell him. Will you wait a moment, sir?" And Eager concluded from his manner that Mr. Kennet had been enjoying himself, and hoped that it might not be, in this case, like man like master.

Sir Denzil, however, received him with most formal politeness.

"You bring me good news, Mr. Eager?" he asked, snuffing very elegantly. "Who is it is a-missing?"

"We can't find Jim, Sir Denzil."

"Ah—Jim! Let me see—Jim! Now, which is Jim?"

"Jim is the hero of the sand-boat——"

"Ah—and is the boat gone again?"

"No, sir. They both pledged themselves not to go out in her alone again."

"Ah—pity! Great pity! I rather counted upon that monstrosity to solve our difficulty. However, Jim is missing!" And he tapped his snuff-box thoughtfully. "And what do you infer from that, Mr. Eager?"

"I'm afraid he may have gone off into the sand-hills and possibly got hurt. We've been down to Seth Rimmer's——"

"Ah—Rimmer! That was, if I remember rightly, the young dolt who bungled the matter so sadly last time. Well?"

"He has not been there. Jack was reading in the kitchen——"

"Jack? Ah—yes. That's the other one."

"And Jim was with him. Jim wandered out, and we cannot find any trace of him."

"Hm! . . . Ah! . . ." And the grim old head nodded thoughtfully over another pinch of snuff. "Well, I don't really see what we can do to-night, Mr. Eager. If, as you suggest, he is lying hurt somewhere in the sand-hills, it would take an army to find him, even in the daytime. We must wait and see. If we don't find him"—hopefully—"if he is gone for good, I shall feel myself under deepest obligation to him or to whoever is concerned in the matter. It leaves us only one boy to deal with—the wrong one, of course—but still, only one."

"Why the wrong one, sir?"

"*If* the other has been purposely removed, as is possible, it is, of course, in order to foist upon us the one who has no right to the position. There could be no other reason. You follow me?"

"I follow your reasoning, of course; but at present we have not the slightest reason to suppose he has been purposely removed. He may be lying in the sand-hills unable to get home."

"In which case he will have a very bad night," said Sir Denzil, as a fury of wind and rain broke against the window-panes—"a very bad night."

"Is there nothing we can do?"

"There's only one thing I can think of."

"Yes?"

"Keep an eye on that old witch's face downstairs. You may learn something from it if you catch her unawares."

Eager slept little that night for thinking of the missing boy.

His anxious mind travelled many roads, but never touched the right one.

Soon after daybreak he was on his way to Knoyle, but returned disappointed, and went on to Carne with a faint hope in him still that Jim might have returned during the night.

"Any news of him, Mrs. Lee?" he asked anxiously, through the kitchen door.

"Noa," said the old lady stolidly. "We none seen nowt on him." And her face was as unmoved as a gargoyle, and the gleam of her little dark eyes struck on his like the first touch of an opponent's foil.

"What on earth can have taken the boy? I've been up to Knoyle, but they know nothing of him there."

"Ay?"

"I'll turn out all the men I can get, and we'll rake over the sand-hills."

"Ay!"

As he turned to go, Jack came trotting in.

"I d'n know what's come of him," he said; "I've been everywhere I can think of."

"I'm going to get all the help I can, and we'll search through the sand-hills, Jack."

"I'll come too," said Jack. And they went away together.

CHAPTER XX

A NARROW SQUEAK

ONCE aboard the smack, Jim was shoved into a small black dog-hole of a cabin forward and the door slid to and bolted. And there, all alone in the dark, he presently passed a very evil time.

In due course he heard the rest of the crew come aboard.

Then the anchor was pulled up, and then his head beg to swim in sympathy with the heaving boat.

Like most boys he had at times had visions of a seafarin life, swinging impartially between that and a military as the only two lives worth living. But the night he spent on that smack cured him for ever of the sea.

It was a black night, with a stiff west wind working round into a south-west gale. They had hoped to get under the lee of the Island before the full of it caught them, but it meant strenuous beating close-hauled, and progress was slow. Before they were half-way across, about midnight, the gale was on them, and they turned tail and ran for their lives, with the great seas roaring past them and like to come in over the stern every moment.

Jim knew nothing of it all. He was sick to death, and bruised almost to a jelly with bumping to and fro in that dirty black hole. While they beat up against the wind, the crashing of the seas against the bows, with less than an inch of wood between him and them, deafened and terrified It seemed impossible that any mere timber could long withstand so terrific a pounding. Each moment he feared to see the strakes rive open and let the ocean in.

But very soon he was past caring what happened. He had never been so utterly miserable in all his life.

When they turned and ran, the crash of the waves against the outside of his dog-hole lessened somewhat, but the up-and-down motion increased so that the roof and the floor alternately seemed bent on banging him to pieces. And at times they plunged down, down, down, with the water bubbling and hissing all about them till he believed they were going down for good, and felt no regret about it.

How long he spent in that awful hole he did not know. Ages of uttermost misery it seemed to him. But, of a sudden, there came an end.

The boat, racing over the great rollers with a scrap of foresail to give her steerage way, brought up abruptly on a bank. The mast snapped like a carrot, the roaring white waves leaped over her, dragged her back, flung her up again, worried her as vicious dogs a wounded rat.

The men in her clung for their lives against the thrashing of the mighty waves, and then, not knowing at all where the storm had carried them, but sure of land of some kind from the bumping of the boat, they scrambled one by one over the bows and fought their way through the tear of the surf to the shore.

All but one. He hung tight to the stump of the mast till the others had gone, each for himself and intent only on saving each his own life.

Then the last man, swinging by one arm from the stump of the mast, caught at the bolt of the dog-hole and worked it back, and reached in a groping arm and dragged out Jim, limp and senseless from his final bruising when the boat struck.

"My sakes! Be yo' dead, Mester Jim?" he asked hoarsely, holding the lad firmly with one arm and the mast with the other.

But the sharp flavour of the gale acted like a tonic. The limp body stretched and wriggled and gripped the arm that held it.

"Aw reet?" shouted the hoarse voice in his ear, and when Jim tried to reply the gale drove the words back into his throat.

The boat was still tumbling heavily in the surf. All about them was howling darkness, faintly lightened by the rushing sheets of foam. Jim felt himself dragged to the side, and then they were wrestling, waist deep, with the terrible backward rush of the surf. His feet were swept from under him, but an iron hand gripped his arm and anchored him till he felt the sand again. Then a thundering wave swirled them on, and they were able to crawl up a steep, hard bank of sand on their hands and knees.

They lay there panting, while the gale howled and the

white waves gnashed at them like wild beasts ravening their prey. And Jim felt cleaner and better than he had done since he boarded the smack.

He turned to his rescuer and laid hold of his arm.

"Who is it?" be shouted.

"Me—Seth," came the hoarse reply into his ear, and he had never in his life felt so glad of a friendly voice, though he would not have known it was young Seth's voice if he had not said so.

For their position was terrifying enough. It was still too dark to see where they were, except that they were on a bank, with the roar and shriek of the gale all about them.

Young Seth stood up to see, if he could, what had become of the others. But he was down flat again in a moment.

"I connot see nowt," he shouted.

"Are we safe here, Seth?"—as a vicious white arm came reaching up the slope at them.

"Tide's goin' down."

So they lay and waited, and it was good for Jim that night that his life on the flats had hardened him somewhat to the weather.

He was soaked to the bones, and the spindrift stung like a whip. But he was so utterly spent with his previous sickness that his heavy eyes closed, and he dozed into horrible nightmares and woke each time with a start and a sob.

And then he found himself warmer, and thought the gale had slackened; but it was young Seth's burly body lying between him and the wind, and he was drawn up close into young Seth's arms, and there he went fast asleep.

He woke at last into a sober gray light and a great stillness. The wind had dropped and the sea had fallen back behind its distant barriers. When he stretched and sat up he could see nothing but sand—endless stretches of brown sea-sand, with the dull gleam of water here and there.

He got on to his feet and felt his bones creak as if they

wanted oiling, and young Seth stood up too and kicked his legs and arms about to take the kinks out.

"Where are we, Seth?" asked Jim, with a gasp.

"I dunnot know. We ran like the divvle last neet. Mebbe when th' sun comes out we'll see."

"Land's over yonder, anyway," he said presently. "But it's a divvle of a way and mos'ly stick-sands, I reck'n."

The clouded eastern sky thinned and lightened somewhat, the sands began to glimmer, and the streaks of water gleamed like bands of steel.

"We mun go," said Seth. "Sun's sick yet wi' last neet's storm. Yo' keep close to me." And they set off on the perilous journey.

For a moment, as they crossed the ridge of their own sand-bank, which stood higher than its neighbours, they caught distant glimpse of yellow sand-hills very far away. Then they were threading cautiously across a wide lower level, seamed with pools and runlets, and could see nothing but the brown sea-sand. And Seth's eyes were everywhere on the look-out for "stick-sands," of which he went in mortal terror.

Where the banks humped up with long rounded limbs as though giants were buried below, he would run at speed; but in the hollows between their progress was slow, because "You nivver knows," said Seth, and tried each foot before he trusted it.

In one wide hollow they came on a mast sticking straight up out of the sand—like a gravestone, Jim thought—and gave it wide berth. And twice they came on swiftly flowing channels which rose to Jim's waist, and it was in the neighbourhood of these that Seth exercised the greatest caution.

"They works under t' sand, here and there, you nivver knows where, an' it's that makes the stick-sands," he said, and breathed freely only when they got on to solid brown ridges again.

So, step by step, they drew nearer to the yellow sand-hills, which looked so like those he was accustomed to that Jim's spirits rose.

"Is that home, Seth?" he asked.

"Ech, lad, no. We're many a mile from home, but we'll git there sometime."

It was when that toilsome journey was over, and the sun had come out, and they were lying spent in a hollow of the yellow sand-hills, that Seth turned to Jim and said weightily:

"Yo' mun promise me, Mester Jim, to forget aw that happened last neet. I dun my best for yo'; an' yo' mun promise that."

"I'm afraid I can't ever forget it, Seth," said Jim solemnly, "and some of it I don't ever want to forget. But I'll promise you I'll never tell about the little barrels and things, or about you, never, as long as I live."

"Well," said Seth, after ruminating on this. "That'll do if yo'll stick to it."

"I'll bite my tongue out before I'll say a word."

"Aw reet. Yo' see, I wur on the boat when they brought yo' aboard, but I couldn' ha' done owt with aw that lot about. 'Twere foolish to fall into their honds."

About midday they came on a fisherman's hut, back among the sand-hills, and got some bread and fish, freely given when Seth explained matters—so far as he deemed necessary; and they lay on a pile of strong-smelling nets and slept longer than Seth had intended. Then, with vague directions towards a distant high-road, they set out again.

"'Twere Morecambe Bay we ran aground in," said Seth, "an' they wouldn' hardly believe as we'd come across th' flats. Reg'lar suckers, they say, an' swallowed a moight o' men in their time."

"And when shall we get home, Seth?"

"It's a long road, but we'll git there's soon as we can," said Seth, with the weight of the journey upon him.

CHAPTER XXI

A WARM WELCOME

FOR two days Eager raked over the sand-hills, from morning till night, with all the men he could press into the service, and all the ardour he could rouse in them.

In long, undulating lines, rising and falling over the hummocks like the long sea-rollers, they scoured the wastes till they were satisfied that no Jim was there.

Each night Sir Denzil met him, when he came upstairs to report, with a repressed eagerness which gave way to cynical satisfaction the moment he saw his face.

"So!" he would say, with a gratified nod, as he helped himself to snuff with studied elegance. "No result, Mr. Eager. I really begin to think we must give him up. You are simply wasting your time and that of all your—er—friends."

"Supposing, after all, the poor lad should be lying, unable to move, in some hollow——"

"Let us hope that his sufferings would be over long before this!"

"It is too horrible to think of. I cannot sleep at night for the thought of it."

"Ah, I am sorry. You should cultivate a spirit of equanimity—as I do. If he is found—well! If he is not found, I am bound to say—better! The problem that has puzzled us these ten years is then solved—in a way, of course, though, as I think I have explained myself to you before, not in the right way. Still we have got only one boy to deal with, and we must make the best of him. I have been considering the idea of a public school. You would endorse that, I presume?"

"Undoubtedly—for both of them, if we can only find Jim."

"We are considering the one we have. Now, which school would you advise—Rugby, Harrow, Eton? There's a new place just opened at Marlborough, I see——"

"Harrow," said Eager decisively. "They are both meant for the army, of course?"

"You will speak in the plural still," said Sir Denzil, with a smile.

"I cannot bring myself to think of Jim as dead and gone."

"Well, well! Let us hope you have more foundation for your higher beliefs, Mr. Eager. Meanwhile, and to lose no time, I will write to my lawyer in London to have this boy entered at Harrow. What delay will it entail?"

"None, I should say. The numbers are low there just now, but Vaughan will soon pull things round, and meanwhile they will stand the better chance."

"They—they—they!" said Sir Denzil, eyeing him quizzically. "You really still hope, then?"

"I shall hope until it is impossible to hope any longer. Have you considered the idea of his having been kidnapped, Sir Denzil?"

"It has occurred to me, of course. But why should any one kidnap him?"

"If it should be so—to leave the other in full possession, of course. But we have no grounds to go upon. I have made inquiries as to all the gipsies who have been within ten miles of us lately. They are all here yet, and know nothing of the boy."

"H'm!" said Sir Denzil thoughtfully. "If it should be that—as you say, it would prove beyond doubt that the boy we have is the wrong one. Gad!" he said presently, "I'm beginning to have a hankering after the other. However——"

Sir George Herapath had seconded all Eager's efforts to discover the missing boy. He and Margaret had ridden with the other searchers each day, and in addition had sought out every gipsy camp in the neighbourhood and made rigorous inquisition as to its doings and membership. Sir George was favourably known to the nomads as a strict but clement justice of the peace so long as they kept within the law, and they satisfied him that they had had no hand in this matter.

He and Margaret were to and fro constantly between Knoyle and Wyvveloe, eager for news, or downcastly bringing none, and when Eager himself was not there it was a very crushed and sober little lady who received them with a sadness greater even than their own.

"It is quite beyond me, Sir George," you would have heard her say, with a gloomy shake of the head. "What can have become of him I can't think. And we do miss him so dreadfully. I always liked old Jim, but I never liked him so much as I do now. It's just breaking Charles's heart."

"It's beyond me too, Gracie," said Sir George, with a worried pinch of the brows. "Where *can* the boy be? I'm really beginning to be afraid we've seen the last of him."

"Charles says we must go on hoping for the best," said the Little Lady forlornly. "But it is not easy when you've nothing to go on."

And to them, talking so, on the afternoon of the fourth day of the search, came in Eager, very weary both of mind and body, and anything but an embodiment of the hope he enjoined on others.

"Nothing," he said dejectedly. "And I do not know what to do next. I'm beginning——"

And then the Little Lady's eyes, which had wandered past him from sheer dread of looking on his hopelessness, opened wider than ever they had done before.

"Charles! Charles!" she shrieked, pointing past him down the path. "Jim!" And she began to dance and scream in a very allowable fit of hysterics.

Eager thought it was that—that her overwrought feelings had broken down, and it was to her that he sprang.

But the others had turned at her words, and had run out of the cottage, and now they came in dragging—as though having got him they would never let him go again—a very lean and dirty and draggled, but decidedly happy, Jim.

Gracie broke from her brother and rushed at him with a whole-hearted "Oh, Jim! Jim!" and flung her arms round his neck and kissed him many times. And Jim, grinning joyously through his dirt, seemed to find it good, but presently wiped off the kisses with the back of his grimy hand.

"Dear lad, where have you been?" cried Eager, all his weariness gone in the joy of recovery. "We have been near breaking all our hearts over you. Thank God, you are back again! . . . Now, tell us!"

And Jim summed up his adventures in very few words.

"I was on the shore. Some men carried me off in a ship. We were wrecked at a place called Morecambe, and I've come home as quick as I could."

"Who were the men? Did you know them?" asked Sir George sternly.

"I can't tell you, sir." And then, looking at Eager, as though he would understand. "It was a promise, a very solemn promise"—and Eager nodded. "You see I was locked up in a little cabin when the ship was wrecked, and I should have been drowned in there——"

"And they let you out on your promising not to tell on them," said Eager.

Jim nodded.

"A promise extorted under such conditions is not binding," said Sir George brusquely. "I want those men. Come, my boy, you must tell us all you know." And Eager watched him anxiously.

"I cannot tell, sir. I promised."

And nothing would move him from this. Sir George, with much warmth, explained to him that no one was safe if such things were permitted to pass unpunished, and that it was his bounden duty to tell all he knew. But to all he simply shook his head and said, "I promised, sir."

And Eager, much as he would have liked to lay hands on the rascals, could not but rejoice in the boy's staunchness. And Sir George gave it up at last, and rode away with

Margaret, baffled and outwardly very angry. But as they rode up the avenue at Knoyle, he said:

"Eager has done well with those boys. They'll turn out men."

Jim was very hungry. They fed him, and then Eager went off with him to break the news to Sir Denzil, and the villagers flocked out and cheered them as they went.

"Well, yo're back!" was Mrs. Lee's greeting when they came into the kitchen at Carne. And Jim, in the joy of his return, ran up and kissed her, but her face was like that of a graven image.

Jack jumped up with a glad shout, and "Hello, Jim! Where you *been*?" and circled round and round the wanderer with endless questions.

Sir Denzil's reception of him was characteristic.

"Well, I'm ——! So you've turned up again." And he eyed his grandson, over a pinch of snuff, as though he were some new and offensive reptile. "What is the meaning of this, sir?" And his hankering after the boy whom, in his innermost mind, he had come to think of as his legitimate heir, and his thwarted satisfaction at what he had hoped was in any case the cutting of his Gordian knot, and a certain anxiety in the matter, which he had very successfully concealed from every one else—all these in combination resulted in an explosion.

He listened blackly to such explanation as Jim vouchsafed, peremptorily demanded more, and the boy refused.

"You will tell me all you know," said the old man sternly—hoping through fuller knowledge to arrive, perchance, at some clue to the great problem behind.

"I promised, sir!" said Jim.

"Hang your promise, sir! I absolve you from any such promise. You will tell me all you know."

But Jim set his lips stolidly and would not say another word.

"You won't? Then, by ——, I'll teach you to do what

you're told." And laying hold of the boy by the neck of his blue guernsey, he caught up his ebony stick and rained savage blows on the quivering little back before Eager could attempt a rescue.

"Stop, sir! Stop!" cried Eager, in great distress at this outbreak, and caught at the flailing arm.

"—— you, sir! Keep off, or I'll thrash you too!" shouted the furious old man, and turned and threatened the interrupter with the heavy silver knob.

"You are forgetting yourself, Sir Denzil," said Eager hotly. "The boy has given his solemn promise in return for his life. Would you have him break it?" And he caught the descending stick with a hand that ached for days afterwards, twisted it deftly out of the trembling old hand, and held it in safe keeping.

"Kennet!" shouted Sir Denzil, "throw this —— person out!" And Kennet came from an adjoining room and looked doubtfully at Eager.

"Kennet will think several times before he tries it," said Eager quietly, swinging the stick in his hand.

And then Eager, eyeing the old man keenly, saw that the fit had passed and reason had resumed her sway.

"Your stick, sir!" and he handed it to him with a bow.

"Your servant, sir!" and the stick was flung into a corner, and a shaking hand dived down into a deep-flapped pocket after its necessary snuff-box. "Kennet, leave us! You've been drinking. And you, boy—damme, but you're a good-plucked one! Of the right stock, surely. Go down and get something to eat—and here's a guinea for you." And Jim, who had never seen a guinea in his life, gripped it tight in his dirty paw as a remarkable curiosity, and went out agape, with squirming shoulders.

The old white hand shook so much that the snuff went all awry, and brown-powdered the waxen face in quite a humorous fashion.

"Mr. Eager, I apologise—and that is not my habit. But you must acknowledge that the provocation was great."

"Not if you had considered the matter. Would you have a Carron break his pledged word?"

"Ay!" said the old man, following his own train of thought, "a true Carron! Surely that is our man! . . . Well, what do you advise next?"

"Send them both to Harrow, and trust the rest to Providence."

And after a brooding silence, punctuated with more than one thoughtful pinch, "We will try Harrow, anyway," said the oracle, and Eager shook hands with him and went downstairs well satisfied.

CHAPTER XXII

WHERE'S JACK?

WITH all diffidence I mention a fact. Whether it had any bearing on a later happening I do not know.

Mr. Kennet, as we know, indulged occasionally in strong waters. The result, as a rule, was only an increased surliness of demeanour of which no one took much notice.

On one such occasion, however, shortly after Jim's return, Kennet, trespassing on Mrs. Lee's domain on some message of his master's, got to words with the old lady, and, rankling perhaps under some sharper reproof than usual from above, snarled at her like a toothless old dog:

"Old witch! foisting your ill-gotten brat on us by kidnapping t'other!" At which Mrs. Lee snatched at her broom, and Mr. Kennet beat a retreat more hasty than dignified.

Mr. Eager did his utmost during these last months of the ear to prepare the boys for their approaching translation.

"It's my old school, boys. See you do me credit there," he would urge on them. "In the games you'll do all right. Just pick up their ways, and never lose your tempers. You'll find the lessons tough at first, but I shall trust to you to do your best. You'll miss the flats and the sand-hills, of course, but you'll soon find compensations in the playing-fields."

They came to look forward with something like eagerness to the new prospect. It would be a tremendous change in their lives, and the call of the unknown works in the blood of the young like the spring.

But they could only stand a certain amount of book-grinding; and the flats and sand-hills, once the autumn gales were past, were full of enticement, and they ranged them, in the company of Eager and Gracie, with all the relish of approaching separation.

When George Herapath and Ralph Harben came home for the holidays, hare-and-hounds became the order of the day, and many a tough chase they had, and went far afield.

And so it came to pass that one fatal day, Jack, being the hare, led them away through the sedgy lands round Wyn Mere, and played the game so well that he disappeared completely.

The course of events that followed was so similar to those in Jim's case that repetition would be wearisome.

Sir Denzil and Sir George Herapath were equally furious and disturbed, but showed it in different ways. Eager, as before, was sadly upset and strained himself to breaking-point in his efforts to discover the missing one.

Once more the sand-hills were scoured, and this time, since the boy had gone in that direction, the Mere was dragged as far as it was possible to do so, but its vast extent precluded any certainty as to results.

And the days passed, and Jack was gone as completely as if he had been carried up into heaven.

"Well, Mr. Eager, what do you make of it this time?"

asked Sir Denzil, one night when Eager called at Carne with the usual report.

"I don't know what to make of it," said Eager dejectedly. "I have thought about it till my head spins."

"Your ideas would interest me."

"When Jim was kidnapped you felt sure that that pointed to him as what you call the 'right one.' Is it possible that has become known to those interested, and this has been done to point you back to Jack?"

"You mean that old witch downstairs. . . . She is capable of anything, of course, and you don't need to look at her twice to see the gipsy blood in her. . . . On the other hand, she may have been cunning enough to anticipate the view you have just expressed. She may have had this boy Jack carried off for the sole purpose of prejudicing the other in our eyes. Do you follow me?"

"You mean as I put it just now—that one would expect them to kidnap our man to leave theirs in possession."

"Go a step farther, Mr. Eager. Suppose they have in some way learned that, in consequence of Jim's carrying-off, I am inclined to think him the rightful heir. They may, as you say, have carried off the other simply to point me away from Jim and so confuse the issue. But it is just possible they are not so simple as all that, and have reasoned thus—'When Jim disappeared Sir Denzil considered that as proof that he was the rightful heir. If we now carry off Jack, that is just what Sir Denzil would expect us to do, and he will probably stick the tighter to Jim in consequence.' If that is their reasoning, then Jack is our man and not Jim. You follow me?"

"It's a terrible tangle," said Eager wearily, with his head in his hands. "It seems to me you can argue any way from anything that happens, and only make matters worse."

"Exactly!" said Sir Denzil, over a pinch of snuff.

"And so we come back to my point. You must treat both exactly alike and leave the issue to Providence."

"It looks like it," said Sir Denzil, and forbore to argue the matter theologically. "If the other comes back we shall have two strings to our bow, which is one too many for practical purposes. If he doesn't, we'll stick to the one we have, right man or wrong, and be hanged to them!"

Seth Rimmer, and young Seth, who had only lately returned home after an unusually long absence, were tireless in their search for the missing boy in their own neighbourhood, in or about the Mere.

After a day's hard work dragging the great hooks to and fro across the bottom of the Mere, old Seth would shake his head gravely as he looked back over the silent black water.

"Naught less than draining it dry will ever tell us all it holds," he would say. "From the look of it there's a moight of wickedness hid down there."

Kattie too was indefatigable, and she and Jim and George Herapath and Harben hunted high and low round the Mere, but found no smallest trace of Jack.

They had all been planning an unusually festive Christmas, but it passed in anxiety and gloom, and the time came round for Jim to go away to school. But going along with Jack was one thing, and going all alone a very different thing indeed, and he jibbed at it strongly.

Sir Denzil, however, having made up his mind, was not the man to stand any nonsense. He prevailed on Eager, as being more conversant with such matters, to see to the boy's outfit, and finally to take him up to Harrow himself.

And so, in due course, Jim, still very downcast at his parting with Gracie and Mrs. Lee and Carne and the flats and sand-hills, found himself sitting with wide, startled eyes and firmly shut mouth, opposite Mr. Eager, in one of the new railway carriages, whirling across incredible ranges of country at a Providence-tempting speed which seemed to him like to end in catastrophe at any moment.

They went from Liverpool to Birmingham, both of which

towns paralysed the little ranger of flats and sand-hills; from Birmingham to London, the enormity of which crushed him completely: spent two days showing him the greater sights, which his overburdened brain could in no wise appreciate; and finally landed him, fairly stodged with wonders, in his master's house at Harrow, which seemed to him, after his recent experiences, a haven of peace and restfulness.

Eager was an old school and college chum of the house-master, and spent a day of reminiscent enjoyment with him. He imparted to his friend enough of the boy's curious history to secure his lasting interest in him, and next day said good-bye to Jim and carried the memory of his melancholy dazed black eyes all the way back to Wyvveloe with him.

And Gracie's first words as she rushed at him and flung her arms round his neck were, "Jack's back!" And the Rev. Charles sat down with a gasp.

"Really and truly, Gracie?"

"Really and truly! Yesterday—all rags and bruises and as dirty as a pig."

"And wherever has he been all this time?"

"Dear knows! He doesn't, except that it was with some men—gipsies—who carried him away and beat him most of the time. He's all black and blue, except his face, and that was dirty brown, and one of his eyes was blackened; one of the men nearly knocked it out."

"Well, well, well! It's an uncommonly strange world, child!"

"Yes. How's old Jim?"

"He was all right when I left him, but anything may happen to those boys, apparently, without the slightest warning. Now, if you'll give me something to eat I'll go along and hear what Jack has got to say for himself."

Jack, however, had very little information to give that could be turned to any account. It was at the far side of the Mere that he had come upon a couple of men crouching under a sand-hill, as though they were on the look out for somebody. They had collared him, tied a stick in his mouth, and carried him away—where, he had no idea—a very long way, till they came up with a party on the road. There he was placed in one of the travelling caravans, fed from time to time, and not allowed out for many days. He had tried to escape more than once and been soundly thrashed for it. His back—well, there it was, and it made Eager almost ill to think of what those terrible weals must have meant to the boy. Then, after a long time, another chance came, when all the men were lying drunk one night and some of the women too. He had crept out, and ran and ran straight on till his legs wouldn't carry him another step. A farmer's wife had taken pity on him at sight of his back and helped him on his road. And through her, others. He knew where he wanted to get to, and so, bit by bit, mostly on his own feet, but with an occasional lift in a friendly cart, he had reached home.

"And what do you say to all that, Mr. Eager?" asked Sir Denzil.

"I say, first, that I am most devoutly thankful that he has come back to us. What may be behind it all is altogether beyond me. If he is their boy would they treat him so cruelly?"

"To gain their ends they would stick at nothing. I see no daylight in the matter."

"You had no chance of seeing how the old woman received him, I suppose, sir?"

"All we know is that when Kennet went downstairs he found the boy sitting in the kitchen, eating as though he had not seen food for a week. Not a word beyond that and what he tells us. The problem is precisely where it was when those damned women came in that first morning each with a child on her arm."

BOOK III

CHAPTER XXIII

BREAKING IN

SMALLER matters must give way to greater. You have seen how that great problem of Carne came about, and how it perpetuated itself in the persons of Jack and Jim Carron, without any apparent likelihood of satisfactory solution, unless by the final intervention of the Great Solver of all doubts and difficulties.

To arrive at the end of our story within anything like reasonable limits, we must again take flying leaps across the years, and touch with no more than the tip of a toe such outstanding points as call for special notice.

Harrow was the most tremendous change their lives had so far experienced. Mr. Eager had indeed prepared them for it to the best of his power. But the change, when they plunged into it—first Jim and then Jack—went far beyond their widest imaginings.

With their fellows they shook down, in time, into satisfactory fellowship. But the rules of the school, written and unwritten, from above and from below, were for a long time terribly irksome and almost past bearing. They were something like tiger-cubs transferred suddenly from their native freedom to the strict rounds of the circus-ring. They were to understand and conform to matters which were so taken for granted that explanations were deemed superfluous. And they suffered many things that first term in stubborn silence, mask and cloak for the shy pride which would sooner bite its tongue through than ask the question which would make its ignorance manifest.

The milling-ground between the school and the racquet-courts knew them well, and drank of their blood, and proved the rough nursery of many a lasting friendship.

Jim used laughingly to say at home that he had seen the colour of the blood of every fellow he cared a twopenny snap for, on that trampled plot of grass by the old courts. If the colour was good, and the manner of its display in accordance with his ideas, good feeling invariably followed, and he soon had heaps of friends. That was doubtless because he had nothing whatever of the swot in him. He delivered himself over, heart and soul, to the active enjoyments of life, and found no lack of like temper and much to his mind.

Jack developed along somewhat wider and deeper lines. He had no great craving for knowledge simply as knowledge. But concerning things that interested him he was insatiable, and slogged away at them with as great a gusto as Jim did at his games.

Jack's ideas of a correct school curriculum, being based entirely on his own leanings, necessarily clashed at times with those of the higher powers, and both he and Jim passed under the birch of the genial Vaughan with the utmost regularity and decorum.

Neither, of course, ever uttered a word under these inflictions. Jack went tingling back to his own private preoccupation of the moment; and Jim went raging off to the playing-fields.

"It's not what he does," he would fume to his chums, "but the way he does it. If he'd get mad I wouldn't mind, but he's always as nice and smooth as a hairdresser, and talks as if it was a favour he was doing you."

"Oily old beast!" would be the return comment, and then to the game with extra vim to make up for time lost in the swishing.

Jim's greatest fight was an epic in the school for many a year after he had left. "Ah!" said the privileged ones—whether they had actually been present in the body on that historic occasion or not—"but you should have seen the slog between Carron and Chissleton! That *was* a fight!"

It was the usual episode of the big bully, whom most public-schoolboys run up against sooner or later, and Chissleton was three years older and a good head taller than Jim. But Jim had the long years of the flats, and all the benefit of Mr. Eager's scientific fisticuffs, behind him. They fought ten rounds, each of which left Jim on the grass, his face a jelly daubed with blood, and his eyes so nearly closed up that it was only when the bulky Chissleton was clear against the sky that he could see him at all. But bulk tells both ways, and loses its wind chasing a small boy about even a circumscribed ring, and knocking him flat ten times only to find him dancing about next round, as gamely as ever, though somewhat dilapidated and unpleasant to look upon. So Jim wore the big one down by degrees, and in the eleventh round his time came. He hurled himself on the dim bulk between him and the sky with such headlong fury that both went down with a crash. But Jim was up in a moment daubing more blood over his face with the backs of his fists, and the big one lay still till long after the pæans of the small boys had died away into an interested silence.

"But didn't it hurt dreadfully, Jim?" asked Gracie, long afterwards, with pitifully twisted face.

"Sho! I d'n know. It was the very best fight I ever had."

The Little Lady found the days without the boys long and slow, in spite of her close friendship with Margaret Herapath.

Meg was everything a girl could possibly be. She was sweet, she was lovely, she was clever, she was a darling dear, she was splendid. She was an angel, she was a duck. She was Lady Margaret, she was dear old Meggums. And never a day passed but she was at the cottage or Gracie was over at Knoyle.

They rode and walked and bathed and read together. They slept together at times, and talked half through the night because the days were not long enough for the innumerable confidences that had to pass between them.

And Eager rejoiced in their close communion, for he had never met any girl whose friendship he would have so desired for Gracie. And he went about his duties, storming and persuading, fighting and tending, with new fires in his heart which shone out of his eyes, and his people all acknowledged that he was "a rare good un," even when he was scarifying them about manure-heaps and stinks, which they suffered as tolerantly as they did his vehemence, and as though such a thing as typhus had never been known in the land.

And what times they all had when the holidays came round!

A little shyness, of course, at first, while the various parties took stock of the changes in one another. For Gracie was growing so tall—"quite the young lady," as Mrs. Jex said; and such a change from the fellows at school, as Jack and Jim acknowledged to themselves.

Girls—as girls—were somewhat looked down upon at school, you know. But this was Gracie, and quite a different thing altogether.

When the first shyness of these meetings wore off she was apt to be somewhat overwhelmed by their effusive worship. They were her slaves, hers most absolutely, and their only difficulty was to find adequate means for the expression of their devotion.

For their first home-coming, each of them, unknown to the

other, had saved from the wiles of the tuck-shop such meagre portion of pocket-money as strength of will insisted on, and brought her a present: Jack, a small volume of Plutarch's Lives, the reading of which gave himself great satisfaction; and Jim, a pocket-handkerchief with red and blue spots, which seemed to him the very height of fashion, and almost too good for ordinary use by any one but a princess—or Gracie.

"You *dear* boys!" said the Little Lady, and opened Plutarch and sparkled—although for Plutarch, simply as Plutarch, she had no overpowering admiration; and put the red and blue spots to her little brown nose in the most delicate and ladylike manner imaginable. "But you really shouldn't, you know!" And they both vowed internally that they would do it again next time and every time, and each time still better.

And, so far, the fact that they were two, and that there was only one Gracie, occasioned them no trouble whatever.

Each time they came home Sir Denzil and Eager looked cautiously for any new developments pointing to the solution of the puzzle, and found none. Developments there were in plenty, but not one from which they could deduce any inference of weight. Was Jim more dashing and heedless and headstrong than ever?—all these came to him from his father. Was Jack developing a taste for study, of a kind, and along certain very definite lines of his own choosing?—could that be cast up at him as an un-Carronlike weakness due to the Sandys strain, or should it not rather be credited to the strengthening admixture of red Lee blood?

Those were the broader lines of divergence between the two, and the most striking to the outward observer, but it must not be supposed therefrom that Jack had foresworn his birthright of the active life. He revelled in the freedom of the flats as fully as ever, rode and bathed and ran, and held his own in cricket and hockey; but, at the same time, the habit of thought had visibly grown upon him, and it made him seem the older of the two.

Time wrought its personal changes in them all, but brought no great variation from these earlier characteristics. Gracie grew more beautiful in every way each time the boys came home; Jack more deliberative; Jim remained light-hearted and joyously careless as ever, enjoying each day to its fullest, and troubling not at all about the morrow. His devotion to the playing-fields gave him by degrees somewhat of an advantage over Jack in the matter of physique and general good looks. His healthy, browned face, sparkling black eyes, and the fine supple grace of his strong and well-knit body were at all times good to look upon.

Charles Eager, who had a searchingly appreciative eye for the beauties of God's handiwork in all its expressions, when he sped across the sands behind the corded muscles playing so exquisitely beneath the firm white flesh, or lay in the warm sand and watched the rise and fall of the wide, deep chest on which the salt drops from the tumbled mop of black hair rolled like diamonds, while up above the clean-cut nostrils went in and out like those of a hunted stag, said to himself that here was the making of an unusually fine man.

He doubted if Jim's brain would carry him as far as Jack's, but all the same he could not but rejoice in him exceedingly.

"Here," he mused, "is heart and body. And there is heart and brain,"—for at heart these two were very much alike still, open-handed, generous, and, by nature and Eager's own good training, clean and wholesome,—"which will go farthest?"

And, following his train of thought to the point of speech, one day when he and Jim were alone, he said:

"God has blessed you with a wonderfully fine body, lad. Where is it going to take you?"

"Into the thick of the fighting, I hope, if ever there is any more fighting," said Jim, with a hopeful laugh.

"One fights with brains as well as with brawn"—with an intentional touch of the spur to see what would come of it.

"Oh, Jack's got the brains—and the brawn too," he added quickly, lest he should seem to imply any pre-eminence on his own part in that respect. "He'll die a general. I'll maybe kick out captain—if I'm not a sergeant-major,"—with another merry laugh. "I'd sooner fight in the front line any day than order them from the rear."

"God save us from the horrors of another war," said Eager fervently. "I can just remember Waterloo. Every friend we had was in mourning, and sorrow was over the land."

"And there is another Napoleon in the saddle," said Jim.

"Ay; a menace to the world at large! An ambitious man, and somewhat unscrupulous, I fear. To keep himself in the saddle he may set the war-horse prancing."

"I'm for the cavalry myself," said Jim, and Eager smiled at the characteristic irrelevancy. "I shall try for Sandhurst. Jack's for Woolwich."

"Even Sandhurst will need some grinding up."

"Oh, I'll grind when the time comes"—somewhat dolefully. "You can get crammers who know the game and are up to all the twists and turns. If I can only crawl through and get the chance of some fighting, I'll show them!"

CHAPTER XXIV

AN UNEXPECTED GUEST

ONE afternoon, in one of their winter holidays, Gracie and the two boys had been down along the shore to visit Mrs. Rimmer and Kattie, especially Kattie.

They were tramping home along the crackling causeway of dried seaweed and the jetsam in which of old they had sought for treasure, and chattering merrily as they went.

"Kattie's getting as pretty as a—as a——" stumbled Jim after a comparison equal to the subject.

"Wild-rose," suggested Gracie.

"Sweet-pea," said Jack.

"I was thinking of something with wings," said Jim, "but I don't quite know——"

"Peacock," said Jack.

"No, nor a seagull. Their eyes are cold, and Kattie's aren't."

"You think she'll fly away?" laughed Gracie. "You think she looks flighty? That was the red ribbons in her hair. She must have expected you, Jim."

"They were very pretty, but I liked her best with it all flying loose as it used to be."

"She's getting too big for that, but she certainly has a taste for colours."

"Well, why shouldn't she, if they make her look pretty?"

"Oh, she can have all the ribbons she wants, as far as I am concerned. I only hope——"

And then they were aware suddenly of the rapid beat of horses' feet on the firm brown sand below, and turned, supposing it might be Sir George or Margaret Herapath.

But it was a stranger, a tall and imposing figure of a man on a great brown horse, and behind him rode another, evidently a servant, for he carried a valise strapped on to the crupper of his saddle. Both wore long military cloaks and foreign-looking caps. In the half-light of the waning afternoon, and the rarity of strangers in that part of the world, there was something of the sinister about the new-comer, something which evoked a feeling of discomfort in the chatterers and reduced them to silent staring, as the riders went by at a hand-gallop.

"Who can they be?" said Gracie, as they stood gazing after them.

"Foreigners," said Jack decisively. "French, I should say, from the cut of their jibs. A French officer and his servant."

"What are they wanting here, I'd like to know," said

Jim, still staring absorbedly. "He's a fine-looking man anyway, and he knows how to ride."

"His eyes were like gimlets," said Gracie. "They went right through me. I thought he was going to speak to us."

"Wish he had," said Jim. "That's just the kind of man I'd like to have a talk with."

They were to drink tea with Gracie, and she had made a great provision of special cakes for them with her own hands. So they turned off into the sand-hills and made their way to Wyvveloe.

Roger came out of a cottage as they passed down the street, and they all went on together.

"Oh, Charles," burst out the Little Lady, as she filled the cups, "we saw two such curious men on the shore as we were coming home——"

"Ah!"—for he always enjoyed her exuberance in the telling of her news. "Two heads each?—or was it smugglers now, or real bold buccaneers?"

"Jack thinks, by the cut of their jibs, they were Frenchmen, one an officer and the other his servant."

"Oh?"—with a sudden startled interest. "Frenchmen, eh? And what made you think they were Frenchmen, Jack, my boy?"

"They looked like it to me. They had long soldiers' cloaks on, and their caps were not English——"

"And they had rattling good horses, both of them," struck in the future cavalryman.

"And where were they going?"

"We didn't ask. We only stared, and they stared back. They were galloping along the shore towards Carne," said Jack.

"H'm! We don't often see Frenchmen up this way nowadays." And thereafter he was not quite so briskly merry as usual, as though the Frenchmen were weighing on him.

And truly an odd and discomforting idea had flashed unseasonably across his mind as they spoke, and it stuck there and worried him.

They were gathered round the fire, and Jim was gleefully picturing to the shuddering Gracie, in fullest red detail, the great fight with Chisleton. And Gracie had just gasped, "But didn't it hurt dreadfully, Jim?" And Jim had just replied, with the carelessness of the hardened warrior, "Sho! I d'n know. It was the very best fight I ever had";—when a knock came on the cottage door, and Eager jumped up, almost as though he had been expecting it, and went out. It was Mr. Kennet stood there, and when the light of the lamp in the passage fell on his face it seemed longer and more portentous even than usual. It was Kennet whom Eager's foreboding thought had feared to see. And his words occasioned him no surprise.

"Sir Denzil wants the boys, Mr. Eager, and he says will you please to come too."

"Very well, Kennet." And if Mr. Kennet had expected to be questioned on the matter he was disappointed. "Will you wait for us?"

"I've a message into the village, sir. I'll come on as soon as I've done it." And in the darkness beyond, a horse jerked its head and rattled its gear.

"Come along, boys. Your grandfather has sent for you. I'll go along with you." And they were threading their way—with eyes a little less capable than of old of seeing in the dark, by reason of disuse and study—through the sand-hills towards Carne.

The boys speculated briskly as to the reason for this unusual summons. A couple of years earlier they would have been racking their brains as to which of their numerous peccadilloes had come to light, and bracing their hearts and backs to the punishment. But they were getting too big now for anything of that kind—except of course at school, where flogging was a part of the curriculum.

Eager guessed what was toward, but offered them no light on the subject.

"Yo're to go up," said Mrs. Lee to the boys, as they

entered the kitchen. "Will yo' please stop here, sir, till he wants yo'." And it seemed to Eager that the grim old face was pinched tighter than ever in repression of some overpowering emotion.

The boys stumbled wonderingly upstairs, knocked on Sir Denzil's door, and were bidden to enter.

Their grandfather was sitting half turned away from the table, on which were the remains of a meal and several bottles of wine. Before the fire, with his back against the mantelpiece, stood a tall, dark man in a very becoming undress uniform, his hands in his trousers' pockets, a large cigar in his mouth. Sparks shot into his keen black eyes as they leaped eagerly at the boys, devouring them wholesale in one hungry gaze, then travelling rapidly back and forth in assimilation of details.

A foreigner without doubt, said the boys to themselves, as they stared back with interest at the dark, handsome face with its sweeping black moustache and pointed beard.

Sir Denzil tapped his snuff-box and snuffed aloofly.

"Gad, sir, but I think they do me credit!" said the stranger at last, in a voice that sounded somewhat harsh and nasal to ears accustomed to the soft, round tones of the north.

"That's as it may be," said Sir Denzil drily. "Credit where credit is due."

"*Sang-d'-Dieu!* you will allow me a finger in the pie, at all events, sir!"

"That much, perhaps!"—with a shrug. "That proverbial finger as a rule points more to marring than to making."

"And you've no idea which is which?" And he eyed the boys so keenly that they grew uncomfortable.

"Not the slightest! Have you?"

"I like them both. I'm proud of them both. But it certainly complicates matters having two of them. Suppose you keep one and I take one? How would that do? I'll wager mine goes higher than yours."

"Suppose you put it to them!"

The boys had been following this curious discussion with certainly more intelligence than might have been displayed by two puppies whose future was in question, but with only a very dim idea of what some of it might mean.

They had at times, of late, come to discuss themselves and their immediate concerns—as to which was the elder, and as to what their father and mother had been like, when they had died, and so on. In the earlier days they had never troubled their heads about such matters. But the exigencies of school life had awakened a desire for more definite information towards the settlement of vexed questions.

And so their holidays had been punctuated with attempts at the solution of these weighty problems, and the piercing of the cloud of ignorance in which they had been perfectly happy. And the unsatisfactory results of their inquiries had only served to quicken their thirst for knowledge.

Old Mrs. Lee gave them nothing for their pains, and her manner was eminently discouraging. "Which was the elder? She'd have thought any fool could tell they were twins! Their mother?—dead, years ago. Their father?—dead too, she hoped, and best thing for him!"

Their only other possible source of information was Mr. Eager. Sir Denzil and Kennet were of course out of the question. And Mr. Eager had so far only told them that of his own actual knowledge he knew as little as they did, and advised them to wait and trouble themselves as little as possible about the matter. He could not even say definitely if their father was dead. He had lived abroad for many years, and had not been heard of for a very long time.

Eager, of course, foresaw that, sooner or later, the whole puzzling matter would have to be explained to them, unless the solution came otherwise, in which case it might never need to be explained at all. But in the meantime no good could come of unprofitable discussion, and there were parts of it best left alone.

And so, when this handsome stranger dawned suddenly upon them, in such familiar discussion of themselves with their grandfather, their first "Who is it?" speedily gave place to "Can it be?" and then to "Is it?"—on Jack's part, at all events, and he stared at the dark man in the foreign uniform with keenest interest and a glimmering of understanding. Jim stared quite as hard, but with smaller perception.

"Well?" said the stranger, his white teeth gleaming through the heavy black moustache. "What do you make of it? Who am I?"

"Can you be our father?" jerked Jack; and Jim jumped at the unaccustomed word.

"Clever boy that knows his own father—or thinks he does—especially when he's never set eyes on him! How would you like to come back to France with me, youngster?"

"To France?" gasped Jack.

"Into the army. I have influence. I can push you on."

"The French army?" And Jack shook his head doubtfully. "I don't think—I—quite understand. Are you an Englishman, sir?"

"A Carron of Carne."

"And in the French army?"

"As it happens. You don't approve of that?"

Jack shook his head. Jim, with his wide, excited eyes and parted lips, was a study in emotions—amazement, excitement, puzzlement, admiration mixed with disapproval—all these and more worked ingeniously in his open boyish face and made it look younger than Jack's, which was knitted thoughtfully.

"If it came to that I should probably claim exemption from serving against England, though, *mon Dieu!* it's little enough I have to thank her for, and it would be to my hurt. Sometime you will understand it all. And you?" he asked Jim, so unexpectedly that he jumped again. "You feel the same? A couple of years at St. Cyr, and then say, a sub-lieutenancy in my own cuirassiers, and all my influence behind you. As a personal friend of the Emperor, Colonel Caron de Carne is not by any means powerless, I can assure you."

But Jim wagged his head decisively. He did not understand how this mysterious, but undoubtedly fine-looking father came to be apparently both a Frenchman and an Englishman, but he himself was an Englishman, and an Englishman he would remain.

"So! Then I go back the richer than I came only in the knowledge of you, but I would gladly have had one of you back with me."

"Go now, boys," said Sir Denzil, "and tell Mr. Eager I would be glad of a word with him." And wrenching their eyes from this phenomenal father, whose advances evoked no slightest response within them, they got out of the door somehow and ran down to the kitchen.

"Sir Denzil wants you to go up, Mr. Eager," began Jack.

"Our father's up there," broke in Jim.

But Mr. Eager had already heard the strange news from Mrs. Lee, and went up at once, full anxious on his own account to see what manner of man this unexpectedly-returned father might be, and rigorously endeavouring to preserve an open mind concerning him until he had something more to go upon than Mrs. Lee's curt but emphatic, "He's a divvle if ever there was one."

"Ah, Mr. Eager, this is my son Denzil, father of your boys," said the old man briefly, and helped himself to snuff and leaned back in his chair and watched them.

"I am glad to make your acquaintance, Mr. Eager,"—and a strong brown hand shot out to meet him. "Sir Denzil tells me that whatever good is in those boys is of your implanting. I thank you. You have done a good work there."

"They are fine lads," said Eager quietly. "It would have been an eternal pity if they had run to seed. We are making men of them."

"I have been trying to induce one of them to go back to France with me——"

"Which one?"

"Either. I don't know one from t'other yet. I could make much of either, and it would solve the difficulty you are in here."

"And they?"

"They won't hear of it."

"I should have been surprised if they had."

"I suppose so. And yet I could promise one or both a very much greater career than they are ever likely to realise here."

Eager shook his head. "They have been brought up as English lads; you could hardly expect them to change sides like that, even for possibilities which I don't suppose they understand or appreciate."

"It's a pity, all the same. There will be many opportunities over there——"

"The Empire is peace——" interjected Eager, with a smile.

"The Empire"—with a shrug—"is my very good friend Louis Napoleon, and peace just so long as it is to his interest to keep it. But"—with a knowing nod—"he has studied his people and he knows how to handle them. I'll wager you I'm a general inside five years—unless he or I come to an end before that."

"I would sooner they died English subalterns than lived to be French generals."

"It's throwing away a mighty chance for one of them."

"Their own country will offer them all the chances they need."

"How?" asked the Colonel quickly. "You think England will join us in case of necessity?"

"I know nothing about that. I mean simply that our boys will do their duty whatever call is made upon them; and no man can do more than that."

"Peace offers few opportunities of advancement,"—with a

regretful shake of the head. "But your minds all seem made up. It is a great chance thrown away, but I judge it is no use urging the matter——"

"Not the very slightest. To put the matter plainly, Captain Carron——"

"Colonel, with your permission!"

"You have forfeited all right to dictate as to those boys' future. Legally, perhaps——"

"*Merci!* I shall not invoke the aid of the law, Mr. Eager."

"It would clear the way here if you took one of them off our hands," said Sir Denzil; "but I agree with Mr. Eager, one Frenchman in the family is quite enough. You will have to go back empty-handed, Denzil."

"I am glad to have seen those boys, anyway. We may meet again, some time, Mr. Eager. In the meantime, my grateful thanks for all you have done for them!"

And next morning he took leave of his sons, and galloped off along the sands the way he had come, and the boys stood looking after him with very mixed feelings, and when he was out of sight looked down at the guineas he had left in their hands and thought kindly of him.

CHAPTER XXV

REVELATION AND SPECULATION

CHARLES EAGER pondered the matter deeply, and was ready for the boys when they tackled him the next morning.

He knew, as soon as he saw them, that they had been discussing matters during the night and were intent on information.

"Mr. Eager," said Jack, "will you tell us about our father? Why is he in the French army?"

Eager told them briefly that part of the story.

"And do you consider he did right to go away like that?" was the next question.

"Under the circumstances I should say he did. At all events it was Sir Denzil's wish that he should go, and he could judge better then than we can now."

"And we two were born after he'd left?"

"So I am told."

"Well now, even in twins isn't one generally the older of the two. Which of us is the elder?"

"That I don't know. I believe there is some doubt about it, and so we look upon you both as on exactly the same level."

"Suppose Sir Denzil should die, and our father should die—we don't want them to, you understand, but one can't help wondering—which of us would be Sir Denzil?"

"That is a matter that has exercised your grandfather's mind since ever you were born, my boy, and I'm afraid we can arrive no nearer to the answer. We can only wait."

"It'll be jolly awkward," protested Jim.

"Very awkward. Some arrangement will have to be come to, of course; but exactly what, is not for me to say. Your grandfather can divide his estate between you, and as to the title——"

"We could take it turn about," suggested Jim.

"Or you may both win such new honours for yourselves that it will be of small account."

"Yes, that's an idea," said Jack thoughtfully. And after a pause, "And you can tell us nothing about our mother, Mr. Eager?"

"No. You were ten years old, you know, when we met for the first time and you stole all my clothes. What a couple of absolute little savages you were!"

"We had jolly good times——"

"We've had better since," said Jack. "If you hadn't come to live here we might have been savages all our lives."

"You must do me all the credit you can. At one time I had hoped to become a soldier myself."

"Jolly good thing for us you didn't," said Jim. "But haven't you been sorry for it ever since, Mr. Eager?"

"There are higher things even than soldiering," smiled Eager. "If I can help to make two good soldiers instead of one, then England is the gainer."

"We'll jolly well do our best," said Jim.

And so they had arrived at a portion of the problem of their house, and bore it lightly.

And as to the grim remainder—"It would only uselessly darken both their lives," said Eager to himself. "We must leave it to time, and that is only another name for God's providence."

CHAPTER XXVI

JIM'S TIGHT PLACE

JACK had set his heart on Woolwich. In due course he took the entrance examinations without difficulty, and passed into the Royal Military School with flying colours.

Woolwich, however, was quite beyond Jim, and, besides, his heart was set on horses. He would be a cavalryman or nothing. But even for Sandhurst there was an examination to pass—an examination of a kind, but quite enough to give him the tremors, and sink his heart into his boots whenever he thought of it. Examinations always had been abomination to Jim and always got the better of him.

He argued eloquently that pluck, and a firm seat, and a long reach would make a better cavalryman than all the decimal fractions and French and Latin that could be rammed into him. But the authorities had their own ideas on the subject. So to an army-tutor he went in due course, a notable crammer in the Midlands, who knew every likely twist and turn of the ordinary run of examiners, and had got more incapables into the service than any man of his time, and charged accordingly.

And there, for six solid months, Jim was fed up like a prize turkey, on the absolutely necessary minimum of knowledge required for a pass, and grew mentally dyspeptic with the indigestible chunks of learning which he got off by heart, till his brain reeled and went on rolling them ponderously over and over even in his sleep.

Fortunately he started with a good constitution, and there was hunting three days a week, or such a surfeit of knowledge might have proved too much for him.

There were half a dozen more in the same condition; and the sight of those seven gallant hard-riders, poring with woebegone faces and tangled brains over tasks which in these days any fifth-form secondary-schoolboy would laugh at, tickled the soul of their tutor, Mr. Dodsley, almost out of its usual expression of benign and earnest sympathy at times. They represented, however, a very handsome living with comparatively easy work, and he did his whole duty by them according to his lights.

The shadow of the coming death-struggle cast a gloom over the little community for weeks before the fatal day, and all seven decided, in case of the failure they anticipated, to enlist in the ranks, where their brains could have well-merited rest.

Jim never said very much about that exam., but he did disclose the facts to Mr. Eager, and chuckled himself almost into convulsions whenever he thought over it and the awful months of preparation that had preceded it.

"There was a jolly decent-looking old cock of a colonel at the table when I went in," he said. "And my throat was dry, and my knees were knocking together so that I was afraid he'd see 'em. He looked at my name on the paper and then at me.

"'James Denzil Carron?' he said. 'Any relation of my old friend Denzil Carron of—what-the-deuce-and-all was it now?'

"'Carne,' I chittered.

"'That's it! Carron of Carne, of course. What are you to him, boy?'

"'Son, sir.'

"'Denzil Carron's son! God bless my soul, you don't say so! And is your father alive still?'

"'Yes, sir.'

"'You don't say so! God bless my soul! Denzil Carron alive! Why, it must be twenty years since I set eyes on him! Will you tell him, when you see him, that his old friend, Jack Pole, was asking after him?' And then," said Jim, "I suppose he saw me going white at prospect of the exam., for he just said, 'Oh, hang the exam.! You can ride?'

"'Anything, sir.'

"'And fence?'

"'Yes, sir. And box and swim, and I can run the mile in four minutes and fifteen seconds.'

"'God bless my soul, I wish I could! You'll do, my boy! Pass on, and prove yourself as brave a man as your father!' And I just wished I'd known it was going to be like that. It would have saved me a good few headaches and a mighty lot of trouble. However, perhaps it'll all come in useful, some day—that is, if I remember any of it."

Jack did well at Woolwich. He passed out third of his batch, and in due course received his commission as second lieutenant in the Royal Engineers.

Jim made but a poor show in head-work, but showed himself such an excellent comrade, and such a master of all the brawnier parts of the profession, that it would have needed harder hearts than the ruling powers possessed to set any undue stumbling-blocks in his way. To his mighty satisfaction, he was gazetted cornet to the 8th Regiment of Hussars, just a year after Jack got through.

CHAPTER XXVII

TWO TO ONE

NONE of them ever forgot the last holiday they all spent together before the great dispersal. Some of them looked back upon it in the after-days with most poignant feelings—of longing and regret. For nothing was ever to be again as it had been—and not with them only, but throughout the land.

It was as though all the circumstances and forces of life had been quietly working up to a point through all these years—as though all that had gone before had been but preparation for what was to come—as though the time had come for the Higher Powers to say, as sensible parents sooner or later say to their children, "We have done our best for you—we have fitted you for the fight; now you are become men and women, work out your own destinies!"

It was amazing to Charles Eager—feeling himself as young as ever—to find all his youngsters suddenly grown up, suddenly become, if not capable of managing their own affairs, at all events filled with that conviction, and fully intent on doing so.

And, so far, the strange story of their actual relationship had not been made known to the boys. Eager had discussed the matter with Sir Denzil many times, but the old man, not unreasonably, maintained the position that, unless and until events forced the disclosure, there was no need to trouble their minds with it. And Eager, knowing them so well, could not but agree that it would be a mighty upsetting for them.

While they were working hard, in their various degrees, for their examinations, it was, of course, out of the question. And when the matter was mooted again, Sir Denzil said quietly:

"Let it lie, Eager. If it has to come out, it will come out; but if anything should deprive us of one of them before it does come out, there is no need for the other to carry a millstone round his neck all his life."

The old man had mellowed somewhat with the years. The problem as to which was his legitimate heir, and the possibility of unconsciously perpetuating the line through the bar sinister, still troubled him at times; but the boys themselves, in their ripening and development, had done more than anything else to alter his feelings towards them.

Well-born or ill-born, they were fine bits of humanity. He had come to tolerate them with a degree of appreciation, to regard them with something almost akin to a form of affection, atrophied, indeed, by long disuse, and disguised still behind a certain cynicism of speech and manner and the very elegant handling of his jewelled snuff-box, whenever they met.

When they were at Carne for holidays, they had their own apartments, and, for a sitting-room, the long, oak-panelled parlour, looking north and west over the flats and the sea; and here they were at last enabled to entertain their friends, and repay some of the hospitalities of the earlier years.

At times Sir Denzil would send for them to his own rooms, and they came almost to enjoy his acid questionings and pungent comments on life as they saw it. Behind his cynical aloofness they were not slow to perceive a keen interest in the newer order of things, and they talked freely of all and sundry—their friends, and their friends' friends, and all the doings of the day. It was very many years since the old man had been in London. He felt himself completely out of things, and had no desire to return; but still he liked to hear about them.

And at times, by way of return, when the boys had their friends in, he would, with the punctilious courtesy of his day, send Mr. Kennet to request their permission to join them, and then march in, almost on Kennet's heels, looking, in his wig and long-skirted coat and ruffles and snuff-box, a veritable relic of past days.

Jack, in the plenitude of his present-day knowledge, and the power it gave him of affording interesting information to the recluse, discoursed with him almost on terms of equality.

Jim, on the other hand, though he could rattle along in the jolliest and most amusing way imaginable with his chosen ones, still found the old gentleman's rapier-like little speeches and veiled allusions somewhat beyond him, and so, as a rule, left most of the talking to him and Jack.

But the first time the boys both came down in their uniforms, modestly veiling their pride under a large assumption of nonchalance, but in reality swelling internally like a pair of young peacocks, they carried all before them. They looked so big, so grand, so masterful, that it took some time even for the Little Lady to fit them into their proper places in their own estimation and in hers.

And as for their grandfather, it took an immense amount both of time and snuff and sapient head-nodding before he could get accustomed to them, and then he was quite as proud of them as they were of themselves.

"By gad, sir!" he said to Eager, in an unusual outburst of suppressed vehemence, "you were right and I was wrong. We can't afford to lose either of them, though what you're going to do about it all, when the time comes, is beyond me. Jack, there, talks like a book, like all the books that ever were, and knows everything there is to know in the world"—Jack had been delivering himself of some of his newest ideas on fortification—"but what can you make of that? It may only be the higher product of a coarser strain. I'm not sure that the other isn't more in the line.

MICROCOPY RESOLUTION TEST CHART

(ANSI and ISO TEST CHART No 2)

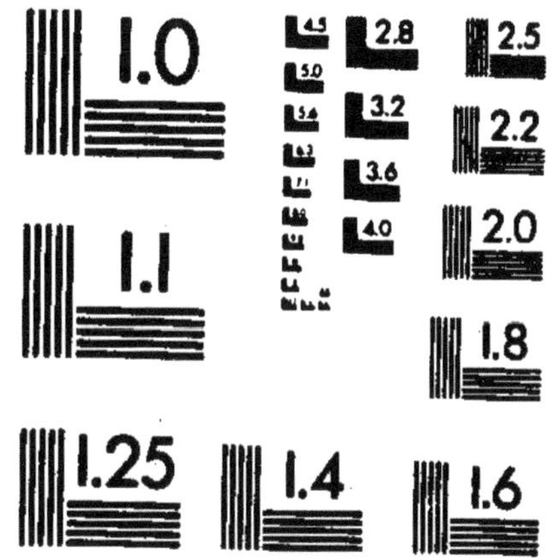

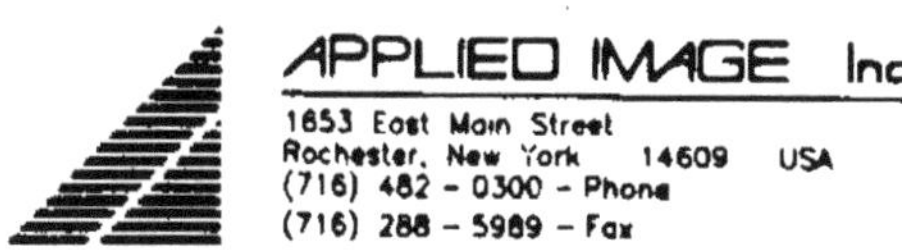

I'm inclined to think he'll make his mark if he gets the chance that suits him."

"They both will, sir. Take my word for it. We shall all, I hope, live to be proud of them both. And as to the other matter, maybe they'll cut so deep, and go so far, that after all it will become of secondary importance."

"That," said Sir Denzil, with a steady look at him over an elegantly delayed pinch of snuff, "is quite impossible. They can attain to no position comparable with the succession to Carne."

And Gracie? With what feelings did she regard these brilliantly-arrayed young warriors?

She had for them a most wholesome, whole-hearted, and comprehensive affection, and she bestowed it in absolutely equal measure upon them both.

She had grown up in closest companionship with them. She could not imagine life without them or either of them: it would have been life without its core and colour. And, so far, they stood together in her heart, and no occasion had arisen for discrimination between them.

When, indeed, Jim had disappeared for a time, and seemed lost to them, life had seemed black and blank for lack of him, and Jack could not by any means make up for him. But when Jack in turn disappeared life was equally shadowed for her, and Jim was no comfort whatever.

She, rejoicing in them equally, had no thought or wish but that things should go on just as they were. But in the boys other feelings began unconsciously to push up through the crumbling crust of youth.

They were nearing manhood. The Little Lady was no longer a child. She had grown—tall and wonderfully beautiful in face and figure. They had met other girls, but never had either of them met any one to compare with Grace Eager. And they met her afresh, each time they came home, with new wonder and vague new hopes and wishes.

It was the party which Sir George Herapath gave in the autumn that brought matters to a head.

Neither of the boys had seen Grace in evening dress before. Indeed, it was her first, and the result of much deep consideration and planning on the part of herself and Margaret Herapath.

When it was finished and tried on in full for the first time, old Mrs. Jex, admitted to a private view, clasped her hands and the tears ran down her face as she murmured, "An angel from heaven! Never in all my born days have I set eyes on anything half so pretty!"—though really it was only white muslin with pale-blue ribbons here and there. But it showed a good deal of her soft white arms and neck, and they dazzled even Mrs. Jex. As for the boys—it was as though the most marvellous bud the world had ever seen had suddenly burst its sheath and blossomed into a splendid white flower.

When she came into the big drawing-room at Knoyle that night, with Eager close behind, his intent face all alight with pride in her, and perhaps with anticipation for himself, she created quite a sensation, and found it delightful.

She came in like a lily and a rose and Eve's fairest daughter all in one; and our boys gazed at her spell-bound, startled, electrified as though by a galvanic shock. And deep down in the consciousness of each was a strange, wonderful, peaceful joy, a sudden endowment, and an almost overpowering yearning. In the self-same moment each knew that in all the world there was no other woman for him than Grace Eager. And, vaguely, behind that, was the fear that the other was feeling the same.

And she? She enjoyed to the full the novel sensation of the effect she produced upon them, and was just the same Gracie as of old—almost.

She sailed up to them and dropped a most becoming curtsey, and rose from it all agleam and aglow with merry laughter at their visible undoing.

"Well, boys, what's the matter with you?" she rippled merrily.

"You!" gasped Jim.

"Me? What's the matter with me? I'm all right. Don't you like me like this? Meg and I made it between us."

Didn't they like her like that? Why——!

"You see," said Jack, "we've never seen you like this before, and you've taken us by surprise."

"Oh, well, get over it as quickly as you can, and then you may ask me to dance with you."

"I don't think I'll ever get over it, but I'll ask you now," said Jim. Which was not bad for him.

And Jack felt the first little stab of jealousy he had ever experienced towards Jim, at his having got in first.

"I'd like every dance," laughed Jim happily, "but——"

"Quite right, old Jim Crow! Mustn't be greedy! You first, because you spoke first, then Jack——"

"Then me again," persisted Jim.

"We'll see. Is that Ralph Harben? How he's grown! His whiskers and moustache make him look quite a man." And Jim decided instantly on the speedy cultivation of facial adornments. "Oh, he's coming! And there's Meg." And she flitted away to Margaret, who was talking to Charles Eager, and so for the moment upset Master Harben's plans for her capture.

With no little distaste the boys had suffered instruction in the art of dancing, as a necessary part of the education of a gentleman. Now they fervently thanked God for it. To have to stand with their backs to the wall while every Tom, Dick, or Ralph whirled past in the dance with Gracie, would have been quite past the bearing. They felt new sensations under their waistcoats even when George Herapath had her in charge, though there was not a fellow on earth they liked better, or had more confidence in, than old George, now a dashing lieutenant in the Royal Dragoons, and quite a man of the world. As for Ralph Harben—well, if either of them could have picked a reasonable quarrel with him, and had it out in the garden, unbeknown to any but themselves, Master Ralph would have undergone much tribulation.

They danced with Gracie many times that night, and grew more and more intoxicated with happiness such as neither had ever tasted before or even dreamed of. And yet, below and behind it all, pushed down and hustled into dark corners of the heart and mind, was that other new feeling which, though it was foreign to them, they instinctively strove to keep out of sight.

Over the incidents of that party we need not linger. There were many fair girls and fine boys there, but they do not come into our story. They all enjoyed themselves immensely, and Sir George, beaming genially, enjoyed them all as much as they enjoyed themselves.

Margaret moved among them like a queen lily, and the boys were somewhat overpowered by her stately beauty. But Charles Eager seemed to find his satisfaction in it, and his eyes followed her with vast enjoyment whenever he was not dancing with her, for he danced as well as he jumped or boxed.

When Mr. Harben—Sir George's active partner in the business, and Ralph's father—chaffed him jovially on the matter, he replied cheerfully that David danced before the ark, and he didn't see why he shouldn't do likewise. And when Harben would have tackled him further as to the ark, he averred that arks were as various as the men who danced before them, and had no limitations whatever in the matter of size, shape, or material—that some men were arks of God and more women—that when he came across such he bowed before them, or, as the case might be, danced with them, and he sped off to claim Margaret for the next round, leaving his adversary submerged under the avalanche of his eloquence.

That night was, for the younger folk, all enjoyment, tinged indeed with those other vague feelings I have named, but quickened and intensified, before they separated, by news from the outer world which strung all their nerves as tight as fiddlestrings and swept them with many emotions.

For, coming upon Sir George and his partner conversing earnestly in a quiet corner one time, Eager, with his eyes on Margaret and Ralph Harben circling round the room, asked—casually, and by way of exhibiting detachment from any special interest in that other particular matter—"Well, Mr. Harben, what's the news from the East?"

And the two older men stopped talking and looked at him.

It was Sir George who answered him, soberly:

"Grave news, Mr. Eager. Harben was just telling me that the fleet is to enter the Black Sea, and that at headquarters they entertain no doubt as to the result."

"You mean war?" asked Eager, with a start.

"War without a doubt, Mr. Eager," said Harben, involuntarily rubbing his hands together. For he was a contractor, you must remember; and whatever of misery and loss war entails upon others, for contractors it means business and profit.

"We are to fight Russia on behalf of Turkey?"

"Russian aggression must be checked," said Harben. "Her ambition knows no bounds. We go hand-in-hand with France, of course."

"H'm! My own feeling would be that it is more for the aggrandisement of Louis Napoleon than for the checking of Russia that we are going to fight."

"Who's going to fight?" asked Lieutenant George, catching the word.

And then of course it was out. For, once more, whatever of misery and loss war entails upon others, to the fighting man in embryo it means only glory and the chances of promotion.

It was the following day that the disturbances nearer home began.

Jack lay awake most of the morning after he got to bed,

thinking soberly, with rapturous intervals when Gracie's laughing face floated in the smaller darkness of his tired eyes, and envying Jim, who slept at intervals like a sheep-dog after a day on the hills. But at times even Jim's heavy breathing stopped and he lay quite still, and then he too was thinking—which was an unusual thing for him to do in the night—though not perhaps so deeply as Jack.

They both felt like boiled owls in the morning, and lay late. It was close on midday when Jack, after several pipes and a splitting yawn, said, "Let's go up along,"—which always meant north along the flats—"my blood's thickening." And they went off together along the hard-ribbed sand, with the sea and the sky like bars of lead on one side and the stark corpses of the sand-hills, with the wire-grass sticking up out of them like the quills of porcupines, on the other.

They walked a good two miles without a word, both thinking the same things and both fearing to start the ball rolling.

"We've got to talk it out, Jim," said Jack at last.

Jim grunted gloomily.

"What are you thinking of it?"

"Same as you, I s'pose."

"It mustn't part us, old Jim."

Jim snorted. Under extreme urgency he was at times slow of expression in words.

"Gracie has become a woman, the most beautiful woman in all the world"—with rapture, as though the mere proclamation of the fact afforded him mighty joy, which it did. "And we are men . . . and—and we've got to face it like men."

And Jim grunted again. He was surging with emotions, but he couldn't put them into words like Jack.

"I would give my life for her," said Jack.

"I'd give ten lives if I had 'em."

"She can only have one of us, and only one of us can have her." Which was obvious enough.

12

"And it all lies with her. We only want what she wants."

"I only want her," groaned Jim.

"Of course. So do I. But we neither of us want her unless she wants us," reasoned Jack.

"I do. She's made me feel sillier than ever I felt in all my life before. All I know is that I want her."

Jack nodded. "I know. I've been thinking of it all night."

"So've I," growled Jim. And Jack refrained from telling him how he had envied him his powers of sleep.

"It seems to me the best thing we can do is to write and tell her what we're feeling."

Jim snorted dissentingly. Letter-writing was not his strong point, and Jack understood.

"Well, you see, we can't very well go together and tell her. But if we write she can have both our letters at the same time, and then she can decide. I'm sure it's the only way to settle it. Can you think of anything better?"

But Jim had no suggestions to offer. All he knew was that his whole nature craved Gracie, and he could not imagine life without her.

In the earlier times, when, as generally happened, they both wanted a thing which only one of them could have, they always fought for it, and to the victor remained the spoils.

But in those days the spoils were of no great account, and the pleasure of the fight was all in all.

This was a very different matter. The prize was life's highest crown and happiness for one of them, and no personal strife could win it. It was a matter beyond the power of either to influence now. It was outside them. They could ask, but they could not take. Forcefulness could do much in the bending and shaping of life, but here force was powerless.

And it was then, as he brooded over the whole matter, that one of life's great lessons was borne in upon Jim Carron

—that the dead hand of the past still works in the moulding of the present and the future, that what has gone is still a mighty factor in what is and what is to come.

He groaned in the spirit over his own deficiencies, the lost opportunities, the times wasted, which, turned to fuller account, might now have served him so well. If only he could have known that all the past was making towards this mighty issue, how differently he would have utilised it.

For, submitting himself to most unusual self-examination, and searching into things with eyes sharpened by unusual stress, he could not but acknowledge that, compared with Jack, he made but a poor show.

Jack was clever. He had a head and knew how to use it. He would go far and make a great name for himself. Whereas he himself had nothing to offer but a true heart and a lusty arm, and Jack had these also in addition to his greater qualifications.

How could any girl hesitate for a moment between them? His chances, he feared, were small, and he felt very downcast and broken as he sat, that same afternoon, chewing the end of his pen and thoughtfully spitting out the bits, in an agonising effort after unusual expression such as should be worthy of the occasion.

His window gave on to the northern flats, and, as he savoured the penholder, in his mind's eye he saw again the wonderful little figure of Gracie in her scarlet bathing-gown, with her hair astream, and her face agleam, and her little white feet going like drumsticks, as they had seen her that very first morning long ago. And, since then, how she had become a part of their very lives!

And then his thoughts leaped on to the previous night, and his pulses quickened at the marvel of her beauty: her face—little Gracie's face, and yet so different; her lovely white neck and arms. He had seen them so often before in little Gracie. But this was different, all quite different. She was no longer a child, and he was no longer a boy. She was a woman, a beautiful woman, *the* woman, and he was a man, and every good thing in him craved her as its very highest good. God! How could he let any other man take her from him? Even Jack——

He spat out his penholder, and kicked over his chair, as he got up and began to pace the room, with clenched hands and pinched face.

CHAPTER XXVIII

THE LINE OF CLEAVAGE

"DEAREST GRACE,

"We two are in trouble, and you are the unconscious cause of it. We have suddenly discovered that we have all grown up, and things can never be quite the same between us all as they have been. Jim is writing to you also, and you will get both our letters at the same time. We both love you, Gracie, with our whole hearts. If you can care enough for either of us it is for you to say which. For myself I cannot begin to tell you all you are to me. You are everything to me—everything. I cannot, dare not imagine life without you in it, Gracie. Can you care enough for me to make me the happiest man in all the world?

"Ever yours devotedly,

"JOHN DENZIL CARRON."

"GRACIE DEAR,

"It is horrid to have to ask if you care for me more than you do for old Jack. But it has come to that, and we cannot help ourselves. I want you more than I ever wanted anything in all my life. You are more to me than life itself or anything it can ever give me. I know I am not half good enough for you, and I wish I had made more of myself now. But I do not thi... any one could ever care for you as I do.

"God bless you, dear, whatever you decide.

"Please excuse the writing, etc., and believe me,

"Yours ever,

"JIM."

When Mrs. Jex brought in these two letters, as they lingered lazily over the tea-table, Grace laughed merrily.

"What are those boys up to now? It must be some unusually good joke to set old Jim writing letters."

But her brother's face lacked its usual quick response. He had been very thoughtful all day, sombre almost; and when Grace had chaffed him lightly as to his exertions of the previous night, instead of tackling her in kind, he had said quietly:

"Yes, you see, we old people don't take things so lightly as you youngsters."

"You are thinking of this war?"

"Yes—partly."

"And——?"

"Oh—lots of things."

"Margaret?"—with a twinkle.

"Oh, Margaret of course. I thought I had never seen her look more charming."

"She is always charming. Charlie, I wish——" and she hung fire lest in the mere touching she might damage.

"And what do you wish, child?"

"I wish you'd marry her. She's the sweetest thing that ever was."

"You have a most excellent taste, my child."

"It's in the family. Meg's taste is equally good"—with a meaning glance at him, but he was looking thoughtfully into his teacup.

"And you really think we shall be dragged into war, Charlie?"

"Mr. Harben seemed to think it certain."

"I don't think I like Mr. Harben very much. I caught sight of his face while you were all talking in the corner, and I thought he must have heard some good news."

"He was probably thinking at the moment only of his own partic. lar aspect of the matter. War means business for contractors, you know."

"Sir George didn't look that way."

"He hasn't very much to do with the firm now, I believe. Besides, one would expect him to take wider views than Harben. He is a bigger man in every way."

Then Mrs. Jex came in with the letters, and Gracie wondered merrily what joke the boys were up to. But Eager, who had not failed to notice their unconcealed enthralment the night before, pursed his lips for a moment as though he doubted if the contents of those letters would prove altogether humorous.

"I thought they'd have been round, but I expect they've been in bed all day." And she ripped open Jim's letter, which happened to be uppermost, with an anticipatory smile.

Eager saw the smile fade, as the sunshine fails off the side of a hill on an April day, and give place to a look of perplexity and a slight knitting of the placid brow.

She picked up Jack's letter, and tore it open, and read it quickly. Then, with a catch in her breath and a startled look in her eyes, she jerked:

"Charlie—what do they mean? Are they in fun——"

"Shall I read them, dear?"

She threw the letters over to him, and sat, with parted lips and wondering—and rather scared—face, looking into the fire, with her hands clasped tightly in her lap.

"This is not fun, Grace dear," her brother said gravely at last. It had taken him a terrible long time to read those very short letters, but he read so much more in them than was actually written. "It is sober earnest, and a very grave matter."

"But I don't want—— Oh!—I wish they hadn't"—with passionate fervour. "Why can't they let things go on as they are? We have been so happy——"

"Yes. . . . But time works its changes. They are no longer boys——"

A wriggle of dissent from Grace.

"——Although they may seem so to us. And you are no longer a little girl——"

"Oh! I feel like a speck of dust, Charlie; and I don't, don't, don't want——"

"I know, dear; but it is too late. You may feel a little girl to-day. Last night you were an exquisitely beautiful woman—and this is the result."

Grace put her hands up to her face and began to cry softly. For there, in the dancing flames, she had seen in a flash what it all must mean—severances, heart-aches, trouble generally. And they had all been so happy.

Eager wisely let her have her cry out. When, at last, she mopped up her eyes, and sat looking pensively into the fire again, he said quietly:

"Let us face the matter, dear! They are dear, good lads, and they are doing you the greatest honour in their power. There being two of them, of course"—and it came home to him that here were he and Gracie up against the problem of Carne also—"makes things very trying, both for them and for you. You like them both, I know——"

"I've always liked them both, and I don't like either of them one bit better than the other."

"Is there any one else you like as well as either of them?"

"No, of course not. I've never cared for any one as I have for Jack and Jim—except you, of course. Oh! what am I to do, Charlie?"

"As far as I can see, there is only one thing to be done at present, and that is—wait."

"Can you make them wait? Oh, do! Some time, perhaps——"

"If this war comes, they will have to go into it. They may neither of them come back."

"Oh, Charlie! . . . That is too terrible to think of——"

"War is terrible without a doubt, dear. It cuts the knot of many a life."

"My poor boys! But how can I possibly tell them?"

"I think, perhaps, you had better leave it all to me, dear. I will just explain to each of them quietly how this has taken you by surprise, and that you feel towards the one just as you do towards the other, and that, for the time being, they must let matters rest there."

"Things will never be the same among us again."

"Not quite the same, perhaps; but there is no reason why your friendship should suffer."

"If they will see it that way——"

"They will have to see it that way. They ought, by rights, to have spoken to me first. And if they had I could have saved you all this. I must scold them well for that."

"The dear boys!"

And presently, since he could imagine from their letters the state of the boys' feelings, and such were better got on to reasonable lines as soon as possible, he set off in the chill twilight for Carne. And Gracie sat looking into the fire, her mind ranging freely in these new pastures—troubled not a little at this sudden break in the brotherly-sisterly ties which had hitherto bound them, with quick mental side-glances now and then at the strange new possibilities, and not entirely without a touch of that exaltation with which every girl learns that to one man she is the whole end and aim of life.

The trouble was that here were two men holding her in that supreme estimation, and that, so far, in her very heart of hearts, she found it impossible to say that she loved one better than the other. And at times the white brow knitted perplexedly at the absurdity of it, while the sweet, mobile mouth below twisted to keep from actual smiles as she thought of it all.

But, naturally, the first result of the whole matter was that her mind dwelt incessantly and penetratingly on her boy-friends who had suddenly become her lovers, and she regarded them from quite new points of view. And she knew that she was right, and that they never could be all quite the same to one another as they had been hitherto.

Long before Charles got back she was feeling quite aged and worn with overmuch thinking.

CHAPTER XXIX

GRACIE'S DILEMMA

"ONE on 'em's up in his room, but I dunnot know which," grunted old Mrs. Lee, in answer to Eager's request for the boys, either or both, and he went up at once. A tap on Jim's door received no answer. Jack's opened to him at once.

"Mr. Eager!" And there was a hungry look in the boy's eyes.

"Hard at work, old chap?"—at sight of a number of books spread out on the table. "I thought this was holidays with you."

"I tried, but I couldn't get down to it."

"Where's Jim?"

"He's off down along—couldn't sit still. Have you brought us any word from Gracie?"—very anxiously.

"Well, I've come to have a talk with you about that." And the Rev. Charles pulled out his pipe and began to fill it. "You ought to have spoken to me first, you know——"

"Oh?—didn't know—not used to that kind of thing, you know."

"I suppose not. Still, that is the proper way to go about it."

"What does Gracie say?" asked Jack impatiently.

"I've come to ask you both, Jack, to let the matter lie for a time." And Jack's foot beat an impatient tattoo. "You see, Gracie had no idea whatever of this, and it has knocked the wind out of her. You can't imagine how upset she is. First, she thought you were joking. Then she had a good cry, and now I've left her staring into the fire, fearing you can never all be friends again as you always have been."

"Why, of course we can!"

"I told her so, but she says things can never be the same."

"We don't want them the same."

"No, I know. But you see, Jack, Gracie has not been thinking of you two in that way; and in the way she has always thought of you, as her dearest friends, she likes the one of you just as much as the other."

Jack grunted.

"After this it will be impossible for her to regard you simply as friends. But you must give her time——"

"Is there any one else?" growled Jack.

"There is no one else. I asked her."

"And—how—long——"

"To name a time, I should say a year."

"A great deal may happen in a year. We may all be dead."

"The chances are that this will be a year of great happenings," said Eager gravely. "The issues are in God's hands. May He grant us all a safe deliverance!"

"You really think it will be war?" asked the boy quickly.

"I fear so."

Jack sat gazing steadily into the fire and limned coming glories in the dancing flames.

"A year's a terrible long time to wait when you feel like a starving dog. But if there's a war . . . yes—that would make it pass quicker."

"Have you said anything to your grandfather about this matter?"

"How could we till we knew which——"

Eager nodded. "Best leave it so at present. How soon will Jim be back? I'd like to have a word with him too."

"I don't know. He's a good deal worked up."

"I'll go along and meet him."

"I'll come too?"

"No. Better let me see him by himself. You can talk it over together afterwards. I hope this won't make any difference between you two, Jack."

"One of us has got to put up with disappointment some time," said Jack steadily. "But we'll just have to stand it."

Eager tramped away along the rim of the tidal sand, well pleased with Jack's reasonable acceptance of the situation. Jim, he felt sure, would be no less sensible, and matters would run on smoothly; and so Time, the great Solver of Problems, would be given the opportunity of working out this one also.

Deeply pondering the whole matter, and letting his thoughts wander back along the years, he tramped on almost forgetful of the actual reason for his coming. It was not till a gleam of light amid the sand-hills on his left told him he had got to Seth Rimmer's cottage, that he knew how far he had come. Jim might have called there, so he rapped on the door and went in.

"Ech, Mr. Eager! It's good o' you to come and see an owd woman like this," said Mrs. Rimmer from the bed.

"It's always a pleasure to see you, Mrs. Rimmer. You're one of the ones that it does one good to see."

"It's very good o' yo'."

"But I came really to look for Jim Carron. They told me he had come down this way, and I thought he might have called in to see you."

"No. I havena seen owt of him."

"And you're all alone? Where's everybody?"

"Th' mester's at his work—God keep him; it's a bad, black night!—and Seth—he's away."

"And where's my friend Kattie? She ought not to leave you all alone like this."

"Ech, I'm used to it. 'Oo's always slipping out. I dunnot know who——" she began, with a quite unusual fretfulness, which showed him she had been worrying over it.

And then the door opened and Kattie came in, ruffled somewhat with the south-west wind, which had whipped the colour into her face. With a bit of cherry ribbon at her throat, and another bit in her hair, and her eyes sparkling in the lamplight, she looked uncommonly pretty.

"How they all grow up!" thought Eager to himself. "Here's another who will set the village boys by the ears; and it seems no time since she was a child running about with scarce a rag to her back!"

"Mr. Eager?" said Kattie in surprise.

"I came to find Jim Carron, Kattie. I suppose you haven't seen him about anywhere?"

"I saw some one walking up along," said Kattie, "but it was too dark to see who it was."

"Jim, I'll be bound. Good night, Mrs. Rimmer! Good night, Kattie! I'll be in again in a day or two." And he set off in haste the way he had come.

A few minutes' quick walking showed him a dim figure strolling along the higher causeway of dried seaweed and drift, and kicking it up disconsolately at times, just as he used to do as a boy when seeking treasure.

"That you, Jim?" And the figure stopped.

"Hello!—what—you, Mr. Eager?"

"Just me. I came to look for you. Kattie told me you'd come on——"

"Kattie?"

"Well, she said she'd seen some one pass, and I guessed it was you. I've been in having a talk with Jack, my boy, and I wanted to see you too." And he linked arms and went on.

"Yes?"

"About your letter to Gracie." And Eager felt the boy's arm jump inside his own. "It was a tremendous surprise to her, you know. She had never thought of either of you in that way, and it knocked her all of a heap. Now I want you all to let matters rest as they are for a year, Jim——"

"A year! Good Lord!"

"I know how you feel, lad, but it is absolutely the only thing to be done. You've been like brothers to her, you know. You are both very dear to her; but when you ask her suddenly to choose between you, she cannot. I couldn't myself. You are both dearer to me than any one in the world . . . almost . . . after Gracie, . . . but if you put me in a corner and bade me, at risk of my life, say which of you I liked best—well, I couldn't do it. And that's just her position."

"I'm afraid . . . I don't suppose I stand much chance . . . against old Jack. . . . He's a much finer fellow. . . . But, oh, Mr. Eager . . . I can't tell you how I feel about her. . . . If it could make her happy I'd be ready to lie right down here and die this minute." And Eager pressed the jerking arm inside his own understandingly.

"I believe you would, my boy. But it wouldn't make for Gracie's happiness at all to have you lie down and die. You must both live to do good work in the world and make us all proud of you. And the work looks like coming, Jim, and quickly."

"You mean this war they're talking about?"

"Yes. I'm afraid there's no doubt it's coming, and war is a terrible thing."

"It'll give one the chance of showing what's in one, anyway."

"Some one has to pay for such chances."

"I suppose so . . . . unless one pays oneself. . . . I don't know that I particularly want to kill any one, but I suppose one forgets all that in the thick of it. . . . Anyway, if it comes to fighting I think I can do that . . . if I haven't got much of a head for books and things."

"I believe you will do your duty, whatever it is, my boy, and no man can do more."

"Well?" asked Gracie eagerly, when Eager got home again. "Did you see them? Quick, Charlie! Tell me!"

"Yes, I saw them. Jack at home—trying to work. Jim down along—couldn't sit still."

"The poor boys!"

"They are very much in earnest, but I have got them to see the reasonableness of waiting—for a year at least."

"I'm glad. I don't know how I can ever choose between them, Charlie."

"Don't trouble about it, dear. Things have a way of working themselves out if you leave them to themselves."

"I wonder!" she said wearily.

CHAPTER XXX

NEVER THE SAME AGAIN

"THINGS can never be the same again," was the doleful refrain of all Gracie's thoughts as she tossed and tumbled that night, very weary but far too troubled to sleep.

And at Carne there were two more in like case.

"Seen Mr. Eager?" asked Jack when Jim came in.

"Yes," nodded Jim, and nothing more passed between them on the subject.

But here too things could never be quite the same again, for, good friends as ever though they might remain in all outward seeming, neither could rid his mind of the fact that the other desired beyond every other thing in life the prize on which his own heart was set. And that ever-recurring thought tended, no matter how they might try to withstand it, to division. Similarity of aim, when there is but one prize, inevitably produces rivalry, and rivalry scission.

They strove against it.

"Jim, old boy, this mustn't divide us," said Jack next day, when both were feeling somewhat mouldy.

"Course not," growled Jim, but all the same the cloud was over them.

Eager had asked them to come in to tea that afternoon, so that he might be with them all at this first meeting and help to round awkward corners.

But they all three felt somewhat gauche and ill at ease at first, as was only natural. For Gracie's face, swept by conscious blushes, was lovelier than ever, and set both their hearts jumping the moment she came into the room. And it is no easy matter for a girl to appear at her ease in the company of two love-sick young men who know all about each other's feelings and hers.

They were both inclined to gaze furtively at her with melancholy in their eyes, and for the time being the old gay camaraderie was gone; and at times, when she caught them at it, it was all she could do to keep from hysterical laughter, while all the time she felt like crying to think that they would never all be the same again.

But Eager exerted himself to the utmost to charm away the shadows, gave them some of the humours of his sharp-witted parishioners, and finally got them on to the outlook in the East, which set them talking and left Grace in comparative comfort as a listener.

Jack gave them eye-openers in the matter of new guns and projectiles. Jim asserted with knowledge that if the cavalry got their chance they would give a mighty good account of themselves. Eager expressed the hope that the Government would awake to the fact that the whole matter was obviously promoted by the French Emperor for his own personal aggrandisement, and would not allow England to be made his willing instrument. The boys knew little of the political aspect of the case, but hoped, if it came to fighting, that they would be in it.

And Grace sat quietly and listened, and wondered what the coming year would hold for them all.

So by degrees the stiffness of their new estate wore off,

and before the boys left they were all talking together almost as of old, but not quite. Still she went to bed that night somewhat comforted, and slept so soundly as almost to make up for the night before.

"What's the matter with those boys?" asked Sir Densil of Eager next day, when they met for the discussion of certain arrangements respecting the boys' allowances. "Are they sick? Any typhus about?" And there was actually a touch of anxiety in his voice.

"No, sir, they are not sick bodily. They're in love."

"The deuce! With whom?"

"Gracie."

"What—both of them?"—suspending his pinch of snuff in mid-air to gaze in astonishment at Eager.

"Yes, both of them."

"So!"—snuffing very deliberately, and then nodding thoughtfully. "So the puzzle of Carne hits you too. And what does Miss Gracie say about it?"

"She is very much upset. They had all been such good friends, you see, that she had never regarded them in that light."

"And you?"

"I have persuaded them to let matters remain on the old footing, as far as that is possible, for at least a year. By that time——"

"Yes, this next year may bring many changes," said the old gentleman musingly; and presently, "Well, I'm glad they have shown so much sense, Mr. Eager—and you too. I have the highest possible opinion of Miss Gracie. Now as to the money. They cannot live on their pay, of course. What do you suggest?"

"Not too much. Jim will be at somewhat more expense than Jack, but it would not do to discriminate. I should say a couple of hundred each in addition to their pay. It won't leave them much of a margin for frivolities, and that is just as well."

"Very well. I will instruct my lawyers to that effect. Three hundred and fifty or four hundred a year would not have gone far with us in my day, but no doubt things have changed. Do your best to keep them from high play. It generally ends one way, as you know."

"I have no reason to believe they are, either of them, given to it. Of course——"

"They've not tasted their freedom yet. It's bound to be in their blood. Put them on their guard, Mr. Eager. We don't want them milksops, but put them on their guard. It will come with more weight from you than from me."

"There is no fear of them turning out milksops, Sir Denzil. They are as fine a pair of lads as Carne has ever seen, I'll be bound, and they'll do us all credit yet. I'll talk to them about the gaming. Jack is too keen on his work, I think. Jim——"

"Ay, Jim's a Carron, right side or wrong. You'll find he'll run to the green cloth like a mole to the water."

"I'll see that he goes with his eyes open, anyway. I don't think he'll put us to shame. Jim's no great hand at his books, but he's got heaps of common sense, and he's true as steel."

"All that no doubt," said the old gentleman, with a dry smile. "But you'll find that boys will be boys to the length of their tether. When they've exhausted the possibilities of foolishness they become men—sometimes," with a touch of the old bitterness.

CHAPTER XXXI

DESERET

NEW men—and women—new manners and customs, to say nothing of costumes.

The accession of the young Queen cut a deep cleft

between the old times and the new. But human nature at the root is very much the same in all ages, no matter what its outward appearance and behaviour.

The wild excesses of the Regency days had given place to the ordered decorum of a Maiden Court. The young Queen's happy choice of a consort confirmed it in its new and healthy courses. But, placid to the point of dullness though the surface of the stream appeared, down below there were still the old rocks and shoals, and now and again resultant eddies and bubbles reminded the older folk of the doings of other days.

Now—as at all times, but undoubtedly more so than during the two preceding reigns—to those who believed in study and hard work as a means of personal advancement, the way was open. And now still, as at all times, but especially in those latter times, to those who craved the pleasures of the table, whether covered with a white cloth or a green, or simply bare mahogany, the way was no less open to those who knew.

Jack, down at Chatham, was much too busy with his books, and such practical application of them as could be had there, to give a thought to the more frivolous side of things.

Jim, cast into what was to him the whirl of London—though his grandfather would have viewed it scornfully over a depreciatory pinch of snuff, with something of the feelings of an old lion turned out to amuse himself in a kitchen garden—Jim found this new free life of the metropolis very delightful and somewhat intoxicating.

Harrow had been a vast enlargement on Carne. London was a mightier enfranchisement than Harrow.

But first of all he was a soldier, very proud of his particular branch of the service, and bent on fitting himself for it to the best of his limited powers.

In the first flush of his boyish enthusiasm he worked hard. His horsemanship was above the average; his swordsmanship, by dint of application and constant practice, excellent; and he slogged away at his drill and a knowledge of the handling of men as he had never slogged at anything before.

He bade fair to become a very efficient cavalryman, and meanwhile found life good and enjoyed himself exceedingly.

His wide-eyed appreciation of this expansive new life appealed to his fellows as does the unbounded delight of a pretty country cousin to a dweller in the metropolis. They found fresh flavour in things through his enjoyment of them, and laid themselves out to open his eyes still wider.

His enthusiasm for their common profession was in itself a novelty. They decided that all work and no play would, in his case, result in but a dull boy, as it would have done in their own if they had given it the chance; and so, whenever opportunity offered—and they made it their business to see that it was not lacking—they carried him off among the eddies and whirlpools of society and insisted on his enjoying himself.

But, indeed, no great insistence was necessary. Jim found life supremely delightful, and savoured it with all the headlong vehemence of his nature.

He had never dreamed there were so many good fellows in the world, such multitudes of pretty girls, such endless excitements of so many different kinds. Life was good; and Jack, deep in his studies at Chatham, and Charles Eager, busy among his simple folk up north, alike wagged their heads doubtfully over the hasty scrawls which reached them from time to time with exuberant but sketchy accounts of his doings, always winding up with promises of fuller details which never arrived.

Gracie enjoyed his enjoyment of life to the full, and wept with amusement over his attempts at description of the people he met, and never suffered any slightest feeling of loss in him, for he wound up every letter to her with the statement that, on his honour, he had not yet met a girl who could hold a candle to her, and that he did not believe there was one in the whole world, and that if there was he had no wish to meet her, and so he remained—hers most devotedly, hers most gratefully, hers only, hers till death, and so on and so on—Jim.

As to Sir Denzil, who received a dutiful letter now and again and got all Eager's news in addition, he only smiled over all these carryings-on, and said the lad must have his fling, and it sounded all very tame and flat compared with the doings of his young days. And if the boy came a cropper in money matters he would be inclined to look upon it as the clearest indication they had yet had as to his birth, for there never had been a genuine Carron who had not made the money fly when he got the chance. None of which subversive doctrine did Eager transmit to the exuberant one in London, lest it should but serve to grease the wheels and quicken the pace towards catastrophe; and he earnestly begged, and solemnly warned, Sir Denzil to keep his deplorable sentiments to himself, lest worse should come of it.

And to Charles Eager, deeply as he detested the thought of war, it seemed that, from the purely personal point of view, as regarded Jim and his fellows in like case, a taste of the strenuous life of camp and field would be more wholesome than this frivolous whirl of London.

Jim, in his joyous flights, met many a strange adventure.

He had gone one night with some of his fellows—Charlie Denham, second lieutenant in his own regiment, and some others—to a house in St. James's Street, where Chance still flourished vigorously in spite of Act 8 & 9 Vict. c. 109, and stood watching the play, with his eyes nearly falling out of his head at the magnitude and apparent recklessness of it all.

It was a curious room—the walls hung with heavy draperies, no sign of a window anywhere about it; and it had a feeling and atmosphere of its own, one to which fresh air and sweetness and the light of day were entirely foreign. It was furnished with many easy chairs and couches, and softly illuminated by shaded gas pendants which threw a brilliant light on to the tables, but left all beyond in tempered twilight.

The entrance too had struck Jim as still more remarkable. A small, mean door in a narrow side-street yielded silently to the Open Sesame of certain signal-taps and revealed a very narrow circular staircase, apparently in the wall of the house. At every fifteen or twenty steps upwards was another stout door, which opened only to the prearranged signal, and there were three such doors before they arrived at first a cloak-room, then a richly appointed buffet, and finally the gaming-room.

If the descent to hell is proverbially easy, the ascent to this particular antechamber was rendered as difficult as possible, to any except the initiated, and he was presently to learn the reason why.

There was a solid group round each of the tables, and some of the players occasionally gave vent to their feelings in an exultant exclamation—more frequently in a muttered objurgation; but for the most part gain or loss was accepted with equal equanimity, and Jim wondered vaguely as to the depths of the purses that could lose hundreds of guineas on the chance of the moment, and could go on losing, and still show no sign.

His wonder and attention settled presently on the most prominent player at the table, an outstanding figure by reason of his striking personal appearance and the size and steady persistence of his stakes.

He might have been any age from sixty to eighty; looking at him again, Jim was not sure but what he might be a hundred. His hair was quite white, but being trimmed rather short carried with it no impression of venerableness. The face below was equally colourless, without seam or wrinkle, perfectly shaped, like a beautiful white cameo and almost as immobile. His eyes were dark and still keen. At the moment they were intent upon the game, and Jim watched him fascinated.

He was playing evidently on some system of his own and following it out with deepest interest, though nothing but his eyes betrayed it.

His slim white hand quietly placed note after note on certain numbers, and replaced them with ever-increasing amounts as time after time the croupier raked them away. Now and again a few came fluttering back, but for the most part they tumbled into the bank with the rest. But, whether they came or went, not a muscle moved in the beautiful white face, and the stakes went on increasing with mathematical precision.

Many of the others had stopped their spasmodic punting in order to give their whole attention to his play. Their occasional guineas had come to savour of impudence alongside this formidable campaign.

Jim watched breathlessly, with a tightening of the chest, though the outcome was nothing to him, and wondered how long it could go on. The man must be made of money. He knew too little of the game to follow it with understanding, but he watched the calm white face with intensest interest, and out of the corners of his eyes saw the slim white hand quietly dropping small fortunes up and down the table and replacing them with larger ones as they disappeared.

Then a murmur from the onlookers told him of some change in the run of luck, but the white face showed no sign. And suddenly the group round the table began to disintegrate.

"What is it?" jerked Jim to his neighbour.

"He's broken the bank. Wish I had half his nerve and luck and about a quarter of his money."

"Who is he?"

"Don't you know? Lord De. eret. Gad, he must have taken ten thousand pounds to-night!"

"Come along, Carron," said one of his friends. "All the fun's over, but it was jolly well worth seeing."

And as Jim turned he found himself face to face with Lord Deseret, who stood quietly tapping one hand with a bundle of bank-notes, folded lengthwise as though they were so many pipe-spills.

"Carron?" he said gently. "Which of you is Carron?"

"I am Jim Carron, sir—at your service." And the keen kindly eyes dwelt pleasantly on him and seemed to go right through him.

"*Jim* Carron?" said the old man, and tapped him on the arm with the wedge of bank-notes, and indicated an adjacent sofa and his desire for his company there. "And why not Denzil? It always has been Denzil, hasn't it?"

"Well, you see, there are two of us, sir, and we are both Denzil, so we are also Jack and Jim to prevent mistakes."

"Two of you, are there?"—with a slight knitting of the smooth white brow, on which all the wildest fluctuations of the tables had not produced the faintest ripple of emotion. "Two of you, eh? And which of you is Lady Susan Sandys's boy? Which is to be Carron of Carne when the time comes?"

"Ah, now! that is more that I can tell you, sir. We are a pair of unfortunate twins, and no one knows which is the elder."

"Twins, eh?" And even to Jim's unpractised eye there was a look of surprise on the calm white face. "That is somewhat awkward for the succession, isn't it? Which is the better man?"

"Oh—Jack, miles away. He's got a head on him. He's at Chatham in the Engineers. I'm in the Hussars."

"There may be work even for the Hussars before long. There certainly will be for the Engineers. You're all looking forward to it, I suppose?"

"Very much so, sir. You think there's no doubt about it?"

"None, I fear, my boy. It will bring loss to many, gain to a few, but the gain rarely equals the loss. Do you play?" he asked abruptly.

"Very little. It's all quite new to me. I've hardly found my feet yet."

"This kind of thing," he said, flipping the bank-notes, "is all very well if you can afford it. Take my advice and keep clear of it."

Jim laughed, as much as to say, "Your example and your good fortune belie your words, sir."

"I can afford it, you see," said Lord Deseret, in reply to the boy's unspoken thought. "When you are as old as I am, and if you have wasted your life as I have," he said impressively, "you may come to play as the only excitement left to you. But I hope you will have more sense and make better use of your time. Will you come and see me?"

"I would very much like to, sir, if I may."

"You are occupied in the mornings, of course." And he pulled out a gold pencil-case and scribbled an address on the back of the outermost bank-note, and handed it to Jim. "Any afternoon about five, you will find me at home."

"But——" stammered Jim, much embarrassed by the bank-note.

"Put it in your pocket, my boy. You will find some use for it, unless things are very much changed since my young days. Your father's son—and your grandfather's grandson for the matter of that—need feel no compunction about accepting a trifling present from so old a friend of theirs. You cannot in any case put it to a worse use than I would. I shall look for you, then, within a day or two." And with a final admonitory tap of the sheaf of notes and a kindly nod, he left Jim standing in a vast amazement.

Lord Deseret had gone out by the door leading to the buffet and staircase. He was back on the instant with his hat and cloak on, just as a sharp whistle from some concealed tube behind the hangings cleft the air, and, in the sudden silence that befell, Jim heard the sound of thunderous blows from the lower regions.

Lord Deseret looked quickly round and beckoned to him.

"The police," he said quietly. "Get your things and keep close to me. It would never do for you to be caught here. There is plenty of time. Those doors will keep them busy for a good quarter of an hour or more. Now, Stepan!" And a burly man, who had suddenly appeared, pulled back the heavy curtains from a corner and opened a narrow slit of a door, and they passed through to another staircase, which led up and up until, through a trap-door, they came out on to the roof. They passed on over many roofs, with little ladders leading up and down over the party-walls, and finally down through another trap, and so through a public-house into a distant street.

"A thing we are always subject to," said Lord Deseret gently, "and so we provide for it. Don't forget to come and see me. Good night!"

"You're in luck's way, old man," said his friend Denham. "Deseret is a man worth knowing. Let's go and have something to eat." And they all went over to Merlin's and had a tremendous supper, for which they allowed Jim to pay because he was in luck's way and had made the acquaintance of Lord Deseret.

And many such supper-bills would have made but a very trifling hole in Lord Deseret's bank-note.

CHAPTER XXXII

THE LADY WITH THE FAN

PERHAPS it was that heavy supper, and its concomitants, that tended to fog Jim's recollection of something in his talk with Lord Deseret which had struck a jarring note in his brain at the time, and had suggested itself to him as odd and a thing to be most decidedly looked into when opportunity offered.

The feeling of it was with him next day, but he could not get back to the fact or the words which had given rise to it. Something the old man had said had caused him a momentary surprise and discomfort, and then had come the abiding surprise, from which the momentary discomfort had worn off, of that enormous bank-note, and after that the hasty exit over the roofs and the tumultuous supper at Merlin's, with much merriment and wine and smoke. It was not easy to get back through all that fog to the actual words of a casual conversation.

But there certainly was something. What, in Heaven's name, was it, that it should haunt him in this fashion?

And then, as he did his best for the tenth time, in his thick-headed, blundering way, to cover the ground again step by step, it suddenly flashed upon him.

"And which of you is Lady Susan Sandys's boy?"

That was it! "Which of you is Lady Susan Sandys's boy?" the old man had asked quite casually, as though expecting a perfectly commonplace answer.

Were they not, then, both Lady Susan Sandys's boys?

To be suddenly confronted with a question such as that—to come upon even the suggestion of a flaw in the fundamental facts of one's life, is a facer indeed.

What *could* the old boy mean? There was no sign of decrepitude about him. That he was in fullest possession of very unusual powers of brain and nerve, his prowess at the tables had shown. What could he mean?

Twin brothers must surely have the same mother. And yet from Lord Deseret's question, and the way he put it, and the searching look of the kindly keen eyes, one might have supposed that he knew, and every one else knew, something to the contrary.

To one of Jim's simple nature, there was only one thing to be done, and that was to go to Lord Deseret and ask him plainly what he meant.

He had already written to Jack, conveying to him his half

of the unexpected windfall, before he had succeeded in getting back to the root of the trouble. And he had simply told him how he had met Lord Deseret, an old friend of their father's, and how he had broken the bank at roulette and bad insisted on making him a present, which was obviously given to them both, and so he had the pleasure of enclosing his half herewith; and Lord Deseret was an exceedingly jolly old cock, and the finest-looking old boy he had ever seen, and the way he followed up that bank till it broke was a sight, and he, Jim, was half inclined to buy himself another horse, as the mare he bad was a bit shy and skittish in the traffic, though no doubt she would get used to it in time.

It was after five before he found out what he wanted to ask Lord Deseret, and so the matter had to stand over till next day, rankling meanwhile in his mind in most unaccustomed fashion, and exercising that somewhat lethargic member much beyond its wont.

That night Denham and the rest were bound for Covent Garden to see Madame Beteta in her Spanish dances.

Vittoria Beteta had burst upon the town a month or two before and taken it by storm. She claimed to be Spanish, but her dances were undoubtedly more so than her speech.

She had a smattering of her alleged native language, and of French and Italian, and, for a foreigner, a quite unusual command of the difficult English tongue.

Whatever her actual nationality, however, she danced superbly and was extraordinarily good-looking, and knew how to make the most of herself in every way.

Her age was uncertain, like all the rest. She looked eighteen, but, as she had been dancing for years in most of the capitals of Europe, she was probably more. What was certain was that she had witching black eyes, and raven black hair, and a superb figure, and danced divinely, and drew all the world to watch her.

Jim was charmed, like all the others. He had never seen anything so exquisitely, so seductively graceful.

He gazed, with wide eyes and parted lips, till the others smiled at his absorption.

"There's your new catch beckoning to you, Carron," said Denham suddenly, but he had to dig him lustily in the ribs before he could distract his attention from the dancer.

"Here, I say! Stop it!" jerked Jim, unconsciously fending the assault with his elbow, while he still hung on to the Beteta's twinkling feet with all the zest that was in him.

"There's Lord Deseret waving to you—in the stage-box, man." And Jim, following his indication, saw Lord Deseret, in a box abutting right on to the stage, waving his hand and beckoning to him.

"You have the luck," sighed Denham. "He wants you in his box. Wonder if he has room for two little ones."

"Come on and try." And Jim jumped up.

"Wait till the dance is over or you'll get howled at, man." And Denham dragged him down again, until the outburst of applause announced the end of the figure and they were able to get round to Lord Deseret's box.

He received them cordially, and as he had the box all to himself Charlie had no reason to feel himself superfluous.

"Yes, she is very charming and dances remarkably well," said Lord Deseret. "It was I induced her to come over here. I saw her in Vienna two years ago, and advised her then to add London to her laurels. Would you like to meet her? We could go round after the next dance. She will have a short rest then."

"Oh, I would," jerked Jim.

And so presently he found himself, with Lord Deseret and Charlie Denham, who could hardly stand for inflation, in Mme Beteta's dressing-room.

She was lying on a couch, swathed in a crimson silk wrap and fanning herself gently with a huge feather fan, over which the great black eyes shone like lamps.

"Señora," said Lord Deseret in Spanish, with the suspicion of a smile in the corners of his eyes, "may I be allowed the pleasure of introducing to you some young friends of mine?" And she struck at him playfully with the plume of feathers, disclosing for a moment a laughing mouth and a set of fine white teeth. And Jim thought she looked hardly as young as her eyes and her feet would have led one to suppose.

"Do you understand Spanish?" she asked of Jim, in English.

"No, I'm sorry to say——"

"Then you see, milord, it is not *comme il faut* to speak it where it is not understood." And she laughed again.

"I stand corrected, madame. We will not speak our native tongue. This is my young friend, James Carron."

And Jim, gazing with all his heart at the wonderful dancer, got a vivid impression of a rich dark Southern face, and a pair of great liquid black eyes glowing upon him through the tantalising undulations of the great dusky fan, which wafted to and fro with the methodic regularity of a metronome.

"And this is Lord Charles Denham. Both gallant Hussars, and both aching to show the colour of their blood against your friends of St. Petersburg."

"Ah, the horror!" she said gently. "But you do not look bloodthirsty, Mr. Carron." And the great black eyes seemed to look Jim through and through.

"I don't think I am really, you know. But if there is to be fighting one looks for chances, of course."

"And the chance always of death," she said gravely.

"One takes that, of course."

"But it is always the next man who is going to be killed, madame," struck in Charlie. "Oneself is always immune. Lord Deseret was at Waterloo, yet here he is, very much alive and as sound as a bell."

"He had the good fortune. May you both have as good!"

"They were anxious to express to you their admiration of

your dancing, madame," said Lord Deseret. "But we seem to have fallen upon more solemn subjects."

"I have never seen anything like it," said Jim.

"It is exquisite beyond words, a veritable dream," said the more gifted Charlie.

"Ah, well, it seems to please people, and so it is a pleasure to me also. You are from—where, Mr. Carron?"

"From the north—from Carne,—the Carrons of Carne, you know."

The dusky plume wafted noiselessly to and fro in front of her face, and its pace did not vary by the fraction of a hair's breadth. Over it, and through it, the great black eyes rested on his face in curiously thoughtful inquisition.

Suddenly, with an almost invisible jerk of the head, she beckoned him to closer converse, and holding the fan as a screen invited him inside it, so to speak.

"Do you play?" she asked gently.

"Very little," he said in surprise. "I have only my pay and an allowance, you see."

"That is right. He"—nodding towards Lord Deseret—"is not a good example for young men in that respect."

"He has been very kind to me. And he warns me strongly against it."

"All the same he does not set a good example. Will you come and see me?"

"I would be delighted if I may."

"Come and breakfast with me to-morrow at twelve. I shall be alone."

She gave him an address in South Audley Street, and then dismissed them all with, "Now you must go. Here is my dresser, and I have but ten minutes more." And they made their adieux and bowed themselves out.

"Is Madame English?" asked Denham, as they seated themselves in the box again.

"Originally, I think so. But she has lived much abroad and has become to some extent cosmopolitan. She certainly is not Spanish, or if she is she has most unaccountably forgotten her native tongue," said Lord Deseret, with his hovering smile.

"She dances in Spanish, anyway," said Charlie exuberantly. "And that is all that concerns us at the moment."

CHAPTER XXXIII

A STIRRING OF MUD

IT is an old saying, founded on very correct observation, that iong-continued calm breaks up in storm. And the same holds good of life, individual and national. Too long a calm leads at times to somewhat of deterioration—at all events to a laxing of the fibres and an indolent reliance on the continuance of things as they are; and that, in a world whose essence is growth and change, is not without its dangers. And—proverbially again—a storm always clears the air.

It seemed to Jim Carron that, of a sudden, the accumulated storms of all the long quiet years burst upon him.

He had intended seeing Lord Deseret at the first possible moment and questioning him as to that very curious remark of his. But he could not broach such a matter at the theatre and in company, and his lordship had driven off to some other appointment the moment the curtain fell.

So, at twelve next day, having scrambled through his morning's duties with a quite unusually preoccupied mind, he presented himself at Mme Beteta's lodgings and was taken upstairs to her apartments.

She welcomed him graciously, and they sat down at once to the table.

He thought she looked decidedly older in the daylight,

but it was only in the texture of her face, devoid now of any artificial assistance, and slightly lined in places.

The two great plaits of black hair showed no silver threads. The luminous black eyes were still bright. The sinewy form the dancer was full of exquisite grace.

"Now tell me about yourself," demanded madame, as they sipped their final coffee, and the maid retired.

"I don't think there's anything to tell," said Jim, with his open boyish smile.

"We have lived all our lives at Carne—Jack and I—until we went to Harrow, and then he went to Woolwich and I came to London."

"Jack is your brother?"

"Yes; we're twins. He's the clever one. That's why he's at Chatham now—in the Engineers. It was all I could do to scramble into the Hussars." And he laughed reminiscently at the scramble, and then told her about it.

"And which of you is the elder? Even in twins one of you must come first."

"That's funny now. Lord Deseret was asking me that the first time we met, and I couldn't tell him. We've really never troubled about it, you see, or thought about it at all until a very short time ago. I suppose it was the fellows at school wanting to know which was the elder that set us thinking about it. We asked old Mrs. Lee—she keeps house for us at Carne, you know—and Mr. Eager——"

"Who is Mr. Eager?"

"Oh, he's a splendid fellow. He's curate at Wyvveloe, and he's done everything for us, he and Gracie"—and madame noted the softened inflection as he said the word.

"And who is Gracie?"

"Mr. Eager's sister. They call her 'the Little Lady' in Wyvveloe."

"Is she pretty?"

"Oh, she's lovely, and as good and sweet as can be."

"You're in love with her, I suppose."

"Yes, I am," said Jim, colouring up, "and I'm not ashamed of it."

"And what about Jack?"

"He's in love with her, too."

"That's rather awkward, isn't it? What does Miss Gracie say to it all?"

"Oh, she was terribly upset. You see she had never thought of us like that. It was after the dance at Sir George Herapath's that we found it out——"

"She had a low dress on, I suppose—bare arms and shoulders, and you had never seen her so before."

"Yes," he said, surprised at such acumen, "I suppose that was it. We all used to bathe together and run about the sands. But that night she seemed to grow up all of a sudden—and so did we."

"And what does her brother say to it—and your grandfather?"

"We're to say nothing more about it for a year. You see, this war is coming on and you never can tell——"

"War is horror," she said, with a shudder. "I have seen fighting in Spain and in the streets of Paris. It is terrible. You may neither of you come back alive. If only one comes, then, I suppose——"

"Yes, that would settle it all."

"And you do not remember your mother?" she asked, after a pause.

"We never knew her," he said thoughtfully, bethinking him suddenly of Lord Deseret and that curious saying of his. "She died when we were born, and nobody has told us about her. Old Mrs. Lee must remember her, but she would never tell us, and Sir Denzil—well, you can't ask him about anything—at least, not to get any good from it."

"He has been good to you both?"

"Oh yes, in his way. But if it hadn't been for Mr. Eager——. We were growing up just little savages, running wild in the sand-hills, you know. And then he came, and it has made all the difference in the world to us."

"You owe him much, then?"

"Everything! Him and Gracie."

In his boyish impulsiveness, having been led on to talk about himself, he was half tempted to consult her about the matter that was troubling his mind in connection with Lord Deseret. But how should this half-foreign woman know anything about such matters. It was not likely that she had ever heard tell of Lady Susan Sandys. How should she? And so he lapsed into a brown study, thinking over it all.

He was aroused from it by another leading question from madame.

"And your father? Is he alive? Can he not help to solve your difficulty?"

"Well—you must think us a queer lot—we never saw our father till a short time ago. He has been living in France. We thought he was dead. He killed a man in a gaming quarrel long ago and had to live abroad, and he's been there ever since."

"Truly, as you say, you are an odd family. Will you bring your brother to see me sometime?"

"I'm sure he would like it, but he's not often in town. You see, he has the brains and he's putting them to use. I'll bring him, though, the first time he's up."

It was not till afterwards that her interest in him and his struck him as somewhat unusual, and then he had other things to think about.

That same afternoon he went to Park Lane, and found Deseret House and asked for Lord Deseret.

"Now, this is good of you," was his lordship's greeting—"to look up an old man when all the world is young and calling to you."

"I wanted to ask you something, sir, if I may."

"Say on, my boy. Anything I can tell you is very much at your service."

"When you were speaking about Jack and me the other night, you said something which has been puzzling me ever since. You asked, 'Which of you is Lady Susan Sandys's boy?'"

"Yes—well?" asked the old man, with a glint of surprise in the keen dark eyes, which rested on the boy's ingenuous face.

"Was Lady Susan Sandys our mother, sir?"

"Good heavens, boy, do you mean to say you don't know who your own mother was?"

"We don't know anything, sir. That was the first time I had ever heard her name."

"Good God!" And there was no doubt about the vast surprise in the calm white face now, as its owner stood for a moment staring at Jim and then began to pace the room in very deep thought.

"Your grandfather? Has he never discussed these things with you?"

"Never, sir. We have never had very much to do with him, you see. Until quite lately we supposed our father was dead too. Then, one day, he came to Carne—from France, where he lives, and it was a great surprise to us."

"And you know nothing about your mother?"

"Nothing whatever, sir. But since you said that, I have been thinking of very little else. You said, 'Which of you is Lady Susan Sandys's boy?' Does that mean that we are not both Lady Susan Sandys's boys? That would mean that we had different mothers. But how could that be when we are both the same age? I wish you would tell me what it all means, for I've thought and thought till my brain is getting all twisted up with thinking."

Lord Deseret paced the long room with bent head and his thin white hands clasped behind him.

It seemed to him shameful that these boys should have been kept in such ignorance of matters so vital. He was not aware, of course, of their strange upbringing in the wilds of Carne.

On the other hand, if their father and grandfather had not thought fit to enlighten them it would hardly become him to do so. Moreover, as he turned it all over in his mind, he perceived that there might be something to be said on the other side.

The boys had obviously been brought up in perfect equality. Any revelation of the mystery of their births could only make for upsetting—must introduce elements of doubt into their minds, might work disastrously upon their fellowship.

Quite unconsciously, supposing they knew all about it, he had stirred up the muddy waters that had lain quiescent for twenty years.

"This is a great surprise to me, my boy," he said quietly at length—"a very great surprise. I should never have said what I did had I not supposed you knew all about it. As matters lie . . . I'm afraid you must absolve me from my promise. If your grandfather and your father have deemed it wise to keep silence in regard to certain family matters, it would hardly be seemly in me to discuss them without their permission. You see that, don't you?"

"I see it from your point of view, sir, but not at all from my own," said Jim stubbornly. "There is something we do not know and we certainly ought to know it. If you won't tell me I must go elsewhere. I wish I had Jack's head. I think I'll go down to Chatham and talk it over with him."

The mischief was done. Lord Deseret saw that the only thing left to him was to direct the boy's quite legitimate curiosity into right channels.

"If I were you I would go straight to Sir Denzil. Tell him just what has happened, and that you will know no peace of mind till you understand the whole matter."

"Thank you, sir. I will do that, but I think I will see

Jack first and perhaps we could go down together. It's right he should know, and he's got a better head than I have."

"It concerns you both, of course. Perhaps it would be as well you should go together," said Lord Deseret, and long after Jim had gone he pondered the matter and wondered what would come of it, and yet took no blame to himself. For who could have imagined that any boys could have grown to such an age in such complete ignorance of their father and mother and all their family concerns?

CHAPTER XXXIV

THE BOYS IN THE MUD

JIM spent a troubled night, tossing to and fro and trying in vain to make head or tail of the tangle.

He was in Chatham soon after midday and made his way at once to Jack's quarters.

He found him hard at work at a table strewn with books and drawings.

"Hello, Jim boy? Why, what's up? You look—— What is it, old boy? Not money, when you sent me that gold-mine, day before yesterday. It was mighty good of you, old chap. Now—what's wrong?"

"I don't know. Everything, it seems to me. I told you about Lord Deseret——"

"Rather! Good old cock! His money comes easily, I should say."

"When he was talking to me, asking about you and Carne and all the rest, he said, quite as though I knew all about it—'And which of you is Lady Susan Sandys's boy?'"

"Who the deuce is Lady Susan Sandys?"

"Your mother—or mine."

Jack's knitted brows and concentrated gaze settled on Jim in vastest amazement.

"Your mother—or mine, Jim? What on earth do you mean?"

"That's just it. I don't know what it means. There is something behind that we don't understand, Jack."

"And this Lord Deseret?"

"I went to him and begged him to explain. He was very much surprised that I didn't know all about it, whatever it is. But he said that since our grandfather or our father had seen fit not to tell us, it would hardly be right for him to do so."

Jack nodded.

"He advised me to go to Sir Denzil and tell him how the matter had come up, and give him the chance to explain. And I suppose that's the only thing to do, but I wanted your advice. We've always been together in everything."

Jack nodded again, and then shook his head over his own bewilderment.

"I don't understand at all, Jim. Do you mean that we are not brothers, you and I? That's nonsense, and d——d nonsense too, I should say."

"I've thought and thought till I'm all in a muddle. But, if words mean anything at all, it means that you and I are not children of the same mother, and Lord Deseret knows all about it."

"You're sure he won't speak?"

"Certain. He's a splendid old fellow. He'll only do what he thinks proper; and the fact that he was so much put out at having started the matter, without understanding that we knew nothing about it, shows the kind of man he is and what there is in it."

"I can't imagine what it all means. Everybody knows we're twins, and to come now and tell us—oh, it's all d——d nonsense!"

"I know. I felt that way too. But all the same we've got to know all about it now. How are you for leave? When can you come down to Carne?"

"Leave's all right. Come now if you like," growled Jack,

very much upset in his mind and temper, as was natural enough.

"Meet me at ten o'clock, at Euston, to-morrow morning and we'll go down and get to the bottom of it all; unless you think it would be better still to go across to Paris and see our father and ask him. I have thought of that."

"If the old man won't speak, we may have to do that," said Jack, in gloomy consideration. "But if there's something queer behind it all, he's the last man to tell us, for he must be mixed up in it, and it can't be to his credit."

"I wish we'd never heard anything about it," said Jim.

"I don't know. If there's anything wrong it's sure to come out sooner or later, and we ought to know. I'd like a proper foundation for my life."

"Seems to me to cut all the foundations away."

"Feels like that. Any one who says we're not brothers is simply a fool. Besides, why on earth should our grandfather bring us up as brothers if we aren't? He's no fool, and he's not the man to play at things all these years. I wonder if Mr. Eager knows."

"I shouldn't think so. We were ten when he came."

"Well, we'll see him first, at all events, and get his advice." And on that understanding they parted, to meet at Euston the following morning.

Jack would have had Jim stop for a while to see round Chatham and make the acquaintance of some of his friends, but he begged off.

"I can think of nothing but this thing at present. It's turned me upside down. I hope nothing will turn up to separate us, Jack."

"We won't let it, Jim boy. That's in our hands at all events, and we'll see to it."

CHAPTER XXXV

EXPLANATIONS

IT was after ten o'clock the next night when they drove into Wyvveloe and knocked on Mrs. Jex's door. Mrs. Jex had gone to bed and so had Gracie. Eager himself answered their knock, and jumped with surprise at sight of them.

"Why—Jack—Jim! What on earth——"

"We'll tell you if you'll let us in," said Jack.

"Now what mischief have you been getting into?" said Eager, as they sat down before the fire, and he knocked the wood into life.

"It's not us this time. We've come to ask you something, Mr. Eager; and if you can't tell us we are going on to see Sir Denzil." And Charles Eager knew, without more telling, that the boys had somehow fallen on the mystery of their birth.

"Go on," he nodded.

"You know what we want to know?"

"I think so; but if you'll tell me I shall be sure."

And Jack, as the better speaker, laid the matter before him, and both eyed him anxiously the while.

"I am glad you came to me first," he said. "I can probably tell you all you wish to know; and you must take it from me, boys, that if it was never told to you before, it was for good reason. Better still if it had never needed to be told at all. Best of all if there had been nothing to tell. The trouble is none of our making. All we can do is to face it like men, and that, I know, you will do."

And he told them, as clearly and briefly as possible, all that he had learned concerning their births.

"To sum it all up," he said in conclusion, "you are sons of the same father, and so are half-brothers. But which of you is the son of Lady Susan and which the son of Mrs. Lee's daughter, no man on earth knows. And again—whether your father was really married to Mrs. Lee's daughter I doubt if any one but himself knows. And so you see the tangle the whole matter is in, and you can understand why it was kept from you. We could only present you with a puzzle of which we did not know the solution. It could only have upset your lives as it has done now. We have gained twenty years by keeping silence."

"Old Mrs. Lee knows which of us is which, I suppose," said Jack. And Jim jumped at the thought.

"I have very little doubt that she does, Jack; but she has never shown any indication of it whatever."

"And is her daughter still alive?"

"I doubt if even she knows that. She has not heard of her for a great many years."

"Does Gracie know anything about it all?" asked Jim.

"Not a word; and I see no reason why she should. You two have given her quite enough to think about without troubling her with this matter."

They quite agreed with that, and Jack, who had been pondering gloomily, summed up with:

"It's all an awful tangle, and I see no way out. It seems to me that it doesn't matter in the least who is who; for even if we learned who our mothers were, we don't know if they were legally married. I'm afraid there is only one thing to be said—and that is, that the one parent we are both certain about was a dishonourable rascal, and we have got to suffer for his sins."

"Morals were very much looser then than they are now," said Eager gently. "He was the product of his age. We may at all events be thankful that things have improved, and you two are the proofs thereof."

"We'd probably have been no better if you'd never come here," said Jim, with very genuine feeling. "We owe everything to you—and Gracie."

"That is so," said Jack heartily; and wished he had said it

first, but he had been too fully occupied with the other aspect of the case.

"One cannot help wondering," he said presently, "what is going to happen if our father and our grandfather should die. What are we going to do then, Mr. Eager?"

"That is a question Sir Denzil and I have often debated, but we never arrived at any conclusion. One of you must be Carron of Carne. There is also another possibility. Lady Susan Sandys was the only sister of the Earl of Quixande. He is unmarried, so far as the world knows, but he also comes of the bad old times and—well, you know his reputation. But if he leaves no legitimate heir the title comes to his sister's son——"

"If he should happen to be legitimate," growled Jack.

"As you say, my boy—if he can be proved legitimate."

"In which case he is both Carron of Carne and Earl of Quixande."

"And, having no need for the two titles, it might be possible to hand one over to his half-brother."

"Could he?" asked Jack doubtfully.

"Under the circumstances it might possibly be sanctioned."

"Failing that, who comes in?"

"Some Solway Carrons. I know nothing of them except that your grandfather detests them. But there is still further possibility for you both."

"What?" And they eyed him anxiously.

"That in your military careers you may both rise to such heights as to cast even the title of Carron of Carne into the shade."

Jack nodded. Jim did not seem to regard it as a very hopeful prospect.

"Well," said Jack, as he got up, "we've got quite enough to think over for one night. We're going to the inn. We told them to make up beds for us there. They'll all have turned in at Carne. We'll go along and see Sir Denzil in the morning."

"Come in to breakfast, and I'll go with you. I shall have to explain to him how it comes that I have had to disclose the whole matter to you."

"The boys came down last night, Gracie," was the surprising news that met the Little Lady when she came down next morning.

"The boys? Whatever for, Charlie? There isn't anything wrong with them, is there?" And the startled colour flooded her face and then left it white.

"Nothing of the kind, dear. They wanted to see Sir Denzil on some family matters, and they arrived too late to go there last night, so they went to the inn."

"You're sure they haven't been getting into trouble?"

"Quite sure. They're coming in to breakfast. You'd better go and talk to Mrs. Jex about supplies. Hungry soldiers, you know." And Gracie flew to the commissariat department.

"You dear boys!" was her greeting, when they came striding in, very tall and large in their undress uniforms. "What *have* you been doing? Over-studying?—softening of the brain?"—to Jack. "Gambling?—and frivolling generally?"—to Jim.

"Quite out," laughed Jack. "My brain was never better in its life, and Jim's pocket never so full. Mayn't a pair of hungry men come all the way from London to see you without being accused of such iniquities?"

"It is nice to get such good reports from yourselves," laughed Gracie. "I wonder how long you can keep it up."

"It depends upon circumstances," said Jack.

"And what are the circumstances?" asked Gracie incautiously.

"You're one," said Jack boldly.

"Here's breakfast. Charlie gave me to understand you had had nothing to eat for a week."

"Nothing half so good as this," said Jack, with an appreciative look at the cottage loaves and golden butter, and the great dish of ham and eggs Mrs. Jex had just brought in.

"My! but yo' do look rare and big and bonny," said that estimable woman. "I do think I'll cook ye some more eggs."

"Yes, do, Mrs. Jex," said Eager. "They don't get eggs like these in London."

And so they got through breakfast; but Jim was the quietest of the party, and Gracie got it into her head that he was in some dreadful mess, in spite of what Charlie had said. And just before they started for Carne she got hold of him for a minute, and asked:

"Jim, what's the trouble? Is it anything very bad?"

"It's nothing we've done, Grace," he said, with so frank a look in his own anxious eyes that she could not doubt him. "Just some old family matters that have cropped up." And though she could not doubt his word, he was so unlike himself that she watched them go in a state of extreme puzzlement as to what could have sapped Jim's spirits to such an unusual extent.

As a matter of fact, the strange disclosures of the previous night were weighing heavily upon him. With a vague, dull discomfort he was saying to himself that, as between himself and Jack, there could be no possible doubt as to which was the better man; and therefore—as he argued with himself—of the true stock. And, if that was so, he was simply superfluous and in everybody's way. He was not much good in the world, anyway. He felt as if he would be better out of it. If he were gone, Jack would take his proper place—and marry Gracie—— All the same, it was deucedly hard that one's life should be broken up like this through absolutely no fault of one's own. And to surrender all thought of Gracie—— Yes, that was the hardest thing of all. But she would go to Jack by rights, along with all the rest.

"Thank God for this war that is coming!" he said to himself. "There will be my chance of getting out of the tangle and leaving the field clear to them."

So no wonder our poor old Jim was feeling in the dumps, and was quite unable to keep them out of his face.

"Hillo? What's brought yo' home?" asked old Mrs. Lee, as they came into her kitchen.

"Business," said Jack curtly, and she was surprised at the dourness of them all.

But Jack was saying to himself—"That old witch may be my grandmother."

And Jim—"She is most likely my grandmother."

And Eager—"If the old wretch would only speak she could tell us all we want to know."

Under which conditions a certain lack of cordiality was really not very surprising.

"Well, well! How much is it?" asked Sir Denzil, eyeing them quizzically over his arrested pinch of snuff as they came into his room. "And how did you manage to get here at this time of day?"

"We slept at the Pig and Whistle, sir," said Jack. "We got to Wyvveloe too late last night to come on here."

"Most considerate, I'm sure. What have you been up to, to make you so thoughtful of the old man?"

"They have run up against the Great Puzzle, sir, as we knew they must sooner or later," said Eager. "They came in to me at ten o'clock last night to ask if I could enlighten them, and I have told them all we know."

"So!" And he absorbed his snuff and stared intently at the boys. . . . "And how do you feel about it?"

"We feel bad, sir," said Jack. "But apparently there is no way out of the tangle."

"We've been trying to find one for the last twenty years," said the old man grimly. "How did it come to you?"

"Ah! I'm surprised at Deseret," he said, when he had heard the story. "He's old enough to know how to hold his tongue."

"How are things shaping? Have they made up their

minds to fight?" he asked. And Eager, at all events, knew how that great question bore upon the smaller.

"I think there is no doubt about it, sir," said Jack. "There is talk of some of our men going out almost at once."

"And you are both set on going?"

"Yes, sir"—very heartily from both of them.

"Well," said the old man weightily, "war is a great clearer of the air. Don't trouble your heads any more about this matter till you come home again. If you both come, we must consider what is best to be done. If only one of you comes, it will need no discussion. If neither,"—he snuffed very deliberately, looking at them as if he saw them for the first, or was looking at them for the last, time—"then, as far as you are concerned, the matter is ended. When do you return?"

"To-morrow morning, sir. We could only get short leave."

"Then perhaps you will favour me with your company at dinner to-night. And Mr. Eager will perhaps bring Miss Gracie."

They would very much have preferred the simpler hospitality of Mrs. Jex's cottage, but could not well refuse. With Sir Denzil's words in their minds they could not but recognise that, for some of them, it might well be the last time they would all meet there.

They picked up Gracie by arrangement, and all went off down along for a quick walk round some of their old haunts.

"How well I remember my first sight of these flats!" said Eager, looking with great enjoyment at the tall, clean-made, upstanding figures striding by his side. Jim, he noticed, was rather the taller and certainly the more boyish-looking. Jack had a maturer air, which doubtless came of study. But both looked eminently soldierly and likely to give a good account of themselves. "You two were just little naked savages, and you stole all my clothes but one sock, and I thought I would have to go home clad only in a towel."

"They were good old times," said Jack. "But I'm

mightily glad you came. What would we have grown up into if you hadn't?"

"Wild sand-boys," suggested Gracie.

"And what a sight you were, the first time we saw you!" laughed Jack: "in your little red bathing things, with your hair all flying, and your little arms and legs going like drumsticks—a perfect vision of delight."

"What a pity we can't always remain children!"

"You can—in all good ways," said her brother.

"One grows and one grows," she said, shaking her head knowingly, "and things are never the same again."

"They may be better," said Jack, valiantly doing his best to allow no sinking of spirits. "It would be a pretty bad look out if one could only look backwards."

Jim was unusually sober. As a rule, on such an occasion, nonsense was his vogue, and he and Gracie carried on like the children of those earlier days.

"If you ask *me*," said Gracie, venturing a flight towards olden times, "I believe old Jim here has got himself into the most awful scrape of his life, in spite of all your assertions to the contrary. *I* believe he's been and gone and lost one hundred thousand pounds at cards, and grandpa has quietly cut him off with a shilling over the usual pinch of snuff."

"No, I haven't. I've lost hardly anything, and I've got heaps of money, more than I ever had in my life before. I'll buy you a pony, if you like."

"All right! I don't mind. Sir George has a jolly one for sale; you know—Meg's Paddy. She's got too big for him, and he's just up to my feather-weight."

"We'll go along and see about him when we've been to the Mere and seen Mrs. Rimmer and Kattie. How's Kattie getting on?"

"She's a wild thing and as pretty as a rose. I'm afraid her mother worries about her. But it must be dreadfully lonely living here all the year round. Just look how grim and gray it all is. How would you like it yourself?"

"I'd like it better than London," said Jim stoutly. "If I hadn't plenty to do I'd get sick of it all—streets and houses and houses and streets, and no end to them."

"But the people! You meet lots of nice people."

"Some are nice, but there are too many of them for me. I can't remember them all, and I get muddled and feel like a fool. I'd swap them all for——"

"For what?"

"Oh—nothing!"

"You flatter them. But you'll get used to it, Jim. It takes time, of course."

"Don't know that I particularly want to get used to it. However, this war will make a change."

"You are certain to go?"

"If we don't, I'll exchange. I want to see some fighting, and to get some."

"Bloodthirsty wretch!"

"No, I don't think I really am. But if there has to be fighting I wouldn't miss it for the world. It's the only thing I'm good for. I'm no good at books, like Jack. But I believe I can fight."

Mrs. Rimmer gave them very hearty welcome, in her surprised spasmodic fashion.

"Ech, but it's good on yo' all to come an' see an old woman," she said, gazing round at them from her bed, with bright restless eyes and a curious anxious scrutiny. "Yo' grow so I connot hardly keep pace wi' yo'. It seems nobbut a year or two sin' yo' lads were running naked on the flats."

"We were just recalling it all as we came along, Mrs. Rimmer, and regretting that we couldn't remain children all our lives," said Gracie.

"Ah—yo' connot do that"—with a wistful shake of the head.

"And how's Mr. Rimmer?" asked Eager.

"Hoo's a' reet. Hoo's at his work."

"And Seth?"

"Seth's away."

"And where's Kattie?" asked Jim.

"Hoo went across to village, but heo'd ought to be home by now. But once the lasses git togither they mun clack, and they nivver know when to stop."

"Girls will be girls, Mrs. Rimmer," said Eager soothingly, "and Kattie's a girl to be proud of. She's blossomed out like a rose."

"A'm feart she's a bit flighty, an' who she gets it from I dunnot know. Not fro' me, I'm sure, nor from her feyther neither."

"Here she is," said Jim. "I hear the oars." And he jumped up and went to the door, and in another minute Kattie came in, all rosy with her exertions in the nipping air, and prettier than ever.

They chatted together for a while, Kattie's sparkling eyes roving appreciatively over the wonderful changes in her former playmates, and a great wish in her heart that the girls up at Wyvveloe could see her on such friendly terms with two such stalwart warriors.

When they got up to go she went out with them, and offered to put them across the Mere in the boat.

"Yo're going back to London?" asked Kattie of Jim, as they threaded their way through the sand-hills.

"We go back to-morrow. They don't give us long holidays, you see."

'London's a grand place, they say."

'In some ways, Kattie, but in most ways I'd sooner live at Carne."

"Ech, I'd give a moight to see London," she sighed.

"You'd soon have enough of it and want to get home again."

"It's main dull here, year in, year out. I'm sick o' sand and sea." And then they were scrambling into the boat and trimming it to the requirements of so large a party.

They said good-bye to Kattie at the other side of the Mere; and when they waved their hands to her for the last time, she was still standing watching them and wishing for the wider life beyond the sand-hills and the sea.

Sir George and Margaret Herapath gave them the warmest of welcomes, and Jim tackled the master at once on the subject of Paddy.

"But, Grace, where on earth can you keep him?" remonstrated the Rev. Charles. "I supposed it was all a joke when I heard you discussing it before."

"Paddy is no joke, as you will know when you've seen him in one of his tantrums. I shall keep him in my bedroom. He will occupy the sofa," said Miss Grace didactically.

"Was ever inoffensive parson burdened with such a baggage before?"

"You silly old dear, I'll find a dozen places to keep him in the village, and a score of willing hands to rub him down whenever he needs it."

"Of course you will," echoed Jim. "And if you can't I'll come and do it myself. Let's go and look at the dear old boy." And they sauntered off to the stables.

"See here, my boy," said Sir George, slipping his arm through Jim's, "if I'd had the slightest idea Gracie would have taken him I'd have offered him to her long since."

"You'll spoil one of the greatest enjoyments of my life if you do that, sir. Please don't!"

"But——"

"I've got heaps of money. If you've anything that would make a good charger knocking about too, I'm your man."

"Ah—you're sure of going, then?"

"If any one goes, I'm going, sir—if I have to exchange for it."

"You're all alike. George writes just in the same strain. God grant some of you may come back!"

"Some of us wouldn't be much missed if we didn't." And Sir George wondered what was wrong now.

They had no difficulty in coming to terms about Paddy, and Jim's pocket did not suffer greatly, but Sir George would not part with any of his horses to be food for powder.

Jack, feeling just a trifle left out in the matter of Paddy, obtained Gracie's permission to send her from London a new saddle and accompanying gear, and vowed they should all be the very best he could procure.

CHAPTER XXXVI

JIM'S WAY

THE boys were back in London the following night, and Jack expressed a wish to go to Covent Garden to see Mme Beteta, whose fame as a dancer had penetrated even to his den at Chatham, and of whose expressed desire to see him Jim had told him, among the many other novel experiences of his life in the metropolis.

"Why on earth should she want to see *me*?" asked Jack.

"No idea. She might not mean it, but she certainly said it. There's a lot of humbug about."

"I'd like to be able to say I've seen her dancing, anyway, though I don't care overmuch for that kind of thing. But every one's talking about her, and most of the fellows have been up to see her."

So they went, and madame's keen eyes spied them out, for, during the first interval, an attendant came round, and asking Jim, "Are you Mr. Carron?" brought him a request from madame that he would pay her a visit in her room and would bring his friend with him.

"I knew it must be your brother," she said, as she greeted them. "Yes, you are much alike."

"We used to be," said Jack, "but we're growing out of it now."

"To your friends perhaps, but a stranger could not mistake you for anything but twin-brothers," she smiled through the dusky plumes of her big fan.

"You, also, are hoping to go to the war?" she asked Jack.

"Oh, we're all hoping to go. It will be the greatest disappointment of their lives to those who have to stop behind."

"You are all terribly bloodthirsty. And yet there are very nice boys among the Russians, too."

"You have been in Russia, madame?"

"Oh yes. I have even met the Tsar Nicholas and spoken with him; though, truly, it was he did most of the talking."

"What is he like?" asked Jack eagerly.

"He is good-looking, very tall, very grand; but—well, that is about all—though, indeed, he was good enough to approve of my dancing. Stay—Manuela!"—to her old attendant—"give me the Russian bracelet out of that little box. I am going out to supper to-night or it would not be here. Yes, that is it. The Tsar gave me that himself, and he tried to smile as he did it. But smiles do not become him. He is an iceberg, and I think he is also a little bit mad. He is very strange at times. Indeed, I was glad when he went away."

"That is very interesting," said Jack; "and this is surely a very valuable present."

"An Imperial present. But I have many such, and some that I value more, though they may not be so valuable."

"You have travelled much, then, madame?"

"I have been a wanderer most of my life——"

Then there came a tap at the door, and an attendant brought in a card. Madame glanced at it and said, "Certainly. Please ask Lord Deseret to come round." And my lord followed his card so quickly that he could not have been very far away.

"Madame is kindness itself," he smiled, as he greeted her. "I saw my young friend here answering a summons, and guessed where I should find him. This"—to Jim—"must be your brother."

"Yes, sir; this is Jack." And the keen dark eyes looked Jack all through and over.

"I am very glad to make your acquaintance, my boy," he said. "I knew your father very well some twenty years ago. You have both of you a good deal of him in you."

"I have to thank you, sir," said Jack, "for my share in your kindness to Jim."

"Oh——?" And my lord looked mystified and awaited enlightenment.

"He sent on to me the half of your very generous gift——"

"Ah! he never told me that. Are you up on leave? You are at Chatham, I think."

"We got three days' leave, sir. We wanted to go down to Carne."

"Ah! I hope you had a good journey. How is Sir Denzil?"

"He is just exactly the same as ever. He has not changed a hair since ever we can remember him."

"I suppose he sticks to the old customs—shaves clean and wears a wig."

"I suppose that is it, sir. He certainly never seems to get any older."

Then madame's warning came, and Lord Deseret carried them off to his box and afterwards to supper.

And he and Jack had much interesting conversation concerning the coming war, and armaments, and so on, to all of which Jim played the part of interested listener, though in truth his mind was busy, in its slow, heavy way, on quite other matters.

"Clever boy, that," said Lord Deseret to himself, as he thought over Jack while his man was putting him to bed that night. "He will probably find his chances in this war and go far. But I'm not sure but what—yes, Jim is a right good fellow. And to think of him sending half that money to the other! I should say that was very like him, though. Now I wonder which, after all, *is* Lady Susan's boy, and how it's all going to work out. If Jack's the man, I wouldn't at all mind providing for Jim. In fact, I rather think I'd like to provide for him. Not a patch on the other in the matter of brains, of course, but something very taking about him. A look in his eyes, I think——"

CHAPTER XXXVII

A HOPELESS QUEST

IT was about a fortnight after their visit to Carne, and Jim, after several hours' hard work outside, was bolting a hasty breakfast in his quarters one morning, when his orderly came up to say that a man was wanting to see him.

"What kind of a man, Joyce?"

"An elderly man, sir; looks to me like a sailor."

"A sailor? And he wants me?"

"Yes, sir; very important, he says, and private."

"Oh well, bring him up, and, Joyce—see to my things, will you? We have an inspection at twelve. The Duke's coming down to see if we're all in order."

"Right, sir!" And Joyce disappeared with a salute, and reappeared in a moment with the fag end of it, as he ushered in—old Seth Rimmer.

"Why—Mr. Rimmer!" And Jim jumped up with outstretched hand. "Whatever brings you so far away from home? Nothing wrong, is there?"—for the old man's face was very grim and gray and hard-set, and he did not take Jim's hand, but stood holding his hat in both his own.

"Yes, Mester Jim, there's wrong, great wrong, an' I cum to see if yo'—if yo'—if—— Where's Kattie?"

"Kattie?" echoed Jim in vast astonishment.

"Ay—our Kattie! Where is she, I ask yo'. If yo'——" And he raised one knotted, trembling hand in commination.

"But—Seth—I don't understand. Sit down and tell me quietly. I know nothing of Kattie. You don't mean that she's gone away? You can't mean that. Kattie!"

"Ay—gone away—day after you wur with her."

"Good God! Kattie! And you have thought—— Oh, Seth! you couldn't think that of me?" And he sprang up and stood fronting him.

And the woeful soul, looking despairingly out of the weather-worn gray eyes into the frank boyish face, saw the black eyes blur suddenly and then blaze, and knew that its wild suspicions were unfounded.

"Ah dunnot know what to think," said the old man wearily. "Hoo's gone an' nivver a track of her. An' yo' wur there last, and yo' wur aye fond of her. An' so——"

"I would no more harm a hair of Kattie's head than I would Grace Eager's, Seth. And you ought to have known that—you who have known us all our lives."

"Ay—ah know! But hoo's gone, an' ah connot get a word of her, an'——" And the tired old arms dropped on to the table, and the weary old head dropped into them, and he sobbed with great heaves that seemed like to burst the sturdy old chest.

Jim was terribly distressed. With the wisdom that comes of deepest sympathy he rose quietly and left the old man to his grief. He found Joyce down below, busily polishing and brushing, and sent him off to procure some more breakfast, and, returning presently to his room, found old Seth as he had left him, with his head in his arms, but fallen fast asleep, and he knew that the outbreak and the rest would do him good.

He sat over against him for close on an hour, cudgelling his brains for some ray of light in this new cloud of darkness. And then, as his time was getting short, he went quietly out again, and Joyce togged him up in all his war-paint, and made him fully fit to meet the critical eyes of all the royal dukes under the sun.

Old Seth was still sound asleep when he went into the room, but he went quietly up to him and laid a hand on his shoulder, and the old man lifted his head and looked vaguely at the splendid apparition, and then began to struggle to his feet.

"It's only me, Seth. Listen now! I've got to go out for an inspection, and it may take a couple of hours or more. You are to stop here till I come back, and then we'll see what is best to be done. Here is food. Eat all you can, and then lie down on that sofa. You're done up. And don't go out of this room till I come back. You understand?"

"Ay—yo're verra good. Ah con do wi' a rest, for ah walked aw the way fro' Wynsloe."

"You must be nearly dead. Help yourself now, and I'll be back as soon as I can." And he went clanking down the stairs and swung on to his horse and away, with a dull sick feeling at the heart at thought of Kattie.

Who could have done this thing? He remembered her expressed wish to get to London, when they were walking down to the Mere that other day. It was, perhaps, not quite so bad—as yet—as old Seth feared.

The girl's longing for what seemed to her the wider, brighter life might have led her to risk her poor little fortune in the metropolis. Or it might be that she had not come to London at all, but had gone away with some village lover. But—on the whole—he was inclined to think London her more likely aim. And as to whether she had come alone he had nothing whatever to go upon.

It was long after midday before he got back to his quarters, but old Seth had not found the time any too long, having been fast asleep ever since he had eaten.

Jim got out of his trappings and lit a pipe, which he had taken to of late as at once a promoter of thought and a soother of undue exertion in that direction.

And after a time old Seth stretched himself and opened his eyes, and then sat up.

"Ah've slep'," he said quietly. "But yo' towd me to."

"You'll feel all the better for it. Now, tell me all you can about this matter, Seth, and we'll see if we can see through it. Where is young Seth?"

"Hoo's away."

"And who have you left with Mrs. Rimmer?"

"Hoo's dead and buried." And the strong old voice came near to breaking again.

"Dead!"

"Ay! It killed her. She wur not strong, as yo' know, and thought of it wur too much for her. Hoo just fretted and died."

"Oh, Seth, I am sorry—sorrier than I can tell you. That's dreadful for you."

"Ah dun' know. Mebbe it's best she's gone. Hoo'll fret no more, and hoo suffered much."

"I am very, very sorry. What could have made you think I could do such a thing, Seth? You know how we've always liked Kattie, all of us, and how good Mrs. Rimmer always was to us. How could you think any of us could do such a thing?"

"One gets moithered wi' grief, yo' know. An' that night after yo'd gone she were talking o' nowt but Lunnon, Lunnon, Lunnon, till I got sick on't. An' I towd her to shut up, and what was it had started her o' that tack? An' she said it was sect o' yo', an' yo'd bin talking o' it to her."

"As we went down to the boat she was saying how she would like to see London, and I told her she was far better off where she was. I think that was all I said, Seth."

"Ah believe yo'. She wur flighty at times, an' she got stowed o' th' sand-hills an' th' sea. It wur a dull life for a young thing, I know, but ah couldna mend it, wi' th' missus bad like that."

"It's a sad business, Seth," said Jim despondently. "And I don't know what we can do about it. If she really did come to London you might look for her here for the rest of your life and never find her."

"Ay, it's a mortal big place. The clatter an' the bustle mazes me till my head spins round. But I conna go whoam till I've looked for her."

"I'll find you a room. My man Joyce is sure to know where to get one. Have you enough money with you?"

"Ah havena much, but it mun do. When it's done ah'll go whoam."

"You must let me see to your board and lodging, at the very least, Seth——"

"Ah con pay my way—for a time. It doan't cost me much to live."

"Whatever you say, I shall see to your board and lodging, Seth, so don't make any trouble about it. I wonder now"—as a sudden idea struck him.

"Han yo' thowt o' something?"—with a gleam of hope.

"There's an old friend of my father who has been very kind to me. I was just wondering if he could help us at all."

The hope died out of Seth's eyes. From all he had ever heard of Captain Denzil he did not place much faith in any friend of his rendering any very reliable help in such a matter.

Nevertheless, it was a good thought on Jim's part.

CHAPTER XXXVIII

LORD DESERET HELPS

JOYCE solved the lodging difficulty off-hand, and old Seth, assured of bed and board, gave himself up to the impossible task of finding a lost girl who had no desire to be found.

Jim made him promise to report himself each day, so

that he could keep some track of his doings. He wrote down his address on a card and put it in his pocket, and watched him go forth the first day with many misgivings.

He saw him go out into the crowded street, bent as he had never been before, peering intently into the bewildering maze of hurrying faces, with a look of dogged perplexity as to where to go first on his own sad gray face. The throng bumped into him, and jostled him to and fro, and passed on, unheeding or vituperative, and at last he turned and went slowly out of sight, and Jim wondered if he would ever see him again.

He was dining that night with Lord Deseret, and determined to ask his advice on the matter. The very look of that calm white face gave one the impression of incomprehensibly vast experience and unusual insight into the depths of human nature. He might be able to suggest something.

My lord's immediate object, apart from his liking for the boy, was to learn the result of their visit to Carne. He had blamed himself, but not unduly, for the incautious words that had set the ball rolling. But who on earth would ever have imagined boys of that age in such ignorance of matters so vital?

He chatted pleasantly throughout the dinner, drawing from the ingenuous Jim many a little self-revelation, which all tended to the confirmation of the good opinion he had formed of him. And he found the modesty which acknowledged many lacks, and was not ashamed to ask for explanations of things it did not understand, distinctly refreshing in an age when self-assertion was much to the fore. He noticed too a lessening of the previous boyish gaiety and carelessness, and traces of the clouds which had suddenly obscured his sun.

"And how did you fare at Carne?" he asked, as soon as they were alone. "I feel somewhat guilty in that matter, you see. From what I know of it I can imagine you heard upsetting and discomforting things. Perhaps now I can be of some assistance to you."

"You are very kind to me, sir, and I wanted to ask your advice. But in that matter"—he shook his head despondently—"I don't see how any one can help. It's all a tangle, but in my own mind I'm sure Jack must be Lady Susan Sandys's boy, and that means that I—that I am——"

"You are yourself, my dear lad, and, unless I am very much mistaken, you will render a very good account of yourself when your chance comes."

"I will do my best, sir, but that does not alter the fact that I am out of it as far as Carne is concerned. And that means a great deal to me. Not that I want it for itself, but—well, there are other things——" And he stuck, with a choking in the throat.

"Don't tell me anything you don't want to, but if I can help I would very much like to."

"It's this way, sir. Jack and I are both in love with Gracie——"

"And who is Gracie, now?"

"Grace Eager—she is the sister of Mr. Eager, our curate at Wynsloe. It is he who has done everything for us——"

"He's a very fine fellow, then, and has done good work."

"Oh, he's the finest man in the world. We were growing up little savages, running wild on the flats, when he came, and he has made us into men—he and Gracie between them. And Gracie is wonderful and lovely and all that is good. And now——"

"Has she chosen Jack?"

"We are to say nothing more about it for a year—just to wait and see. You see we all grew up together, and she had never thought of us in that way, and it upset everything——"

"I think I understand. Now, my dear boy, will you take it from an old man, who has seen more of the world than perhaps has been good for him, that there is not the slightest ground for your feeling as you do. I knew your father very intimately. We had many failings in common. He behaved as we most of us behaved in those days—according to our lights, or shadows, and in accord with the times in which we lived. I cannot exonerate him any more than the rest of you. Still, do not think too harshly of him! He was the product of his age. Now, what valid grounds have you for believing your brother to be in any way better circumstanced than yourself?"

"He's so much the better man, sir. Jack's got a head on him and will——"

"If you applied that to the peerage generally, I'm afraid you would bar many escutcheons," said the old man, with a smile. "Brains by no means always follow the direct lines of descent. In fact, as you ought to know, a cross-strain frequently produces a finer result. From that point of view you may set your mind at ease. As to how the matter is to be settled eventually, that is beyond me. Time works out his own strange solutions of difficulties. I'm afraid you'll have to leave it to him. Then, again, you are both going into this war. If only one of you should come back——"

"Yes, that would settle it. I have been looking to that as the only settlement," said Jim solemnly.

"Meaning that Jack would most likely come back, and that you would most likely not."

"I think that would be the best settlement, sir. The better man should get the prizes, and there can be no question which is the better of us two."

"Jim, my boy,"—and the long thin white hand came down gently on the boy's strong brown one, and rested on it impressively—"there are better things in this world even than brains. Clean hearts, clean consciences, clean lives——"

"Jack has all those, sir."

"And so have you, and they are worth more than all the

brains in the world in some people's eyes. Did brains ever win a girl's heart?—or any one else's?"

"I'm afraid I don't know much about them, sir," said a touch of the old Jim.

"And as to the tangle," continued the old man, very well satisfied with his work, "it may be considerably more involved than you imagine. Supposing, for instance, that your father was actually married to the other girl before he married Lady Susan! Where do you find yourselves then? It is by no means impossible—such very strange things were done in those times. I could tell you of infinitely stranger things than that."

"I have hardly thought of it in that light," said Jim.

"Take my advice and think no more of your tangle. Just go ahead with the work you have in hand, and when your chance comes, as it will, make the most of it."

"You have done me good, sir. May I ask you about another matter?"

"Surely, my boy. Another tangle?"

And Jim told him briefly about Kattie, and old Seth's visit and impossible quest.

"He's a fine old fellow, and young Seth saved my life twice. I'd like to help him if I could, but I don't know what I can do. Besides, Kattie was a nice girl. She used to play with us all on the sands, you know."

"You don't know, for certain, that she has come to London?"

"Old Seth seems sure of it."

"Who else was there when you all used to play together on the sands?"

"Oh, Gracie, and Margaret and George Herapath, and Ralph Harben——"

"Who is Ralph Harben?"

"Son of Mr. Harben, Sir George's partner. They're the big army contractors, you know."

"And where is he now?"

"Up here in London. He's in the Dragoons—lieutenant. So is George."

"Any one else?"

"Mr. Eager and Sir George, and Bob Lethem, their groom. They all used to ride over, you see, and we needed all hands, so we used to press Bob into the service."

"And you don't think there is any entanglement there?"

"What—Kattie and Bob? No, I'm sure there isn't. You see, Kattie got rather large ideas, and she was certainly very pretty. She would never have looked at Bob, I'm certain."

"I will see if I can learn anything. There are ways if you know how to use them."

"Thank you, sir. I thought if any one could help us it would be you."

"How are you mounted? You ought to have a second horse if you're going out. They will allow you two, I suppose."

"I believe so. I was thinking of buying one out of that money you gave me."

"Keep it, my boy. You may need it all. You never know what may happen when you get abroad. If you'll take my advice you'll always carry a good supply in a belt next your skin when you're campaigning. I'll find you a horse up to all your requirements. You want height and bone and muscle for a charger on campaign. Beauty is a fifth consideration. Your life may depend upon your horse."

"There is no doubt about our going, then, sir?" asked the boy, with a sparkle in his eyes.

"No doubt, I'm afraid, my boy; but their plans are very undecided. I was speaking with Clarendon only last night, and, as far as I can make out, what our Government would like would be to coerce Russia by making a demonstration in force, and the Tsar is much too pig-headed for that—as they would know if they knew him as well as I do."

"You know him, sir?"

"I was ambassador there for nearly ten years, and in ten years one learns a man fairly well. He is an unusually strong-willed and determined man, bigoted too, and believes absolutely in his mission——"

"What is that, sir?"

"Oh—briefly—to conquer the world on the lines laid down by his ancestor, Peter the Great. But the man who sets out to conquer the world always finds his Waterloo sooner or later."

And Jim went home that night feeling very much less under a cloud on his own account, and not unhopeful on Seth's. For this new old friend of his impressed him deeply as one who knew a great deal more than most people, and as the kind of man who, if he took a matter up, would not rest till he attained his end.

But as for Kattie, if she had indeed come to London, he had nothing but fears.

CHAPTER XXXIX

OLD SETH GOES HOME

OLD Seth had a heart-breaking time of it.

To all intents and purposes he found himself in a foreign country. He wandered bewilderedly here and there, thinking that where the crowds were thickest there would be most chance of finding her he sought. But, to his amazement, the crowds seemed equally thick wherever he went, and every single person seemed to him to be hurrying for his or her life on business that did not admit of a moment's delay.

He lost himself regularly every day. From the moment he loosed from his quiet little harbour of refuge in the morning, till, by means of the address on his card, he found himself eventually and miraculously piloted back there by a series of top-hatted policemen, he was simply tossing to and fro on the swirling waves of the mighty whirlpool, without the slightest knowledge of where he was, except that he was in London, and Kattie was somewhere in London too.

He tried to talk to people, policemen and cabmen on the stands, who were the only ones who seemed not to be spending themselves in aimless rushings to and fro. But his uncouth speech was Hebrew to them. At first they grinned and shook their heads. Then, catching what sounded like a rough attempt at English, they tried to understand, but soon gave it up in spite of his woeful face and evident distress, and it was only when at last he wanted to get home, and produced his card, that they were able to assist him.

Fortunately the weather was cold and damp—conditions to which he was accustomed. Hot summer days and the airless, evil-smelling streets would have knocked him over in a week.

It seemed to Jim that the sad old face grew grayer and gaunter each day when he came in to give his monotonous report, which was comprehended in a dismal shake of the head and the simple word, "Nowt!"

And Jim, hopeless himself of anything coming of the disheartening quest, still did his best each day to cheer him. And Seth was glad of the chance of speaking a word or two with some one who understood his talk and sympathised with his woes.

"A most 'mazing place," he said, one time, "an' thicker wi' folk than ah could ha' believed. An' ah connot understand them an' they connot understand me. Ah wish——"

But the poor old fellow's wishes were never to be realised—not the obvious ones at all events. He was neither to find Kattie, nor to find himself safe home again in the spoiled cottage by the Mere.

Perhaps it was best so.

The inevitable happened—that which Jim had feared for

him from the time he saw him drift helplessly away into the crowd that first day.

He had written all about the matter to Jack, and Jack's reply, while it lacked nothing in sympathy for old Seth in his bereavements, yet expressed in unmistakable language the writer's astonishment and indignation that he could for one moment have thought any of them guilty of such a deed.

Jim had also waited hopefully on Lord Deseret, to see if his efforts had met with any success. But, so far, they had not.

"I confess I had certain ideas on the subject," said his lordship, "and I have had them followed up, but quite without result. My people are entirely at fault. Is it possible we are all on a false scent and she is nearer home all the time? The indications pointing to her having come to London are, after all, exceedingly slight and vague."

"I've no idea," said Jim despondently. "I wish the old chap would go home. He can do no good here and he's on my mind day and night. I'm certain he'll get run over one of these days."

And, sure enough, there came a day when no Seth put in an appearance, and Jim's fears felt themselves justified.

He sent Joyce round to his lodgings. The old man had never turned up the night before.

It came at a bad time too, for they were working might and main at their preparations for the coming campaign. The Guards had left for Southampton the day before. They themselves were down for service and the call might come any day. War, indeed, had not yet been formally declared, but that was a minor matter. There was no doubt about what was going to happen.

So Jim packed off Joyce in a hansom, with orders to make the round of the hospitals and report at once if he got any news.

He was back at midday. The old man was lying at Guy's, broken to pieces and not expected to last the day out.

Jim jumped into the cab with a very heavy heart. It was just what he had feared, and it was terribly sad. And yet, as his cab wormed its slow course through the traffic about London Bridge, there came to him a dim apprehension that what seemed to them so sorrowful a happening might, after all, in some inscrutable way, be the better way for old Seth. For his life, if he had lived, must have been a sad and broken affair, and now——

He found the old man lying quietly in his bed, with the screens already drawn round it. He was only just in time.

The gaunt gray face brightened at sight of him, as Jim took his hand gently and sat down beside him.

"Ah'm fain to see yo'," he said, with difficulty. "'Twur a waggin . . . aw my fault. . . . Tell her. . . . Tell her . . ." —the crushed chest laboured in agony,—"tell her to come whoam. . . ."

And presently, without having spoken again, the dim light failed suddenly in the weather-worn gray eyes, and the life faded out of the gnarled brown hand, and Jim, boy still, put down his head and sobbed at the grim sadness of it all.

A nurse peeped round the screen and was surprised at the sight, for the eagerness of the splendid young officer to get to the uncouth old wreck, of whom, beyond his mortal injuries, they had been able to make so little, had impressed them all.

It was not till Jim had mopped himself up at last, and stood taking a last sad look at the tired old face, that she came in again.

"You knew the old man, sir?" she said sympathetically, behind which lay considerable curiosity.

"I've known him all my life. He's one of our people from Carne. It's terribly sad, you know. His daughter left home, and he came up to look for her. Think of it—to look for her in London! And I was afraid, all the time, how it would end. And it has. Poor old Seth!"

He told them all they wanted to know, and arranged with them to have the old man decently buried, and gave them money for the purpose and something for the hospital, and his own name and address.

"Then you're going to the war," said the nurse, with an animated face.

"Oh yes; we may go any day now."

"You ought to take some of us with you. You'll need us, you'll see."

He had promised to call on Mme Beteta that afternoon, and would have put off the visit but that he knew she would be disappointed, and she had shown herself so very kindly disposed towards him.

So he went, but madame's shrewd eyes fathomed his state of mind at once.

"Now you have some trouble, and perhaps it is my chance to be of use," she said, and bit by bit drew from him all the story of Kattie's disappearance and old Seth's death.

"If any one can find her, Lord Deseret will. He is a very, very clever old man, and in some things very young. She is pretty, you say?"

"We always thought her very pretty, even as a wild girl about the sands, and she has grown prettier still."

"London is a bad place for a pretty girl such as she. Even if you find her——" And she broke off and looked at him musingly. "What could you do if you did find her?"

"Get her to go home."

"And if she would not?"

"Then—I don't know. It is horrible to think of Kattie running loose in London."

"When Lord Deseret finds her, bring her to me and I will see what I can do," said madame thoughtfully; and there the matter rested.

CHAPTER XL

OUT OF THE NIGHT

JIM reaped—and duly passed along to Jack—the benefit of Lord Deseret's long and wide experience of life under many conditions. As a young man he had served with Wellington in the Peninsula, and he had also been with him at Waterloo, where he had, as fellow aide-de-camp, Fitzroy Somerset, now Lord Raglan, who was to command the present expedition to the East.

So Jim and my lord between them evolved, by process of continuous elimination, a campaigning kit, which, if to Jim's inexperienced eyes it lacked much, comprehended, according to his lordship, everything that was absolutely necessary, and probably even yet some things which he would hasten to throw away under pressure of circumstance.

"How long it will last it is hard to say," said Lord Deseret. "If you should by any chance be kept there till the winter I will send you out all you will need."

"Oh, surely we and the Frenchmen between us can clean it all up before then," said innocent Jim.

"We shall know better when we learn where you're bound for, and what you've got to do. At present no one seems to know. They are all very mysterious about it, which is all right if it's policy, but if it's ignorance——"

Jack was first to go, and Jim was mightily put out that engineers should get ahead of cavalry. They had hoped to be able to run down to Carne to say good-bye, but that was quite out of the question. The army had been rusting, more or less, for forty years, and, now that the call had come, every man on the roll was hard at work scraping the accumulated deposit off his bit of the machine, and oiling the parts. The days were all too short for what had to be done, and leave was out of the question.

Jim was here, there, and everywhere, helping to buy horses for the coming wastage, for if he had no head for business he certainly knew horses from tail to muzzle, from hoof to shoulder, and all in between. He was kept hard at work till the call came for the cavalry, and then every minute of every day was over-full, and his head spun with the calls upon his forethought and ingenuity.

He made long lists of the things he had to see to, on scraps of paper with a pencil that was always blunt and often missing, and as each item was attended to he duly scored it off, and so kept fairly straight.

His men had taken to him, and consulted him now as an oracle, and within his capacity he enjoyed it all immensely.

Lord Deseret's munificence knew no bounds. In addition to a great brown charger, whose peculiar delights were military music and the roar of artillery—the first of which enjoyments the campaign was unfortunately to offer him few opportunities of indulging in, though he had his fill of the other—his lordship presented Jim with a pair of unusually fine silver-mounted revolvers, of a calibre calculated to make short work of the biggest Russian born, and one of these he was to hand over to Jack as soon as they met out East. And for Jim himself, as a very special mark of his goodwill, he bought a sword, selected out of many and suiting his grip and reach as if it had been made for him.

"A most gentlemanly weapon," said the old man, as he poised it with knowledge in his thin white hands. "May it help you to carve your way to much honour! But war is not a gentlemanly business nowadays. That other brutal little thing will probably serve you better."

And so we come to the very last night. The 8th were to leave at six the next morning for Southampton, and Jim was making his way back to his quarters, dead tired, but vaguely hopeful that he had failed in none of the multifarious calls on these last short hours.

His list had been an unusually long one that day. But he had ploughed doggedly through it, and reduced it item by item, till it was cleared off. After his actual military duties had come final letters to Gracie and Mr. Eager and his grandfather—he might never see any of them again. All the same he wrote in the best of spirits, though in grievous regret at not being able to run down and say good-bye.

Then he had made a round of farewell calls among the friends he had made in London, and had even made time to drop in on Mme Beteta for a cup of tea. He had finished up with a quiet dinner with Lord Deseret in Park Lane, and now, in the spirit, England lay behind him, and his compass pointed due east.

Out of the depths of his very large experience, Lord Deseret had given him many a useful hint and much wise advice over their cigars and coffee, and had finally shaken his hand and bidden him "God-speed!" with more emotion than Jim had believed it possible for that calm white face to show.

And Mme Beteta, too, had held his hand as he said "Good-bye," and said, with much feeling, "I would have been glad if you had got into some mischief so that I might have had the pleasure of helping you. I will hope all the time to see you come back alive and whole."

"You are all too good to me," laughed Jim, overcome by the kindness he was everywhere meeting with. "I feel as if I was getting more than my proper share. If Jack had been here now, you'd have thought ever so much more of him."

"Perhaps!" smiled madame. "We will see when you both come back."

He was hurrying back to his quarters, bent on getting a good night's sleep if possible, since the coming nights on board ship might be less conducive thereto, when, as he swung round a corner where a gas lamp hung, deep in his own thoughts and with his head bent down, a timid hand fell on his arm, and as he hastily shook it off, a soft voice jerked:

"Jim!"

He whirled round in vast amazement, and got a shock.

"Kattie! . . . oh, *Kattie!*"

"I did so want to see you before you went. I only heard to-day——"

She looked so pretty in the fluttering light of the lamp, so touchingly soft and sweet, like some beautiful wild bird drawn to a possibly hostile hand by stress of need and prepared for instant flight.

She was very nicely dressed too, better than he had ever seen her before, in well-fitting dark clothes and a little fur pork-pie hat, like the one Gracie used to wear in the winter. And under it her eyes shone brightly and her face glowed and quivered with many emotions.

The passers-by were beginning to notice and look back at them. He led her into a quieter side-street where there was almost no traffic.

"But what are you doing here, Kattie? We have been searching for you for a month past, and now——"

"I couldn't help it, Jim. I had to come——"

"But why, Kattie? Why? Do you know what you've done by running away like that?" And he could not keep the feeling out of his voice, as he thought of poor old Seth, and her mother, and the broken home. "Your mother is dead. It killed her." Kattie's hands were over her face and she was sobbing. "And your father came to London to look for you, and got run over. His hand was in mine as he died, and his last words were for you, 'Tell her to come home!' he said, and then he died."

The slender figure shook with sobs. Perhaps he had been too brutal to blurt it out like that. He ought to have broken it to her by degrees.

"Oh, why did you do it, Kattie?" he said, more gently.

And Kattie, shaken out of herself by his news and his manner, sobbed out her secret.

"Jim, Jim, don't be so hard to me! It was for you, you, you——"

"*Kattie!*" he cried, aghast.

"Yes," she choked on, in a passion of surrender and self-revelation. "It was you I wanted—you—always. And I thought if I could only get to London where you were——"

"Oh, Kattie!" And he could say no more for the feeling that was in him, and Kattie hung on to his arm and he did not shake her off.

"Kattie," he said at last, in a deep hoarse voice, "has it been my fault? I did not know——"

"No, no, no! It was not your fault. But I could not help it."

"I am very sorry, dear. If I had known—but I never dreamt of it. How did you get here?"

She hesitated, and then said, briefly:

"I got some one to bring me."

"Who?"

"I cannot tell you."

"It was an evil thing to do, whoever it was, and I hope some of the sorrow will fall upon him," he said hotly. "But you must not stop here, Kattie. You must go home."

"Home!" she said wildly. "I have no home. I will wait here till you come back from the war, Jim——"

"Kattie! . . . For God's sake, don't talk like that! You don't know what you are saying, child. I may never come back at all . . . And if I do——"

"Oh, Jim! *Jim!*"

She hardly knew what she was saying. She only knew that for months she had been longing for Jim, and now he was here, and he was going, and she might never see him again.

The pretty, quivering, wild-rose face was turned up to his. Her eager arms stole round his neck.

"*Jim!*"

Now, thanks be to thee, Charles Eager, muscular Christian and strenuous apostle of clean living and the higher things!—sitting by your dying fire in Mrs. Jex's cottage at Wyvveloe, thinking much of your boys and praying for them, perchance,—nay, of a certainty, for thoughts such as yours are prayers and resolve themselves into familiar phrases—"that they fall into no sin, neither run into any kind of danger"—"from battle and murder and from sudden death,"—at which the thinker by the fire fell into deeper musing. And thanks be to all your teaching of the Christian virtues and truest manhood, both by precept and example!

For Jim Carron was only a man like other men, and young blood is hot. And Kattie, in her fervour, was more than pretty.

Jim's big chest rose and fell as if he had been running a race—say with the devil, or as if he had been engaged in mortal combat. Perhaps he had—both.

He broke her hands apart with a firm, gentle grip.

"Kattie dear! You don't know what you are saying. You know it can't be. God help us! What am I to do with you?"

And then he bethought him of Mme Beteta and saw his way.

"Come with me!" he said, and drew her arm tightly through his and led her down the street, and on and on till they came to a thoroughfare where there were cabs. He hailed one, handed her in, gave the driver the address, and sat down beside her.

Kattie asked no questions. She was with Jim. That was enough. Her arm stole inside his again and nestled and throbbed there. She would have asked no more—not very much more—than to ride by his side like that in the joggling cab for ever.

The cab stopped at last before the house in South Audley Street. Jim jumped out and rang the bell, paid the man, and led her up the steps.

"Is madame in?" he asked of the maid who opened the door.

"Just come in, sir."

"Will you beg her to see me for a moment?" And she showed them into a small sitting-room and went noiselessly away.

"Will you please to come to madame's room, sir?" And they were ushered into the cosy room where Mme Beteta had just sat down to supper before a blazing fire. Her wraps lay on the sofa where she had flung them on entering.

She looked laxed and tired, all except her face, and her great dark eyes opened wide at sight of Kattie. Jim had indeed told her that the girl they were searching for was pretty, but this girl, with all that was working in her still in her face and her eyes, was very much more than pretty.

"Mme Beteta, will you do something for me?" began Jim impulsively.

"I have only been waiting the opportunity, my boy, as I told you this afternoon. What is it now—and who is your friend? Won't you sit down, my dear?" to Kattie. "You look very tired."

Kattie sank into the proffered chair, and Jim stood behind it.

"This is Kattie Rimmer, a friend of ours from Carne. She finds herself suddenly alone in London. If you will take care of her I would be so grateful to you."

"Indeed I will, if she will stop with me for a time. You are much too good-looking, my dear, to be alone in this big place. I shall be glad to have something young and pretty about me. My dear old Manuela is worth her weight in gold, but, truly, she is no beauty. And when I go abroad, presently, you shall come with me there also, if you feel so inclined."

Madame understood—partly, at all events, and possibly guessed wrongly at the rest. But there was no mistaking her kindliness. She saw that the girl was under the influence of some overpowering emotion, and she talked on for the sake of talking and to give her time.

"Kattie dear, will you promise me to stop with madame?" asked Jim anxiously. For it was one thing to have got her there—and a great thing; but it might be quite another thing to get her to stop.

"Must I, Jim?" And the great eyes, swimming with tears, snatched a hasty glance at him.

"Yes, Kattie, you must. And, madame, I cannot thank you enough. Sometime, perhaps—if I come back alive——"

And at that, Kattie sprang up and flung her arms round his neck again, crying, "Oh, Jim! Jim!"

And he kissed her gently and put her away, and she sank down into the chair, a convulsive heap of sobs.

He mutely begged madame to follow him, and left the room.

"It is terribly sad," he said to her, in the other room. "I met her near my quarters to-night. She had been waiting for me, and she says—she says"—he stumbled—"well, she says she came to London after me. And, you know, I never had a thought of her—poor little Kattie! And I didn't know what to do with her, and so I brought her to you."

"You did quite right, my boy. For your sake—and, yes—for her own—I will do my best for her. She is a pretty little thing—much too pretty to go to waste in London."

"You are very good, madame, and I am very grateful. Perhaps you would consult Lord Deseret about her too, if you think well. He has been very kind in the matter."

"And you have no feeling for her at all?"

"There is only one girl in all the world for me, and that is Gracie Eager. You'll understand when you see her."

Then he wrung her hand very warmly, and said a final good-bye, and went away,—very tired, but with something of a load off his heart as regarded Kattie at all events.

CHAPTER XLI

HORSE AND FOOT

THE dullest pages in history are those which record the long, slow years of peace and progress, when everything goes well and nothing lively happens.

Jack's term of service at Chatham had been such. His record was one of simple hard work, considerable acquirement, and a methodic, level life.

His work appealed to him, and he gave himself up to it heart and soul, and might have given his health as well if the authorities had not seen to it. Brains in an officer were very acceptable, and the concentrated application of them still more so—to say nothing of the comparative rarity of the combination. But brains without body would obviously be of small service to the country, and so Jack was kept fairly fit in spite of himself. He won the golden opinions of his instructors and examiners, and was looked upon as a reliable officer and a coming man.

"Give us a good tough bit of siege work," he had said, with hot enthusiasm, as they tramped the frozen sands at Carne that last time, "and we'll show them what we are made of."

"A good open country and plenty of room for cavalry to manœuvre, that's what *we* want," said Jim, with relish, "and we'll show the world what British squadrons can do."

"Tough sieges somehow seem a bit out of date," said Mr. Eager. "I should say Jim's horses are more likely to be in it."

"I'd sooner have the siege," said Gracie; and they all clamoured to know why, and Jim felt humpy.

"Oh, just because you're all farther away from one another and not so likely to get hurt," said she. "When you fight on horses you're bound to get close to one another."

"That's what we want," growled Jim. "The closer the better."

"And then the poor horses!" said Gracie, with a shiver.

"To say nothing of the poor men!" growled Jim once more.

"It's all horrid and hateful and wicked. I don't mean you two," she added hastily, "but the people who bring it about. If they all had to fight themselves, instead of sending other people to do it for them, they wouldn't be so ready to begin."

"They'd make a pretty poor show, some of them," laughed Jack. "Think of little Johnny Russell facing up to the Tsar."

"David and Goliath," suggested the Rev. Charles.

"Goliath got the stone in his eye—well, in his head, it's all the same—and so he will this time," said Jim.

"Artillery!" said Jack triumphantly.

"David cut off his head," said Gracie.

"Infantry assault after we—I mean the artillery—had made the breach."

Involved military operations, and especially the complicated strategy of the siege, had fascinated Jack from the time he could read. He absorbed the elements of his profession with keenest delight; and driest details, which to some of his fellows were but dull drudgery, were to him like the necessary part of a puzzle of which he held the clue, and their essentiality was clear to him.

What would be the course of the coming war none could tell, for the simple reason that no one seemed to know exactly where they were going or what they were going to do. All arms were to be represented, however, and each separate branch hoped ardently that the tide would run its way.

Jack and Jim, at parting, had undertaken to correspond regularly. They had also mutually pledged themselves to write not more than one letter a week to Gracie.

If Jim's scrawls had hitherto been the more interesting

to their recipients, it was certainly not by reason of their penmanship, or their spelling, or their literary qualities, but simply that, living in London and somewhat in the whirl of things, and with more time and mind for outside matters than Jack had, he had always something to tell about, and that, after all, is what people want.

Very sympathetic—and certainly very charming—little smiles used to lurk in the corners of Gracie's flexible little mouth as she read Jim's epistles. And she would murmur, "The dear boy!" as she thought of the time and labour he had given to their production. For to Jim the sword was very much mightier than the pen and infinitely more to his liking.

He told Gracie, in his letters, most of what befell him in London, much about Lord Deseret, and much about Mme Beteta, but concerning Kattie and old Seth Rimmer, after much ponderous consideration, he had thought it best to keep silence.

Jack had waxed mightily indignant over old Seth's half-blown suspicions, and on the whole it was perhaps just as well that the old man fell into Jim's hands.

Of the final episode Jim told none of them. In the first place, he felt bound to keep Kattie's secret. In the second, he went straight home to his bed that night as tired as a dog, and was *en route* for the East soon after six o'clock next morning. And in the third place, as to telling Jack, Jack was on the high seas nearing Gallipoli, and they did not see one another again for months to come.

CHAPTER XLII

DUE EAST

JACK, to his immense delight, found himself detailed for duty with a large number of his men to assist General Canrobert in the fortification of the long narrow peninsula on which Gallipoli is situated.

No matter that the fortifications were little likely to be of any actual benefit, it was active service and turning to practical account the theoretical knowledge of which he was full.

The men, who had left England ablaze with warlike fervour amid the cheers of the populace, had found their long detention at Malta very trying and relaxing. Warlike fervour cannot keep at boiling-point unless it has something to expend itself upon. And so they welcomed this diversion, and planned, and built earthen ramparts, and bastions, and barbettes, and ravelins, and redoubts, to their hearts' content; and felt very much better both in mind and body than when they were kicking their heels and frizzling in the tawny dust of Malta.

There were many discomforts, however, chiefly in regard to the provisioning. Even at this very first stage in the proceedings the men had little to eat and less to drink; and if curses could have assisted the commissariat, or blighted it off the face of the earth, its movements would have been mightily quickened. But forty years of peace do not make for efficiency in the fighting machine. It had grown rusty through disuse, as all machines will, and the ominous creakings which began at Gallipoli never ceased till—too late for the hosts of gallant souls who died of want before Sebastopol—England awoke at last to the shame of her relapse, and set her house in order with a roar of righteous, but belated, indignation.

Jack and his men fared better than most, through their intimacy with the Frenchmen, who had the knack of living in plenty where others starved. Jack brushed up his French, and found welcome, and still more welcome hospitality, among the officers, and his men learned how tasty dinners could be made out of the scantiest of rations if only you knew how to do it.

But the slow weeks dragged on; there was no sign of an enemy, and the fighting for which they had come out seemed as far off as ever. And the little advance army growled and grizzled and cursed things in general, and began to get a trifle mouldy. And meanwhile the Turks, under Omar, were valiantly holding the Danube against the Russians, and the allied generals were in communication with the allied ambassadors at Constantinople, and the ambassadors were in communication with the un-allied diplomatists at Vienna, and the diplomatists were seeking instructions from London, Paris, Berlin, and St. Petersburg, and futile talk blocked the way of warlike deeds.

It was the middle of May before the welcome order came to move on, and their spirits rose at the prospect. They had come out to fight, and anything was better than moulting at Gallipoli.

But the diplomats were still chopping words at Vienna, so they were all dumped down again at Scutari, till the wise men should see which way the cat was really going to jump.

More weary weeks followed, though, since they gave Jack the chance of seeing a great deal of Constantinople, he at all events had no cause for complaint. The neat little steamer, which the Sultan had placed at the disposal of the British officers, ran across in a quarter of an hour and plied to and fro constantly; and having no duties to perform, Jack missed none of his opportunities and saw all he could, and that included many strange sights.

He made many new acquaintances, and began to lose somewhat of the studious concentration which had hitherto stood in the way of his making any very close friendships even at Woolwich and Chatham. He had given heart and brain to his work, and now only craved the opportunity of applying his knowledge and climbing the ladder. While frivolous Jim, with a modicum of the brains and still less of the application, somehow possessed the knack of making friends wherever he went. And having mastered his drill and won the hearts of his men, he also considered his military education completed, and longed only to get the chance of showing what was in him and them.

Jim would have had a delightful time in Constantinople, and, with all his desire for glory, would still have enjoyed himself thoroughly; but Jack, with most of his fellows, felt keenly that all this was not what they had come out for; and when, in June, orders came to embark for Varna, up along the coast of the Black Sea towards the Danube, he was heartily glad. For there had been heavy fighting on the Danube, and if they could only get there in time there might still be a chance of showing what they were made of.

It was four months since they left England, and so far they had practically done nothing more than mark time, and there is a certain monotony about that necessary but fruitless operation which has a depressing effect on spirits and bodies alike.

However, they were getting on by degrees at last, though what their ultimate objective really was no one seemed to know, unless, perhaps, Lord Raglan and Marshal St. Arnaud, and they kept their own counsel.

Jack had been a fortnight at Varna, and was beginning to get sick of it as he had of Malta and Gallipoli, when one day the stately *Himalaya* steamed quietly in among the mob of smaller craft which crowded Varna Bay, and began to discharge the first of the cavalry that had put in an appearance. This looked like business, and Jack joined the crowd watching the disembarkation.

"Hello, Jim, old boy!"

"Hello, Jack! That you?" And the boys of Carne had met again.

"Hardly knew you in those togs. Took you for a tramp," grinned Jim.

"You loaf here for half a dozen weeks, my boy, and you'll come to it. Have you any news? Are we going on? We're all sick to death of the whole business."

"*I* dunno. We've come straight through. We began to be afraid we'd be too late and miss all the fun."

"You've not missed much so far. We've been frizzling

and grizzling all this time. Never seen the ghost of a Russian so far."

"Waiting for us, I expect. Can't get on without cavalry."

"If that's what we've been waiting for we're all mighty glad to see you. All this hanging about is the hardest work I've ever done yet."

"Where are you living?"

"Up on the hill there. You'll be going on to Devna, I expect. That's twenty miles further up."

"I've got to look after the horses. They've done splendidly so far. Not lost a leg. We'll have a talk when we knock off." And Jim turned to the congenial work of seeing his equine friends safely ashore.

When he had seen them all picketed on the stretch of turf near the beach, and enjoyed for a time their rollings and stretchings and kickings of cramped heels, he walked away up the shore, had his first delicious swim in the Black Sea, and then made his way into the dirty little town and struggled slowly through its narrow streets, packed with such a heterogeneous assortment of nationalities as his wondering eyes had never looked upon before.

Guardsmen, Fusiliers, Riflemen, Highlanders, Dragoons, and Hussars, Lancers, Chasseurs, Zouaves, Artillerymen, and Cantinières; Greeks, Turks, Italians, Smyrniotes, Bashi-Bazouks, and nondescripts of all shapes and sizes; dark, windowless little shops with streaming calico signs in many languages, offering for sale every possible requirement from pickles to saddlery, but especially drinks; a slow-moving, chattering, chaffering, and occasionally quarrelling, mob of shakos, turbans, fezes, Highland bonnets, *képis*, and wide-awakes, with bearded faces under them in every possible shade of brown and mud-colour,—no wonder it took Jim a long time to get through.

But he got out into the open country at last, and breathed clean air again, and climbed the hill and found his way to Jack's tent, and demanded something to drink.

"What a place!" he gasped. "Never saw such a sight in my life!"

"Beastly hole!" growled Jack. "I wish to Heaven they'd get us on and give us some work to do."

"Why don't they?"

"Ah—why don't they? Some one may know, but I'm beginning to doubt it. When we came up here we had hopes again, but now they say the Russians have had enough on the Danube and are bolting, so that's off. What's the news from home? I've hardly had a letter since we left."

Jim gave him of his latest, and handed him Lord Deseret's present, which Jack found greatly to his taste.

"No more news of Kattie?" he asked presently, when other subjects seemed exhausted, and in a tone that anticipated a negative reply.

"Yes. I found her—the very last night," said Jim quietly.

"You did? How was it?"

"I had been dining with Lord Deseret, and saying good-bye all round, and was dead tired. We were to start at six next morning and I was hurrying home to get some sleep, when suddenly Kattie stepped up and spoke to me."

"Good God! Did she know it was you?"

"Oh yes. She hadn't got so low as all that. But it gave me a shock, I can tell you, Jack, to meet her like that, though we had been doing all we could to find her."

"And how did she seem? And what had she to say for herself?"

"She looked prettier than I'd ever seen her—better dressed, you know, and all that."

"And what did she say?"

"She flatly refused to tell me who had brought her to London. She had heard we were leaving in the morning and she wanted to say good-bye—so she said."

"Deuced odd! What did you do?"

"Well—I was knocked all of a heap and didn't know what to do. Then I suddenly bethought me of Mme Beseta. She had been very kind to me, and only that afternoon, when I was saying good-bye, she had laughed and said her only regret was that I hadn't got into any scrape that she could help me out of. It was jolly nice of her, you know. So I bundled Kattie into a cab, and took her straight to madame, and left her with her."

"Poor little Kattie! She was too good for that kind of thing. And you got no hint as to who——"

"Not a word. I asked her straight, and she said she would not tell."

"I'd like to wring his neck for him, whoever he was."

"She probably knew we would feel that way, and that's why she wouldn't speak. And how have you been keeping, Jack? Seems to me you look thinner. Perhaps it's the way you dress—or don't dress. I never saw such a seedy, weedy-looking set. You'd certainly be taken for tramps in England."

"Just you wait, my boy. If you get four months of this infernal loafing in dust and dirt and blazing sun, you'll come to it. And I may well be thin. I'd hang every commissary in the service. They starve us half the time and give us rubbish the rest."

"That sounds bad. What's got them?"

"Everything's at sixes and sevens. All the food and drink in one place and all the hungry and thirsty souls in another, some hundreds of miles away. If I was the Chief I'd hang a commissary every time the men go short. And the amount of red-tape! Oh, Lord! But you'll know all about it before you're through, my boy. Some of the fellows have chucked it and gone home."

"Rotters!"

"I don't know. It's been almost beyond endurance at times, and all so senseless, and nothing comes of it. Starving for a good cause is one thing, but starving simply because the men who ought to feed you are fools is quite another."

"Overworked, I expect."

"Undertrained, I should say. I'll ask you three months hence what you think about it all."

Jim was very busy the next few days getting his men and horses on to Devna. His chiefs had found out that he could get more out of men and horses than most, and that when he took a thing in hand he did it. So work was heaped upon him and he was as happy as could be.

He messed with Charlie Denham in a little tent on the shore, bathed morning and night, and Joyce and Denham's man saw that their masters—and incidentally themselves—were properly fed.

CHAPTER XLIII

JIM TO THE FORE

CAVALRY transports were coming in every day now; the Varna beach looked like a country horse-fair, and to Jim was given the task of superintending the debarkation of the horses and their dispatch to their appointed places.

One day, when the great raft on which the horses were floated to the shore bumped up against the little pier, a nervous brown mare broke loose and jumped overboard. There happened to be no small boats close at hand, and the poor beast, white-eyed with terror at the shouts of the onlookers, struck out valiantly for the open sea.

To Jim, in the thinnest and oldest garments he possessed, and sweating heartily from his labours, an extra bath was but an additional enjoyment. He leaped aboard, ran nimbly along outside the horses, and launched himself after the snorting evader. His long swift side-stroke soon carried him alongside.

He soothed her with comforting words, turned her head shorewards, and presently rode her up the beach amid the bravos of the onlookers. It was little things like that that won the hearts of his men. They knew he would do as much and more for any one of them.

As he slipped off, with a final pat to the trembling beast, a hearty hand clapped his wet shoulder.

"Well done, old Jim! It was Carne taught you that, old man." And the voice of the gigantic dragoon, whose clap was still tingling in his shoulder, was the voice of George Herapath, though Jim had to look twice at his face to make sure of him.

"Why, you hairy man, I'd never have known you. Just got here?"

"This minute, my boy, and glad to see you old stagers still alive and kicking. Here's Harben. I say, Ralph, this dirty wet boy is our old Jim."

"Hanged if I'd have jumped into the sea after an old troop-horse," said Harben, looking somewhat distastefully at the dishevelled Jim.

"A horse is always a horse," said Jim, "and an extra bath's neither here nor there. Can't have too many this weather, if you work as I've been doing lately."

"Deucedly dirty work, it seems to me. Why don't you let your men do it? That's what they're here for."

"They are doing it," said Jim, waving a benedictory wet hand towards the horse-fair along the beach. "I'm only keeping an eye on them."

And before they could say more, a very splendidly accoutred horseman rode down to them, with a still more gorgeous one behind him.

"Very smartly done, my boy," said the first in English, though he wore the uniform of a colonel of Cuirassiers. "An officer that looks after his horses will certainly look after his men."

"Hello, sir!" jerked Jim. "Glad to see you again! Sorry I'm so dirty."

"It's the men who get dirty who do the work." And then he

turned to the magnificent personage behind, who sat looking on with a suave smile on his clean-shaven face, and said in French, "This is one of my cubs, Your Highness, though I'll be crucified if I know which." And turning to Jim—"Let me see, now, you're——"

"I'm Jim, sir. Jack's in the Engineers."

"Ah, yes—Jim. It was the Prince who bade me come down and thank you for saving that mare, and it was only when I heard your friend mention Carne that I recognised you. Monsieur——?" to the Prince, who addressed some remark to him in French, to which he laughingly replied, and then turned again to Jim.

"His Highness says he would like to see you cleaned up, and invites you to his table to-night—both of you, if you can come.. I suppose you can fig out all right?"

Jim saluted Prince Napoleon and bowed.

"It is a great honour," he said. "I'll find Jack, sir, and we'll fig out all right."

"Eight o'clock, then. We're camped over there for the night. Any one will show you the Prince's quarters." And the two horsemen saluted generally and galloped away.

"You're in luck, old boy," said George. "Dining with princes and big-pots. Who's the other? He talks uncommonly good English for a Frenchman."

"My father," said Jim quietly.

"Your—— Good Lord! Well, I—— Yes, of course, now I remember."

"All the same," said Jim, "princes are not much in my line, and I'd just as soon he hadn't asked me."

"Man alive!" said Ralph, with exuberance. "Why, I'd give my little finger for the chance."

"And where's old Jack?" asked George.

"Up on the hill there behind the town."

"And where do we go?"

"You stop the night here and get on to Devna to-morrow. It's about twenty miles up-country."

Jack was mightily astonished when Jim gave him his news, and showed no modest reluctance in accepting the invitation.

"It's always interesting to meet people like that," he said. "Is he like the Emperor?"

"He's not like his pictures. More like the first Emperor, I should say. But he seemed pleasant enough."

"And our paternal?"

"He was all right. They seemed on very good terms with one another."

"And he really is as big a man as he led us to believe that night?"

"Why, yes, he seemed so. Did you doubt it?"

And so, all in their best, they duly presented themselves at the Prince's quarters a few minutes before eight, Jack, in his modest Engineer uniform, feeling somewhat overshadowed by Jim's gorgeous Hussar trappings.

"By Jove! but don't they know how to make themselves at home!" said Jack, as they came in sight of the handsome tent, with a great green bower made of leafy branches in front and an enclosure of the same all round it.

The sentries passed them in at once, and their father came out from the tent and met them with cordial, outstretched hands. He held both their hands for a moment, and looked from one to the other.

"Jack is the Engineer, and Jim is the Hussar, and both of you very creditable Carrons. We must get to know one another better, my boys. The coming campaign should afford us plenty of opportunities."

"Is there to be a campaign, then, sir?" asked Jack. "We'd about given up all hopes of it."

"Oh, we're not through yet by any means," smiled the Colonel.

"I don't know how it is with your men, sir, but all this dawdling about is doing ours no good."

"It is good for nobody, my boy, but we've got to obey orders, and those who pull the strings are far away. However,

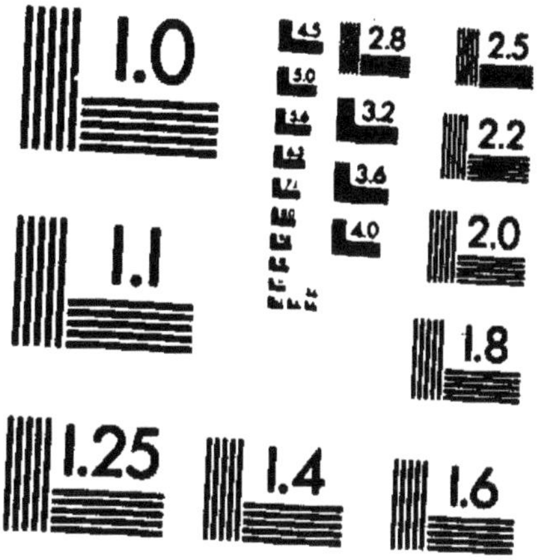

you need have no fear. The Tsar is far too stiff-necked to give way till he's had a good thrashing, and we have not only to fight him, but distance and climate to boot. Here is His Highness."

And when he introduced them, the Prince, with a smile at Jim, and a pat on the shoulder, told him he would certainly have had difficulty in recognising him again, and he was a "brave boy," which set the brave boy blushing furiously under his tan.

"They are grumbling at getting no fighting, Your Highness," said the Colonel.

"Young blood! Young blood!" said the Prince, with a smile. "Let us hope they will have plenty left when the fighting is over."

A number of other bravely dressed officers came in, and in the long green bower they sat down to a dinner such as they had not tasted for months, and of which they many times thought enviously in the lean months that followed.

CHAPTER XLIV

JIM'S LUCK

JIM, by force of circumstance, acquired a very wholesome reputation as the best-mounted man in the Light Brigade, as a tireless rider, and as an officer who doggedly carried out his instructions. The result was much hard work, which he enjoyed, and much commendation, which he thoroughly deserved.

When the Russians retired from the Danube and disappeared into the wilds of Wallachia, Lord Cardigan was ordered to follow them with a party of gallopers and learn what route they had taken.

The first man picked for his troop was Jim Carron, and

Jim was wild with delight. Here, at last, was something out of the common to be done, something with more than a spice of danger in it, and altogether to his liking.

They were away for seventeen days, camping as best they could without tents, and they rode through three hundred miles of the wildest and most desolate country Jim had ever set eyes on. For one hundred miles at a stretch they never saw a human being, but finally got on the track of the Russians and found they had gone by way of Babadagh. Then they rode up the Danube to Silistria and returned to camp by way of Shumla, somewhat way-worn as to the horses, but the men fit and hard as nails.

But they were the fortunate ones, and their satisfaction with their lot could not leaven the seething mass of growling discontent represented by the remaining fifty thousand would-be warriors, who had come out all aflame with martial ardour, but had so far never set eyes on an enemy; who were ready to die cheerfully for a cause which not one in a hundred properly understood, but found themselves like to moulder with ennui and lack of proper provisioning.

Their hopes had been constantly raised only to be dashed. They were to go up to the Danube to help the Turks against the Russians. They were aching to go. But fifty thousand men need feeding, and the commissariat was in a state of confusion, and transport non-existent and unprocurable. So they stayed where they were, and mouldered and cursed, and began to look askance at the whole business and to doubt the good faith of every one concerned.

Many officers fell sick, some threw up their commissions in disgust and went home. The men would have liked to follow.

In July came the inevitable consequences of ill-feeding, ill-temper, enforced idleness, and mismanagement—the men became as sick in body as they had long been at heart. The heats and rains of August turned the camps into steaming stew-pans, and the men, who would have faced death by shot and steel with cheers, died miserably of cholera and typhus, and dying, struck a chill to the hearts of those who were left.

The officers did their best—got up games for them and races. But the more intimate companionship between officers and men which obtained in the French army was lacking in the British, and could not be called into spasmodic existence on the spur of the moment.

The races alone excited a certain amount of enthusiasm, and whenever Jim happened to be in camp he carried all before him.

With quite mistaken grandmotherly solicitude, too, the bands were all silenced, lest their lively music should jar on the ears of the sick and dying. The men tried sing-songs of their own, but sorely missed their music, and those near any of the French camps would walk any distance to share with them the cheery strains they could not get at home.

The camps were moved from place to place in vain attempt at dodging death. But death went with them and the men died in hundreds. And those who were sent to the hospitals at Varna wished they had died before they got there.

Through all that dreadful time, when the doctors were next to powerless and burying-parties the order of the day, our two boys kept wonderfully well. And for that they were not a little indebted to Lord Deseret, to a certain amount of fatherly oversight on the part of Colonel Carron, and perhaps most of all to the fact that they were kept busy.

Jack and his fellows beat the country-sides for game until they had swept them bare.

Jim, still in luck, was sent out to buy horses, and travelled far and wide, and still farther and wider as the nearer provinces became depleted. And when Jack's game was finished he got permission to go with him, and in those long, venturesome rides they two renewed their youth together, and rejoiced in one another, and found life good.

Many a lively adventure they had as they scoured the long Bulgarian plains in search of their four-legged prizes, for which they paid a trifle over a pound a leg in cash, whereby they beat their French opponents, who only paid in paper which had to be cashed at French Head-quarters, one hundred or more miles away.

To the boys it was all a delightful game; and getting the horses home, when they had found and bought them, was by no means the least exciting part of it. But the chief thing was that it took them out of the deadly camps, kept them fully occupied, and in soundest health when so many sickened and died.

The risks of the road were comparatively small, and they always went well armed and with an e[illegible].

Danger, indeed, lurked nearer home. For the twenty miles of road between Varna and the camps at Aladyn and Devna began to be infested with the baser spirits from among the great gathering of the off-scourings of the Levant which had flocked after the army.

Outrages were of daily occurrence, and every man who went that way alone rode warily, with his hand on his revolver and his eyes on the look out.

One day Jack had ridden up to the plateau by the sea, where the Dragoons were, to visit George Herapath and Harben, who were both down with dysentery, and Jim had been delayed at the commissary's office by the only part of the business in which he took no delight—the settlement of his accounts, which never by any chance came out right.

They were cantering home in the cool of the evening, when cries of distress at a short distance from the road turned their horses' heads that way, and galloping up in haste they came on a band of Bashi-Bazouks—cut-throat ruffians whom General Yusuf was trying to lick into shape—dragging away a young country girl, whose terrified eyes had caught sight of the British uniforms. Already that uniform carried with it greater guarantee of right and justice than any of the many others with which the country was overrun. So as soon as she saw them she shrieked for help, and they answered.

"Let her go, you beasts!" shouted Jack, as he dragged out his sword.

And then, as dirty hands fumbled in waist-shawls full of pistols, Jim's revolver cracked out, and two of the rascals went down. Curses and bullets flew promiscuously for a second or two, and then the remaining Bashis bolted, leaving four on the ground and the girl on their hands.

"What the deuce are we to do with her?" said Jack, as the spoils of war clung tearfully to his leg.

"Where?" asked Jim, in one of the few native words he had picked up in the course of business.

"Pravadi," panted the girl.

"That's over yonder, past Aladyn," said Jim. "We'd better take her home, or those brutes will get her again. I'll take her up—my horse is fresher than yours. Come along, my beauty!" And he stuck out his boot for a foot-rest, and held out his hand to the girl.

The uniform was her sufficient guarantee, and she climbed up and straddled the horse, and locked her arms tightly round Jim's waist.

"All right?" he asked. And they turned to the road.

Two minutes later they fell in with a Turkish patrol galloping up at sound of the firing, and had some difficulty in making them understand that they were not carrying off the girl on their own account. They were only convinced by being led back to the place where the wounded Bashis lay. Then they offered to take care of the girl and see her safely home. But she knew them too well and would have none of them. She clung like a leech to Jim, and at last they were permitted to go on their way.

They had many little adventures of the kind, and they tended to keep their blood in circulation, and the blues, which afflicted their fellows, at a distance.

Lord Deseret had laid down the law for Jim as regards eating and drinking.

"I have lived in Turkey," he said. "Drink no water unless

it has been boiled, and then dash it with rum. Tea or coffee are better still. And eat as little fruit as possible; it's tempting, but dangerous."

And Jim used to get wildly angry with his men, when he saw them devouring cucumbers by the half-dozen, and apricots and plums by the basketful, under the impression that these things were good for their health. They laughed at his remonstrances at first, but remembered them later; and those who did not die foreswore cucumbers for the rest of their lives.

CHAPTER XLV

MORE REVELATIONS

COLONEL CARRON was constantly looking the boys up, and carrying them off to the best meals they ever got in that country. His Chief, Prince Napoleon, had gone down to Therapia with a touch of fever, and the Colonel was in charge of his quarters and saw to it that His Highness's cooks did not get rusty in his absence.

Over these delightful dinners in the leafy arbours which always marked the Prince's quarters, they all came to know one another very much better than they might have done under any ordinary circumstances.

And the burden of the Colonel's talk was chiefly regret that one or both of them had not taken his offer and joined him in the French service.

"Sorry I am to say it," he said one night, as they sat sipping coffee such as they got nowhere else, and smoking cigars such as their own pockets did not run to, "but your army is only a fancy toy—in the way it's run, I mean. Your men are the finest in the world, what there are of them; but England is not a soldierly nation, say what you like about it."

"What about the Peninsula, sir?—to say nothing of Waterloo!" murmured Jack, after a discreet look round.

"Oh, you can fight and win battles, just as you can do pretty nearly anything else you make up your minds to do—regardless of cost. But with us the army is a science—an exact science almost—and every single detail is worked out on the most scientific lines. You only need to look round you to see the difference. England is never ready because she is not by nature a fighting nation. Her army rusts along, and then when the sudden call comes you have got to brace up and win through—or muddle through—at any cost, and the cost is generally frightful. The men and money you have wasted—absolutely wasted—in your wars do not bear thinking of."

"I'm afraid it's true, sir. And we don't seem to learn much by experience. I suppose it comes from having sea-frontiers instead of land. You have to *be* ready. We always have to *get* ready."

"And how about the horses, Jim?" he asked. "I'm told you manage to get more than we do. That's one for you, my boy."

"We pay cash, sir. You pay in paper promises, and a man a hundred miles away will sooner part for gold than for paper."

"Truly; I would myself. Do you lose many *en route*?"

"Not two per cent, sir. Some of them are pretty wild, and they make a bolt at times, but it adds to the fun, and we nearly always get them back. Did you see Nolan's Arabs?"

"I saw them—beauties. The Prince wanted to buy two or three, but I dissuaded him. They're too delicate for a winter campaign. That big brown of yours, that Deseret gave you, is worth four of them—as far as work is concerned."

"You think we're in for a winter campaign, sir?" asked Jack eagerly.

"No doubt about it, I think. We've got to do something before we go home—some of us. Our coming up here has cleared the Russians off the Danube, but our dawdling here has given them every chance of strengthening themselves in the Crimea. The biggest thing they have there is Sebastopol, on which they have squandered money. Therefore I think it will be Sebastopol, and anything but an easy job."

"We shall get our chance, then," sparkled Jack. "We did a bit at Gallipoli, but a real big siege would be grand."

"I hope your commissariat will play up better then, or we shall have to feed you," said the Colonel, with a smile.

He liked to draw them out and get their views on men and things, and watched them keenly the while, but all his watching brought him not one whit nearer a solution of the problem of Carne than had Charles Eager's and Sir Denzil's.

In the course of one such talk, however, they made a discovery and received a shock which knocked the wind out of them.

Their father was delightfully open and frank with them as regards the past, and it drew their liking.

"I have behaved shamefully to you both," he said one time, "and still worse to one of you. And I have nothing to plead in extenuation except that I did as my fellows in those days did—which is a very poor excuse, I confess. I must make such compensation as I can. One of you will have to become Carron of Carne, and the other M. le Compte de Carne—maybe M. le Duc by that time. There's no knowing."

"There's the Quixande matter too," said Jack thoughtfully.

"An empty title, I fear, by this time. And the Carrons were of note ages before the Quixandes were heard of. You seem to have got on very good terms with Deseret"—to Jim.

"He was very good to me, sir. I don't know why, unless it was because of his old friendship with you. He always spoke very handsomely of you."

"He was always a good fellow, but a terrible gambler. And yet I don't think he suffered on the whole. He was so confoundedly rich that it made no difference to him in any way. I have seen him win and lose £10,000 in a night at Crockford's, without turning a hair."

"I saw him win somewhere about that at a house in St. James's Street and——"

"And how much did you lose?"

"Nothing, sir; I was only looking on. Charlie Denham took me there—just to see it, you know. When Lord Deseret heard my name he came up and spoke to me. He asked me to call on him, and scribbled his address on the back of a bank-note, and gave it to me, and insisted on my keeping it."

"Just like him!"

"Then the police came and we had to get out over the roofs——"

"I would dearly have liked to see Deseret getting out over the roofs," laughed the Colonel.

"He seemed quite used to it, sir."

"I haven't a doubt of it. And he never suggested you should play?"

"On the contrary, he never ceased to warn me against it. So did Mme Beteta——"

"Mme Beteta!" And the Colonel's cigar hung fire in mid-air, and he sat staring at Jim as if he had called up a ghost.

"The dancer, you know. She has been awfully kind to me. Did you know her too, sir?" asked innocent Jim.

"How did you come to make *her* acquaintance?" asked his father, with quite a change of tone, and an intenseness that struck even Jim.

"We had gone to see her dance——"

"Both of you?"

"Charlie Denham and I. And Lord Deseret saw us and sent for us to his box, and at the interval he offered to take us round."

"Deseret?" And he said something under his breath in French which they did not catch. "Well—and how did she receive you?"

"She was very pleasant. She asked me to call and see her, and I've been several times."

The Colonel resumed his cigar and smoked in silence for some time, with his eyes fixed meditatively on a distant corner. Then he seemed to make up his mind. He blew out a great cloud of smoke and said very deliberately:

"In view of what is coming it is perhaps as well you should know, though it will not help you to a solution of your puzzle—at least—I don't know. . . . It might—yes—probably it might, if one could be sure of her telling the truth for its own sake and apart from all other considerations. Mme Beteta is your mother"—and he nodded at Jim, who jumped in his chair; "or yours"—and he nodded at Jack, who sat staring fixedly at him. "She may know which of you is her own boy. I cannot tell. But she will only tell what she chooses—if I know anything of women."

"Yes," he said presently, while the boys still sat speechless, "Beteta is old Mrs. Lee's daughter. The old woman knows also, I expect, but she certainly will only tell what suits her, and you could put very little reliance on anything she said. Has madame met you both?"

"Yes, sir. She asked me to bring Jack to see her the first chance I got, and I did so."

"Well?"

"She was just the same to him, as nice as could be, anxious we should get into some scrape so that she could be of some use to us, and that kind of thing—very nice."

"Ay—well! It is just possible—it is very probable," he said weightily, "that some of us three may never get home again. We don't know for certain what we're going to attempt, so it is impossible to forecast the chances. But, in view of what may be, it is only right that you should know. Is there anything else you wish to ask? I have had great cause to regret many things in my life, but nothing, perhaps, more than this. Though, *mon Dieu!*" he said very heartily, "even this has its compensations in you two boys. However, I have no desire to refer to it again. So, if there is anything more——" And he waited for their questioning.

"There is one thing, sir," said Jack, unwillingly enough, and yet it seemed to him necessary. "You will pardon me, I hope, but it might be of importance. Did you—were yon—was your marriage with madame all in order?"

The Colonel nodded as though he had been expecting the question.

"In justice to her, I must say that she believed so at the time, but there were irregularities in it which would probably invalidate it if brought to the test, and I think she is now aware of it."

"You have met her since?"

"Oh yes. We have been on friendly terms for some years past."

"And you believe she could solve the question that is troubling us all, if she would?"

"I think it likely, but—you must see," and he addressed himself more particularly to Jack—"that most women, in such a case, would lie through thick and thin to establish their own cause."

"I don't know," said Jack doubtfully. "I suppose it is possible."

"It is certain. However, the solution to the puzzle may come otherwise,"—they knew what he meant—"so now we will drop the matter, and you must think of me as little unkindly as you can. Jean-Marie," to an orderly outside, "bring us fresh coffee and more cognac."

"Do you know that Canrobert lost three thousand of his men up in the Dobrudscha?"

"Three thousand!" gasped Jim.

"They got into some swamp full of rotting horses and dead Russians and consequent pestilence, and the men died like flies."

"It is hard to go like that," said Jim. "I'd sooner die ten times over in fair fight than of the cholera. That's what's knocking the heart out of the men, that and having nothing to do but watch the other fellows die."

"Ay—well, we'll give them something to do at last. Every Tom, Dick, and François is to set to work making fascines and gabions."

"That means a siege, then," said Jack, with delight. "And our time's coming after all."

CHAPTER XLVI

THE BLACK LANDING

FROM that time on there was no lack of work. The spirits of the men went up fifty per cent, and the general health improve in like ratio. Hard work proved the best of tonics.

And, of a truth, a tonic was needed. It took the Guards—the flower of the British army—two days to march from Aladyn to the sea at Varna, a distance of ten miles. So reduced were they by sickness, that five miles a day was all they could manage, and even then their packs were carried for them.

For those in charge there was no rest, by day or night, until the embarkation was complete. When Jim Carron followed his last horse on board the *Himalaya*, he tumbled into a bath and then into a bunk, and slept for twenty-four hours without moving a finger.

But he had ample time, when he woke up, fresh and hungry, to admire that most wonderful sight of close on seven hundred ships, of all shapes and sizes—from the stately *Agamemnon*, flying the Admiral's flag, to the steam-tug *Pigmy*, wrestling valiantly with a transport twenty times her size—as they crept slowly across the Black Sea, with 80,000 men on board for the chastisement of the Russian

Bear. A sight for a lifetime, indeed, but one which no man who remembers or thinks of would ever wish to set eyes on again.

Jim and his fellows, however, rejoiced in it, for without doubt it meant business at last, and they had almost begun to despair.

So, in due time, they came in sight of the tented mountains and the coast; and after what seemed to the ardent ones still more vacillation and delays, the launches and flat-boats got to work, and the long strip of shingle which lay between the sea and a great lake behind became black with men.

All was eagerness and anticipation. The voyage had had a good effect on bodies sorely weakened by disease, and the prospect of active employment at last a still better effect on hearts that had grown heavy with disappointment.

But ten days of life-giving sea cannot entirely undo the mischief of the sickly months ashore. Numbers died on the voyage. Of those who landed, few indeed were the men they had been when they left England six months before, but hearts ran high if bodies were worn and weak.

That was the busiest day those regions had seen since time began. To the few bewildered inhabitants it seemed as though the whole unknown world was emptying itself on their shores.

Before sunset over 60,000 men were landed, and still there were more to come. All that coast, from Eupatoria to Old Fort, was like an ant-hill dropped suddenly on to a strange place, over which its tiny occupants swarmed tumultuously in the endeavour to accommodate themselves to the new conditions.

The weather, which had held up during the day, broke towards evening. The surf roared viciously up the shingle beach, and the rain came down in torrents. The tents were still aboard ship; men and officers alike sat and soaked throughout the dreary night in extremest misery. Jack among them. He had been sent on in advance of his corps to make observations and dispositions for the accommodation of the ordnance, and carried—according to instructions—nothing but his great-coat rolled up lengthwise and slung over his shoulder, a canteen of water, and three days' provision of cooked salt meat and biscuit in a haversack. The men had their blankets in addition, and their rifles and bayonets and ammunition.

When the deluge broke on them, and the spray came flying up the beach in sheets, drenching them alike above and below, the men huddled together and tried to improvise shelters with their great-coats and blankets. But Nature was pitiless and seemed to bend her direst energies to the task of damping their spirits. With their bodies she had her will, but their spirits were beyond her, for they were on Russian territory at last, and that meant business.

Jack sat on the wet shingle, back to back with one of his fellows, and the rain soaked through him, till his very marrow felt cold.

Some of the men near him, crouching under their sopping blankets, started singing, and "God save the Queen" and "Rule Britannia" rolled brokenly along the lines for a time. But by degrees the singing died away, the wet blankets exerted their proverbial influence, and silent misery prevailed.

The weather had broken before the cavalry got ashore, so Jim spent that night very gratefully in the comfort of his bunk on the *Himalaya*, and wondered how they were faring on land.

He was up before sunrise, however, and hard at work, though the waves were still high, and landing horses would be no easy matter.

He was sent ashore to see if it was possible, and was sickened and saddened by the sights that met him. Everywhere drawn, blanched faces, strained and bloodshot eyes, and stiffened bodies that stretched in vain for limberness. And worse

He came on Jack prowling anxiously among the black masses just wakening into life again.

"Hello, Jim!" he said hoarsely. "Where were you? Did you get damp?"

"We're not landed yet. Too rough for the horses."

"Lucky beggars! I never had such a night in my life. It was ghastly. Why the deuce couldn't they let us have some tents? Those French beggars had theirs, and the beastly Turks too. We're the worst-managed lot I ever heard of."

"What's this?" asked Jim, staring open-mouthed at a muffled figure at his feet—stiff and stark, though all around were stirring. "Why doesn't he get up?"

"He's got up," said Jack through his teeth. "He's dead, and there's a score or more like him. Dead of the cold and want of everything. Hang it all, why aren't we Frenchmen or Turks!" A sore speech, born of great bitterness.

And Jim felt it almost an insult be so warm and hearty and well-fed, with that dumb witness of the dreadful misery of the night lying silent at his feet.

And the thought of it all bore sorely on him and brought the lump into his throat. To pull through the bad times at Varna; to come all that way across the sea, indomitable spirit overcoming all the weaknesses of the flesh; to land at last in the high flush of hope,—and then to die like dogs of cold and misery, on the wet shingle, before their hope had smallest chance of realisation! Oh, it was hard! It was bitter hard!

When he reported on board it was decided to make for Eupatoria, where there was a pier, but before they got under way the weather showed signs of improvement, and presently the landing began, and for the next two days both the boys had so much on their hands that they had no time to think of anything but the contrarinesses of horses and guns, and the disconcerting effects of high seas on things unused to them.

In spite of all they lacked, however, the men's spirits rose as soon as the sun shone out and warmed them. They were on Russian soil at last, and that made up for everything. All they wanted now was Russians to come to grips with—Russians in quantity and of a fighting stomach.

Sebastopol was thirty miles to the south, and between them and it lay rivers, and almost certainly armies; and on the third day they set off resolutely to find them. And that day Jim had his first trying experience of playing target to a distant enemy in deadly sober earnest.

He had wondered much what it would feel like, and how his inner man would take it. As for the outer, he had promised himself that that should show no sign, no matter what happened.

The Hussars were feeling the way in advance, when a bunch of Cossacks appeared on the hills in front, and representatives of Britain and Russia took eager stock of one another. They were rough-looking fellows on sturdy horses, and carried long lances. They rode down the hill as though to offer battle, and the Englishmen were keen to try conclusions with them. But behind them, in the hollows, were discovered dense masses of cavalry waiting for the game to walk into the net. And when the wary game declined, the cavalry opened out and disclosed hidden guns, and the game of long bowls began.

The first shots went wide, and Jim watched them go hopping along the plain with much curiosity. Then came the vicious spurt of white smoke again, and the man and horse alongside him collapsed in a heap; the horse with a most dolorous groan, the man—Saxelby, a fine young fellow of his own troop—with a gasping cry, his leg shorn clean off at the knee.

Jim's heart went right down into his stomach for a moment as the blood spirted over him, and he felt deadly sick.

His first impulse was to jump down and help poor Saxelby, but he feared for himself if he did so—feared he would fall in a heap alongside him and perhaps not be able to get up, for he felt as weak as water.

He clenched his teeth till they ached. He dropped his bridle hand on to his holster to keep it from shaking, and clasped his horse so tightly with his knees that he resented it and began to fret and curvet. Jim bent over and patted him on the neck, and two troopers got down and carried Saxelby away. The horse stopped jerking its legs and lay still, with its eyes wide and white, and its nostrils all bloody, and its teeth clenched and its lips drawn back in a horrid grin.

The guns had found their range and were spitting venomously now. Half a dozen more of his men were down. He was quite sure he would be next. He thought in a whirl for a moment,—of Gracie; she would marry Jack, and all that matter would be smoothed out;—and of Mr. Eager, the dear fellow!—and his father, and he wished they had seen more of one another;—and Sir Denzil, he was not such a bad old chap after all. He thought they would be sorry for him. And Mme Beteta, he wondered—— Well, maybe he would know all about it in a minute or two.

Then his heart rose suddenly right up into his head, and he was filled with a vast blazing anger at this being shot at with never a chance of a stroke in reply. If they would only let them go for those d——d Russians he would not feel so bad about it! But to be shot down like pheasants! It was not business! It was all d——d nonsense! He began to get very angry indeed.

His quickened ear had caught the rattle of artillery coming up behind. But it had stopped. Why the deuce had it stopped? Why couldn't someone do something before they were all bowled over?

Then at last there came a roar on their flank, and some of the newer horses kicked and danced, and Jim, staring hard at the Russians, saw a lane cleft through them where the shot had gone.

He clenched his teeth now to keep in a wild hurrah. It was an odd feeling. He knew nothing about these fellows under the hill, but he hated them like sin and rejoiced in their destruction. He would have liked to slaughter every man of them with his own hand. If he had been able to get at them he would have hacked and slashed till there wasn't one left.

No more balls came their way now. The guns turned on one another, and presently the Russians limbered up and retired—and it was over, and he was still alive. And then he was thankful.

Jim went off in search of Saxelby and the other half-dozen wounded men, as soon as he came in, and found them trimmed up and bandaged, just starting in litters for the ships, and all very angry at being knocked out before they had had a chance.

Then they crossed the Bulganak and bivouacked for the night, in grievous discomfort still from lack of tents and shortage of provisions, but strung to cheerfulness by the fact that they were really in touch with the enemy at last—triumph surely of mind over matter. Notwithstanding which, the morning disclosed another pitiful tale of deaths from cold and exposure—brave fellows who would not knock under in spite of pains and weakness, and had dragged themselves along lest they should be "out of the fun," and died silently where they lay for lack of the simple necessities of life.

Rightly or wrongly the blame fell on the commissaries, and the dead men's comrades flung them curses hot enough to fire a ship. For meeting the Russians in fair fight was one thing, and altogether to their liking; but this lack of foresight and provision took them below the belt in every sense of the word, and was like an unexpected blow from the fist of one's backer.

CHAPTER XLVII

ALMA

AT noon next day they came to a shallow river winding between red clay banks, a somewhat undignified stream whose name they were to blason in letters of blood on the rolls of fame—the Alma.

The Russians were strongly entrenched on the hills on the other side and in great force, and every man knew that here was a giant struggle and glory galore for the winners.

It was a great fight, but it was mostly rifle and bayonet and the grim reaction from those deadly slow months at Varna. And the Engineers had little to do but watch the others, as they dashed through the muddy stream, and climbed the roaring heights in the face of death, and captured the great redoubt at dreadful cost. And the cavalry were miles away on the left, covering the attack on that side from five times their own weight of Russian cavalry, who never came on, and so they had nothing to do and were disgusted at being out of it.

So neither Jack nor Jim were in that fight, but afterwards they climbed the hill with separate searching parties and met by chance in the redoubt on top, and looked on sights unforgettable, which made a deep and grim impression on them both.

It was the first battlefield they had ever set eyes on, and they spoke very little.

"God! Isn't it awful?" said Jack through his teeth, as they stood looking down the hill towards the river flowing unconcernedly to the sea, just as it had done when they came to it at noon, just as it had done all through the dreadful uproar when men were falling in their thousands.

The ground between was strewn and heaped and piled with dead bodies.

But Jim had no words for it. He could only shake his head.

While they were still gazing awe-stricken at the ghastly piles of broken men, among which the litter-men were prowling in anxious search for wounded, a group of brilliantly clad officers came up from the French camp, where the rows of comfortable white tents set English teeth grinding with envy and chagrin. And among them they saw Prince Napoleon and Colonel Carron.

Their father saw them in the redoubt and came up at once.

"Glad to see you still alive, boys," he said cheerfully. "Hot work, wasn't it?"

"Awful, sir. Were you in it?" asked Jack.

"Oh yes. We came across there"—pointing to a burnt village on the river-bank—"and then up here. Here's we got the guns up to relieve Bosquet. We've paid heavily, but it's shown them what we're made of. weren't in it, I suppose, Jim?"

"No, sir; we were waiting over yonder for some cavalry to come on, but they wouldn't. Worse luck!"

"Your chances will come, my boy. And you, Jack?"

"We had very little to do, sir. We were away in the rear there."

"Your men did splendidly. Canrobert was just saying that he doubted if our men would have managed that frontal business as yours did."

"They paid," said Jim.

"And are still paying," said the Colonel, as they stood watching the French ambulances, with their trim little mules, trotting off towards the coast, carrying a dozen wounded men in quick comfort, while the English litter-men crept slowly along on their jogging four-mile tramp, which proved the death of many a sorely wounded man and purgatory to the rest.

"Truly, your arrangements are not up to the mark," said Colonel Carron. "How have you stood the nights? Somebody was saying you had no tents."

"Last night was the first time we've had any, and they've all been sent on board again," said Jack gloomily.

"That's too bad. It's hard on the men."

"We lose a number every night with the cold."

"Bad management—— The Prince is off. I must go. Good luck to you, boys! I shall come over and look you up from time to time. Keep out of mischief!" And he waved a cheery hand and was gone, and the boys went down among the ghastly piles to do what they could.

But it was heart-breaking work; the total of misery was so immense, and the means of alleviation so feeble in comparison.

The French wounded were safe on board ship within an hour after they were picked up. It was two days before all the English were disposed of, though who could be spared set his hand to the work.

In the afternoon of the second day after Jim was going wearily down the hill, after such experiences among the dead and wounded as had made him almost physically sick.

All the French, and he thought almost all the English, wounded had been seen to. The Russians had necessarily been left to the last.

As he passed a grisly pile he thought he caught a faint groan from inside it, and set to work at once hauling the dead men apart, with tightened face and repressed breath. The job was neither pleasant nor wholesome, but there was no one else near at hand and he must see to it.

Right at the bottom of the pile, soaked with the blood of those who had fallen on top of him, he came upon a young fellow, an officer, just about his own age. And as he dragged the last body off him, he opened his eyes wearily and groaned.

Jim put his pocket-flask to the white lips, and the other sucked eagerly and a touch of colour came into his face. He lay looking up into the face bending over him, and then his chest filled and he sighed.

"Where are you hurt?" asked Jim, expecting no answer, but full of sympathy.

"Leg and side," said the wounded one, in English with an accent.

"I'll fetch a litter."

"Stay moment. Only dead men—two days. Good to see a live one. . . . Did you win?"

"Yes, we won, but at very heavy cost."

"Glad you won."

"That doesn't sound good," said honest Jim, with disfavour.

"You would feel same. Hate Russians. . . . Pole."

"I see," said Jim, whose history was nebulous, but equal to the occasion.

"Forced to fight," said the wounded man. "Done with it now."

"Take some more rum—it'll warm you up; and I'll find a litter for you."

"Have you bread? I starve. . . ."

"I'll see if I can get you something."

"Open his roll." And the wounded man turned his eyes hungrily on the nearest dead body. And Jim, opening the linen roll which each Russian carried, found a lump of hard black bread and placed it in his hand.

"I thank. You will come again?" asked the young Pole anxiously.

"I'll come back all right, as soon as I've found a litter." And he left the wounded man feebly gnawing his chunk of black bread like a starving dog.

He found a litter in time, and the weary eyes brightened a trifle at sight of him.

"You are good," he murmured. "You save me."

And Jim, thinking what he would like himself in similar case, went along by his side till they found a doctor resting for a moment, and begged him to examine the new-comer.

"His leg must go. The body wound will heal," said the medico. "Seems to have had a bad time. Where did you find him?"

"I found him under fifteen dead men."

"Then he owes you his life."

"Yes, yes," said the wounded one. "I am grateful. Take the leg off."

"He's a Pole, forced to fight against his will," said Jim, at the doctor's astonishment.

"I see"—as he screwed a tourniquet on the shattered limb. "We're sending all their wounded to Odessa."

At which the young man groaned.

"Hold his hand," said the doctor. "He's pretty low." And Jim held the twitching hand while the knife and the saw did their work, and was not sure whether it was his hand that jumped so or the other's.

The other hand suddenly lay limp in his, and he thought the man was dead.

"Fainted," said the doctor. "He's been bleeding away for two days."

He came round, however, and tried to smile when he saw Jim still there. And presently he murmured:

"I thank." And then he looked down at his hand all caked with blood, and tried feebly to get a ring off his finger.

"Take!" he said. But Jim shook his head.

"Yes, yes." And he wrestled feebly again with the ring.

"Better humour him," said the doctor. "It'll do him more good than to refuse."

So Jim worked the ring off for him, and slipped it on his own finger, and the wounded man said "I thank!" and lay back satisfied.

Jim saw him carried down to the boat and wished him luck, and then strode away to his own quarters, which consisted of a seat on the side of a dry ditch—dry at present, but which would be soaking with dew before morning—with his brown horse picketed alongside, as hungry and low-spirited as his master.

Jim looked at his ring and thought of its late owner, and hoped he would get over it, and wondered how soon his own turn would come. For the thing that amazed him was that any single man could come alive out of a fight like that at the Alma.

His horse nuzzled hungrily at him, and he suddenly bethought him of the black bread in the Russians' linen rolls. He jumped up, tired as he was, and strode away to the battlefield again, and came back with chunks of hard tack and black bread enough to make his brown and some of his neighbours happy for the night.

Marshal St. Arnaud, sore sick as he was, was eager to press on at once after the discomfited Russians. But "an army marches on its stomach," and it was two full days before Lord Raglan could make a move. Those two lost days might have changed the whole course of the campaign, and saved many thousands of lives. The defective organisation of the British transport and commissariat slew more than all the Russian bullets.

On the third morning, as the sun rose, all the trumpets, bugles, and drums in the French army pealed out from the summit of the captured hill, and presently the allied armies were *en route* again for Sebastopol.

The next day, however, saw a sudden change of plans and most remarkable happening. The allied chiefs gave up the idea of attacking the town from the north, on which side all preparations had been made for their reception, and decided, instead, to march right round and take it on its undefended south side. And so began that famous flank march to Balaclava which was to turn all the defences of the fortress.

And on that selfsame day the Russian chief, Menchikoff, decided to march out of Sebastopol into the open, and so

19

turn the flank of the allies. And the two lines of march crossed at Mackenzie's farm.

The Russians had got out first, however, and it was only their rear-guard upon whom the English chanced, and immediately fell, and put to rout. They chased them for several miles and took their military chest and great booty of baggage which, being left to the men as lawful prize, cheered them greatly.

When Jim got back from the chase the new owners were offering for sale dazzling uniforms, and decorations, and handsome fur coats, at remarkable prices. He had no yearning for Russian uniforms or decorations, but as he suffered much from the cold of a night he bought two of the wonderful coats for five pounds each, and, when they halted, he sought out Jack and made him happy with one of them.

CHAPTER XLVIII

JIM'S RIDE

NEXT day the allied forces crossed the Tchernaya by the Traktir Bridge and marched on Balaclava.

And here Jim's threefold reputation as a hard rider, the best-mounted man in his regiment, and a man who did, brought him a chance of fresh distinction.

In abandoning the coast and marching inland, the army had cut itself off from its base of supply—the fleet. It was urgently necessary that word should be sent to the admirals to move on round the coast past Sebastopol and meet the army in its new quarters.

Just as they were crowding over Traktir Bridge a rider came galloping up with dispatches for Lord Raglan—Lieutenant Maxse of the *Agamemnon*. He had left

Katcha Bay that morning, and offered at once to ride back with orders for the fleet to move on. A brave offer, for the country was all wild forest and lonely plain and valley, infested with prowling bands of Cossacks, and the night was falling.

An hour later Maxse, on a fresh horse, was galloping back to the coast.

"If anything should happen to him," said the Chief, "we shall be in a hole." And he sent for Lord Lucan.

"I want your best horseman and your best horse, Lucan, and a man who will put a thing through."

"That's young Carron of the Hussars, sir."

And Jim, paraded for inspection on his big brown horse—quite filled out and frolicsome with its load of black bread the day but one before—seemed likely in the Chief's eyes.

"Mr. Carron," he said. "I have a dangerous task for you. I am told you are the man for it. Lieutenant Maxse left here an hour ago for the ships. They must get round at once and meet us at Balaclava. Here is a copy of the order. If Maxse has not got through you will deliver it to Admiral Dundas in Katcha Bay. Don't lose a moment. The welfare of the army depends on you."

Jim saluted.

"How will you go?"

"Mackenzie's farm and the post-road, sir."

"You are armed? You may meet Cossacks."

"Sword and revolver. I shall manage all right."

"Come round with the ships and report to me at Balaclava."

Jim saluted once more, and spurred away.

The distance was only some twenty miles, an easy two hours' ride. The dangers lay in the hostile country and the prowling Cossacks, for in the long defile from the farm to the Belbec, and then again in the broken country between the Belbec and the Katcha, there were a thousand places where a rider might be picked off from the hill-sides and never catch a glimpse of his adversary.

However, it was no good thinking of all that, and Jim was not one to cross bridges before he came to them, or to meet trouble half-way. His big brown had a long, easy stride which was almost restful to his rider, and Jim had a seat that gave his horse the least possible inconvenience, and between them was completest sympathy and friendship.

And as to the dark, unless he absolutely ran into Cossacks he reckoned it all in his favour. It kept down his pace indeed, but at the same time it hid him from the watchful eyes on the hill-sides and the leaden messages they might have sent him.

He received warm commendation for that night's ride, but, as simple matter of fact, he enjoyed it greatly, and had no difficulties beyond keeping the road in the dark and making sure it was the right one. Plain common-sense, however, bade him always trend to the left when cross-roads offered alternatives, and after leaving Mackenzie's he never set eyes on a soul till he found the Belbec an hour before midnight, and rode up through the wreathing mists of the river-bed to the highlands beyond.

The dew was drenching wet and the night cold, but he got into his big fur coat, which had been rolled up behind his saddle, and suffered not at all.

His thoughts ran leisurely back to them all at home,—Gracie, and Mr. Eager, and his grandfather, and Lord Deseret, and Mme Beteta, and his father's amazing revelation concerning her. He wondered whether they would ever learn the truth, and if not, how the tangle would be straightened out. He thought dimly, but with no great fear now, that they would probably both be killed if there was much fighting such as that at the Alma, so there was no need to trouble about the future.

Charlie Denham, indeed, never ceased to philosophise that it was always the other fellow who was going to be killed; but if every one thought that, it was evident, even to Jim's unphilosophic mind, that there must be a flaw somewhere.

Anyway, when a man's time came he died, and there was no good worrying oneself into the blues beforehand.

A hoarse challenge broke suddenly on his musings, and a darker blur on the road just in front resolved itself into half a dozen horsemen. They had heard his horse's hoofs, and waited in silence to see who came.

He had pulled the hood of his fur coat right up over his busby, and the heavy folds covered him almost down to the feet. He decided in a moment that safety lay in silence, so he rode straight on, waved a hand to the doubtful Cossacks, and was past Telegraph Hill before they had done discussing him.

He wondered if Maxse had met them and how he had fared.

An hour later he forded the Katcha and turned down the valley towards the sea. Boats were still plying between the sandy beach and the ships. The Jacks eyed him for a moment with suspicion, but gave him jovial welcome when they found that only his outer covering was Russian.

Lieutenant Maxse had just been put aboard the *Agamemnon*, he found, and a minute or two later he was following him. So Jim had the pleasure of steaming past the sea-front of Sebastopol to Balaclava Bay, where they found the ancient little fort on the heights bombarding the British army with four tiny guns.

They brought it to reason with half a dozen round shot, and presently steamed cautiously in round the awkward corners, and dropped anchor opposite the house where Lord Raglan had taken up his quarters.

CHAPTER XLIX

AMONG THE BULL-PUPS

AND now force of circumstances left the cavalry stranded high and dry, with nothing to do but range the valley now and again in quest of enemies who never showed face, and growl continually at the untowardness of their lot.

They had indeed had little enough to do so far, but always in front of them had been the hope of active employment and its concomitant rewards. But what use could cavalry be in a siege? And had they lived through all those hideous months at Varna, and come across the sea only to repeat them outside Sebastopol? They grizzled and growled, and expressed their opinions on things in general with cavalier vehemence.

And the worst of it was that the other more actively employed arms were inclined to twit them with their—so far—showy uselessness.

What had they done since they landed, except prance about and look pretty? Why hadn't they been out all over the country bringing in supplies? Where were they at the Alma, when hard knocks were the order of the day?—asked these others.

And, indeed, among themselves they asked bitterly why they had been chained up like that and allowed to do nothing. They had held all the Russian cavalry in check, it is true; but that was but a negative kind of thing, and what they thirsted for was an active campaign and glory.

But now it was Jack's turn, and the Engineers were in their element. Not a man among them but devoutly hoped the place would hold out to the utmost and give them their chance.

It was almost too good to be true—an actual siege on

the latest and most approved principles! And they tackled it with gusto, and were planning lines and trenches in their minds' eyes before their tents were up.

As a matter of fact, tents were still things to be looked forward to with such small faith in commissaries and transport as still lingered in their sorely tried bodies, for it had long since left their hearts; food was so scarce that for a couple of days one whole division of the army had tasted no meat; and every morning the first sorrowful duty of the living was to gather up those who had died in the night of cold and cholera, with bitter commination of those whom they considered to blame.

However, all things come in time to those who live long enough, and the tents came up from the ships at last, and rations began to be served out with something like regularity. The busy Engineers traced their lines, and, as soon as it was dark each night, the digging parties went out and set to work on the trenches, and the siege was fairly begun, and Jack and his fellows were as busy and happy as bees.

But Jim, if officially relegated to comparative inaction, found no lack of employment.

He was intensely interested in all that was going on. He rode here and there with messages to this chief and that. For when he reported himself to Lord Raglan at Balaclava, according to instructions, his lordship was pleased to compliment him in his quiet way.

"You did well, Mr. Carron," he said. "I am glad you both got through safely. Much depended on you. By the way, you know my old friend Deseret, I think."

"Lord Deseret was very kind to me in London, sir."

"I remembered, after you left last night, that he had spoken to me of you. And surely," said his lordship musingly, "I must have known your father. Is he still alive?"

Jim hesitated for half a second, and then said simply:

"Yes, sir; he is on the staff of Prince Napoleon."

"With Prince Napoleon?" said his lordship, and stared at him in surprise. And then the old story came back to his mind. "Ah, yes! I remember. Well, well! . . . And I suppose you're growling like the rest at having nothing to do?"

"We would be glad to have more, sir."

"I'm afraid it won't be a very lively time for the cavalry. But you seem to like knocking about. I must see what I can do to keep you from getting rusty."

"I shall be very grateful, sir."

And thereafter many an odd job came his way, for the allied lines, from the extreme French left at Kamiesch Bay in the west, to the British right above the Inkerman Aqueduct on the north-east, covered close upon twenty miles, and within that space there was enough going on to keep a man busy in simply acting as travelling eye to the Commander-in-Chief—in carrying his orders and bringing him reports.

And this was business that suited Jim to the full. He saw everything and was constantly meeting everybody he knew, and many besides.

He was galloping home from the French lines one evening, through the sailors' camp by Kadikoi, just above the gorge that runs down to Balaclava. The jolly Jacks were revelling in their lark ashore, and showed it in the labelling of their tents with fanciful names. Jim had already seen "Albion's Pets," "Rule Britannia," and "Windsor Castle," and every time he passed he looked for the latest ebullitions of sailorly humour. This time, to his great joy, he found "Britain's Bull-Pups," and "The Bear-Baiters," and "The Bully Cockytoos."

The Bull-Pups and the Bear-Baiters and the Bully Cockytoos, and all the rest, fifty in a line, were hauling along a Lancaster gun, with a fiddler on top fiddling away for dear life, and they all bellowing a chantie that made him draw rein to listen to it. The bands in the French camp were playing merrily as he left it, but in the British lines there was not so much as a bugle or a drum, and the men were feeling it keenly.

So the rough chorus struck him pleasantly, and he stopped to hear it out.

When the gun was up to their camp, the men cast loose and began to foot it merrily to the music, just to show what a trifle a Lancaster gun was to British sailormen. And Jim, as he sat laughing at their antics and enjoying them hugely, suddenly caught sight of a familiar face. Not one of the dancers, but one who stood looking on soberly—it might even be sombrely, Jim could not be sure.

He jumped off his horse and led him round.

"Why, Seth, old man!" he said, clapping the broad shoulder in friendly delight. "What brings you here?"

And young Seth turned and faced him, and had to look twice before he knew him.

"Ech—why, it's Mester Jim!" he said slowly.

"Of course it is. And but for you he wouldn't be here, and he never forgets it. But how do you come to be here, Seth?"

"I come with the rest to fight the Roosians, Mester Jim."

"I wish they'd give us a chance, but it's going to be all long bowls, I'm afraid."

But there was that to be said between them which was not for other ears.

The tars had watched the meeting with much favour, for greetings so friendly between officer and man were not often seen among them in those days, though more possible between sailormen than in the army. When they saw Jim slip his arm through Seth's and draw him along with him, they started a lusty cheer. "Three cheers for young Fuzzy-cap! Hip—hip!" And Jim grinned jovially and waved his hand in reply. And Seth Rimmer, in spite of the taciturnity which they could not understand, was a man of note among them from that day.

"Did you hear all about your poor old dad, Seth?" asked Jim quietly.

"Yes, Mester Jim. Th' passon told me all about it."

"It was a grievous thing. But I don't think I was to blame, Seth. He would go out and ramble about. I did all I could for him."

"I know. I know."

"And Kattie, Seth! *You* surely never thought I had anything to do with that matter?"

"No, Mester Jim. I knowed it wasn't you."

"Do you know who it was, Seth? I would hold him to account if ever I got the chance. But she would not tell me."

"You found her?" asked Seth, with a start that brought them both to a stand.

"She came to me in the street the very last night before we left——"

Seth gave out something mixed up of groan and curse.

"She said she had heard we were going in the morning, and she wanted to say good-bye."

"Th' poor little wench! . . . What did you say to her, Mester Jim?"

"I was knocked all of a heap at meeting her like that, Seth. But when I got my wits back I did the only thing I could. I took her to a lady friend who had been very kind to me, and she promised to look after her. And I am quite sure she will. If Kattie only stops with her I think she may be very comfortable there."

"It were good o' yo'. . . ." And then, reverting to Jim's former question, "I know him," he said hoarsely, "an' when th' chance comes——" And the big brown hands clenched as though a man's throat were between them. And Jim thought he would not like to be that man.

"I'm afraid I feel like that too, Seth, though I suppose—I don't know. Poor little Kattie!"

And presently he wrung the big brown hands, that were

meant for better work than wringing evil throats, and swung up on to his horse.

"I must get along, Seth. But I'm often through here, and we'll be meeting again. We're about two miles out over yonder, you know. Good-bye!" And he galloped off to his quarters.

He frequently rode across of a night for a chat with Jack, but Jack was a mighty busy man these days, and nights too. He had an inordinate craving for trenches and gabions and fascines and parallels and approaches, and could talk of little else, and confessed that he dreamed of them too. And if he could have accomplished as much by day as he did by night, when ne was fast asleep—though as a matter of fact it ought to be the other way, for most of the actual work had to be done under cover of darkness and he slept when he could—Sebastopol would have been taken in a week.

As the trenches began to develop, he would take Jim through them for a treat, and explain all that was going on with the greatest gusto. And at times Jim found it no easy matter to conceal the fact that it was all exceedingly raw and dirty, though he supposed it was the only way of getting at them.

And at times shot and shell would come plunging in over the sand-bags and gabions, and then every man would fling himself on his face in the dirt till the flying splinters had gone, and Jim would go home and try to brush himself clean—for Joyce had died of cholera two days out from Varna—and would thank his stars that he belonged to a cleaner branch of the service.

Still, it was fine to watch the shells come curving out from the town with a flash like summer lightning, and hear them singing through the darkness, and see the fainter glare of their explosion; and when he had nothing else on hand he went along to the trenches almost every night to watch the fireworks.

CHAPTER L

RED-TAPE

THE siege of Sebastopol was quite out of the ordinary run, and about as curious a business as ever was.

For one usually thinks of a besieged town as surrounded by the enemy and cut off from the rest of the world. And that was never the case with Sebastopol.

The allied forces drew a ring round the south and east sides of the town, and the sea guarded it on the west, but by way of the north and north-east the Russians had free passage at all times, and could introduce fresh troops and provisions and all the material of war at will, and so the defence was in a state of continuous renewal, and fresh blood was always pouring in to replace the terrible waste inside.

By those open ways also they sent out army after army to creep round behind the besiegers, to harry and annoy them, and this it was that led to some of the fiercest battles of the campaign. The knowledge also that great bodies of Russians were at large in their rear, and only waiting opportunity to attack them, kept the Allies perpetually on the strain, and hurried musters in the dark to repel, at times imaginary, assaults were of almost nightly occurrence.

Failing complete investment—when starvation, added to perpetual and irretrievable wastage, must in time have brought about a surrender—the Allies could only pound away with their big guns, and hope to wear down the heart and pride of Russia by the sheer dogged determination to pound away till there was nothing left to pound at.

The later attempts to breach and storm, to which all these gigantic efforts were directed, were but a part of the same policy. Russia was to be crushed by the combined weight of England and France and Turkey, and, later on, Sardinia. It was very British, very bull-doggy, but it was also terribly wasteful and costly all round.

The Russians had expected the attack on the north side, and had made it almost impregnable. When, by their flank march, the Allies came round to the south, the town was absolutely open and unprotected, the streets running up into the open country. Before the Allies could gird up their loins for a spring, earthworks and forts had sprung up in front of them as though by magic, and the only means of approach was by the slow, hard way of parallels, trenches, and zigzags. And all this it was that made up the Crimean War.

But our boys were busy, and so kept happy in spite of discomforts without end.

Every single thing the army needed, either for fighting or for sheer and simplest living, had to be brought to it by sea, and the one door of entrance was tiny Balaclava Bay—with the natural consequence that Balaclava Bay became inextricably blocked with shipping discharging on to its narrow shores, and its shores became inextricably piled with masses of war material and stores, with no means of transport to the camps six and eight and ten miles away. And so confusion became ten times confounded, and brave men languished and died for want of the stores that lay rotting down below. Add to this the fact that every British official's hands were bound round and round, and knotted and thrice knotted, with coils of stiffest red tape, and no man dared to lift a finger unless a dozen superiors in a dozen different departments had authorised him to do so, in writing, on official forms, with every "t" crossed and every "i" carefully dotted, and you have the simple explanation of the horrors of the Crimea.

Our own red-tape and sheer stupidity wrought far more evil on our men than all the efforts of Menchikoff and Gortschakoff with all the might of Russia at their backs.

The trenches wormed their zigzags slowly down the slope towards the Russian lines, and never was there more zealous zigzager than Jack. The Russians poured shot and shell on him and his fellow moles; but they dug on, mounted their heavy guns, and dosed him with pointed Lancaster shells, which were new to him, and impressed him most unpleasantly.

And Jim galloped to and fro and worried more over his horse's feeding than his own, and kept very fit and well.

He went over now and again to the Heavies, to see how George Herapath and Ralph Harben were standing it, and found them generally on the growl at having so little to do and none too much to eat; and they all condoled with one another, and expressed themselves freely on such congenial subjects as the Transport and Commissariat Departments, and felt the better for getting it out.

Letters from home came with fair regularity now, and they swapped their news and had time to write long letters back—except Jack, whose whole soul was in his trenches, and who was too tired and dirty for correspondence when he came out of them.

So upon Jim devolved the duty of keeping Carne and Wyvveloe posted as to the course of the war, and his painfully produced scrawls were valued beyond their apparent merits by the anxious ones at home, and treasured as things of price.

For Gracie, at all events, said to herself, when each one came, "It may be the last we shall ever get from him"; and, "They may both be lying dead at this moment. This horrible, horrible war!"

But she wrote continually to both of them; and if the dreadful feeling that she might only too possibly be writing to dead men was with her as she wrote, she took good care that no sign of it appeared in her letters. They were brave and cheery letters, telling of the little happenings of the neighbourhood, and always full of the hope of seeing them again soon. And if she cried a bit at times, as she wrote and thought of it all, be sure no tear-spots were allowed to show. They had quite enough to stand without being worried with her fears.

And she prayed for them every night and every morning with the utmost devotion, though, indeed, at times she remained long on her knees, pondering vaguely. For she knew that what must be, must be, and that her most fervent prayers could not turn Russian bullets from their destined billets—that if God saw it well to take her boys, they would go, in spite of all her asking. And so she came to commending them simply to God's good care, and to asking for herself the strength to bear whatever might come to her.

When the Alma lists came out, she and the Rev. Charles scanned them with feverish anxiety, and with eyes that got the names all blurred and mixed, and hearts that beat muffled dead marches, and only let them breathe freely again when they had got through without finding what they had feared.

And both of them, grateful at their own escape, thought pitifully of those whose trembling fingers, stopping suddenly on beloved names, had been the signal for broken hearts and shattered hopes and desolated lives.

And, any day, that might be their own lot too; and so, like many others in those times, they went heavily, and feared what each new day might bring.

Margaret Herapath spent much of her time with them, and Sir George was able to bring them news in advance of the ordinary channels.

And the grim old man up at Caine read the news-sheets and the lists, which smelt of snuff when he had done with them, and was vastly polite and unconcerned about it all when Gracie and Eager went to visit him; but Kennet led somewhat of a dog's life at this time, and had to find consolation for a ruffled spirit where he could.

CHAPTER LI

THE VALLEY OF DEATH

THE Cavalry, Light and Heavy, but more especially the Light, were, as we have seen, rankling bitterly under quite uncalled-for imputation of showy uselessness, and chafing sorely at their enforced inaction during the siege operations. The campaign, so far, had offered them no opening, nor did it seem likely to do so. Moreover, forage was scarce, their horses were on short rations, and before long, unless those infernal transport people woke up, they would be padding it afoot like the toilers on the heights, who were having all the fun—such as it was—and would reap all the glory.

But Fortune was kind, and sore, on them.

For some days past they had, from time to time, caught the sound of distant bugles among the hills to the north and east of the valley in which their camp lay, and their hopes had been briefly stirred.

It might mean nothing more, however, than the passage of reinforcements into Sebastopol, for those northern ways by Inkerman gorge were always open and impossible of closing.

In front of them on the plain was a line of small redoubts occupied by Turks. Behind them on the way to Balaclava lay the 93rd Highlanders under Sir Colin Campbell.

Jim Carron was awakened from a very sound sleep one morning by a lusty kick from Charlie Denham, and the information that "Lucan wanted him."

Five minutes later he was pressing his horse to its utmost, with the word to Head-quarters that the Russians were pouring down the valley towards Balaclava, that they had already captured Redoubt No. 1, that the Turks could not possibly hold the others against them, and that unless our base at Balaclava was to go, the sooner the army turned out to stop them the better.

Lord Raglan sped Jim on at once to French Head-quarters with the news; and as he galloped back in headlong haste lest they should be starting without him, all the camps were a-bristle and troops hurrying from all quarters to the scene of action.

As he came over the hill leading down to the Balaclava road, he could see the vast bodies of Russians pouring out of the hills, the Turks from the redoubts were running across the plain towards the long thin line of Highlanders, and the Cossacks and Lancers were in among them cutting them down as fast as they could chop.

All this he saw at a glance, as he sped on to join his own men, drawn up on the left of the Heavies. And as he took his place, panting, both he and his big brown, like steam-engines, he heard the roll of the Highlanders' Miniés on the right as they broke the rush of the Russian cavalry.

The next minute a great body of horsemen, brilliant in light blue and silver, topped the slope in front of the Heavies, and looked down on their insignificant numbers as Goliath did on David.

He saw old Scarlett haranguing his men, and then with a roar—he knew just how they felt!—like starving tigers loosed at last on long-desired prey—the Greys and Enniskillens dashed at them and through them, and wheeled, and through again, first line, second line, and out at the rear. And then, as the broken first line gathered itself again to swallow the tigers, the rest of the Heavies, the Royals, and Dragoons shot out like a bolt and scattered them to the winds.

And Jim and all about him yelled and cheered in a frenzy—but down below it all was a bitter sense of regret at being out of it. Truly it seemed as though malignant fate had the Light Brigade on her black books and was bent on defrauding them of their rightful chances.

By this time the allied troops were coming up from their

distant camps, and the rout of the Russian horse enabled them to take up their positions in the valley.

It looked like being a pitched battle. All hearts beat high, and none higher than those of the Hussars and Light Dragoons. Their chance might come after all. They twitched in their saddles. Give them only half a chance and they would show the world what was in them.

And it came.

Messengers sped in haste to and from the Chief, on the heights above, to the various commanders down below. And then came young Nolan of the 15th, Lord Raglan's own aide, his horse in a white sweat, himself aflame.

He spoke hurriedly to Lord Lucan, and Jim saw his lordship's eyebrows lift in astonishment. He seemed to question the order given.

Nolan waved a vehement arm towards the Russians. Lord Lucan spoke to Lord Cardigan, and his brows too went up. Every tense soul among them, whose eyes could see what was passing, watched as if his life depended on the outcome.

Then in a moment the word rang out, and they were off.

Where? He had not the remotest idea nor the slightest care. Enough for him that they were off and that they meant business.

And away in front of them, where he had no earthly right to be, since he did not belong to them and had only brought a message, went young Nolan, waving them on with insistent arm.

They swept along at a gallop in two long lines, and the rush and the rattle got into Jim's blood, and the blood boiled up into his head, and he thought of nothing—nothing but the fact that their chance had come at last—least of all of fear for himself.

Fear? There were Russians ahead there!——them all!—and every faculty in him, every nerve and muscle, every drop of boiling blood, every desire of his mind and heart and soul rushed on ahead to meet them. He wanted at them, he wanted to hew and thrust and kill. He wanted blood.

Head down forward a bit, sword-hilt fitting itself to his hand as it had never done before, knees so lightly tight to the saddle that he could feel the great brown shoulders working like machinery inside them, a glance forward from under his busby and an impression of a vast multitude of men—and the roar and crash of numberless guns in front and on both flanks—a scream just ahead, and young Nolan's horse came galloping round at the side, with young Nolan still in the saddle—but dead—his chest ripped open by a shell.

Men were falling all round now, men and horses hurling forward and down in rattling lumbering heaps.

Jim's face was cast-iron, his jaw a vice. Not the Jim we have known—this! His dæmon—nay, his demon, for he had but one thought, and that was to kill. No man who knew him would have known him.

Belching guns in front. Shot and bullets coming like hail. Men falling fast. Lines all shattered and anyhow. But the thick white smoke and the venomous yellow-red spits of flame were close now, and so far it had not struck him as wonderful that he still rode while so many had gone down.

He had felt hot whips across his face, something had tipped his busby to the back of his head, several other somethings had plugged through the flying jacket which covered his bridle arm. Then he had to swerve suddenly from the smoking black muzzle of a gun, and he was among flat-caps and gray-coats, and his sword was going in hot quick blows, and every blow bit home.

A big gunner struck heavily at him with a smoking mop. He had an honest brown hairy face and blue eyes. The sweep of Jim's sword took him in the neck, and . . . .

An infantryman behind had his gun-stock at his chest to fire. Jim drove the big brown at him, the man went down in a heap, arms up, and the gun went off as he fell.

Then it was all wild fury and confusion. Deseret's sword was wonderful, as light as a lath and as sure as death. He was through the smoke, fighting the myriads behind—single-handed it seemed to him.

—!—!—!—!—he could not tackle the whole Russian army! He whirled the big brown round and plunged back through the smoke, saw the others riding home, and bent and dashed away after them.

He was almost the last. A thunder of hoofs on his flank, and a vicious lance-head came thrusting in between his right arm and his body. His sword swept round backwards—and the Lancer's empty horse raced neck-and-neck with his own, its ears flat to its head, its eyes white with fear.

Then the guns behind opened on them again, and bullets came raining in on each side as well—on Russian Lancers and British Hussars and Dragoons alike.

Jim was swaying in his saddle, he did not know why. But dashing at those guns was one thing, and retiring was another, and the hell-fire had burnt out of him and left him spent.

He saw the long unbroken lines of the Heavies sweeping up to meet and cover them, and wondered dizzily if he could hold on till they came.

There were Lancers ahead of him, thrusting at his men as they rode. A whole bunch of them went down in a heap just in front of him, riddled by the murderous fire of their comrades behind, and he lifted the brown horse over them as if they had been a quick-set.

The Heavies parted to let them through, and the splendid fellow on the thundering big horse at the side there, who stood high in his stirrups cheering on his men, was good old George. There was no mistaking him, he was such a size and weight.

A couple of Lancers, who had been making for Jim, swerved to face the new attack and made for George instead, bold in the advantage of their longer reach. And Jim would have been after them to equalise matters but that it was all he could do to keep his seat.

He saw George rise in his saddle, with his great sabre swinging to the blow. Then a whirling blast of canister shore them all down, and they lay in a heap, men and horses riddled like colanders. And Jim, with a sob, clung to the pommel of his saddle and let the brown horse carry him home.

Jack had just got up to camp from night duty in the trenches when the alarm sounded in the valley, and he made his way with the rest to the edge of the plateau to see what was going on.

When he saw the cavalry drawn up for action he hurried down the hill as fast as he could go, hung spell-bound half-way at the terrible and amazing sight below, and then tumbled on with a lump in his throat to learn the worst, as the broken riders came reeling back in twos and threes.

It was he lifted Jim out of his saddle, and found it all sticky with blood from the lance-thrust in his side. His face was streaming from a graze along the scalp, and he had a bullet through the left shoulder—small things indeed considering where he had been.

The miracle of that awful ride was, not that so many fell, but that any single man came back alive.

CHAPTER LII

PATCHING UP

AS soon as matters settled down, Colonel Carron rode over at once for news of his boy. He knew he must have been in that brilliant madness, about which every tongue in the camps was wagging, and he feared he had seen the last of him.

He had some difficulty in finding what was left of the Light Brigade, for the Russians still held the lowlands in force. They had, in fact, drawn a cordon round the allied forces and were, to an extent, besieging the besiegers, and the cavalry camps had to be moved up on to the plateau.

But he came at last on the handful of laxed and weary men, lying about their new quarters, some fast asleep with their faces in their arms, while willing hands did all their necessary work for them, and every man of them still bore in him the very visible effects of that most dreadful experience.

He almost feared to ask for Jim, lest it should kill his last spark of hope.

"You had a terrible time," he said, to one on his knees by a big brown horse, which stood there with an occasional shiver as he applied healing ointment to its many wounds. "The whole world will ring with it."

"All blamed foolishness, sir," growled the man—who had lost his own horse and most of his chums in the foolishness, and so was in a mighty bad humour—and lifted a casual sticky finger in recognition of the Colonel's brilliant uniform.

"I'm afraid it was, but you did it nobly. Can you tell me anything of Cornet Carron? Was he in it?"

"In it and out of it, sir, thanks be! He's too good a sort to lose. He's inside there. This is his horse I'm patching up, 'cos he wouldn't lie quiet till I done it." And the Colonel dived into the tent with a grateful heart, and found Jim fast asleep on a hastily made couch. His wounds had been bound up, and there were even mottled white streaks on his face where a hasty sponge had made an attempt to clean it. But he was sleeping soundly, and it was the very best medicine he could have.

The Colonel went quietly out again to wait. He gave the horse-mender a very fine cigar, and lit it for him along with his own.

"Bully!" said the man. "Best thing I've tasted since I left Chelsea."

"Your losses must be very heavy."

"Under two hundred at roll-call, sir, and we went in over six."

"Awful!"

"Set of —— fools we were, sir; but we showed 'em what was in us, an' now mebbe they won't talk about us any more as they have bin doen."

"They'll talk about you to the end of time," said the Colonel heartily.

"That's all right, sir. That's a different kind of talk."

"We knowed it was all a mistake," he went on, with his head on one side, as he laid on artistic patches of ointment; "but we'd bin aching for a slap at the beggars, just to put a stopper on the mouth-wagglers nearer home. And we *did* slap 'em too, by——!"—and he lost himself for a moment in admiring contemplation of their prowess. "But they're vermin, them Roosians! Shot down their own men when we got all mixed up with 'em coming home, so they say."

"Yes, they did that. We saw it all from the heights."

"Well, that's not what I call right, sir."

"It was barbarous and damnable. No civilised nation would do such a thing."

"That's it, sir—barbarious and damnable and no civilised nation would do such a thing." And he said it over and over to himself, and gained considerable éclat by the use of it in discussion with his fellows later on.

"Jackson!" said a drowsy voice inside the tent. "How's Bob? And what the deuce are you preaching about?" And the brown horse gave a whuffle at sound of the voice.

"That's it. Thinks more of his hoss than he does of himself," said Jackson, with a wink at the Colonel. "Bob's patching up fine, sir. He's a good bit ripped up, but no balls gone in, s'far as I can see. He'll be ready for you, sir, by time you're ready for him, I should say. Gentleman called to see you, sir."

"My dear lad," said the Colonel, sitting down by his side

on a stained-red saddle. "I am grateful for the sight of you. We doubted if one of you would come back alive."

"I don't know that we expected to, sir. But we hadn't time to think about it."

"Whose mistake was it? Lucan's?"

"I don't think so, sir," he said thoughtfully, as he strove to recall it all. "I remember the look that came on his face when Nolan brought him the order. . . . I think both he and Cardigan knew there was something wrong. But Nolan was hot to have us go——"

"Is it true that he and Lucan were not on good terms?"

"I don't know anything about that, sir. There's so much talk. He's dead, anyway. His horse came galloping back with him still in the saddle and all his chest ripped open. It was horrid."

"He had no earthly right to go with you. There was some strong talk about it up there. A brave fellow, from all accounts, but hot-headed. . . . I'm going to take you to my quarters, my boy. We want you on your legs again as soon as possible."

"All right, sir. I don't think it's much. A rip or two here and there and some bullet-grazes. And the doctor's patched me up nicely."

"It's a wonder there's anything left to patch."

"You'll bring old Bob along too?"

"Oh yes, we'll take you both together. I'm glad it's in life you're not to be divided, not in death."

"He went like a bird," said Jim. And then, as the recollection of it all came back on him—the belching guns, the hairy brown gunner, the venomous Lancers, George Herapath,—"My God!" he said softly, "I wonder we ever got back at all."

CHAPTER LIII

THE FIGHT IN THE FOG

IN the comparative luxury of Colonel Carron's quarters, which were far beyond anything he could have got in the English camps, Jim pulled round rapidly. He was in the best of health, his wounds showed every intention of healing readily, and the Colonel saw to it that he lacked nothing.

He found himself, somewhat to his confusion, something of a lion there, and never lacked company anxious to discuss with him the details of that mad ride up the Valley of Death and back again.

His French visitors were unanimous in their grave disapproval and admiration; and Jack, whenever he could get away from his trenches for a chat with the invalid, reported the same feeling everywhere.

Jack himself had had a hand in the tussle with the enemy, the day after Jim's affair. But he came out of it untouched, and made light of it.

He reported Harben severely wounded, in the second charge when George Herapath was killed, and the body of the latter had been recovered and buried.

It was sad to think of old George gone right out like that. He had died bravely, hastening to the rescue of his fellows, and the boys hardly dared to think of the bitter sorrow at Knoyle and Wyvveloe when the news should get there. It would, they knew, bring right home to them all the dreadful possibilities of the war, as nothing else could have done. George gone, Ralph sorely wounded. Who would be the next to go?

Here, in the camps, with sudden death hurtling through the air night and day, and sickness still claiming more victims than all the whistling shells, they were getting somewhat case-hardened, and accustomed to sudden disappearances and vacant places. But, to the anxious scanners of the lists at home, each death in each small circle made all the other deaths seem more imminent, and weighted every heart with fresh fears.

The zigzags and trenches in which Jack held a proprietary interest were creeping nearer and nearer to the town, and he was well satisfied with the progress made. But on one other point he and his fellow Engineers were anything but content.

The right flank of their position, opposite the Inkerman cliffs and caves and very close to the road by which the Russian forces got in and out of the town, seemed to their experienced eyes but ill-defended and not incapable of assault from the lower ground. And such assault, if successful, must of necessity entail the most serious consequences on the Allies.

They spoke of the matter, harped on it, but nothing was done, save the erection of a small sand-bag battery on the slope of the hill, and no guns were mounted on it lest the sight of them should tempt the Russians to come up and take them; and so—that grim and deadly hand-to-hand struggle in the early morning fog, known as the Battle of Inkerman—which, for all who were in it, for ever stripped the fifth of November of its traditional glamour, and left in its place a blind, black horror—a nightmare struggle against overwhelming odds, which seemed as if it would never come to an end.

Oh, we won; we won of course—but, as we do win, at most dreadful cost which foresight might have saved.

Jack was in the midst of it. He had just come up from the front, soaked with rain and caked with mud, and was making a forlorn attempt at cold breakfast before lying down, when heavy firing, in the very place where they had all feared sooner or later to hear it, took him that way in haste to see what was up.

He could see nothing for the fog and rain, but a hail of shot and shell was coming from the heights across the valley and he bent and ran for the shelter of the sand-bag battery. And for many hours—and every hour an age—the sand-bag battery was "absolute hell," as he told Jim that night, with a very sober face and no enthusiasm.

Endless hosts of gray-coats came surging up out of the fog, yelling like demons, and fighting with their bayonets as they had never fought before. They were slaughtered in heaps, but there always seemed just as many coming on, yelling and stabbing, and our men yelled and stabbed, and the piles of dead grew high.

But Jack saw very little. It was all a wild pandemonium of clashing steel and yells and groans and curses, with streaming rain above, swirling fog all round, and what felt like a ploughed field heaped with dead bodies below. He picked up a rifle and bayonet, and jabbed and smashed at the gray-coats with the rest.

Through the fog he could hear the same deadly sounds all round, but whether they were winning or losing, or indeed what was going on, he had not the slightest idea. All he knew was that hosts of Russians kept on coming up in front out of the fog, that they had to be stopped at any cost, and that, from the time it was lasting, the cost must be awful.

He stumbled inside the battery one time, after a bang on the head from a clubbed musket which made him sick and dizzy; and as he sat panting in a corner for a moment till his wits came back, he told Jim afterwards that he remembered wondering if he had died and this was hell. He had a flask in his pocket somewhere, and he tried to get it out, and found his left arm would not act, though he had felt nothing wrong with it till he sat down.

He was drenched with rain and sweat—and blood, though he did not know it at the time. He got out his flask with his right hand at last, and took a long pull at it and felt better. Blood out, and brandy in, made his bruised head feel li^ht and airy. He picked up his heavy rifle and bayonet and staggered out to join the wild mêlée again—one hand was better than none where every hand was needed.

But he tumbled blindly down the slope and fell, and men trampled to and fro over his body till he felt all one big bruise. Then the grim dim struggle swayed off to one side for a moment, and he tried to crawl away.

A tall Russian—an officer by his sword—lunged down at him as he leaped past in the fog, but the point struck on his flask and the blow only rolled him over again, and the other had not time to repeat it.

And presently he crawled away up the hill, and got out of it all, and down the other side towards his own camp.

It was there his father found him, late in the afternoon, spent and bruised, and weak from loss of blood, and he went off at once and got a litter, and took him away to his own tent and set him down beside Jim. For the English doctors had their hands very much more than full, and Colonel Carron, rightly or wrongly, had much greater faith in the nursing arrangements of his adopted service than in those of the British camps and field hospitals.

When he came in at night, Jack was all bandaged up and as comfortable as could be expected, with bayonet wounds in his arm and shoulder, a badly bruised head, and a bodyful of contusions.

"I was just thanking my stars and you, sir, that I was here, and not shivering to pieces over yonder," he said gratefully.

And with reason. For the Colonel's tent was as cosy a little habitation as even the French camps could show. He had taken advantage of a slight hollow, and had had it deepened and the earth piled high like a rampart all round it, so that only its top showed above ground-level, and the keen night winds whistled over it with small effect. And inside was a cheerful little stove, and Tartar rugs, of small value perhaps, and of crude and glaring colour and design without doubt, but very homely to look at to boys who had grown accustomed to bare trodden earth. And for couches, instead of waterproof cloth and a couple of blankets spread on the ground, they had clever little bedsteads, consisting of a springy network of string inside an oblong wooden frame which rested on folding legs like a campstool.

"We certainly know how to do for ourselves better than you do. Have you had anything to eat?" asked the Colonel.

"Just had the best dinner we've had since—well, since we dined with you last, sir," said Jim, with great satisfaction. "I don't know what it was, but it was uncommonly good."

And Jack asked anxiously: "Have you any news for us, sir? We heard they were driven back. Are any of our people left?"

"A few; but your loss is very heavy. Ours also; but you bore the brunt of it over there where the work was hottest. They came up out of the town at us, just below here, while you were busy there, and they made a feint also just above Balaclava. It has been a hot day all round. I hope they'll give us time to breathe now."

"I wonder what lies that fellow Menchikoff will stuff into the Tsar this time," said Jim.

"He can hardly claim a victory, anyway," said his father, with a smile.

"I bet he will, sir."

"Did you hear anything as to casualties, sir?" asked Jack, whose mind could not get far away from that grim struggle in the fog.

"Only outstanding ones. Your loss in big men is terrible. Cathcart is dead, and Strangways——"

"Poor old Strangways!"

"A dear old chap!" echoed Jim.

—"and Goldie,—all killed. George Brown and Codrington and Bentinck wounded, and I believe Torrens and Buller and Adams also. Some of your regiments are almost without officers. Our most serious loss is de Lourmel, down in front here, repulsing the sortie. They estimate 15,000 Russians killed and wounded——"

"There seemed millions of them lying round that battery," said Jack.

"They reckon there were 8,000 English and 6,000 of our men in the fight, and between 50,000 and 60,000 Russians. So that every one of our men put at least one of theirs *hors de combat*—a remarkable performance indeed."

"I've been thinking, Jim," he said presently, "that a few days on the sea would set you up again quicker than anything else. What do you say?"

"I'd like it immensely, sir, if it could be managed. It's awfully good of you."

"You're creditable boys, you see, and I'm anxious not to lose either of you. I wonder how soon the medico would let you go too, Jack?" And he looked at him with a practised eye. "Not for a week anyway, I expect."

"I feel as if I could sleep for a week, sir. It's so mighty comfortable here," he said drowsily.

"They've had such a stomachful to-day that I think they'll keep quiet for a time now. It was a great scheme and they did their best. It'll take them a little time to work up a new one. Well, we'll see about it to-morrow. You think you'll be able to sleep, Jack?"

"Sure, sir, when I get the chance. Jim's been talking ever since the doctor went."

CHAPTER LIV

AN ALLY OF PROVIDENCE

THE Colonel was away on business soon after sunrise, long before the boys were awake. The Russians had had enough for the moment and gave them a quiet night. He came in while they were breakfasting, with a satisfied look on his face.

"Well, Jack, how goes it? You were both sleeping like tops when I left you."

"I feel like a jelly-fish on Carne beach, sir," said Jack. "I have a very great disinclination to move."

"Cuts twingy?"

"When I think of them, sir. At present I can think of nothing but this coffee. They give us ours green, you know, and nothing to roast or grind it with."

"So I heard. I would like to see what would happen if they sent ours like that; but, *mon Dieu!* I wouldn't like to be in their shoes! The good old fashion of hanging a commissary whenever anything went wrong was certainly effective. Jim, my boy, I've got your matter arranged all right. You are to get away to-morrow with a fortnight's leave. That should pull you round."

"It's awfully good of you, sir. It's just what I'm needing."

"Talking of hanging commissaries," said the Colonel, with a whimsical smile on his dark face, "it was all I could do to keep my hands off one of your pig-heads down at Balaclava yonder." And he switched his long mud-caked riding-boot with his whip as if it were the gentleman in question.

"I called on Lord Raglan to ask his permission to my plan, and at first he was a bit stiff and stand-offish. But he came round and spoke very nicely of you, my boy. He wouldn't discuss that foolish charge of yours, and I did not press it. He granted you leave at once, and gave me a written order for your passage to and from Constantinople by first ship that was leaving."

"But that's only the beginning of the story," he said, as Jim's mouth opened with thanks again. "I thought I'd make sure of the whole business, so I waded down to Balaclava. *Mon Dieu!* what a travesty of a road! My poor beast was up to his knees in the filth at times. And the place itself when I got there! The harbour is a cesspool, an inferno of evil smells and pestilence. And I think the evil vapours have got into the heads of your people there. I never saw such disorder and confusion in all my life. I found the harbour master at last, and asked him for information as to sailings. But he was only the Inner Harbour Master, it seems, and he referred me to the Head of the Transport. The transport people referred me to the Naval Authorities, and a naval officer, whom I caught on the wing, told me I would have to apply to the Outer Harbour Master, who was somewhere outside among the fleet. I was consigning them all to warmer quarters than Balaclava, when I spied a man I knew—Captain Jolly of the *Carnbrea*, who had brought some of our troops over to Kamiesch Bay. He was bursting with complaints and nearly mad, said he'd like to tie the heads of all the departments in one big bag and sink them in the cesspool. He said he was sailing to-morrow with a load of sick and wounded, and he'd been up trying to get a few stoves from the official who had charge of them, as the sick men were dying of the cold. 'He'd got hundreds of them lying there,' said old Jolly, almost black in the face, 'and he wouldn't let me have one. Said I must get a requisition and fill it up and get it signed at Head-quarters. I told him the men were dying meanwhile. He could do nothing without a requisition signed at Head-quarters. I asked him to lend me some stoves. He couldn't. I asked him to sell me some. He wouldn't. I told him those men's deaths would lie at his door. He said if I would get a requisition, etc., etc. So then I—well, I told him what I thought of him and all the rest, in good hot sailor-talk, and came away.

"I asked him if he could find room for one more on his ship, and told him about you, and, like a good fellow, he said, 'Send 'em both along and I'll make room for 'em.' So you're all right, Jim, and Jolly will make you comfortable, I know."

"It's awfully good of you, sir," said Jim once more. "I'm sorry we're such a bother to you."

"It's not every man can boast of two such young warriors,

you see. On the whole I'm inclined to think Providence served us well in making me an ally, eh?"

"Your people are very much better off than ours, sir," said Jack. "Our camp is like London on a foggy day."

"And ours is like Paris," laughed the Colonel. "You see we understand the art of war better than you do, and, candidly, I think your officers are much to blame for the little interest they take in their men. Here we are all *bons camarades*, whereas your men are left entirely to themselves."

"We mix in the trenches," said Jack in defence.

"Of necessity, I suppose, since the space is limited. But even there you don't mix as we do."

"Your music alone is worth coming for," said Jim. "It did me as much good as the doctor almost."

"Yes; I notice a lot of your men come across to hear it whenever they get the chance. Great mistake shutting up your bands. The men always like music, and expect it."

"You don't think I'll miss anything by going, sir?" asked Jim anxiously.

"You'll gain a great deal more than you'll miss, my boy. I shouldn't wonder if we have a fairly quiet time here now."

"And you'll see to my horse?"

"He shall have every attention, I promise you."

CHAPTER LV

RETRIBUTION

THE following day saw Jim joggling down the miry way to Balaclava Harbour on a French mule-cacolet. He had said good-bye to the others in camp, and begged his father not to venture down into the inferno again. So the Colonel sent his own servant in charge of him, with full instructions where to find the boat Captain Jolly had promised to have waiting.

The hopeless confusion in the little harbour appalled Jim, and the dank misery of the rows of wounded men awaiting shipment, with ill-bound wounds, cold blue faces, and heavy hopeless eyes, chilled him to the heart.

And suddenly a familiar face caught his eye, and he stopped the mule and sat up.

"Why, Seth, old chap! I'm sorry to see you like this"—for Seth's left leg was gone, and the roughly bandaged stump stuck out forlornly along the ground.

"My fightin's done, Mester Jim. 'Twere a shell took it off in the battery."

"When are you going over?"

"God knows. We bin waiting over a week."

"An' dyin' as quick as we could, just to save 'em trouble," said his neighbour.

"I wish I could take you all," said Jim, and the bleached leather faces turned wistfully on him. "But I can take one, and I must take you, Seth. You understand, boys: he's from my own part, and twice he's saved my life."

"That's right, sir. You take 'im home, and God bless you! Wish there was more like you! We'll die off as quick as we can, just to save 'em trouble," said the jocular one, who had lost both an arm and a leg. "If they ask where 'e is we'll tell 'em 'e's gone on in front to engage us quarters."

"Lift him in," said Jim, and with the assistance of the bystanders Seth was lifted into the other side of the cacolet.

An official came hurrying up with a brusque, "Now then, what's all this?"

"Oh, go and hang yourself!" said Jim, sinking back wearily. "Can't you see I'm saving you trouble by taking him off your hands?"

"Yes—but——"

"Go ahead!" said Jim, and left the other staring after them.

Captain Jolly's boat was waiting for them, and presently they were swung up on to the deck of the *Carnbrea*.

"So you've both come, after all?" said the hearty old fellow to Jim, who came up first.

Jim explained, and the captain said he had done quite right, and they would find a corner for Seth between decks, though they were pretty full already; and then he helped him across to a seat by the wheel, and the *Carnbrea* crept away out of the noisome harbour at once, and Jim counted no less than six dead horses, washing about in the water or cast up on the rocks, before the sweet salt air outside gave him something better to think about.

They passed the warships, and a multitude of vessels hanging about outside, and the monastery perched up on the cliff, and the white lighthouse at the point, and presently, through a rift in the dull November sky, the sun shone red on Sebastopol, and set it all aglow. Here and there, on its outer edge, there were little cotton-woolly puffs of white smoke, and the plateau behind was dotted with similar ones.

Captain Jolly was as good as his name and Colonel Carron's opinion of him. He made Jim very much at home, got him to tell him all he could about the great charge, and in return gave his own free and unrestrained opinions on men and things in general, with a special excursus on harbour masters and transport officials.

"Too many head cooks—that's what's the matter, and not a man below 'em dare lift his little finger unless he's got permission in writing. Why, sirs, there's things rotting there in that harbour that'd be worth their weight in gold up above, but it's nobody's business to send 'em up, and there they stop. It's a crying shame and—and an infernal sin! What do you say to it all, doctor?"

This was a grave, thin-faced young fellow who had joined them in the cabin for a cup of tea, and Captain Jolly had simply introduced him with a wink as Dr. Subrosa.

"It's heartbreaking," he said, with deepest feeling. "We

have lost thousands of good men from sheer want of the simplest necessaries, and almost every one of them might have been saved. For weeks I had not a single drug except alum! Think of it! And to see those poor fellows in torture, and dying like flies, when you knew you could save them if you could only lay your hands on the proper remedies!"

"I'll be bound there's piles of all you wanted stowed away in Balaclava somewhere," said the captain.

"I fear so. I came down, day after day—and it was no easy matter, I can assure you—and begged them to give me any mortal thing they had for my fevers and rheumatisms and diarrhoeas; and the reply was always just a parrot-like 'Haven't any—Haven't any—Haven't any,'—till I would willingly have poisoned every man who said it. They're getting calloused to it all, and, as Captain Jolly says, not a man among them dare lift his finger without a written order."

"Take my own case," he said, turning to Jim. "The continuous wear and tear, and the constant sight of nothing but sickness and death and broken men, were beginning to tell on me——"

"My God, I don't wonder!" jerked Jim.

"My chief on the medical staff told me I must get away for fourteen days or so or I'd break down, and he signed me the proper form for the purpose. I found it had to be countersigned by the quartermaster-general, then by the colonel of the regiment to which I was attached, then by the general of the division, and finally by the adjutant-general. It is probably still going round among them, if it hasn't got lost. I waited six days and could get no word of it, and my chief advised me to take French leave and bring back some drugs if they're to be had. I'm told there is a *Times* man come out with money, to help make good some of the shortcomings in the official providence, and I'm hoping he'll help me. I'm actually a deserter, you see. That's why this dear old chap calls me Subrosa. My name is McLean, and I'm attached to the 63rd."

"And a rare good sort he is," said Captain Jolly. "Did I tell you about my load of boots?"

"No; what was it about the boots?"

"Last voyage I came out with nothing but boots—more boots than you ever dreamt of, thousands and thousands of pairs. The whole ship stank of 'em—smelt like a tannery. Well, when they let us into Balaclava Harbour at last, and we were hoping to get rid of the boots——"

"They're going barefoot yet, many of them," said McLean.

"I know. Well, before we could begin to break cargo there came a couple of dandy fine gentlemen, with a peremptory order to take them to Constantinople as fast as we could go, and we were hustled away before you could say 'boots.' We were less than a day's sail from Constantinople, when one of the dandy men mentioned in confidence to me that the men up there were barefoot and they were going to buy boots for them."

"What did you say?" asked Jim expectantly.

"Well, I said more'n I should perhaps. Dandy men or no dandy men, I said, 'Why, you —— fool, I'm loaded to the hatches with boots and nothing but boots! Why in thunder couldn't you open your mouth sooner?' 'Our instructions,' says he, 'were to buy boots, captain, not to go talking about it, and I'll thank you not to use language unbecoming a gentleman when talking to me.' And he walked away to talk to the other, who was sick in his bunk."

"And what did you do?" asked Jim.

"I shut off steam," said the captain, with a meaning wink, "and presently he came up again and said they'd decided we'd better turn back again and take the boots to the feet that were waiting for them. And I've no doubt they're rotting on Balaclava Quay now with all the other things. Why, if my owners did their business as the Government does its they'd be bankrupt in a year."

After his cup of tea Jim went below to see that Seth was comfortably stowed.

He found him, with a couple of hundred others, lying in long rows in the 'tween decks, which had been adapted to their use as far as it was possible to do so. They lay pretty close, and each man had a couple of blankets to soften the wood and keep out the cold.

At one end were half a dozen wounded officers. Between them and the men had been left a space of a few feet, and that was the only distinction between them. To make room for Seth this space had been encroached upon, and he lay next the officers.

As Jim rose from his knees after a short chat with him, in which he had done his best to put a little heart into the poor fellow, by assuring him that he should be properly provided for when he got home to Carne, he heard his name called weakly from the officers' quarters, and, bidding Seth good night, and promising to see him first thing in the morning, he turned that way.

"Why, Harben!" he said. "I'm sorry to see you here. What is it?"

"Nothing. I'm sick—very sick. Who is that they've put there?" asked Ralph, in a low eager whisper.

"That? Why, it's Seth Rimmer—young Seth, you know, from down along."

"He's a dangerous man that, Jim. Put him somewhere else! Take him away!"

"Nonsense, old man. Seth's as true as they make 'em. Besides, he's lost a leg. And anyway I couldn't ask them to move him now. There's no room anywhere else."

"He's dangerous, I tell you," said Harben, with a shiver. "He thinks . . . he thinks . . . but I haven't, Jim. I swear I haven't. I'd nothing to do with it. I swear I hadn't."

"Don't you worry, old man," said Jim soothingly, for it all sounded to him like the ravings of a disturbed brain. "Can I get you anything, or make you more comfortable?"

"Only take him away," whispered the other insistently.

But that Jim could not do. He and Seth were only there

on sufferance, as it were, and he wanted to give as little trouble as possible.

Captain Jolly had insisted on giving up his own bunk to him, but had only prevailed on him to take it by asserting that he would be on deck most of the night. And the clean cold sheets were so delightful, after the threadbare amenities of the camp, that he felt as if he could sleep on for a week.

Very early next morning Jim was wakened by a hand on his shoulder. He jumped up so vehemently—forgetful of the narrowness of his quarters, and with a mazy impression that the Russians were upon them—that his head was sore for days after it.

"Mr. Carron," said a grave quiet voice, "there is trouble on board." And he saw that it was Dr. McLean.

"Trouble? What trouble, doctor?"

"We want you to explain it if you can. Slip on some things and come along." And Jim tumbled wonderingly into his jacket and trousers and followed the doctor—to the 'tween decks—to the officers' quarters.

And there lay the end of a tragedy.

Seth's pallet was empty. Seth himself—what had been Seth—lay partly on the body of Ralph Harben. His rough brown fingers still gripped Harben's throat, with a grip that had started the dead man's eyes almost out of his head and had prevented him uttering a sound.

And Seth lay in a pool of his own blood, for his vehemence had burst his hastily bandaged amputation, and he had bled to death in the act of wreaking his vengeance.

"Good God!" gasped Jim, and felt sick and ill at the sight.

"Are they dead?" he whispered, as though he feared to wake them.

"Both quite dead. Been dead several hours," said McLean, and led him back to the captain's cabin, where the steward brought them hot coffee.

"Do you know what it all means, Mr. Carron?" asked the captain.

"I'm afraid I do, captain, but I'd no idea of it, and it's a terrible shock to me." And he briefly explained as far as was necessary.

"Ay, ay," said the old man soberly; "I can see it all. He came out on purpose to find the other, to pay him out for the wrong he'd done him, and when his chance came he took it. . . . I don't hold with murder myself, but . . . well, I'm bound to say I can feel for this poor lad."

There were eight others who had died in the night, and they buried them all at the same time, and Captain Jolly read the service over them, and entered in his log the simple fact that ten died and were buried.

And Jim said no word of it in his letters home, and only told Jack about it when he got back to camp.

CHAPTER LVI

DULL DAYS

THE ten days' voyage there and back, in Captain Jolly's bunk and cheerful company, did Jim a world of good. They lay off Scutari six days, and were back in the Cesspool, as Jolly persisted in calling Balaclava Bay, on the twenty-second of November, having just missed the great gale, which tore the camps to pieces and piled the wild Crimean coast with the wreckage of over forty ships and millions of pounds' worth of the goods that were so badly needed on shore.

Nearly every ship they passed, as they drew in, was dismasted and looked half a wreck, and Jim, when he had said good-bye to the genial Jolly, and had waded through the muddy gorge and climbed the heights, found everything and everybody in the camps in very similar condition.

In spite of his own fitness, and the healthy frame of mind induced by sixteen days of clean salt air and the companionship of Captain Jelly, his spirits sank with every step he took. It was like climbing through a charnel-house—dead horses and mules stuck up out of the mud on every side, just as they had fallen under their loads and been left to die; and Jim's love for every dumb thing that went on four legs was sorely bruised before he got to the plateau.

And when he did get there the sights were more painful still—mud everywhere, and dirty pools and trickling streams, sodden tents, and gaunt, hungry-looking men in rags, trudging to and fro, with bare feet or with boots that only added to the dilapidated looks of their wearers. Truly, he thought, though not perhaps in so many words, this was the seamy side of war, and the glory and glamour were remarkable only by their absence.

He reported himself at Head-quarters, but saw only an aide-de-camp, who was the only clean and wholesome and fairly-fed person he had met since he landed. He learned that his chief, Lord Cardigan, was sick, and that his brigade was to go down to Balaclava as soon as possible, as the horses could not stand the miseries of the heights.

Then he went across to the French camps, and found things in very much better condition there, and Jack getting on famously and eager for all his experiences.

Jim told him of Seth and Ralph Harben, and he was profoundly surprised and saddened by it all.

"And you really think it was Ralph took Kattie away, Jim?" he asked, after a long stare of amazement.

"Seth wouldn't have done a thing like that unless he had good reason," said Jim simply.

"I can't imagine Kattie caring for a fellow like Ralph, you know," said Jack thoughtfully. "He was always such a—well, he's dead, so it's no good saying it, but you know yourself what he was. . . . . . But it's horrible to think of—four lives gone by reason of it."

And Jim said no more, except that he had thought it best to say nothing about it in his letters home.

There were two letters from Gracie to read, one to himself and one to Jack, both so bright and cheerful and full of hope that they could not by any possibility have imagined what it cost her to write like that, when her heart was so full of fears for them. She told Jim of Paddy's admirable behaviour, and of long delightful rides with Meg and Sir George on the flats. And she told Jack of visits to Sir Denzil, and how the Rimmer cottage was still shut up and empty. But from neither letter could the most discriminating judge have drawn any clue as to the writer's heart tending more to the one of them than to the other.

There were also letters from Charles Eager, with comments on the course of the war and the feeling at home, and fervent hopes for their safety and that of George Herapath—who lay out there in the cemetery on the cold hill-side. And there was also one from Lord Deseret to Jim, which contained, among other things, the somewhat surprising news that Mme Beteta had gone to St. Petersburg to fill an engagement there.

Then Colonel Carron came in and gave him hearty welcome, and wanted all his experiences over again.

"And how's my horse?" asked Jim, as soon as he got the chance. "I was thinking of him all the way up from the harbour. The road is thick with the poor beasts who have died there."

"He's first-rate. I've been riding him myself to keep him in condition. I shall be quite sorry to part with him. Deseret knew what he was about, my boy, when he chose him for you."

He was very pleased with Jim's eulogiums on Captain Jolly, and forthwith decided that Jack must make the next trip with him.

So they had a very pleasant time in the banked-up tent, in spite of the dreariness of things outside. But all too soon it came to an end, and Jim had to go off to his own Spartan quarters, where the heartiness of his greeting almost made up for the lack of everything else.

He settled down into the rut of camp life again, but found it all very slow and dull and dirty.

There was little doing. It was as much as they could do simply to live.

The dull routine of the trenches went on. The batteries spat shot and shell at the town at intervals, and Russian shot and shell came singing back in reply, and sometimes did a little damage.

And at times the camps would be wakened by furious fusillades in the advanced French lines, when the Russians enlivened matters with a sortie. But these alarms were spared the English, on account of the bad ground in their front, which did not lend itself to such matters.

More than once, too, they all turned out *en masse* in the middle of the night—and always on the bitterest nights—to repel attacks in the rear which never came off.

And every day there went down to Balaclava the long slow procession of sick men, and to the cemetery another procession of those who had died in the night.

Jack duly got his leave and went away with Captain Jolly, and Jim busied himself, as well as the authorities would let him, in providing for the reception of the men and horses of the Light Brigade on the hill-side above Balaclava Bay.

A slow, dull time, wearing on body, mind, and spirit—and yet, not the worst time possible.

CHAPTER LVII

HOT OVENS

JACK was back, in the best of health and spirits.

"I'm almost sorry I didn't join the navy," he said, as he trudged with Jim through the mud to the Picket House, to see how things had gone on in his absence. "They do keep things clean, anyway."

"That's the only place where they have any fun nowadays," he said, as they stood looking down on the lines and zigzags, creeping nearer and nearer to the town, and pointed to a deep gully which ran up from the head of the Admiralty Harbour and separated the British position from the French.

"The Ovens," said Jim. "Couldn't we go down some night and see some of it?"

"Any night you like when I'm not on duty."

"Why not to-night? You won't start work till to-morrow, I suppose."

"All right! To-night! The 50th are down there, and there are some capital fellows among them."

And that was how it happened that, for the sake of a little fun, or, in other words, the chance of a brush with the enemy, the boys found themselves that night stumbling along the deep trench which zigzaged down from Chapman's Battery towards the Green Hill, and so into the deep gully which ran up into the plateau from the head of Admiralty Harbour in Sebastopol. The sides of the gully contained numerous caves, formed by the decay of the softer strata in the rocks, and these caves had for some time past been the stakes for which small parties on each side played sharp little war-games, and paid at times with their lives.

First they were Russian, then they were British, then again Russian, till the 50th had ousted them and remained in possession.

It was a bitterly cold night, but the boys, in the great fur coats Jim had bought out of the loot at Mackenzie's Farm, had nothing to complain of.

They found a strong picket of the 50th making themselves very much at home in the Ovens, and received a warm welcome from the officers in charge.

"Any chance of any fun to-night?" asked Jack.

"We can never tell what's going to happen. Keeps us on the jig the whole time, but it's better than doing nothing upstairs."

"And it comes off sometimes," said another.

"And when it does, the Ovens get hot," laughed a third, and they squatted on the floor and discussed zigzags and such matters.

"Almost took you for Russians in those big coats," said one enviously. "Did you steal 'em?"

"Somebody else stole 'em," laughed Jack. "We're only receivers. Jim bought them that day at Mackenzie's, when Menchikoff bolted and left us his baggage."

"Talking of spies," said another, sliding off on an inference, "did you hear of the one who walked about our lines for half a day as cool as a cucumber? He was dressed in full French uniform, asked heaps of questions in very bad English, and said we were doing wonders, and made himself quite pleasant all round. And then he caught sight of some more Frenchmen, coming down with the Colonel towards the battery to have a look at the Lancasters. As soon as he saw them he began to edge off down the hill, and when he saw his chance he just made a clean bolt of it, with our men blazing away at him as hard as they could, but he got clear away under the Redan there. And now we're a bit suspicious of men in big fur coats. If you'll take my advice you'll leave 'em behind you here. Save you a heap of trouble maybe."

"Any sentry would be justified in shooting any man he saw in a coat like that," said another.

"All right, my boys! We'll keep our coats and take our chances. What's that?" And they all pricked up their ears to listen.

An order in French came to them from the opposite side of the gully.

"Their sentries and pickets are just over there. This is Tommy Tiddler's Ground, between England, France, and——"

A hoarse shout outside, and shots and yells, and they were all out in a moment and found the gully packed with Russians, and their own men, taken by surprise, falling back in some confusion.

"Brace up there, men!" shouted the officer in charge. "They're only a handful and only Russians."

It was very dark, except where the fires inside the caves sent out a dull glow here and there on the bare space between the combatants. Then the whole place blazed with a Russian volley, and again with the reply to it.

"Bayonets, men! And down with them!" And with a yell the Englishmen plunged down past the dull-glowing Ovens, and Jack and Jim raced with them, revolver in hand, blazing away into the darkness in front as they ran.

But the Russian plans for that night had been well laid. It was a miniature Balaclava charge over again.

A ripping volley met them, not from the front, but from both sides, and then masses of men closed in behind them and swallowed them up, and every man was fighting for his life against unnumbered odds.

Jim, elbow to elbow with Jack, and yelling with excitement, felt him suddenly trip and fall. He stooped to help him up again. But Jack lay still.

He straddled across him to keep him from being trampled on, and men lunged into him and tumbled over Jack, and he hurled them aside. Hand-to-hand fights were going on all round, and the place was full of the clash of steel on steel and pantings and groanings and hearty British curses.

But they were outnumbered twenty to one, and the last dozen were borne to the ground by sheer weight of Russians on their backs. The Ovens changed tenants and were occupied in force, and their late occupants were dragged away down the sloping valley towards the Harbour.

Jim found himself the centre of a raging mob. He had snatched up a rifle, and, swinging it by the muzzle, kept a rough circle clear of Jack's body. But vicious bayonets were jabbing at him all round, and a bullet went singing past his head.

"Cowards! Murderers! Do you call this fighting fair?" he shouted savagely.

And of a sudden the mob parted, and an officer was belabouring his men with the flat of his sword and strong words.

"Vous vous rendez?" he cried to Jim.

"Suppose I must," he growled.

"All right!" said the Russian. "Go there! Allez!" and pushed him towards the gorge.

Jim stooped and endeavoured to lift Jack.

"Quoi donc? What?"

"My brother. I must take him."

"Dead?"

"My God!" gasped Jim at the word, as all that would mean to them all flashed upon him. "No, no! I hope not—only wounded."

"We cannot take him."

"We must."

The Russian used language, then called to one of his men, who sulkily took Jack's limp legs while Jim took him under the arms, and they stumbled away downhill, leaving a strong force in possession of the Ovens.

Skirting a dark sheet of water, they came on a road where some rough carts were waiting. The wounded were bundled into them, and a place found for Jack, and Jim trudged behind with his hand on the tail of the cart, and his heart full of bitterness. Their fun had become, of a sudden, grimmest earnest.

They turned to the right over a bridge, where many lights gleamed on the water in front, and so came at last to a great building which proved to be the hospital.

CHAPTER LVIII

CHILL NEWS

THE first news of trouble reached Carne in a brief letter from Colonel Carron to Sir Denzil.

Gracie and the Rev. Charles were sitting over their tea one

afternoon in the quiet, hopeful despondency—if the expression may be permitted—which had become the natural state of all who had dear ones at the war. They were full of fears; they cherished hope; they waited with quiet resignation what each day might bring forth.

When Kennet rapped on the door of the cottage, Gracie's heart jumped and sank, and Eager incongruously thought of the old Latin Grammar tag: *Mors æquo pede* . . . ("Death with equal foot knocks at the door of rich and poor").

"Sir Denzil begs you will come and see him at once, sir."

"Bad news, Kennet?" asked Eager, as he reached down his hat.

"He didn't say, sir; but he's in a bad-enough humour. Not that that's much to go by, though, these days"—from which one gathers that even Sir Denzil's equanimity was not entirely unaffected by the disturbances of the times.

Gracie had slipped on her cloak and little fur turban. He looked at her doubtfully. But she shook her head with decision.

"I could not possibly wait here, fearing everything," she said; and they went along together.

Sir Denzil expressed no surprise at sight of her.

"I have just received a letter from my son, Colonel Carron," he said, in a voice perhaps a trifle too unnaturally even and unmoved. "The boys, I am sorry to say, have met with a misfortune." Gracie's heart sank, and braced itself as best it could for the worst. "It is not, however, as bad as it might be." Her heart gave a hopeful kick. "They are both prisoners in the hands of the Russians, and one of them is wounded again; but, so far, he has not been able to ascertain which. That is all; but I thought it better to let you know the full extent of the matter. The newspaper accounts are so garbled at times that one is apt to get wrong impressions. When you come across their names among the missing, you will understand. It does not necessarily mean anything more than I have told you. In fact"—with an appreciative pinch of snuff—

"it may well be that they are safer inside Sebastopol than outside."

"Prisoners!" jerked Gracie. "Will they be well treated?"

"Oh yes; I should say so. The rank and file of the Russian army are doubtless somewhat boorish, but their officers are civilised—gentlemanly, indeed, I believe, if you don't go too far down. I do not think you need fear any ill-treatment for them, Miss Gracie. It is annoying, of course, not to know which of them is wounded, and to what extent. But the authorities will, no doubt, do their best to ascertain, and we may hear shortly."

"I am inclined to think with you, sir, that they will probably be safer inside than outside," said Eager thoughtfully. "From all accounts, the state of things in the camps is awful."

"Extremely British," said Sir Denzil. "Matters will improve in time. When the Many-headed One awakes to the fact that all this waste and misery are quite unnecessary, it will roar loud enough, I warrant you. Then our men will be properly looked after—that is, if there are any of them left to look after, which seems somewhat doubtful."

"It is shameful!" broke out Gracie, with vehemence. "I wish I could have gone with Miss Nightingale to help them."

"You would have died of atrophy and paralysis, my dear, if you had come in contact with the red-tape of the services. If Miss Nightingale succeeds in her mission she will be the one woman in ten million, and will deserve well of her country."

And so they were left in doubt and much distress of mind as to the welfare of the boys.

Margaret Herapath, in her deep mourning and her own bitter sorrow, came over to share their anxiety and distress. Her father had suddenly become an old and broken man. Charles Eager was much with him, and he was the only person, outside his own household, whom Sir George cared to see. And Eager, with the wisdom of deepest love and sympathy, let the old man's grief run its course, and then strove to build him up anew by diverting his grief from the one to the many.

Bitter sad times were those in the happy homes of England: Sorrow lay on the land like a chill black frost; but below it were simmering all those forces of passionate indignation which presently rose into that inextinguishable roar which swept men from their high positions, and in time carried somewhat of relief to the remnant of the army before Sebastopol.

CHAPTER LIX

TOUCH AND GO FOR THE COIL

JIM followed Jack's body with the single-minded persistency of a faithful dog whose master has come to grief. His original captor would have taken him elsewhere, but he flatly declined to go anywhere but where Jack went. He thrust aside all interfering hands, and to all attempts at coercion in any other direction simply pointed to Jack and himself and said, "My brother!"—but with so grim and determined and dejected a face that at last the other gave way and followed them into the hospital.

It was very full—crammed with broken and dying men—but Jim had no thought save for Jack. Whether he was alive or dead he did not know, but he must stick to him and do what he could.

There was difficulty in finding room for him. A harassed surgeon, to whom the officer spoke, shook red hands at them and poured out a spate of hot words, but, arrested by something the other said, looked worriedly round and at last pointed to a corner; and Jim's captor explained to him, in his peculiar English, that the man who lay there would be dead in a minute or two, and then they could put Jack in his place.

And presently the attendants came along and carried the dead man away, and Jim and the officer lifted Jack on to the pallet, and the worried surgeon came round and knelt down and opened up his things, and examined him with quick, practised hands and a keen eye for causes and effects.

Jim's heart ran slow at sight of a bullet-hole in the white breast, and he watched the surgeon hypnotically as he carefully turned the body over and pointed to the place where it had come out at the back, just under the shoulder, and then spoke hurriedly to the officer.

"He says," said the other, in his broken English, helped out with very good French—which it would be but a hindrance to attempt to reproduce in detail—"he cannot tell. It has gone right through. He may live, he may die. It will take time to tell. Now you come."

"May I come again to see him?"

"I will try. You will give your parole?"

"Yes," said Jim; for Jack was more to him than all the chances of escape.

"Then we will see. Now come!"

"Beg him to do everything he can for him. Couldn't we take him somewhere else?"

"He is better here, for the present. Later we will see. Now come!" And since he could do no more at the moment, Jim went with him.

"For to-night you will come to the guard-room. To-morrow you will go to Head-quarters and be properly paroled. Then we will see."

And Jim spent the rest of the night on three chairs in the guard-room, brooding gloomily most of the time on the disastrous results of "seeing the fun" of the Ovens, and full of fears as to the end of it all.

In the morning his keeper came for him, and Jim, for the first time, took the opportunity of looking at him. He had been too busy with other matters the night before.

He was a young fellow of about his own age, dark-haired, and of a thin sallow face, bright-eyed, pleasant-looking. Under other circumstances Jim thought they might have become friendly. He had certainly treated him well.

"How is my brother?" asked Jim anxiously.

"We will see as we go. Have you eaten? No?" And he took him away to a mess-room just alongside, where a number of officers were drinking coffee from bowls, and smoking and talking.

They saluted Jim politely, and stared at him without restraint while he ate a chunk of very good white bread and drank his coffee, which was excellent, and meanwhile they plied his friend with questions.

And one, after much observation of Jim's uniform, suddenly made some remark which carried all eyes to him and made him extremely uncomfortable at so much observation.

"He is saying that your regiment was in that mad charge outside Balaclava," said his particular officer.

"Yes; I was in it," said Jim quietly.

And at that, to his immense surprise, every man in the room sprang to his feet and gravely saluted him again.

"And you got through whole?" was the next question.

"No. I had a lance wound and three bullets into me, but I've been a voyage to Constantinople since then, to brace up, you know."

And they crowded round him, and pressed cigars on him, and showed themselves right good fellows.

Then his new friend took him along to the hospital, and they learned that Jack had come to himself and was sleeping, and so they went on across the bridge of boats, and through the public gardens, and past the cathedral, to Head-quarters.

After waiting some time, they were conducted down many long passages to a room where a tall fair man, of high face and autocratic bearing, sat at a table piled with papers and plans. Another stood looking out of the window, with his back turned to them, and a white English terrier, standing by his side on its hind legs, was trying hard to make out what he was looking at.

Jim's keeper saluted deferentially and made his statement to the tall man at the table.

"I understand you are prepared to give your parole not

to attempt to escape, or to hold any communication with the outside?" said he, somewhat brusquely, first in French and then in understandable English.

"I am," bowed Jim. And at the sound of his voice the white dog came dancing across to him as though he were an old friend, and accepted his caresses with delight.

"And your brother is also a prisoner, in hospital, and you wish to attend on him."

"I do."

"What is your name and standing?"

"James Denzil Carron—cornet, 8th Hussars." And at that the man at the window turned suddenly and looked at him, and came and stood by the table.

"You were, then, in the mad charge at Balaclava, perhaps?"

"I was."

"It was a foolish business."

"It was."

"Ah—you agree? How was it?"

"Some mistake. But no one quite knows."

"What are your total forces up there now?"

At which Jim's lip curled in a smile.

"You can hardly expect me to tell you that," he said quietly.

The tall young man who had been standing by the window said a word or two to the other, who seemed surprised, and turning to Jim, said: "Very well, Monsieur Carron. I accept your parole, and Lieutenant Greski will be personally answerable for you."

The lieutenant bowed, and plucked Jim backward by the sleeve, and Jim bowed, and gave the white dog's ear a final friendly pull, and they went out.

"Who is he?" he asked, as soon as they were in the corridor.

"Menchikoff, the one at the table. The other is the Grand Duke Michael. How does he know you?" And he looked at Jim with new curiosity.

"Who—Menchikoff?"

"No—the Grand Duke."

"Know me?" jerked Jim. "Some mistake. I never set eyes on him before."

"He told Menchikoff to do what you wanted, and said he knew you, or something about you, or something of the kind. He dropped his voice so that I couldn't catch it all."

"That's odd. I certainly know nothing of him."

"He thinks he knows you, anyway, and so much the better for you. You shall come with me and stop at my house. It is not far."

"You are very good. I shall have a better opinion of Russians in future."

"Russians! I am no Russian. I am a Pole. I hate the Russians, and would love the English if I might."

"I see. But why do you fight for them, then?"

"Because if I didn't my kin in Poland would have to pay for it."

"That's jolly hard, to have to risk your life, and maybe give it, for people you hate."

"There are many more like me. But what can we do? If we go against them they visit it on the innocent ones at home. If I could destroy the whole of Russia, Tsar and Grand Dukes and all, at one blow, I would strike it so"—and he dashed his fist into the palm of his other hand—"and then I would die with a glad heart. . . . But one does not talk of these things, you understand, except among one's friends."

He stopped at a house which stood about midway down the slope overlooking the harbour, and led Jim into a room on the ground floor. From the window he could see Fort Constantine, shining white in the sun on the other side of the water, and the bristling line of the masts of the sunken ships, and the harbour itself dotted all over with plying boats.

"One moment," said Greski, and left him there, but came back in an instant with a very beautiful white-haired old lady, whom he must have met in the passage. Her dark eyes were shining like stars at the joy of seeing her boy again.

"My mother," said Greski, and explained matters to her in a torrent of Polish.

She assented without any demur to all her son's proposals, and shook hands very heartily with Jim, giving him what was evidently warm welcome, in a tongue he did not understand.

Then the door opened again, and a girl rushed in and flung her arms round the lieutenant's neck, and kissed him, between broken ejaculations of joy, as one come back from the dead, while two long plaits of black hair gyrated wildly at her back.

When the tails had settled down, Greski laughingly swung her round facing Jim, and introduced her as his sister Tatia, and Tatia blushed charmingly, and said, in very passable English: "You must excuse us, sir. You see, when he goes out we are never quite certain that we shall ever see him again. And when he does return our hearts are joyful. Those terrible pointed shells you send us—ah, *mon Dieu!* one came through the side of the cathedral this morning when I was there praying for Louis, and we all ran and ran."

"They are not supposed to fire at the cathedral," said Jim.

"Ah, when one plays with monsters you never know what may happen."

Then they all three spoke together for a minute or two in Polish, since madame knew no tongue but that and Russian, and a little French, and then the ladies went off on household duties.

"I hope I shall not put you to any trouble," said Jim, "and—and"—he stumbled—"you will please let me pay my way. I have heaps of money——"

"We can discuss that later. We shall be glad to be of service to you. Our hearts go out to Englishmen."

But it was a little later, when they sat down to breakfast, that a new and very surprising development took place.

Madame Greski's eye suddenly lighted on Jim's ring—the one pressed upon him by the young officer whose life he had saved on the heights of Alma. She stared hard at it, and then said a quick word to the others, and, to Jim's surprise, Greski caught hold of his hand, held it for the others to see, and they all stood up in great excitement, and all spoke at once as they stared down at the ring.

"Where did you get it?" asked Greski quickly.

"It was given me by a Russian officer at the Alma. He was wounded and I gave him a hand, and he made me take this in return."

And madame came round and put her trembling white hands on his shoulders and kissed him on both cheeks, and her eyes were full of tears. Tatia looked as if she would have liked to do the same, and Jim would not have minded very much if she had.

"It was my brother John," said Greski. "He wrote to us from Odessa telling us all about it. You saved his life."

"I am very glad I was able to be of service to him."

"And now we will repay you as far as we can," said Tatia joyously. "Oh, I am glad! But the marvel that you should fall into Louis's hands!"

Madame spoke quickly to her son, and he translated.

"My mother says your brother must come here too and they will nurse him."

"I am very grateful. Can we go and see him after breakfast? Are you on duty?"

"Not again all this week, *Dieu merci!* There are many more of us than are needed for the batteries, you see. If there were any signs of a general assault we should all be called, of course. But that is not likely yet."

So Jim had fallen more than comfortably, and, for Jack's sake especially, he was glad. For if the hospitals inside were anything like those outside, it might make all the difference between life and death to a sick man, to be in such good hands.

They set off at once for the hospital. It was a cold raw day, and up on the hill-sides, as they crossed the bridge of boats, the dull boom of the guns sounded now and again at long intervals. In that quarter, however, there were but few results of the bombardment visible, and when Jim remarked on it, Greski said,

"So far you are kind to us: you keep your fire for the forts and batteries and Government buildings. But in time you will lose patience, and then we shall suffer. Why didn't you come straight in when you landed? After Alma you might have done it, I think."

"I don't know why," said Jim. "But I wish we had. It would have saved much loss on both sides. You must have suffered terribly in the last fight—Inkerman."

"Horribly, horribly!" said Greski, with an expressive gesture.

At the hospital they found Jack looking very white and washed out, and visibly in great pain.

His face brightened at sight of Jim, but a bad spasm twisted it as he tried to smile, and the smile faded like a winter sunbeam and left his face hard and set.

"Dear old boy," said Jim, kneeling down by his side and holding his hand, "I've got good news for you. We've found friends, and you're to come to their house and get the best of nursing and attention."

Jack brightened again at the prospect, and Jim told him how it all came about, and introduced Greski, who nodded and smiled encouragingly.

When the doctor came round he made no difficulty about Jack's removal. He was only too glad to get another bed. He talked with Greski for a few seconds, and then hurried away to his work.

"I will get an ambulance," said Greski, "and we will take him at once. He will be happier there." And Jim had no chance to ask him what the doctor had said, until they were walking slowly behind the litter, which, on second thoughts, Greski had brought as entailing less discomfort.

"He says it is a very bad wound. The bullet went right through the lungs, but we will do everything that is possible for him." And Jim went heavily, and his heart was full of fears.

"But you must not look like that," said Tatia reprovingly to him, when they had got Jack stowed away in bed, in such outward comfort as soft clean sheets and a warm pleasant room could afford. "That is not the face of a good nurse, no indeed! I shall not let you in to see him till you look more cheerful." But Jim found a cheerful face no easy matter.

They had, however, still another surprise during the afternoon, which raised his spirits somewhat if it did not at the moment kindle his hopes.

The special doctor attached to the Grand Duke Michael came in, and informed them that the Grand Duke himself had ordered him to take the English officer in hand. He had been to the hospital and had been sent on to Mme Greski's house. So, between them all, no possible chance for Jack would be missed.

He examined his patient most carefully, and when Jim followed him anxiously out of the room he told him plainly, and in excellent English, that the hospital doctor was right—it was a very serious case, and they could only do their best and trust in Providence. If he did pull through it would probably leave him weakly all his days; but —— and the great man pursed his lips and shook his head doubtfully.

CHAPTER LX

INSIDE THE FIERY RING

NOTHING could exceed the kindness of their new friends to the strangers cast so curiously on their care.

Brother John's ring had been an Open Sesame to their hearts, and they vied with one another in the repayment in kind for all that the absent one had received at Jim's hands.

Madame Greski and Tatia devoted themselves to Jack as if he had been brother John himself. No single thing that could make for his comfort and well-being was lacking on their part. Never was wounded man tended with more loving and unremitting attention.

And when Jim thought of the bleak miseries of the camps up there on the hill-sides, and the long-drawn horrors of the passages on the hospital ships, he thanked God in his heart that Jack was where he was.

For himself, although the rôle of prisoner of war was little to his taste, it was still mightily interesting to be inside Sebastopol after gazing at it so long from the outside. There was so little doing outside that it seemed to him that he was not missing much; in due course they would probably be exchanged; and meanwhile the difference between the mud-and-canvas life of the camps and this warm and cheerful home in the town was somewhat in the ratio of hell and heaven.

In view of the abounding comforts with which they were surrounded, it was indeed difficult at times to realise the actual and astounding fact that they were undergoing a siege that would rank as one of the great sieges of the world's history; that this comfortable town was an almost impregnable fortress; and that England and France, outside there, were bending all their energies to its reduction.

For they lacked nothing. Supplies were abundant. They were warm and well-fed, and, beyond the dull boom of the distant guns, they heard nothing of the siege. Through that uncloseable northern door, by night and by day, long strings of carts brought in to them everything that was necessary, and much besides. Contrary to custom, it was the besiegers who suffered, not the besieged.

And Jim, when Tatia drove him away from Jack's bedside, to seek exercise and fresh air lest she should have another patient on their hands, quietly observing everything—the rude strength of the defences, the unlimited, even wastefully profuse stores of guns and ammunition, the teeming barracks full of men, and that ever-open door though which the limitless supplies could still be drawn upon—said to himself that the siege might go on for ever.

Jack, however, was in most distressing condition. The slightest exertion, any movement almost, brought on painful fits of coughing which seemed to shake his wounded chest to pieces. Speaking was out of the question, for even breathing was difficult to him; and all Jim could do, to show him what he felt about it all, was to sit by his bedside, holding his hand at times, and at times forcing himself to unnaturally cheerful talk lest the dreadful silence should bring him to foolishness in other ways. For he felt certain, from Jack's appearance and the doctor's manner, that his case was hopeless and the end not far off, and the thought of it was terrible to him.

Of the consequences—of the results to himself, at Carne and Wyvveloe—not one thought. The fluttering of the shadowy wings put all other considerations to rout. This that lay so still on the bed was dear old Jack, and the fear that he was going filled all his heart and mind.

But Tatia, pretty as she was, and of a most vivacious disposition, possessed also much common-sense.

Again and again she insisted on Jim quitting the room and the house, and threatened him with penalties if he came back under a couple of hours. And when her brother was available she would send them off together, begging them only to beware above all things of pointed shells and to turn up again in due course whole and undamaged.

"I would nurse you with enjoyment," she said, her soft dark eyes dwelling appreciatively on Jim's sorrowful long face, in which they seemed to find something that appealed to her strongly. "But, for yourself, you will be better to keep well. If you come back in less than two hours you shall have only half a dinner. Louis, you will see to it."

And Greski would march him away to the harbour front where walking was safe, since the shells rarely topped the hill, and they would discuss matters from both sides as they went.

On that side of the town there was little sign of the siege beyond the activities of the quays, and an occasional roar from the man-of-war moored under Fort Nicholas. But when they strolled along the front, and came round the hill, and up by St. Michael's church and the tower whose clock bore on its face the name of "Barraud, London," then all the grim actualities met them full face.

Up there, across the Admiralty Harbour—whose head ran up into the gorge wherein lay the fatal Ovens out of which they had come into captivity—beyond the great barracks and the hospital, up there on the hill-side lay the huge works which Jim knew as the Malakof and the Redan, but which Greski spoke of as the Korniloff and No. 3—very different in the rear from what they were in front, grim and forbidding, but crude and rough and unfinished-looking. And those little zigzag piles of earth just beyond them were the British trenches, and up on the plateau beyond were the tents, which shone so white in the morning sun, but were so horribly thin and cold of a night, and so dirty when you got close to them.

He could see the Picket House, and knew just what the usual crowd about it would look like; and he could see the gunners moving about the platforms inside the Russian works, and now and again white clouds of smoke rolled over them and the angry roar came bellowing across the quiet waters of the harbour, and the mole-heaps on the hill-side spurtled out in reply.

Now and again a shell came hurtling into the town from the Lancasters or the French batteries, but did little damage on that side, since there was little damage left to be done.

Up there to the right, as they went on past the Admiralty buildings and the cathedral, the houses were mostly in ruins, the streets were already barricaded in anticipation of assault, and the whole scene was one of dismal desolation.

And at times they would meet stretchers carrying broken men, and again, strings of carts carrying rough red coffins up to the cemetery.

But Jim deemed it wise, from every point of view, to keep, as a rule, away from the actual scene of operations. It was slow work watching at a distance the very leisurely operations, and it gave him little to report. But he had an idea that if he showed too great an interest in their concerns the authorities might perhaps tighten his tether, and that might mean separation from Jack. Now and again, however, the desire to see for himself how things were going on got the better of him, and he would creep into some deserted corner of the hot side of the town and endeavour to estimate the possibilities.

And from such observations he always came away downcast and disheartened, for, as far as he could see, the besiegers made no progress whatever, while the besieged toiled unremittingly at the strengthening of their defences, and blocked every possibility of entrance with their mighty earthworks. Up that side of the town went an unceasing stream of men and carts carrying fascines and gabions and shot and shell, and strings of straining horses dragging big guns from the arsenal; and new works, fully equipped, sprang up like mushrooms in a night.

But there were dark days also, when Greaki was on duty in the bastions, or nominated for a sortie. And then madame and Tatia went about very quietly and nervously, and started at any unusual sound, and showed their fears in their faces.

But he was very fortunate, and came home each time to their joyful welcome with his tale of catastrophe to others whom they knew, but himself escaped unhurt, and they all breathed freely till his turn came round again.

Christmas slipped by almost unnoticed. When he did, by accident, awake to the fact that it really was Christmas Day, the difference between this and other Christmas Days gave Jim an unusual fit of the blues.

He thought of them all at Wyvveloe, and wondered if Gracie had decked the church with holly. He knew they would all be thinking about them, probably in great distress of mind. What news concerning them had reached home he could not tell. After much discussion with Greski, who assured him it would be useless, he had requested permission from the authorities to write home, subject to their inspection. But his request was returned to him with a brief inscription in Russian, which Greski translated as "out of the question."

So he could only hope that Colonel Carron would have been able to make inquiries under one of the occasional flags of truce, and had sent word home. But operations were slow at the moment; there had been neither assaults nor sorties of any consequence, and so flags of truce and opportunities of communication were of rare occurrence.

Yes, he knew it must be a bitter, sad Christmas for them all at home—for the many who had already got their fatal news, and for the more who awaited theirs in fear and trembling. And he knew too well what a shockingly thin and sore one it must be for the gaunt, shoeless, half-starved and ill-clad men in the thin white tents on the heights over there.

And when, through the weight of their colouring, his dismal thoughts plumbed deeper depths than was his wont, the grim irony of this most unchristian Christmas sat heavily on him. Christmas!—bristling with raw yellow earthworks, shattered with bursting shells, ghastly with crawling processions of broken men and more peaceful red coffins! Christmas!—peace on earth and goodwill——! And yet, after eighteen hundred years, here were so-called Christian nations at one another's throats, tearing and rending the image of God into raw red fragments, and with no thought but for destruction.

They were, many of them, very good fellows, these Russians. hey would stop him in the street—those whom he had et that first morning, those who were left—and greet him ordially, and ask after his brother, and express their regrets, nd he had no more desire to kill them than he had to kill Lord Raglan himself. And yet, set him on the hill-side up there, and all his thought would be towards their destruction.

Truly it was a queer world, and there must be something wrong somewhere! But it was all beyond him, and he could only brood and wonder.

Their New Year was ushered in on the night of the twelfth with great illuminations, much ringing of church bells, and a solemn service in the cathedral—by a terrific bombardment of their fellow Christians on the hill-side, and two furious sorties, which effected nothing beyond an increase in the tally of broken men and in the cart-loads of red coffins creaking away to the cemetery.

"Absolutely useless," acknowledged Greaki, when his mother and Tatia released him from their warm embraces on his return. "But the Chief thinks it does the men good to go out occasionally after all their dirty work on the new bastions."

CHAPTER LXI

WEARY WAITING

"NOTHING yet," said Sir Denzil to Eager, on his twentieth anxious call after further news of the boys. "I am surprised Denzil has not written. But so many things may happen out there. His letter may have gone astray. There may be difficulty in communicating with Sebastopol. He may be wounded himself. He may be dead. We can do nothing but wait. I will send you word the moment I have any news. Miss Gracie well?"

"Quite well, sir, but sorely troubled about the boys."

"Ay, ay! That is the woman's part—to sit at home and nurse her fears."

"No news, Charlie?" asked the Little Lady hopelessly, from her chair by the fire.

"No news yet, dear. Sir Denzil promises to send round the moment he gets anything."

"I'm beginning to fear they're all lying dead in that horrible Crimea. This waiting, waiting, waiting, is terrible."

"Yes, it's hard work, the hardest work in the world. But we can only wait and hope, dear. Whatever is is best, and we cannot alter it."

It was a weary time for all of them, and all over Britain and France and Russia the same black cloud lay heavily. The only ones who were happy were those whose warriors had come home maimed, so long as the maiming was not absolute and irretrievable. For such were at all events safe from further harm.

So the slow dark days dragged on until at length one night, when Eager had just got in from his rounds and the usual fruitless call at Carne, there came the long-expected knock on the door, and Gracie ran to answer it.

"Is it you, Kennet?"

"Me, miss. Sir Denzil would like to see Mr. Eager."

"He has got some news at last?"

"Ay, some papers just come in. But I don't know what it is. Bad, I should say, from the looks of him—he was so mortal quiet."

"We will come at once. Let me go alone, Charlie. You're tired out."

"Not a bit of it, my dear. I feel like a hound on the scent at the word 'news.' Don't you think you'd better wait here till I bring you word?"

"I can't wait," she said breathlessly. And they went along together.

Sir Denzil met them with ominous impassivity.

"I trust Kennet did not raise your hopes," he said, with he corners of his mouth drawn down somewhat more even han usual, and a glance that never wavered for a moment.

"This arrived just after you left, Mr. Eager. It explains, of course, to some extent——"

It was a letter from General Canrobert, informing Sir Denzil, with many complimentary phrases as palliatives to the blow, that Colonel Carren had met his death while gallantly repelling a sortie on the night of the 12th January. He had left instructions, in case of need, for word to be sent to Sir Denzil and it was in pursuance thereof, etc. etc.

"That, of course, explains why he has been unable to pursue his inquiries after the boys," said Sir Denzil, in an absolutely unmoved voice.

"I need not say our deepest sympathies are yours, sir——"

"It is the boys I am concerned for," said Sir Denzil, with an impatient double wave of the hand, whose finger and thumb held his pinch of snuff. "Denzil put himself out of the running twenty years ago. This is only an incident. But"—and he snuffed very deliberately—"it may not be without its consequences in the other matter. There is no one out there now who has any special interest in them, you see. And, under present circumstances, they may quite easily be overlooked and lost track of. Personally, I should not be in the least surprised to learn that they are both dead. This war seems to me to be carried on in quite unusually wasteful fashion."

Gracie never said a word. The callousness of the old heathen chilled her heart, though it was boiling with many emotions. If she opened her mouth she feared it would all come out in a torrent that would astonish him for the rest of his life.

"We can only go on hoping for the best," said Eager quietly. "Sir George is making inquiries for us——"

"He is quite outside things," said Sir Denzil brusquely, and gazed at Eager with thoughtful intensity for a moment, as though on the point of offering some other suggestion. "However," he said abruptly, at last, "at the moment, as you say, we can only wait and see what comes of it all. If

I hear anything I will send you word at once." And they left him and went soberly home, feeling death still a little nearer their dear ones in this new loss.

"What a terrible old man he is!" said Gracie. "I think he must have been born without a heart."

"It is mostly assumed, I think. Inside, I have no doubt he is feeling his loss bitterly, but he prides himself on not letting it be seen. It is the old fashion. Thank God, we have come to recognise the fact that a man may be a strong man and yet have a heart! It makes for a better world."

And as the slow weeks dragged on, and still brought them no news of the missing ones, their hearts were heavy with fears.

CHAPTER LXII

FROM ONE TO MANY

THE great heart of the nation at home had been wrung with pity and indignation at the altogether unnecessary sufferings of the men who had gone out to fight her battles in the East, and who, through miscalculation, muddle, and incapacity, had died like flies, of sickness and want.

The roar of anger with which the news was greeted shook the mighty in their seats and hurled Ministers and Cabinets 'nto the dust. Still more to the purpose, the sympathy sed set itself promptly to the cure of official abuses by e administration of private charity; which word is used its high apostolic sense, for private munificence and public bscription provided the miserable, gallant remnant of our my only with those things which were theirs by right, of which they had been defrauded by sheerest stupidity d the inexorcisable demon of Red-tape.

The *Times* fund was a mighty help; Florence Nightingale

a still mightier, in that noblest attribute of personal service and sacrifice which touches all hearts to higher things.

But there were also many private benefactors, who set to work at once on their own account to do what they could, and among them was Sir George Herapath.

When the dreadful disclosures of the camps and hospitals came home, he was still bending, almost broken, under the weight of his own loss. His son's death had beaten him to the ground and shortened his span by years.

But the thought of the miseries of those other brave fellows, out on the bleak hill-sides above Sebastopol, stirred him out of the depths of his sorrow. He sent for Charles Eager.

"Eager," he said, "I can't get any sleep for thinking of it all."

"He died as a gallant man should die, Sir George."

"It's the others I'm thinking of—the poor fellows who are mouldering away out there for want of everything that has been forgotten or sent astray."

And a spark came into Eager's eye, for here was sign of grace and hope after his own mind—a sorely stricken heart rising superior to its own loss in helpful thought for others.

"Yes, they're having dreadful times. What were you thinking of?"

"Helping, if you'll take a hand."

"I'm your man, sir, and God be thanked for your good thought! I'll thank you in my own way."

"Help me to make a list of the most necessary things, and I'll charter a ship to take them straight out. Will you go with her and see to it all?"

"Will I?" blazed Eager. "Will I not? It's almost too good to be true. I want to find out what's become of those boys too."

"I wouldn't like it all to go astray like the rest, you see."

"I'll see to that. It may be the saving of hundreds. God bless you, sir! George's death will be a blessing to many through you. It is just what he would have done himself."

Sir George shook his head sadly. The wound was too raw yet. "Let's get to work!" he said; for in work, and especially in such work, there was something of healing.

So they formed themselves into a committee of four, and Sir George insisted on Eager and Gracie coming to stay with them at Knoyle so that the work might go on without interruption.

He went down to Liverpool, and with difficulty secured a steamship—the *Balclutha*, 1,000 tons burden, James Leale, master, at a very high price, for Government charters had made a tight market.

He went over all their lists carefully, knew just where to lay his hand on everything, and the work went forward rapidly.

Eager had secured a locum and was keen to be off, for every day's delay meant so many wasted lives. Gracie was to stay on at Knoyle with Margaret. And so the very last night came, and found them sitting round the fire in Sir George's study after dinner.

"You must all give an eye to my people while I'm away," said Eager. "Bratton is a good sort, I think, but it'll take some time for him to get to know them; and the vicar——"

"The vicar is resigning as soon as you come back," said Sir George quietly. "The South of France is the only place where he can live, Yool says. I want you to take it when you get home."

"That is very good of you, sir. I want you to give me something else too"—and he slipped his hand inside Margaret's arm.

"I knew," said Sir George. "Meg has told me, and I could not wish her better."

Gracie flung her arms round Margaret and kissed her heartily.

"Oh, I am so glad!" she cried. "That is what I have been wanting all the time."

"So have I," laughed Eager. And then more soberly, as he lifted Margaret's hand to his lips—"And truly, I am grateful. My cup is full—almost to the brim——"

"I wish I could go with you," said Margaret.

"So do I," said Gracie eagerly.

"Yes, I know, but——"

And they knew too that the "but" must keep them at home.

"You'll find out all about the boys, Charlie," ordered Gracie.

"I'll do my best, dear, you may be sure. It all depends on what there is to find out and what an outsider can do. The possibilities are so tremendous. All we can do is to hope for the best and keep our hearts up. I have letters from Lord Deseret to Lord Raglan and several others, and I have no doubt they will give me all the help they can."

And next day he sailed, very happy in his mission, happier still in what lay behind and before him; troubled only on account of the boys who had disappeared into the smoke-cloud, and of whom for many weeks they had been able to obtain no tidings whatever.

The master, the supercargo, and the crew of the *Balclutha* were all of one mind in the matter, and so she made a record passage, was through the Straits fourteen days after she hauled out of the Mersey, and two days later lay off Balaclava Bay awaiting official permit to enter.

The Bay was crowded, but a corner was found at last, and Eager's wondering eyes travelled over the amazing activities and manifold nastinesses of that historic port, though these last were nothing now to what they had been.

He landed at once, introduced himself and his business to Admiral Boxer and Captain Powell, found favour in their sight, and made arrangements for the unloading and forwarding of his cargo.

Sir George had furnished him with ample funds and the best of advice. He organised his own transport, saw to it himself, with the hearty assistance of Leale and his two mates and some picked men of the crew, and drove things forward at such astonishing speed that the harbour-master broke out one time.

"Man! Was it a parson you said you were, Mr. Eager? It's head of the Transport you ought to have been. You get more out of those lazy scamps than any man we've had here yet."

It was the same wherever he went. His strenuous cheerfulness, his masterful energy, his unfailing good-humour—in a word, his Eagerness infused itself into all with whom he came in contact and carried him royally through all difficulties. He was an object-lesson in what might be done when Officialism and Red-tape had no fingers in the pie.

To tell all he did, and saw, and thought, during those days, would take a volume. He cheered and comforted, and lifted from misery and death many a stricken soul, both in the hospitals and in the camps.

He came across old Harrow and Oxford friends, who welcomed him with open arms and tendered him advice enough to sink a ship. And when he had finished his distributions, and so eased the ways of all the needy ones within the range of his powers, he turned with keen anxiety to that other quest which lay so near his heart.

He paid a visit to British Head-quarters, in the low white houses on the road leading from Balaclava to Sebastopol, delivered Lord Deseret's letter to an aide-de-camp, and intimated his intention of waiting there till he could see Lord Raglan in person.

When at last he was admitted, he found the Chief sitting at a huge table heaped with papers, and two secretaries writing for dear life at tables alongside.

Lord Raglan had already seen him about the camps and hospitals, and had heard of his good works, and received him with courteous kindness. Eager was struck with his thin, worn face—the face of a brave man wrestling with unwonted problems and innumerable difficulties.

MICROCOPY RESOLUTION TEST CHART

(ANSI and ISO TEST CHART No. 2)

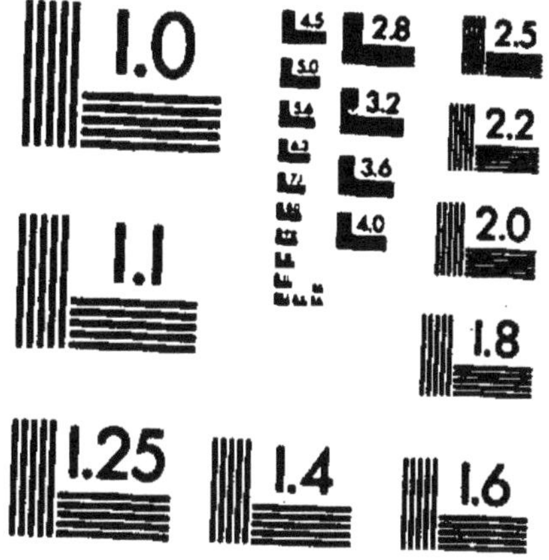

1653 East Main Street
Rochester, New York 14609 USA
(716) 482 - 0300 - Phone
(716) 288 - 5989 - Fax

"I don't know what we can do to help you in your quest, Mr. Eager," said his lordship, with Lord Deseret's letter in his hand, "but anything we can do we will. I am sure you will understand that it has been through no intentional neglect that these young friends of yours have slipped out of our sight. The demands upon one's time from the people at home"—with an expressive glance at the mountainous heaps of forms and papers before him—"have afforded one small chance of attending to individual cases. The last we know was that they were prisoners in Sebastopol."

"I thank your lordship, and I am very loth to trouble you," said Eager; "but there is so much dependent on these two boys that I must do all I possibly can to learn what has become of them. One could not ask by letter, I suppose?"

"Did I not write to Menchikoff, Calverly, soon after they were taken? I seem to remember——"

"You did, sir," replied one of the overwrought secretaries, without stopping his work for a moment. "And we got no answer."

"Would it be possible for me to get in under a flag of truce?" asked Eager.

"Quite possible," said his lordship, with a faint smile; "but decidedly risky, and you certainly would not come out again."

"There are occasional truces for picking up the wounded, are there not?"

"We have never asked for one. As a rule the Russians request it after one of their big sorties. If you wait a while—one never knows what night they will come out. What was your idea?"

"Simply to inquire among the Russian officers. There could be no objection to that, I presume?"

"Not the slightest. You might learn something. It is just a chance."

"Then I will wait for that chance, with your lordship's permission."

"By all means, Mr. Eager, and I wish you all success; also

please convey to Sir George Herapath our thanks for all he has done for the men here, and accept the same yourself. They have suffered grievously. His son's death was a great loss to us. He was a fine young fellow."

And Eager bowed himself out.

CHAPTER LXIII

EAGER ON THE SCENT

EAGER'S lean and lively face became well known in the camps and trenches. He was keen to see all he could, and was everywhere welcomed with acclaim, but perhaps the greetings he most enjoyed were the rough grateful words of men whom he had helped and heartened in the field hospitals, and who had recovered sufficiently to get back to their work. These would do anything for him, and from morning till night he was all over the place, seeing everything, mightily interested in it all, and leaving, wherever he went, a trail of uplifting cheerfulness which was a moral tonic.

He watched the perpetual fierce little fights over the rifle-pits, and went down into them and tended the wounded when chance offered. He mingled with the frequenters of the Picket House, and watched the effect of the somewhat desultory pounding of the batteries by the big guns. He crept cautiously through untold miles of muddy trenches, both French and British, and viewed with wonder the gigantic tasks which prepared the way for the second bombardment. And in the hospitals he soothed many a sufferer's passage to more peaceful quarters, and put fresh heart into those whose lot it was to go back to the front.

In the officers' tents and huts he was hail-fellow-well-met everywhere, and the only fault found with him was that he could not be in many places at the same time.

He heard matters discussed there with an outspoken freedom which would have set ears tingling at home; and when he asked how soon it was going to end, was told, "Never, my boy. It's going on for ever and ever." And an irreverent one added, "As it was in the beginning, is now, and ever shall be, world without end, amen!"

"End, my dear fellow? Why should it end?" said still another, waving an old briar at him, with the smoke curling like a flag of truce from the stem. "They've got unlimited supplies to draw upon, and an open road to get 'em in. As fast as we kill 'em they bring in fresh ones. As fast as we knock down their earthworks they build 'em up again——"

"Faster!" growled another.

"Yes, faster. I don't see why it should not go on till the year 2000—going on as we are. It's not a siege; it's a discipline—a chastisement for our sins! I only wish——"

"Hear, hear!" grunted another, who had heard that wish many times before.

"What do you wish?" asked Eager.

"I wish all the Red-tape and Routine people at home could be driven into the trenches here and kept there for a month. They'd learn a thing or two."

"Die . . . never learn," growled the other.

"If we'd gone right in when first we got here, it would have been a most enormous saving, even if the cost had been heavy. For some reason we lost the chance, and it's never going to come back. We're like a prize-fighter pummelling away at the other fellow's leg and hoping to break him in time that way. We may tire him out, of course, but it's a deuced slow business."

"Do they never exchange prisoners?" asked Eager.

"We never take any worth exchanging. It's only the ruck we get, and they're mostly dead."

"Their boots are the best part of 'em," said the other. "Our men are always better shod after a sortie. Gad! sir, it would have made you blaze to see our fellows—Guardsmen and all—tramping about in mud and snow with no soles to their rotten boots! I hope the man who made 'em will spend his eternity in a snowy hell with raw bare feet!"

But one night they were all out in haste, at the sound of heavy and continuous musketry down in the trenches on the left attack; and Eager, tumbling out and rushing on with the rest, found himself where a noncombatant had no right to be.

He had gone plunging downwards with the others, in order to see all he could, till he fell bodily into a trench. He picked himself up and joined the stream of men hastening towards the firing, and found himself suddenly in the thick of things—bullets humming venomously past his head, men falling with groans and curses by his side, and a big man, standing just above him on the rough parapet of the trench, shouting to his men to "give it 'em hot with the steel," and meanwhile picking up the biggest stones he could find and hurling them at the oncoming Russians in front.

The men clambered up and swept away into the darkness with shouts and cheers and clash of steel, and Eager was left alone in the trench with the fallen ones. Up from below rose an awful turmoil, lit now and again by receding flashes, then a final British cheer, and one more sortie was repulsed.

It was only next morning that he learned the size of it.

"They say there were about fifteen thousand of them out last night," said one of his friends. "One lot went for the French over by the Mamelon, and the rest came up here."

"Gordon's men say he was on top of the trench chucking stones at the beggars as they came up——"

"I saw him," said Eager. "He was standing just above me, shouting to his men and flinging stones as hard as he could. Then they fixed bayonets and went downhill like an avalanche."

"You'd no right to be there, my boy."

"I suppose not. I went to see what was up, and fell into a trench, and ran on with the rest. Was the Colonel hit?"

"Couple of bullets in him, but not deadly."

"It's amazing to me that any one comes through alive."

"Yes, it feels like that at first, but you get used to it."

"Did we lose many?"

"Pretty heavy; but there are four or five Russkis to each of ours. Ground's thick with 'em. They'll want an armistice to clean up, I expect—generally do."

And, sure enough, the Russians presently requested a truce to pick up their men; and before long the white flags were flying on the batteries, and the men of both sides streamed out into the open, picked up their dead and wounded, and took stock of one another.

This was the chance Eager had been waiting for, and he went down to the debatable ground between the lines with the rest.

It was a horrible enough sight—a couple of thousand dead and wounded men strewn thick in that narrow space; but the stretchers were busily at work, and he had his own inquiries to make.

A number of Russian officers were strolling about, dressed in their best and smoking their best cigars, and quite ready for a talk.

He approached one, lifted his hat, and asked in French:

"I wonder if monsieur could afford me some information?"

At which the Russian smiled, and his blue eyes twinkled.

"With pleasure, monsieur. We have at this moment one hundred thousand men in there and five thousand guns, and provisions for fifteen years, and when they are used up we have five times as many more to come."

"If you could give me a satisfactory word about two young officers, prisoners in your hands, you would ease some very sore hearts at home, monsieur. That is all I ask. I have come all the way from England to get news of them."

"If I can, monsieur. What are their names?"

"Carron; two brothers—one in the Engineers, the other in the Hussars."

"*Tiens!* Yes—Carron! I know them. Some of our guns have the same name. They are well, monsieur. I saw them only yesterday."

"Thank God for that! And I thank you, monsieur, most gratefully."

"It is nothing. One of them was sorely wounded, but the Grand Duke sent his own doctor, and he is recovered. They were walking together yesterday, and we spoke. I shall tell them of your inquiry. What name, monsieur?"

"Eager—Charles Eager. Will you tell them all are well at home and very desirous of seeing them. If only this terrible war would come to an end!"

"Yes, indeed; *le malheur!* But I assure you, monsieur, we will stop fighting at once if only you will all go home."

"I wish I could make them," said Eager. "It is terrible work." And he looked round at the broken men lying so thickly all about.

"It is rough play. Whether the omelets are worth all the broken eggs, I cannot say. Have you any idea what we're fighting about, monsieur?"

"General principles, I suppose."

"Ah, he is a costly leader, this General Principles," said the other, with a twinkle. "Permit me to offer you a cigar."

"We will exchange," said Eager, producing some of Sir George's extra specials. "Let us smoke to a speedy peace."

"With all my heart." And they parted friends, and both went their ways wondering why such things must be. And if the Russian never delivered Eager's message it was not his fault, for he was killed by a shell that same afternoon in Bastion No. 4.

The ground was cleared at last. There was a moment's pause. Then the white flags came fluttering down, and a gun from the Redan sent a shot hurling up the trenches, to show that playtime was over.

Eager was much comforted in mind by his interview with the Russian. He had seemed a good fellow, and could have no object in deceiving him. He wrote long letters home, and resolved to wait on and see if the great bombardment, to which all efforts were now directed, would bring the end an nearer.

And so it came about that he stood with the rest on Cathcart's Hill, in the misty drizzle of that bleak Easter Monda morning, and watched the opening of the second bombardment of Sebastopol.

They could hear enough up there. All round the vast semicircle more guns were crashing than had ever roared in concert before. But they could see very little. The gunners themselves could not see. They knew Sebastopol lay over there and they were bound to hit something.

And Eager strained his eyes into the chill white mist to see all he could, and felt sick at heart at thought of the destruction any one of those wildly flying shot and shell might wreak.

CHAPTER LXIV

THE LONG SLOW SIEGE

IT was the most trying time Jim had ever spent. He had had no experience whatever of sick-beds, beyond his own short spell after Balaclava, and even that was as different from this deadly monotony as well could be. But he stuck to it valiantly, and was only saved from physical and mental collapse himself by Tatia's arbitrary oversight.

If there had been anything going on outside he might have found the change from the sick-room bracing, but both besieged and besiegers were too busy girding their loins for another struggle to waste time or powder on useless display.

The Allies had found the nut too hard to crack, and were working hard on preparation for the next blow; and those inside, fully informed of everything that went on in the camps, were straining every nerve to resist it.

So big guns and mortars went toiling up to the heights from Balaclava Bay, and mountains of gabions and fascines and more big guns went toiling up the heights inside to face them, and for days hardly a shot would be fired on either side.

It was towards the end of February that Greski said to Jim, one day when Tatia had turned them out-of-doors—"Come, and I will show you something new." And they went round to the eastern slope, looking out towards the Karabelnaia suburb and the Malakoff and Redan—all of which Jim knew by heart.

And at the first glance Jim saw a change in the look of things.

A new fort had sprung up in the night between the Malakoff, which till now had been the foremost Russian work on that side, and the French trenches—a fort of size too, all abristle with gabions and fascines round the crown of the flat hill. The thousands of men still working at it made it look like a great ant-heap.

"French!" said Jim, after his first quick glance, with a feeling of exultation, for the new work must seriously menace, if not command, the Malakoff.

"French?—no, my friend!—Russian! Truly your people are not very wideawake. Todleben has been expecting them to seize that hill ever since they crept so close, and it would have been bad for the Korniloff Bastion, you see. So, as they did not, and it seemed a pity no one should use it, he occupied it last night, and ten thousand men have been busy on it ever since."

"Hang it! What fools we were to let it slip!"

"Undoubtedly! And without doubt you will now try o recover it, and it will cost you many men, and us also, nd so the game goes on."

And that very same night, when Jack had at last fallen sleep, Greski said to Jim, as though he were inviting him a theatre party:

"At midnight we will take a little walk, and you will se your friends attempt to recover the new fort, the Mamelon.

"You seem to know all about it," said Jim incredulously.

"Of course. That again is where we beat you. We kno all your plans. We have plans of every trench you cut with every gun you place in it."

"Not from any of our men," said Jim, with heat, for under hand work such as that struck him offensively.

"Oh no. But your men talk too much among themselves, and our spies are through your camps night and day. The all speak French, you see, and uniforms are easy to get, whereas none of your people speak Russian well enough to pass muster for a moment. I can even tell you that the attack will be all French—Zouaves, Marines, and Chasseurs, under three thousand in all, and the General Monet will be in command. They will walk right up into the trap and will all be killed or captured."

"It is sheer murder."

"What would you? It is war; and after all, though I hate Russia, one cannot help remembering that she did not invite you to come here. We will wait here. It is not yet time."

"Why aren't you up there yourself?"

"I was in the last sortie and it is not my turn, *Dieu merci!* for it will be hot up there to-night. There are plenty of us, you see, and we take fair turns."

All was dark and still up along the distant hill-side, so void of offence that Jim began to wonder if Greski had not made a mistake. But after several impatient glances at his watch by the glow of his cigar, he said at last:

"Now—it is time! Watch!—over there!"

But the minutes passed—long, long minutes, almost the longest Jim had ever lived through.

"Doesn't seem coming off," he jerked.

"Wait!" jerked Greski, at tension also. "They were to start at midnight. They have a quarter-mile to cover, and they will go cautiously because the ground behind them is bad. We are to let them come right up and—ah—*voilà!*" as the darkness behind the new fort blazed and roared and became an inferno of deadly strife: terrific volleys of musketry and the hoarse shouting of men—no big guns, and presently even the firing became desultory, but the turmoil waxed louder and louder.

Greski danced with excitement.

"*Mon Dieu!* but they are fighting!—hand to hand! They are devils to fight, those Zouaves. I wish—I wish—but it is not safe here to wish."

The turmoil came rolling round this side of the hill; the Russians were falling back. Then flaming volleys broke out on each side of the turmoil.

"Ah—ah—ah! Supports from Korniloff," jerked Greski.

And then suddenly the Malakoff and Redan big guns blazed out, and poured an avalanche of shot and shell and rockets on the gallant attack, and it withered and melted away.

"Two—three thousand men in pieces, and as you were!" was Greski's summing up.

"Infernal butchery," growled Jim, much worked up.

"What would you, my friend? It is war." And they went soberly home, thinking of the horrors of the red hill-side and all the broken men who lay there, while all the church bells in the town clashed pæans of victory overhead as they went.

The one bright ray to Jim, in this time of gloom, was the fact that Jack was without doubt slowly improving, to the great satisfaction and greater surprise of his wearied but unwearying nurses and the Grand Duke's doctor.

"He has no right to live," said the latter, "and yet he lives, and may live. It is marvellous." But then he had not known how the open-air life on the flats prepared a man for contingencies such as this.

It was long before Jack could speak above a whisper without suffering, and then at last be was able to sit propped up with pillows and to take an interest in things in general. But the gardens were full of hyacinths and crocuses, and there were even patches of them on the troubled hill-sides, among the white tents and muddy trenches, before he tasted fresh air again.

Then Jim would lead him on his strong arm, very slowly and with many a rest, to a sheltered place whence he could see what was going on, and so keen was his interest that it was no easy matter to get him home again. And the officers they met on the road would stop them, and politely inquire after Jack's health, and express their pleasure at his recovery, and discuss matters with them, and gallantly express their conviction that the siege would go on for ever, but admit all the same that if it could honourably end they would not be sorry.

They had another ray of hope when the news came of the death of the Tsar. Would it mean an end of the terrible struggle, and release, and home? Their hearts—and not theirs only—beat high with hope, and fell the lower when the word came that the fight was to go on to the bitter end.

CHAPTER LXV

THE CUTTING OF THE COIL

WITH the better weather things quickened somewhat—the things of Nature, to life; the things of Man, to death. Man strove with all his might to end his fellow man, and drenched the earth with blood: and the spring flowers pushed valiantly through the blood-soaked sods and seemed to wonder what it was all about.

The boys learned from Greski that the chief bones of contention now were the rifle-pits.

The lines and burrows of attack and defence had by this time run so close to one another that in places you could almost throw a stone from one to the other. No smallest chance of harassing the enemy was lost on either side. Both sides had learnt by experience what damage and annoyance to the working parties could be effected by small bodies of picked marksmen hidden in sunken pits in advance of the lines, and the struggles over and round and in these tiny strongholds were endless, and furious beyond description.

He told them how sixty Russians had held their pits near what he called the Korniloff Bastion, but which Jack and Jim knew more familiarly as the Malakoff, against five thousand Frenchmen, until reserves came up and the Frenchmen had to retire. And how some crack shot in one of the English pits was potting their men even in the streets of the town, twelve hundred yards away, so that passage that way · as no longer permitted.

He told them that the Allies were mounting more and more big guns, and prophesied hot work again before long, and feared that this time "he"—by which simple comprehensive pronoun the Russian soldiers always referred to the hundred thousand men out there on the hill-side—the enemy—just as Jack and Jim had always used the term to designate Sir Denall in their early days—Greski feared that "he," out of patience with the long delay and the sufferings it had entailed, would no longer confine his efforts to battering the forts, but would probably try to make an end of the town itself.

"In which case," he said, "we may have to move over to the other side of the water. He can knock down the bastions to his heart's content; we can build them again faster than he can knock them down. But the town—that would be another matter."

All the streets leading in from the hill-sides were barricaded, and a new line of huge entrenchments sprang up among the houses inside the town, half-way up the slope on which it was built.

From their chosen look-out on that eastward slope the boy watched all that went on, inside and outside, with hu anxious eyes. They noted the immense activities on bot sides, and it seemed to them, as it had done before to Jim that things might go on like this for ever.

"If we are really going to try another bombardment," sai Jack slowly—he always spoke slowly and quietly now, a wa he had got into through fear of straining his chest—"and they keep it to the earthworks, it is all wasted time. The only way to end it is to smash the town and rush it over the pieces. It is doubtful kindness to spare it. Far better end the matter for all concerned. Then we could all go home and become human beings again. I've no fight left in me, Jim."

"A couple of months on the flats will make you as sound as a bell," said Jim cheerfully. "The air here is full of gunpowder and dead men. What you want is Carne."

"I've thought a good deal about it all while I lay there and couldn't talk," said Jack. "You'll have to take it all on, Jim. I shall be a broken man all my life—I feel it inside me; and Carron of Carne must be a whole man. You must take it on, Jim."

"Don't let's talk about it, old man. We're not home yet. Time enough to go into all that when we get there. I wish to goodness Raglan would come right in and make an end of it."

"It would be an awful business. But I don't see how we're going to end it any other way. And truly I wish it were ended, for I long to get home. All I want is to get home."

Their friend Greski had so far escaped the dangers of his unpalatable duties in a manner little short of marvellous. He shirked nothing, and took his fair turns with the rest. And, though he hated Russia with all his heart, he laughingly confessed that when he was in the thick of things he forgot it all in his eagerness to win the fight.

But such phenomenal luck was too good to last. He went out one night to join in a sortie, and the morning came without him, and found his mother and Tatia in woeful depths, certain he was dead.

Jim went off at once for news, and found him at last in the hospital, with a bullet in the thigh and a bayonet wound in the shoulder.

"It is nothing, it is nothing," said the hurrying surgeon. At which Greski made a grimace at Jim, and said:

"All the same, if it was only himself now! And the way he hacked that bullet out! We are getting callous to other folk's sufferings."

"Why, you hardly felt it," said the surgeon. "You said so."

"When one's helpless under another man's knife one says what he wants. It hurt like the deuce."

"When can I take him home?" asked Jim, in stumbling French.

"After two days, if he behaves and goes on well."

So Jim went home and comforted madame and Tatia; and two days later they were happier in their minds than they had been since the siege began, in that they had him there all the time and safe from further harm.

He grizzled somewhat at being shelved "just when the fun was going to begin," for he felt assured in his own mind that "he," outside, was preparing for a general assault, and he would have liked to see it. And so the boys did their best to keep him posted in all that went on.

They were wakened at daybreak one morning by an uproar altogether out of the common—one vast, unbroken, terrific roll of thunder, so deep, so ominous, so far beyond anything they had ever heard in their lives before that it sounded as though the whole of heaven's artillery had been mounted on the hill-sides, and brought to bear on the devoted town, and was bent on battering it to pieces.

Greski called them from his room, and they went in.

"Hurry, hurry, or you'll miss it all! We knew it must be soon, but could not learn the day. They will come in on top of this, I think. Keep under cover, and come back and tell me all about it. Oh, —— this leg!"

It was a bad morning for any conscious possessor of a chest—heavy with mist and thick with drizzling rain; a black funereal day, sobbing gustily, and drenching the earth with showers of bitter tears. The chill discomfort of it told even on Jim.

"Jack, old man, I wish you'd go back," he said, before they had gone a hundred yards. "I'll bring you word as soon as I can. They're not likely to come in at once, and you'll have plenty of time to see all that's going on. They'll probably bang away at the forts for the whole day. Do go back."

"Get on!—get on!" coughed Jack. "I want to see." And they pushed on through the gloomy twilight.

The streets were alive with all the others who wanted to see, and long compact lines of gray-coats were pressing stolidly towards the front, to strengthen the lines against the expected onslaught.

Jim was doubtful how far they should venture, but Jack was intent on seeing. This was history. This was the consummation of all the hopes, and the weary days and nights, that had gone into those mighty zigzags up on the hill there. This was his own arm striking as it had never struck before since time began, and he must see it at its best.

But, though they could hear enough, they could not see much, because of the mist and the rain and the dense clouds of smoke rolling down the hill-sides.

The Russian batteries were only beginning to reply, by the time the boys reached their usual look-out on the eastern slope near the cathedral, and then the uproar doubled, and the very ground beneath them seemed to shudder under it.

Jim helped his brother to his usual seat in a niche in the broken wall of a garden, and tucked his cloak carefully about him, for between his boiling excitement and the rawness of the morning, he was all ashake and his teeth were chattering.

"Every gun we have," gasped Jack . . . "hard at it!"

"If they can't see more than we can, they're going it blind," growled Jim, as he strode about to get warm.

And then, like a bolt from the sky, without an instant's warning, out of the chill white mist in front came a great round black ball, which dropped with a thud into the ground almost at Jack's feet. It lay there, hissing and spitting like a venomous devil gloating over its anticipated villainy, and Jim rushed at it with an unaccustomed oath of dismay. It was sheer instinct. He had no time for thought. The devilish thing was close to Jack, and Jack could not move.

He got his right hand under it to hurl it down the slope. His feet slipped from under him as he heaved. Then with a splintering crash the thing burst. . . .

And the Coil of Carne, cut by a stray British shell, lay shattered about the eastern slope of Sebastopol.

CHAPTER LXVI

PURGATORY

JIM came to himself in purgatory. It seemed to him that he came slowly out of a dead black sleep into a horrible wakening dream.

He was in a vast room, low-roofed, with massive arches which obstructed his view and lay like weights on his brain. Small, heavy windows let in a murky light. All about him were dismal groanings, and mutterings, and curses, and a most evil atmosphere, which turned his stomach.

He tried to move, and was seized with grinding pains up his right side and arm and shoulder.

He tried to grope back into the meaning of it all, and suddenly he remembered the shell.

It must have burst and wounded him. His right hand shot suddenly with burning pangs.

He wondered how Jack had fared. He could not remember whether he had succeeded in pitching it down the slope or not. He had done his best; but he remembered that the fuse was very short. . . .

Was he really alive? . . . or was he dead, and this hell? . . . The groans and curses . . . that awful smell of blood and dead men! . . .

He came to himself again, and it was all black about him—thick, heavy, chill darkness, full of groans and curses and the smell of blood and dead men.

The heavy little windows came slowly out of the black void first, then the massive pillars, and after a long, long time he saw dim figures moving slowly about in the twilight.

One passed close to him, and he wanted to call to him to ask him about Jack, but when he tried to speak he found he could not.

Then two more men came and dragged away the bodies of the two who lay in the straw on each side of him. Their clothes rubbed his as they went. He had not thought about them because they had lain so quiet.

The men came back with another man, who groaned as they laid him down, and then with another on the other side who groaned also, and Jim wished they had left him the quieter ones.

It was a very long time before a surgeon came round to look at the new-comers, and Jim had had plenty of time to think as well as he was able to.

If he lay there much longer he would die. He must get them to take him away. How?

His dulled wits, roaming for possibilities, came on thought of the Grand Duke's doctor who had pulled Jack through. If he could get them to send for him. . . . Though why he should come was quite beyond him. . . . Still it was a chance.

The surgeon took off his right-hand neighbour's leg where he lay, by the light of a lamp. The man gave a sudden gasp and a choke, the surgeon said "Ach!" and they carried the body away.

He took off the left-hand man's arm and strapped it up.

Jim with a mighty effort said, "Monsieur!" And the rumpled surgeon looked down at him and wiped his fingers on a piece of dirty rag.

"I beg you," said Jim, and the surgeon bent down to him.

"Well?" he said brusquely, for loads of broken men lay waiting for him, and he had cut and carved till his hands and arms were tired and his back stiff with bending.

"I want . . . the Grand Duke's doctor," murmured Jim.

"The deuce you do? Anything else?" And he was going.

"The Grand Duke's own orders. . . . He will tell you." And then he went out into the darkness again.

But the feeble words had caused the surgeon to look more closely, and then to make inquiries, and when Jim came back to life he was in bed at Mme Greski's, and Tatia was sitting by the bedside. And to Jim it was like a sudden leap from hell to heaven.

Tatia nodded cheerfully to him.

"Where's Jack?" he asked in a whisper.

"They've not found him yet. They're searching for him," said Tatia, after a moment's hesitation. "You're not to talk, or to think, or do anything but what I tell you. Drink this." And he drank, and fell asleep again.

It was not until many days afterwards, when he had grown accustomed to the fact that he would have to go through life with one sleeve looped up to a button—though he still complained at times of pains in that hand—that Tatia gently broke the news to him that Jack was gone. The shell had killed him on the spot, had literally blown him to pieces.

And she broke down at sight of his face; and when he turned it over to the pillow and sobbed silently, she crept quietly out of the room and left him to his sorrow.

Jack gone! *Jack!* He felt stupid and newly broken.

Dear old Jack! . . . smashed by that cursed shell! A Britis shell, too, unless he was very much mistaken. That was lines, after coming through so much. Hard lines! Hard lines

He was very weak yet, and the tears welled out again an again, as he lay thinking dreamily of all the old times o the flats, and how close they had been to one another a through their lives. And Jack was gone . . . killed by British shell! And he was so much the better man of th two. And now, if he himself lived, he would have to go home—some time—if this wretched war ever came to an end—and break all their hearts with the news. In his weakness and sorrow he wished that cursed shell had made an end of them both.

It was early summer before he was about again, for the bursting shell had ripped open his side and shoulder, in addition to shattering his arm beyond repair, and had given a shock to his system from which it recovered but slowly.

And still the siege dragged on. Early in June came the third bombardment. All the southern portion of the town had long been a heap of grass-grown ruins. Now, even the northern slopes became almost untenable.

The theatre was shattered out of all knowledge; in every barricaded street the roadway was furrowed like a ploughed field by the shot and shell which came raining in, and these were collected each day and piled into pyramids ten feet high. Not a house but was damaged, many were in ruins; the vertical shells from the mortars came down like bolts from heaven and spread destruction where they fell.

It was death to walk the streets, and no safer to stop indoors. Many crossed the harbour to the northern heights. The Greskis and Jim fitted up their cellars and lived there as in a bomb-proof.

Greski himself had made but a slow recovery. The bullet-wound in his thigh took long to heal, and left him limping still and quite unfit for service—at which his mother and Tatia rejoiced greatly, and he did not greatly repine.

"As a soldier," he said, "I would shirk nothing; but all the same Russia is not my country, but my oppressor, and it makes a difference. For Poland I would die ten deaths. For Russia I grudge a finger."

When the bombardment slackened again, he limped out on Jim's sound arm to gather news, and managed to keep a portentously long face as his fellows in the café told them of the taking of the Mamelon and Sapoune by the French, and the closing of the harbour road leading out to Inkerman.

But alone with Jim and his own people, he let his feelings have play.

"Now we're getting on a bit. I mean you are. The Mamelon is one of the keys to the door. I see the end in sight. But your people are strangely dilatory or overcareful. From what they were saying down there you could have got in more than once if you'd only come on."

"I wish they had come on," said Jim heartily. "Maybe there are too many cooks at the pie."

Ten days later came the fourth bombardment, and in the comparative safety of their cellars they heard the neighbours' houses crumbling and falling, and the upper part of their own came down with a crash which blanched the women's faces, till the ruins settled into position and left them still alive.

Then one day, in an appalling cessation of the thunders to which their ears were accustomed, Jim and Greski, stealing out to the south slope, heard on the hill-side the solemn wail of the Dead March, and presently a great salute of unshotted guns, and learned later that Lord Raglan was dead, and, according to Greski, was succeeded by one Sampson, whom Jim failed to recognise under so large a name.

Sebastopol was becoming one great hospital, one might almost say charnel-house, for the wounded were beyond their capacity for tending, and the dead lay for days in the streets unburied. And over it all the summer sun shone brightly, and flowers bloomed gaily among the shattered columns and fallen walls of houses which had once made this one of the fairest cities of the East.

The siege lapsed again into dullness, in spite of Greski's prophecy. The thinned ranks behind the bastions were replenished from the northern camps. All day long the harbour was alive with the boats that brought them across. And the bastions themselves grew stronger and stronger, with the myriads of men working on them and the tons of shot rained into them from the outside.

Working parties streamed up to the front all day long, carrying great stakes and poles for the abattis, and fascines and gabions for the ramparts, and in this work every English and French prisoner they had taken was employed.

Jim found it refreshing to hear the hearty British oaths which rattled about such fatigue parties, and he generally hailed the speakers and got a hearty word in reply.

"God bless you, sir, but this ain't no work for British sailormen, an' it does one a sight o' good to cuss 'em high an' low, even if they doesn't understand it."

"Perhaps just as well," said Jim. "Can you use any money?"

"Try me, sor! God bless your honour! This night I'll be as drunk as a lord, an' so will all me mates. 'Twill lighten the day an' the weight of these —— stakes. ———— all Rooshians! They don't know how to treat a sailorman."

CHAPTER LXVII

THE BEGINNING OF THE END

AND so, at last, we come to the end of that titanic struggle in the East—so far, that is, as we are directly concerned in it.

It was in the first days of September, just twelve months after the Modern Armada sailed from Varna in hopes of settling matters out of hand, that the great bombardment opened; the earth shook and the heavens shuddered, and men grown used to the sound of big guns were amazed at the hideous uproar. Fifteen hundred of the heaviest guns in existence thundered back and forth in concert, and the hot hail of more than half of them rained ceaselessly on the stricken town. The sky was hidden by the smoke, and through the smoke, along with the bursting shells, shot flights of fiery rockets to add to the inferno inside.

Within that fiery pale no soul ventured forth. Jim and Greski paced their gloomy quarters like restless animals—hopeful of the end, doubtful what it might entail. The women sat in corners in momentary expectation of death.

All who could go had crossed the harbour to the safety of the northern heights. Greski, as the result of many discussions with Jim, had resolved to stay where he was and trust to luck and the Allies.

For four days and nights the doomed city suffered that most awful scourging, and then there came a lull, and the taut-strung men in the cellar looked meaningly at one another.

And presently they crept cautiously out into the sulphurous upper air, just as day was breaking.

"It is ended," said Greski, for the low thick clouds of smoke rolling over the town were all aglow with the flames of burning buildings. Wherever they turned, fresh fires were bursting out. And as they stood looking, a mighty explosion shook the earth and half a dozen shattered houses near at hand came crashing into the street.

Another tremendous explosion, and another and another.

"It is all over," said Greski quietly again. "They are blowing up the bastions and burning the town. That, I know, was decided on long since, if it came to the point. Moscow over again."

From where they were they could not see the explosions and they did not dare to venture far. But presently all the harbour was red with the blaze of burning ships, and they could see the new bridge of boats, leading across to the north side, black with crowds of hurrying fugitives. Then Fort Nicholas below them burst into flame, and the smoke from Fort Paul, just across from it, rolled along the roadstead. It was a most amazing scene, beyond description, almost beyond imagination.

The firing had ceased with the blowing up of the bastions. Up on the heights the besiegers clustered thick as bees, watching with awe the results of their long and arduous labours. Below them a thin trickle of creeping looters was already making its way through the ruined suburbs into the burning city.

Jim and Greski returned to their cellar; Jim to fig himself out in the remains of his uniform, Greski to collect such of the family valuables as could be easily carried; and then, with madame and Tatia on their arms, they set off, by devious ways which avoided burning and tottering buildings, crossed the black desolation of the southern suburbs, and came out on this side of the Quarantine Ravine, nearly opposite the cemetery.

The looters, mostly red-trousered Zouaves, looked askant at Jim's uniform and slipped past quietly. All they wanted was plunder, and they feared to be stopped. How this young English Hussar officer had managed to get in so quickly puzzled them, but he had evidently got all he wanted. So—*allons, mes enfants!* and let us lay hands on all we can, before the rest of our brave allies arrive!

Jim knew his way as soon as they had been passed through the lower trenches, and made straight for his father's tent. The camps were almost empty. Everyone was down at the front staring at the burning town. Outside the well-known tent in the hollow, however, an orderly was hard at work scraping the mud off his master's overcoat.

"Where is Colonel Carron?" asked Jim expectantly.

But the man looked back at him stolidly and said, "I do not know, monsieur."

"But this is his tent."

"Monsieur is mistaken. This is the tent of M. the Colonel Gerome—if he is still alive, *mon Dieu!* He went into Malakoff yesterday and we have not seen him since."

"And where is Colonel Carron, then?"

"I do not know, monsieur. It is only three months since I came out. Is it all over, as they say?"

"We have Sebastopol," said Jim, "or part of it." ıd he pushed on along the road to French Head-quarters.

A squadron of lancers came down the road at a fast trot, gleaming in the sun and jingling bravely. Their leader looked curiously at the odd little company, for ladies were refreshingly rare in camp. Then he suddenly drew rein and saluted, and Jim knew him. They had met many times in the tent in the hollow.

"You, M. Carron? Why, we gave you up for dead long ago!"

"Where is my father, du Bourg? I've been to his tent——"

"*Mon Dieu!*—and you have not heard? I am sorry to have to tell it, but you would have to hear. Colonel Carron was killed six months ago, repulsing a sortie." And, as he saw Jim's face fall, he added: "If you have had no news for six months, *mon ami*, be prepared for the worst. You will find very few of your friends left. Where have you been?"

"Prisoner inside since December."

"*Mon Dieu!* you've had hard luck! Well, I must get on or our lively red-legs won't leave a stick in Sebastopol. We've been doing all we could to get in, and now my orders are to let no one in ^n any account. Adieu!" And they went off at a clanking gallop to make up for lost time.

Jim set off again in gloomy spirits for British Head-quarters on the other side of the Balaclava road.

Jack gone! His father gone! George Herapath and Ralph Harben gone! His little world seemed devastated. He wondered if any of the home folk were left.

Gracie—Good God!—suppose Gracie were dead! And

Charles Eager, and Sir Denzil! In six months anything mig have happened to any or all of them.

Tatia was the only fairly cheerful member of the party. her it was like heaven to be out of that dreadful prison-hor below. She had grown so used to the smell of gunpowder t the keen sweet air intoxicated her with delight. Her moth was very weary with the long walk; and as for Greski, his thig was giving him pain, and the only thing he wanted now was t sit down and rest it.

Except for the sentries and a few underlings, British H quarters was deserted like the rest of the camp. All the world wa down at the front, watching the end of Sebastopol. So they sa on a bench in the sunshine, and waited for some one to turn u

The first to come was McLean, the young doctor with who Jim had crossed to Constantinople on the *Carnbrea*. He wa looking older, but well and cheerful.

"Hello!" he cried, as soon as his eyes lighted on Jim. "It's good to set eyes on some one alive that one knew si months ago. Where have you been all this time? I see you've suffered too"—with a glance at the empty sleeve.

"Been in Sebastopol for last nine months. Glad to get out."

"About as glad as we are to get in. Going home, I suppose?"

"Just as quick as I can. Come to report myself, but there's no one to report to."

"All at the front, I suppose. It's a great day this. We're shipping off loads of sick men as fast as we can fit them for the voyage. Our old friend Jolly's in Balaclava Bay. He'd be delighted to take you, I know, if you can fix matters up quickly here."

"Things any better than they used to be?"

"Oh, we're all learning by experience. Even the red-tape isn't as red as it used to be; it's not much more than pink now. We've got everything we need for the sick, anyway, and that's something. By the way, there was a man here inquiring for you a short time ago—came out on purpose, I believe, and brought a shipload of just the things we were needing most."

"Oh? Who was that?"

"A lean-faced chap—a parson, and better than most. What was his name now?—Earnest—Eager? that was it—Charles Eager."

"Eager? The dear old chap! Just like him! How long since?"

"Oh, months—four or five at least. Here's the Chief!"—as a thin, quiet-looking man with a tired face rode up with a couple of aides, saluted the little party, and went inside.

"Sick men first," said Jim; and McLean nodded, and went in.

He was back again in five minutes. "Come down to me at Balaclava as soon as you're ready," he said, "and I'll help you on. I'll have a word with Jolly too." And he sped away.

General Simpson greeted Jim, when at last he was admitted, with simple kindliness but evident preoccupation. His hands and mind were very full at the moment, and Jim's only desire was to get on towards home. All his requests were granted without hesitation, the necessary papers were promised him before night, and they set off again, first to the cavalry camp, whose location he had learned from one of the aides, and then to the railway which lay a little beyond.

At the camp he came across his own orderly, who greeted him with a mixture of jovial delight at meeting again an open-handed friend and master, and of deferential awe at encountering one returned from the dead.

"Quite thought you was dead, sir," said he, with a big shy smile.

I've been next door to it once or twice, Jones. Where's my horse?"

"Ah, then! Dear knows, sir! The French gentleman took him to's own quarters an' I never set eyes on him since."

"Ah! Anybody left here that I know? Denham?"

"Lord Charles Denham, he died six, seven months ago of the fever, sir."

"Mr. Kingsnorth?"

"Invalided home in the winter, sir."

"Captain Warren?"

"Killed in the rifle-pits while he was potting the Russians. There's hardly anybody left that was here when you was here, sir, 'cept some of us men. You going home, sir?"

"As quick as I can, Jones. Here's a guinea for old times' sake. Good-bye!" And he went soberly on, feeling himself a stranger in a strange place and as one risen from the dead.

They got a lift on the railway, and Jim hardly knew Balaclava, so little of the old was left—just as in the camp up above. But he tumbled up against Captain Jolly almost at once, and then his difficulties were over.

"Take you?" cried the jovial master. "Take you all the way home if you like. My charter's up and I'm to get back as quick as the weather'll let me. Taking a cargo of broken pieces to Scutari, and then straight for Liverpool. Right! We'll find room for you all if we have to sleep in the bilge. Your servant, madam, and yours, miss! Glad to get away from all the noise and nastiness, I'll be bound. Come on board any time you like, Mr. Carron. Shipboard's a sight cleaner and more comfortable than any place you'll find ashore." And Jim felt happier than he had done for very many months back.

CHAPTER LXVIII

HOME AGAIN

DR. McLEAN snatched half an hour to say good-bye as they were weighing anchor. And among other things he happened to ask Jim:

"Have you sent word home that you're coming? I don't believe in surprises."

"No, I haven't. I'm only learning to write, you see."

"Tell me what you want to say and I'll telegraph it from here."

"Can you?" said Jim, with a look of surprise, for this too was all new since he went into captivity. "I wish you would. Just say 'Coming home—Jim,' and send it to Sir Denzil Carron, Carne, Sandshire."

"Right! I'll see to it."

And he duly saw to it, but in the mighty pressure on the wires, consequent on the great events of those latter days, the private dispatch got mislaid, or was lost on the road—somewhere under the Black Sea, maybe, or in the wilds of Turkey; anyway, it never reached its destination.

And so it came about that Jim, satisfied that they knew of his coming, walked up to the door of Mrs. Jex's cottage, three weeks later, and found it occupied by young John Braddle, the carpenter's son, and his newly married wife.

"My gosh!" said young John at sight of him. "But yo' did give me a turn, Mester Jim! An' yo've lost an arm! Was that i' th' big charge?"

"No; I left it inside Sebastopol, John. But where's everybody? Mr. Eager and——"

"They're all up at Vicarage, Mester Jim. He's vicar now, and Mrs. Jex she keeps house for him. An' so Molly and me——"

But Jim was off, with a wave of the workable arm. He had not come home to hear about John and Molly Braddle.

Mr. and Mrs. Charles Eager had just got back from their honeymoon. Mrs. Jex had been in residence for a month past, getting things into shape for them, with Gracie's very active assistance. And—"Bless her 'art! She couldn' do no more if 'twas her own house she was a-fittin' up. And may I live to see that day!" said Mrs. Jex with fervour.

Gracie had been living at Knoyle, for the comfort an consolation of Sir George, who found his great house very lonely, and talked of selling it and coming to live with them at the cosy old ivy-covered Vicarage.

They were all sitting round the dinner-table still; Meg—Mrs. Charles—and Gracie cracking a surreptitious walnut now and again, Sir George sipping his own excellent port, and smoking one of his own extra-specials with a relish he had not experienced for months past; while the Rev. Charles—the vicar, if you please—recalled some of the delightful humours of their travel. For never since the world began had there been a month so packed with wonder and delight.

The drift-logs on the hearth crackled and spurted, and the many-coloured flames laughed merrily at their own reflections in the Jex-polished mahogany and old walnut panelling. And Rosa, the little maid, had tapped three times on the door and peeped in, and gone back to Mrs. Jex with word that he was a-talking and a-talking as if he'd go on all night, and they all looked so happy that she hadn't the heart to disturb them. To which Mrs. Jex had replied, "All the same, my gel, we've got to wash up, and so we'll begin on these."

"I'm so glad," said Gracie, during a brief pause, and she knitted her fingers in front of her on the table and gazed happily on them all. "You two make me happy just to look at you——"

"Then is the object of our wedding attained," said Charles, with a smile and a bow.

"Almost quite happy," continued the Little Lady. "If only the boys were here, now——"

"We ought to hear something soon," said Sir George. "I was hoping the dispatches might bring some news of them. You don't suppose the Russians would carry them across with them?"

"I wouldn't like to say what the Russians might or might not do," said Eager thoughtfully. "They're a queer lot, from all accounts. I didn't tell you we called on Lord Deseret as we came through London. He was very friendly and as nice as could be. Among other things he told us that, as the result of all his inquiries, he learned from St. Petersburg that the boys were being kept in Sebastopol of set purpose."

"That's odd! Why?" asked Sir George.

"For the still odder reason, as it was reported to him, that they were safer inside than outside."

"And who was it was playing Providence to them like that?"

"He could only surmise, but I am not at all sure that he told us all he knew. He is an old diplomat, you know."

"And to whom did his surmises point?"

"I gathered it was towards Mme Beteta, the Spanish dancer. You remember she made something of a furore in London when she was over here."

"But what on earth has she got to do with our boys?" asked Gracie, kindling.

"She seemed to take a fancy to them. You remember how Jim used to write about her."

"But how could a woman such as that exercise any influence in such a matter?" asked Sir George.

"Ah!——"

Then there came a knock on the front door, and they heard Rosa trip along to answer it.

And the next moment Rosa's white face appeared at the dining-room door, and Rosa's pale lips gasped:

"Oh mum, miss, 't's 'is ghost—Master Jim!"

And Jim pushed past her into the room, and they all sprang up to meet him.

Gracie was nearest, and she just flung her arms round his neck crying, "Oh Jim! *Jim!*" And he put his left arm round her and kissed her, and put her back into her chair.

It was many minutes before they could settle to rational

talk, for Mrs. Jex must come hurrying in, and Jim kissed her too, and seemed inclined to go round the whole company.

But then they came to soberness with the inevitable question:

"And Jack?"

And an expressive gesture of Jim's left hand prepared them for the worst.

"The shell that took this," he said, glancing down at his empty sleeve, "took Jack too. I did my best"—and he looked anxiously at Gracie and Eager—"I tried to fling it away, but it burst, and—and—that was the end. It was days before I knew."

By degrees he told them all the story; and saddened as they were by the loss of one, they could not but soberly rejoice that one at all events had been spared to them.

He told them of the Greskis and all their kindnesses, and how he had brought them home with him, since Greski was set on ending his servitude with Russia, and now it would be supposed that they had perished in the bombardment, and so no consequences could be visited on their friends in Poland because of his desertion. He had settled them for the time being in a quiet hotel in Liverpool, and later on they would decide further as to their future.

Eager had been very thoughtful while Jim talked. Now he said:

"Do you feel able to come along with me to Carne, my boy? Mrs. Jex was telling me that old Mrs. Lee is lying at the point of death. It is just possible—— But I don't know," he said musingly, with a tumult of thoughts behind his fixed gaze at Jim "It does not matter now. . . . Still, I imagine your grandfather. . . . Yes, I think we must go."

"I'm ready," said Jim, and they two set off at once for Carne, and the others gathered round the fire and talked by snatches of it all, and Gracie mopped her eyes at thought of all those two boys had suffered, and of Jack, and of Jim's poor arm—and everything.

"He has become a very fine man," said Sir George. "A man to be proud of, my dear."

And Meg kissed her warmly and whispered, "Make him happy, dear!"

CHAPTER LXIX

"THE RIGHT ONE"

A WOMAN from the village opened the door, and stared at Eager and Jim in vast surprise.

"How is Mrs. Lee to-night, Mrs. Kenyon?" asked Eager.

"'Oo's varry low. 'Oo just lies an' nivver spakes a word."

"Well now"—very emphatically—"I want you not to go in, or speak to her, till we come down again. You understand?"

"I understand, and I dunnot want to spake to her."

They went quietly along the stone passage, past the door of the room where the sick woman lay, and tapped on the door of Sir Denzil's apartments.

Kennet opened it with a wide stare, and they went in.

Sir Denzil was lingering over his dinner.

"So you've got home, Mr. Eager——" he lifted his glass of wine to his health. Then catching sight of Jim behind—"Ah, Jim, my boy, so you've come home at last!"

"All that's left of me, sir."

"Ah—I see. Well, well! Better half a loaf than no bread." And he stood up and got out his snuff-box, tapped it into good order inside, and extracted a pinch. "I've been expecting you ever since we got news of the fall of Sebastopol. And Jack——?"

"Jack is dead, sir."

"So!" And the grizzled brows went up in inquiry for more.

"He was killed by the same shell that took my arm. Why it did not take us both I do not know."

"Dear, dear! The ways of Providence are past our finding out. Let us accept her gifts without questioning. I am delighted to see you, my dear boy—delighted. Now that we have got you safe home we must make the most of you." And for the first time in his life Eager got glimpse of a Sir Denzil he had never known before, and could hardly have imagined, had it not been his custom to credit every man with more possibilities of grace than outside appearances might seem to warrant.

"And now," continued Sir Denzil, with anxious warmth, "I hope you've had enough of war, and are ready to settle down here and make the most of what is left to you."

"It has been a trying time, sir. I shall be glad of a rest."

But Sir Denzil was gazing at him with something of the fixity of Charles Eager's look before they left the Rectory. He took a thoughtful pinch of snuff, with a sudden relapse into his old manner. Then he nodded his head slowly several times, and said, "No . . . I think not . . . No need—now. . . ." And he looked across at Eager and said: "It occurred to me that if he went down and saw that old woman . . . but it is not necessary now. Nothing she could say——"

"I would like to see her, by your leave, sir," said Jim. "After all, she was good to us boys, in her own way, you know."

"Very well," said Sir Denzil, after a moment's hesitation, as though he shrunk from subjecting his new-found satisfaction to any test whatever. "Only—remember! Her whole life has been a lie, and we cannot trust a word she says." And they went downstairs, and along the stone passage, to the side-room in which Nance Lee's baby had slept his first sleep at Carne, that black night one-and-twenty years before.

"Yon other woman will have told her," said Sir Denzil, stopping short of the door as the thought struck him.

"No; I told her not to," said Eager.

"Ah!"—with a quick look at him—"then you had the same idea." And they went quietly in.

Mrs. Lee was lying motionless on her back, and her thin gray face in its frilled white nightcap looked so set and rigid that at first they thought her dead.

Sir Denzil nodded to Eager to speak to her, and stepped back out of sight.

"Mrs. Lee," said Eager, bending over her, "here is one of our boys come back from death. He wished to see you."

The dim old eyes opened and stared wildly at them all for a moment, then settled on Jim in a long, thin, piercing gaze.

"Don't you know me, Mrs. Lee?" he asked.

"Ay—shore! . . . Yo're——" and she struggled up to her bony elbow to look closer, and caught a glimpse of Sir Denzil behind—"yo're Jack!" and fell back on to her pillow.

They thought she was gone; but she suddenly opened her eyes again and laughed a thin, shrill little laugh, and said:

"So t'reet un's come back, after aw!"

And then her meagre body straightened itself in the bed, and she lay still.

"I knew we'd get nothing out of her," said Sir Denzil, when they had got back to his room. "But whatever she said would have made no difference. You are Carron of Carne, my boy; and, thanks to our friend here, Carne will have a better master than it has had for many a day."

CHAPTER LXX

ALL'S WELL!

"GRACIE, dear!" said Jim, "will you make me the happiest man in all the world? I've hungered and thirsted for you all these months, and I believe old Jack would wish it so if he knew."

"Oh, Jim!"—and she put up her arms and drew down

Lightning Source UK Ltd.
Milton Keynes UK
UKHW010752221118
332685UK00007B/1212/P